"I AM DONE WITH WORDS," MY HUSBAND SIR ROLAND SAID.

With a slow, deliberate movement, he turned around.
... As he moved over me, his knees grazed the inside
of my thighs and his broad chest brushed my breasts.
All thoughts fled at his touch. His hands, strong and
ungentle, commanded all sensations, bruising my
softness, and the heavy thud of his heart drummed
mine to insignificance. Just as his mouth came down
on mine silencing all further objections, his powerful
body against mine obliterated the world...

*   *   *

I would not know until much later how little
freedom I had from him once he had made me his,
how I would depend on him for much more than
protection and shelter.

For Love of Lord Roland

Julie Tetel

Popular Library

An Imprint of Warner Books, Inc.
A Warner Communications Company

O, faire Marguerite, thou art well named!
The Greeks knew to ally thy gentle beauty to the
fields and thy sweet, secret wisdom to the sea.
For doth not μαργαρον embrace both
the daisy and the pearl?

—*Thirteenth-century inscription*

Chapter 1

I had thought once, such a very long year ago, that spending a fortnight in the royal court at Westminster in the Year of Our Lord 1250 would be the full sum of happiness. Nothing exceeded my joy when my father unexpectedly unleashed me last summer from the plodding predictability of life at Shrivenham Castle to discover the world and its sweet promises. My first visit to court began as an uncomplicated wonder and delight, and I lost no opportunity in tasting all that life had to offer me. It was usual, of course, for young ladies of my station to sally forth in groups on the arms of obliging cavaliers from Westminster into Town, crowded with merchants and trading booths and rich burghers ("Nauseously rich," King Henry had snorted once years ago in a now oft-repeated phrase) strutting the streets in their neat-fitting garments and cocky hats. I could imagine few pleasures finer that first week than wandering through the goldsmiths' shops in Cheapside, exclaiming at the silks and samites in Thread Needle Street, or marveling over the spices and drugs and other luxuries on display by the clever Italian merchants who had invaded, and conquered, Lombard Street. My mouth sticky sweet with a fresh honey pasty and the warm summer sun overhead, I innocently deemed life full to bursting in Londontown. There were plays and mysteries, the acrid smell of stout English ale at a tuppence the stein, rowdy laughter spilling from the countless taverns, and a robust barmaid jeering a beggar from her busy doorstep. Throughout this buzz of haggling and hawking could be heard the coarse threads of a droll, bawdy song warbling on the lips of a goliard strumming his gittern and strolling the markets.

1

There was, to dazzle further my avid, secular eyes, the magnificence of the Plantagenet Court. Although King Henry III was refurbishing Windsor Castle (at a crippling expense to the royal exchequer, as court gossip had it) because his beautiful and unpopular queen, Eleanor La Belle of Provence, found the royal quarters at Westminster dingy, I was quite sure that I had never seen anything quite as grand as Westminster's Great Hall with its soaring vaults and brilliant tapestries, or as awesome as the adjacent Tower that frowned down upon all of London. Given this magnificence, I could not imagine what Windsor would look like when it was completed. However, one glance at Henry's queen assured me that if the new residence were to equal the elegance of its mistress, it would be splendid indeed.

Since Queen Eleanor was not inclined to circulate among her English subjects, I saw her only once during my stay, at a lavish court feast. She was easily discernible even among that fashionable throng of peers, and her entrance created quite a stir. I would have been able to recognize her, though, without the hushed silence that marked her appearance, for she was all that was queenly and aloof. She wore a parti-colored *cotte* with wide goring at the hips and the daring effect of red silk damask and decorations of gilt quatrefoil to enhance her lithe ivory-and-brown southern beauty. At her waist a silver girdle was slung in which a dagger was carelessly thrust, the mantle of honor cast over the shoulder, and therewithal sat a very high and very new type of wimple (making my crisp, white coif sadly old-fashioned by comparison) into which her pretty head receded until her face seemed a flower in an enveloping spathe, topped by a saucy pillbox cap. I guessed that she would start a fashion, and that was all that Alicia, Yvette, Marie-Ange, and I could talk about the next afternoon when we came together to stitch.

Because I was a neophyte, my friends eagerly initiated me into all the conventional court stories, and I listened with enthusiasm. I was fascinated to learn, for instance, that the Provençals—those who had come with Queen Eleanor—were a disagreeably superior lot and voiced the greatest contempt for everything English. They looked down their long, finely boned noses at us and shuddered at the weather and sang mournful songs about their beautiful, sunny weather so far away. But they were only too glad to stay and in many cases probably never would go back to beautiful, sunny Provence. The courtiers had understandably begun to hold them in dislike, while the Londoners had conceived an open hatred for them. There was Alicia's forthcoming wedding to Herbert Longchamps to be discussed, too, and we spent many an hour prattling over the details of the nuptials that would take place the next month at Castle Burford. Every little *affaire*, every intrigue, every event of even mild significance that rippled through the castle found its way into our talk, and I formed the conviction that the courtier's first duty in life was to stay abreast of the latest gossip.

Perhaps it was all that lightheaded chatter that eventually turned my head and spread in my idle brain the first seeds of dissatisfaction that was to warm and leaven over the next few days. Perhaps it was the expectant air of plots and counterplots, throbbing under the glittery surface of court life, that awoke in me the desperate desire to become part of the mysterious, vital heartbeat of the castle. Perhaps it was my own girlish giddiness that compelled me to try my inexpert hand at contrivance, however harmless I judged it to be. I do not know. But one night during the second sennight of my first, all too brief visit to the royal court, I convinced myself that it was not enough to have a vicarious taste of life before I settled back down to the dull rhythms of Shrivenham. No, I wanted the full course of danger and adventure, and I was prepared to meet it head on.

Since that night and all the unforeseen consequences it brought, I have had many long hours to ponder the sober truth that a reckless yearning for life holds its own risks, that danger and excitement are not bartered cheaply, that it is vastly safer and far more comfortable to know nothing of passion or desire and to leave unprobed the dark corners of the soul. I wish, on occasion, when there is nothing else to soothe the unbearable torment, that I could recapture the girl in me who once thought the total of earthly happiness was a well-stocked stillroom, newly laid rushes, and a neatly dressed evening meal for my castle folk. That was the girl whose simple innocence had not yet been touched by Roland's urgent hand, who had not yet been filled, slowly, painfully with the realization that my happiness belonged to him whether he wanted it or not, a gift freely given, an invisible, golden chain more tenacious and inescapable than all the other bonds that made me his.

I have heard it said by our churchmen that patience is a virtue and that virtue is its own reward, but I doubt—and I shall repent my sinful doubt one day when I am free or indifferent or empty—I doubt that these well-meaning men with their eyes pinned piously heavenward have ever known the wicked ache of longing or the slow, hot tears of loneliness. They do not know that while the body waits tensely for the return of a lover, the heart weeps with the sure knowledge that seeing him will only make things worse. They do not know that despair and misery and heartbreak, once born and bred in the soul, are constant companions, like small, cross children who whine and sob for attention and pull incessantly at one's skirts. They do not know that errant memories may not be plucked and discarded like a vagrant growth, or that even the very garden below my sewing-room windows, neatly trimmed and weeded like a clear conscience, provides me no solace now on a sweet summer's day, for it reminds me unpityingly of a similar garden that I gazed down upon, surely a hundred years ago, the night I met Roland, when I first tasted excitement and danger and life.

I remember well the hour I met him at Westminster, in a small, close chamber just after nightfall.

It was a sticky July evening, heavy with impending rain, an evening not conducive to repose or to sleep. I stood at my window, sighing deeply and trying to convince myself that I did not mind spending this time alone.

Leaning on the casement, chin in hand, I frowned against the moonlight. The air was redolent of roses, and the full moon, creeping into the sky, cast ebony shadows on the ground. It showed the castle gardens etched against a sky of deepest sapphire, and made it easy for me to perceive the shadowy walks that meandered among high, luxuriant hedges and the thin thread of the rivulet that slept silently in the depths of the thick copse. Yet, in my faintly dissatisfied humor, I was not receptive to the poetry of the scene spread before me, for I did not admire the effect of the trees against the night sky or the sheen of moonlight on the lily pond.

I stood there for a long while in the summer darkness. The honey-laden breezes came in wafts through the open window and set me dreaming. A rare indulgence, my dreams, and certainly not a credit to the experience and wisdom of my twenty years. And, while I was about it, I gratified myself with a bout of petty, tiresome self-pity that I was not able to partake more fully of all the court had to offer, as I fancied Alicia and most of my other friends did. Another sigh escaped my lips.

At length the melancholy call of the watch assured me and other restless spirits at the castle that night had fallen and all was wearily well. I wondered wistfully what other souls were alone this hour, dreaming idle dreams, and then a flash of inspiration visited me. My Lady Constance Hartford! Upon my departure from Shrivenham, Father had bidden me give my Lady Constance a note, but he had made so little of it and I had such a dislike of the caviling woman that I had conveniently forgotten this small errand.

Two things stood out in my mind about the Lady Constance, besides her repulsive son, Charles, pimply faced and fourteen. The first was that she had a high, whiny voice and the second was that that voice always carried some complaint of her fragile health. There was no entertainment arranged for the court this evening, and so I guessed that she, like me, was alone at that very moment.

I went to one of my trunks, dug to the bottom, and withdrew a neatly folded parchment, aged and yellowed like the back of my father's hand. I did not stop to think of the oddity of visiting my Lady Constance without prior appointment, and since I guessed her to be alone, I guessed also that she would be secretly pleased to have an audience for the newest of her ailments. What was more, I was suddenly delighted at the prospect of an independent adventure, feeding the rebellion I felt in my breast after so many years of routine in the convent and at Shrivenham and now an exciting, but singularly un-eventful, week at court. A touch of lunacy seemed to have penetrated my being, as if I had bathed too long in the moon-light, and I was intoxicated by my sense of freedom and daring.

I pulled a gray homespun kirtle over my thin shift and slipped into soft leather shoes. I did not bother with a girdle, nor did I think to hide my long braids in the perfunctory coif. I slid my father's message into a cleverly hidden pocket in my pendant sleeves and smiled to myself that such was my "ad-venture" in delivering a message bearing news no doubt that my father's stomach pains were better, mayhap worse. I quietly unlatched the door that led to the outer room where my two women lay on small pallets. I picked my way noiselessly around them, having enough sense to realize that a genteel lady did not in fact go galivanting at night alone, and I did not need Bess and Gertrude to tattle to my father, for I would imme-diately be returned to the predictable rhythms of Shrivenham.

I cautiously opened the outer door of my small apartment, but once the door was closed behind me, I had the urge to run. In the cool, dimly lit hallways, I felt a surge of relief and liberation, little wry devils nipping at my heels, urging me mischievously onward. I knew very well where Lady Con-stance resided, although I had not yet visited her, and so de-scended two flights of stairs and turned down another long, dark hallway.

The sound of footsteps approached me and I took to the shadows. As the crisp steps died away, so did the pounding of my heart. I had met and evaded my first foe, I thought dra-matically, and congratulated myself on the deft maneuvering so essential to the successful completion of my mission. To this purpose I was, to make a clean breast of it, rather pleased with my inconspicuous dress. My dark kirtle blended with the shadows, and my dark hair unadorned by a white coif would not give me away.

So absorbed was I in my moon-drunk world of make-believe

adventure that my senses did not immediately register the pale yellow light cast across my path from an open door as I turned a corner. It was then, when I least expected it, that I was literally and bodily pulled into a new, all too sobering reality.

"Hey! A wench! Jus' what we've been needing, lads, to really sh-shelebrate!"

Of a sudden I found myself in a small chamber, in the rough, unsteady grip of a stocky man of indeterminate age. In the close room the air hung with the odor of ale and the heavy scent of the tallows guttering low in their sockets. I pushed away my captor with the strength of indignation just as I was grabbed by another, who flung his arms about me and planted a slobbery kiss awry on my eyebrow, his breath reeking of wine and ale.

The stocky one seized me again before I had a chance to protest and shoved me into a chair. I glared at him with a mixture of confusion, disbelief, and wrath, entirely bereft of speech. He thrust a horn of ale in front of me and with an exaggerated drunken gesture ordered me to drink it.

"Thish one'sh for Guy. Ju' his type," he pronounced with satisfaction, cocking his head to the far end of the massive table where sat a third man, presumably named Guy, sullenly contemplating his drinking horn. He did not look up.

"Guy'sh the one to shelebrate tonight, ain't you, Guy? It'sh not every day a man in-inherits a fortune!" He punctuated this with a loud belch.

Guy merely grunted an inarticulate reply.

"'S my turn!" the second, older man argued with drunken tenacity. "You had the lash' one—thish one mine!" He leaned across the table to touch me and added rather simperingly, "An' on our lash' night at court..."

I bolted out of the chair in a mounting rage, my senses restored.

"Unhand me, you oaf!" I cried, too furious at this outrageous gesture to be afraid. "I am no court whore!"

I headed with ruffled dignity toward the door. The second man, far more in his cups than I had at first realized, blocked me. I retreated a strategic step and eyed him narrowly.

The two men looked at each other, winked, and whistled low.

"D'you hear that? No common whore, thish one," the other one taunted.

I was too familiar with the lewd looks and leers of my father's friends to be undone by his crude appraisal of me. Being tall for a woman, I stared level into the bleary eyes of this man who looked back at me as if I existed in duplicate.

He made an unbalanced movement toward me.

"Don't touch me," I threatened, calling forth all the epithets I had often heard the scullery maids use.

He grinned back at me, his face flushed.

"Yer've got shpirit. I like shp-shpirit. Ye're a pretty one, too, a real beauty."

Since I had scant acquaintance with mirrors and no suitors to sing me of my charms, I was disinclined to believe such high praise. With the portion of my mind that stood apart surveying this incredible, quite ridiculous scene, I noted with something akin to humor that this grizzled, ugly man swept away by his ale-inspired aesthetics would find even the oldest strumpet with sagging bosom, few teeth, and hair on her lip worthy of his tribute.

The stocky one now joined his friend, the two of them closing in on me, very much enjoying their game. I took one more step back and found myself against the wall.

"Aye, she's a pretty one. And fresh," the stocky one agreed.

"Fresh from the king's bed, no doubt," slurred the second, as he picked up one of my braids, my hair woefully supporting the theory that I had indeed just come from bed.

"Hold off! I warn you, I am a noblewo—"

The rest of the word was checked by a searing slap across my cheek. I reeled under the impact, held steady only by the wall.

"A noble whore to be sure! An' we likes ours that don't talk so much, eh?"

A brown hand reached out and fondled my breast. My eyes widened in sickened shock, and I stiffened as the comprehension dawned that I was in real danger of losing my virtue. The two surrounded me, and I felt suffocated with the stench of ale and sweat. Then I heard the bodice of my kirtle rip and felt a damp palm on my bare breast. My flesh crawled.

"Ooooh, lovely, my sweet. None of that wadding like some of them other flat-chested doxies."

Without another thought, I hauled off and slapped the stocky one with a blow that knocked him down and left my hand stinging for moments afterward.

The second one staggered forward and lunged at me.

"Why, you vicious . . ."

I stepped to the side and tripped him. He collided full force with the wall and, exhaling in a long groan, slid to the floor. Then he lay silent at my feet.

For the length of a heartbeat I stared at them lying there, stunned at my success, for it had been too easy. But my wits had not fled me completely, and I realized how small my accomplishment was, given their advanced state of intoxication. Fear of being discovered now pricked me. I lifted my skirts to run and spun in the direction of the door.

I halted abruptly. Before me was the third man, whose presence I had forgotten, leaning leisurely against the trestle between me and the door. He was a powerfully built man and tall, towering a good hand above me. My eyes flew to his face and met the astonishing cold blue of his eyes unclouded by the effects of strong drink. Paralyzed by a new, more intense fear, still clutching my skirts, I was unable to command my hands to cover my breasts, which lay partially exposed to his view. I was not immediately conscious of my state of undress—remembering it only much later with considerable consternation—for my attention fastened on the lean, irregular features in the tanned face framed with sun-lightened locks. For a moment, I dispassionately assessed the face, which was neither handsome nor ugly but which held a rugged masculinity far more appealing than beauty.

"Do you think to dispose of me as easily as you did the others?" he said at last as his eyes flickered sardonically over my disheveled garments.

The sound of his voice jolted my senses and freed me at

last of my paralysis. I clasped the two halves of my bodice together.

A strange exhilaration had me momentarily in its grip, and I did not hesitate to cross swords with my opponent. I had a desire to show him that he had more than met his match in composure and ease.

"As you can see," I said, hoping the coolness of my voice equaled his, "I am unarmed." I allowed my eyes to sweep him as his had so disdainfully measured me, my gaze resting significantly on the sheathed dagger at his waist. Brazen it out, I told myself, and I lifted my chin a notch. "And I can see that no man, and surely no woman, is your match."

"No match at all," he agreed, not in the least diverted by this artless piece of flattery. His eyes did not leave my face, nor did they, I reckoned from their continued chill, find anything there to please them. I found myself unable to look boldly back at him as I would have liked to do. I lowered my eyes, hiding cowardly from his cold, rather cynical gaze, to study instead the steady pulse in his sun-darkened throat.

"Do you intend, demoiselle, to discourage me or lure me on?"

"I have certainly given you no reason," I said evenly, "to presume that I would lure you on."

"Do I indeed presume too much?" he retorted.

There was a space of silence. He was clearly the superior player at this game, for, as the long silence stretched perilously thin, I had ample time to exaggerate the fate that surely awaited me, and he had time to further disconcert a most unworthy opponent.

I felt the necessity at least to try for an escape. I lifted my eyebrows haughtily and said, "You and your friends have detained me long enough. Pray, let me pass."

"Certainly. As soon as you tell me what brings you out alone at such an hour."

"I cannot imagine why my affairs should interest you," I said, and at once regretted the ill-bred note in my voice.

"They are of no interest to me," he answered flatly. "But there are those who need to know when a serving maid has abandoned her post." His eyes held a challenge that I could hardly refuse.

My dress was simple, but surely he could tell from the quality of my French that I was no common serving maiden. For that matter, there was nothing about him, except his speech, to distinguish him as a peer of the realm. He had nothing over me in rank, and judging from the company he kept and his clothing, unadorned by the fashionable silver cords and absent of pearls and other ornamentation, he must have come from a lower order. However, now was clearly not the time to boast the privileges of one's station.

"It seems, sir, that I have incurred your displeasure, but need you insult me?"

"I wish you would tell me how I may insult so bold a piece as yourself," he responded, faintly contemptuous. I had no chance to respond, for at that moment he bent down with a careless grace to retrieve a folded letter. It was the note that had fallen from my sleeve during my struggle. He held it out to me. "Now I have guessed the reason for your movements but not the motive. Do you do it for money or for power?" he questioned mockingly.

I took the proffered letter, and in a detached manner I noticed that my hand did not shake and was vaguely pleased. For an interminable moment I could think of nothing to say. I had the wild impulse to tell him my real destination, but checked it almost as it rose. As for my motive, how could I explain to him the effect of moonlight, the boredom and constraint I had felt for so many years, and my need for adventure? How could I convince him that every movement I would make had been planned since my birth and that tonight I had given myself completely over to impulse? Indeed, how could he understand my yearning for adventure, when, as I looked at him, I felt that his life had known very few of the fetters of mine? He did not give the appearance of a man who tolerated opposition to his wishes, and what for me was a grand undertaking could appear to him only as singularly foolish.

If I was not sure until that moment in what light I had impressed him, he made it very plain with his next words. I chanced to look up and saw the unpleasant curl to his lip when he said, "I care little for women who sell themselves to men."

The color flamed up into my cheeks, yet I managed to gather what little pride was left in me to salvage and to answer, "Then I have nothing to fear from you, my lord, since I have no intention of selling you anything."

"And you have nothing I want."

Since I could no longer command my voice for the constriction in my throat, I nodded deferentially, beyond shame, hoping now that if I conceded defeat he would let me go.

I lifted my skirts to walk past him, and in so doing, to my chagrin, grazed him slightly. He must have felt me stiffen, for he shifted his weight to bar my passage, and I stood stock against his chest. I was acutely aware of the smell of him, and I could almost feel his soft tunic next to my cheek, and I noted its delicate weave. So close to him, I was at once attracted and repelled by the power balanced in his body.

"I trust," he said low, "that we shall meet again in more unexceptionable circumstances." The menacing note in his voice did not escape my notice, and I wondered for a moment exactly what deep dealing he attributed to my actions.

I had bandied words just enough to know that I would not emerge from the exchange a winner, so I vouchsafed no response. I left the room then, every instinct urging me to run, to flee from him, and the strange feeling welling from the pit of my stomach to my breast. But I did not run. Nor did I feel any comfort in the cool, dark hallways down which I had only minutes before imagined myself floating. For my cheeks still burned from the intensity of his penetrating blue gaze on me and with the shame, the humiliation, that I, a silly and imprudent woman, should fancy myself so brave and adventuresome.

My heart was still pounding when I regained my chambers, and my one desire at that moment was to throw myself in bed and hide forever under the covers. I was momentarily relieved to find Bess and Gertrude snoring lightly, but for some minutes after regaining the security of my chamber I sat on the edge of my bed before I undressed with trembling fingers.

With my adventure, such as it was, at an end, there was

nothing more to do except sigh, toss once more in my bed, and wait desperately for sleep.

I greeted the morning reluctantly, clinging to my sweet dreams of innocence and simplicity. Like a child who will shape her mouth into a button and refuse to take her medicine, I would crack my eyes, blinking against the morning light, and nestle down farther under the covers. I hovered thus on the selvages of wakefulness for some time, aware only of not wanting to pull back the heavy curtain of sleep that protected me from the honest light of day.

Even the noises from the next rooms, where Bess and Gertrude bustled, could not persuade me from my craven repose. Finally, two short raps on the door signaled that my solitude was to be violated and that I could no longer hide from the new day. I turned down the covers and peeked over their edge only to learn that I was being critically regarded by a buxom woman bearing a large salver upon which were a wooden goblet, a trencher of bread and cheese to break my fast, and a ewer of water for the morning wash. Her rather plump form was neatly attired in a kirtle of Kendal green, cut generously, and unadorned by any braiding or embroidery. She was a round, rubicund woman with a smiling countenance for all, but at the moment it looked as if I were about to receive a scold.

"My Lady Marguerite," Bess began, "'tis not seemly for a gentlewoman to loll about till the sun is halfway up in the sky like some court hussy! You'll ruin your figure and my reputation. Now, out of bed with you and eat!"

"Thank you, dear Bess. But I fail to see how prolonged sleep spoils the figure," I countered, as I swung my legs over the side of the bed. I groped somewhat sleepily for my light shawl.

She clucked her tongue and exclaimed, "Why, my lady, you do look pulled this morning. How did you sleep?"

"Wonderfully," I replied, perjuring my soul without hesitation. As the disagreeable churning of a guilty conscience could easily double for gnawing hunger, I added that it was perhaps only that I was very hungry. I bade her place the tray on the small table near the window and asked if she had been abroad and inquired as nonchalantly as possible for the latest news.

"Have I been abroad yet?" she echoed indignantly. "My heavens, Lady Marguerite, I have already been to the laundry to wash your white clothes hours ago it was! Gertrude has been busy sewing and mending since dawn. The only news you'll be getting out of me, you laggard, is that you've missed the better part of the new day!" Embroidering on this theme, a privilege of old and trusted servants, Bess regaled me with the story of the Lady Adela, who slept late every day and was eventually discovered one morning dead in her bed. But as I knew this respected lady to have had some seventy years in her dish at the time of her death, I observed that late sleeping seemed rather a prescription for long life, and won an opprobrious look from Bess, who briskly withdrew.

While I applied myself to my food, I began, upon sober reflection, to convince myself that there was no way anyone would learn of my nocturnal misadventure. No one had seen me the night before who would recognize me again, except for the Unknown Guy, and even he did not know my name, nor had he ever seen me before. From what one of the drunken men said, it was their last night at court, and so I could safely suppose them gone. I congratulated myself on having had the prudence not to indicate my rank to the Unknown Guy, for now that I had time to collect my thoughts, I realized that such a disclosure could have left me open to a very unsavory attack indeed, which my active imagination did not hesitate to exaggerate into blackmail. While on this fertile topic, I mused on the Unknown Guy's words to me. He had insinuated that I myself was engaged in some sort of plot, perhaps blackmail or murder, or was there even the hint of some sordid love affair? I soon lost myself to the weaving of several highly improbable adventures in which I played a central role and finally had to shake my head clear of these imaginings.

With a facile resolve to unburden my soul of its waywardness by the dispensing of a few coins to the most wretched beggar I could call to mind, I washed the last of my fears down with my watered wine and at last gained the courage to dress for the day and face my fate.

I summoned Bess to attend me, and she promptly sailed into my chamber, her wimple billowing with busyness. She called to my mind my mid-morning meeting with Alicia, which had become a daily rite with us. I thanked her duly for the reminder, wondering anew that I, sole mistress of Shrivenham and a grown woman, would never be anything to her but the shy, gawky girl of fourteen who suddenly inherited the keys to the castle when the seneschal's wife died.

Bess neatly laid out my clothing for me, and I dressed with more than usual care this morning, wishing belatedly that I had thought to complete my toilette of the night before with a bliaut or at least an embroidered girdle. With my white, starched coif finally in place, I felt less exposed and somewhat more proper as befitted a lady of my station.

Bess secured a silver clasp around my throat, stepped back to survey her work, and exclaimed, "My, how lovely you look today, my lady! Wouldn't your father be proud of you!"

I doubted that but kept it to myself. Not even mention of my sire, however, reminded me of my unaccomplished errand. Such must have been the state of my guilty conscience, that I, who chose to consider myself a responsible young lady, simply forgot about delivering my father's missive to Lady Constance. I proceeded instead to the day's business.

I emerged from my room into the antechamber and found Gertrude, whom my father had once described as looking more like a skinned rabbit than a woman. Although she was certainly very thin, I felt it unjust to liken her to a skinned rabbit, and if asked to continue in this vein of comparisons, I would have said she had very much more of an aquiline appearance and sharp, birdlike movements. Indeed, I found her in one of the outer chambers brooding over her sewing, like an eagle in her aerie. She glanced up at me sharply when I bid her good morrow. My heart quailed for a moment under her scrutiny, and I expected a severe reprimand for my errant behavior. My misgivings vanished when she merely replied with a curt, "Good morrow, my lady."

I nodded and smiled at her and gave my kirtle a last pat before stepping into the long corridor. Never, I thought, as I found my way through the castle, could two women have formed a stronger contrast to each other than Bess and Gertrude! They might have served as models for Dame Aplenty and Dame Penury, one so corpulent and cheery, full-featured and with thick, gray hair, the other lean and somber, with severe lines, her whole person suggesting austerity rather than abundance. In looks and manner, they differed as night and day, Gertrude as dour as the moors in winter, and Bess as sunny as a May morning.

Alicia was already awaiting me at the designated bench under a plantain tree that fascinated me because it was the scene of a most scandalous murder a half-century before during the reign of John Lackland and thus fulfilled my need for adventure, however vicarious. We hugged briefly, exchanged greetings, and sat down together with hands clasped. Her presence always exercised a calming effect on me, for I felt comfortable with her prettily feminine face with its flyaway eyebrows that gave her a vague air of perpetual surprise and innocence.

"Marguerite, you are looking out of sorts," Alicia said in her soothing voice, adding with a twinkle in her soft gray eyes, "Never tell me you had a late-night tryst in this very garden without my knowing it!"

I laughed a bit uncomfortably. "No," I said ruefully. "You know I did not, Alicia. In truth, I did not sleep well, for it is hot and stuffy in my chamber. July is not the month to plan a trip to London."

"I understand perfectly, for so it is with me! But I have the most delicious news to discuss with you, Grita," Alicia said, her eyes aglow with excitement. "And it concerns you most particularly. What is it, my dear? You are suddenly so pale! Ah, so you do have a lover, and you think I have just found out!"

"Don't tease me, Alicia," I managed weakly. "Why is it that when one is in love, one believes all others to be in love, too? Pray continue with your story." I decided it would be better to hear her version before I jumped to my own defense.

She patted my hand fondly. "You will tell me in your own good time, but first you must hear the very latest in court gossip. It so happens that the betrothal between Isabelle Beauvais and Roland of Guimont has been mysteriously dissolved and under the most unusual circumstances—"

I was so distracted by this unexpected beginning that I could not help but interrupt. "How does this concern me?" I asked.

Alicia looked mildly taken aback, but she was too kind to call me a silly goose. "I mean only, of course, that the Guimont lands border on yours and that any change of alliance with that house is bound to have an effect on you at Shrivenham."

"Oh, why, yes, of course. You're quite right," I said, shaking my head clear of its confusion. "You can see that I slept poorly and have not put my head on aright this morning."

I could not suppress a laugh of self-mockery. Silly woman! I saw in a flash that even if it were known that I had been abroad last night, what I had done was too unimportant to raise the brow of even the most conventional courtier. The activities of a lone, insignificant woman were hardly the stuff that court gossip was made of. Births, deaths, marriages, wars won and lost: that was the stuff to keep tongues active.

I would be reproachably less than honest to say that my curiosity was not stirred, and I also forgot my express intention of asking Alicia as casually as I could about the possible identity of a man named Guy. "Tell me about it, and spare me no details so that I may steal the march on Marie-Ange when next I see her!" I laughed. "However, I am not hopeful. She has a way of knowing everything and being everywhere!"

A dark look crossed Alicia's face. "Marie-Ange may certainly be everywhere, but she does not know everything!"

"Of course she does not. I will wager that she has not yet heard the news about Sir Roland and Lady Isabelle, for instance."

"That is not what I mean!" Alicia said with uncustomary severity.

Marie-Ange, who in addition to being a sad rattle was a practiced flirt, had never been a favorite with me, but this embittered reference to her from the gentle, uncritical Alicia seemed to call for an explanation. "What has Marie-Ange done to warrant your censure, Alicia?" I asked.

"Nothing, I assure you!"

"Pray excuse me, then, for the odd interpretation I put on your words."

Alicia ignored my attempt to coax her back into humor. "Her want of decorum makes me blush, while her behavior last night was—was indecent!"

"So I have always thought. Still, I fail to see how her behavior distinguished itself in any way last night."

"She was casting out her lures to Herbert in a most unseemly way!"

"Ah!" I exclaimed, as the infamy of Marie-Ange's behavior became apparent. I should have guessed that in defense of Alicia's husband-to-be, the kitten could become a tigress, but the worst was yet to be disclosed.

"And Herbert seemed to enjoy it!" she said with an indignant flush.

"Well, of course he did!" I said. "But you have nothing to worry about, for he is head over tail in love with you. Besides, men do not like teasing women—that is, in the long run! I will allow her to be a very pretty woman, but if you have discovered more wit in her than may be stowed in your thimble, and leave room to spare, you have remarkable powers of discernment, my dear Alicia!"

"But you are so clever, Grita!" she said simply, her pique with Marie-Ange forgotten.

"I?" I could scarcely explain how lamentably less than clever I felt today.

"Oh, yes! At the convent, the things you would read, and the adventures—"

"Those adventures, as you call them, were more foolhardy than clever and belong to my rebellious girlhood. They are the things one outgrows, *should* outgrow," I amended hastily, "and display little common sense. But we've strayed from the topic and I want to hear the news. I had in fact been bemoaning my fate to have appeared at court in such a fallow season."

"Then you are in luck! Herbert says that there has been

nothing like it since the scandal caused when the queen surprised King Henry in the gardens with a half-naked Madeleine of Nantes, and that was ages ago! All the main events surrounding this fresh topic occurred a week ago at Castle Hungerford on the Guimont demesne. Since then, the rumors have been so conflicting and the speculation so intense that it is quite difficult to sort it all out!"

"How is it, then, that I have heard nothing of it until this moment?" I asked. "Not from Marie-Ange, who loves to talk more than we do"—this elicited from Alicia a gurgle of laughter—"or even from Yvette, with whom I stitch every day."

"I myself did not hear until yesterday evening from Herbert. As it was, Roland of Guimont was summoned by King Henry to court shortly after the happenings. He arrived a few days ago but kept his presence a secret. However, he was in circulation yesterday as if nothing had happened, and now all tongues are wagging. I am sure Yvette will be informed on the subject when you see her later today. It will be all over the castle by nightfall."

"But you have yet to enlighten me. What exactly happened?"

"As you may know, Roger of Guimont, Sir Roland's elder brother, was known to be a heavy drinker whose life seemed doomed to failure. Did you ever meet him or hear about him, being such close neighbors?"

"We are vastly uninformed and isolated at Shrivenham due to my father's reclusive habits," I said, sighing. "I know almost nothing of them or their lives."

"Surely you knew, though, that Sir Roger's first wife died in childbirth along with a stillborn son, and his second wife died about two or three months ago in a riding accident, leaving Sir Roger without an heir."

"I seem to recall some talk about the incident from Bess, though certainly no news of it came from my father."

"Well, Roger and Roland never got along well, although many say that there was never precisely any enmity between the two. I understand Roger to have been a rather dull man, while Roland is known to be very needle-witted, and for all of his being a second son, he never assumed the role, for he made most of the decisions on managing the estates after it became apparent that Roger was unsuited to the position. There was also talk that the two would quarrel violently. Apparently Roland never curbs his sharp tongue and would anger Roger into speechlessness."

"I have never heard any of this! I am sure that the servants at Shrivenham know more about the Guimont family than I do."

"Anyway," Alicia continued, "last week Roger had a fatal fall down a flight of stairs at Guimont, and this has left Roland as the sole heir, which is of course normal. The curious thing about all of this is that Isabelle was at Hungerford Castle on the evening of the accident—some say Roger was drugged, others say he was pushed. He had definitely been drinking, and so had Roland, although Herbert assures me that he is known for his hard head. In any case, the servants claim that Isabelle and Roland had had a bitter argument earlier that evening, or at least Isabelle's voice was heard to be near hysterical. One cannot help but think that Roger's death was in some way related."

I paused to digest this. "You mean he was killed? By Sir Roland?"

"Again, none of it is clear. Roland's squire swears he was with his master on the other side of the castle when Roger fell, and Isabelle has retired to her domain in Northumberland, apparently so upset that she is unable to see or talk to anyone. Herbert says that Roland parries all inquiries deftly and comports himself as befits a man whose brother has just died."

"Then maybe it was a natural accident," I countered.

"The situation could not be more ambiguous. One would almost say deliberately so, for even if it were a natural accident, the circumstances are such as to give rise to speculation in any case. To make matters worse, it seems that Isabelle petitioned the king to revoke officially the betrothal between her and Roland, which the king has done. The implication would then be that Roland killed his brother for the inheritance, and Isabelle wants to be free from such a man. Nevertheless, the king is so far from repudiating Roland that he has actually bestowed upon him a property in Wales, all under the pretext that Roland's recent service in Aquitania was invaluable to the well-being of the kingdom. That was why King Henry summoned Sir Roland to court in the first place—or rather this event happily coincided with Isabelle's petition. The timing of the gift can give no rise to comment, since it would have come naturally at this time; and since Sir Roland returned to England only a few short weeks ago after having spent almost a year in Aquitania, Sir Roland can in no way be connected with Sir Roger's wife's riding accident. It seems, then, that he merely took advantage of a ready-made situation. It is only that one would think that if Roland had indeed killed his brother, the king would hardly be disposed toward gift giving. I do not believe the affair can be any more tangled!"

"Holy Mother," I said irreverently, reflecting on the implications. "Exactly what services did Sir Roland perform for the King? What makes him so valuable?"

"That is a piece with the rest!—few people know what he is about! Not even Herbert, although it is whispered that he works directly for the king. Doing what, I don't know. I do know that my Herbert holds him in high esteem and is counted among his friends, but Sir Roland has powerful enemies. He is a strange sort of man. He is known to keep very low company, besides being a drinker like his brother, and his reputation with women—! Well! I cannot wonder at Isabelle's wanting to break off the betrothal."

"Not a love match, then?"

"On this it seems that you may choose the rumor that is to your taste. Isabelle is undoubtedly the most beautiful woman in the kingdom—after the queen, of course!—but her lands in Northumberland are in bad heart, so it cannot be said that Sir Roland, being a second son, was making an advantageous match. And then, too, it was not advantageous for her either, so it may well have been love that inspired the match, but I doubt it. They were not often seen together, and when they were, they quarreled."

"Sir Roland does not seem to get along with too many people," I interposed.

"Well, no," Alicia conceded, "and there must have been something unsure about the alliance to have had such a long engagement. They were betrothed over four or five years, and it is not as if they were waiting for Isabelle to come of age, since she is now already four-and-twenty, and it may be very difficult for her to marry anyone now that there has been this scandal."

I found myself in sympathy with the poor Isabelle, but I did not believe the world to be as callous as that. "But if she is so beautiful and has tried to extricate herself honorably from such a tangled situation, surely she will be able to establish herself creditably after the worst has passed."

"Yes, perhaps you are right. I suppose that I should reserve my pity for Sir Roland, who will have difficulty making a match. And he is well past his thirtieth summer!"

"Alicia, do but consider! His lands are extensive and he is now even richer with his revenues from Wales. He is also apparently in the good graces of the king. I should not be surprised that he finds himself with an excellent match, not that his bride will have anything to say in the matter. I think we should save all of our sympathies for this as-yet-unknown woman!"

"And yet," Alicia said thoughtfully, "many women are very attracted to him. I might have felt it myself, had I not been so in love with Herbert."

"You have met Sir Roland?" I cried in accents that betrayed envy. "Pray, what is he like?"

"Yes, I met him only once. I was at Herbert's castle at the occasion of our formal betrothal. Sir Roland and two other men came unexpectedly one night to deliver some urgent message or other to Herbert's father. I should say that I *heard* Sir Roland before I saw him. The evening he and his men rode in, I had been in the undercroft inspecting the grain bins, and when I came up I strayed a little and came upon the livery. Before entering it, I heard a man ringing a fine peal over what I believed to be his squire. The man was in a black humor and his voice was angry but controlled. My curiosity was roused, so I stayed a moment, but I never understood the nature of the squire's offense. I could just see around the corner the frightened youth who was the object of this tirade, and he was quaking in his chausses. I was quite in a quake myself and fled the scene before I heard any more and before anyone saw me"—she paused slightly before resuming—"but that is hardly to the point! It was bad of me to eavesdrop!"

"Alicia, I would have done just the same thing!" I laughed. "Only I would have stayed to hear the entire discourse in hopes of acquiring some choice phrases to use when dealing with impertinent and incompetent subalterns!"

Alicia gasped. "I could never scold. Even when my women squabble among themselves and must be brought to order."

"And never will you have to. Your serving maids will invariably obey you through your kindness and gentleness, and any other situation will be handled by Herbert, I am sure."

"While you, Grita, have had to manage your castle alone with no help from your father. I do appreciate your iron fist in these matters, and you hide it admirably, my dearest, in a velvet glove. But as I was saying, I met the squire later that evening at dinner and there seemed to be no hint of tension between him and his master. The squire is a shy, engaging boy. McLaughlin is the name, I think. A more perfect Scotsman I never saw!"

A thought struck me. "A tall, gangling youth, a shock of red hair, a splay of freckles across his nose, and an Adam's apple that bobs?"

Alicia laughed. "Yes! That's the one."

"I have seen him once or twice recently. In fact, I thought once that he was following me, but I am sure I was imagining it! I must keep a sharp eye out for his mysterious master. Tell me more about him."

"I do not know if it was what I had heard about his reputation with women or the memory of the terrible dressing down of his squire, but the man frightened me. Not that he wasn't the model of courtly manners and most charming! Perhaps it was the direct look in his eye, as if he could see through you, or the fact that I could not follow the conversation that he was leading." She turned this over in her mind. "I suppose that I was not exactly afraid of him. I mean only that I would fear him as an enemy."

"From all I have heard of him, one is probably wise not to have him as an enemy! But surely reports of his successes with the ladies are exaggerated, just like this new scandal. I own that I am curious to know what he has to recommend himself to women. From what you say, even as an impecunious younger son, he met with success."

Alicia drew her brows together. "He is not precisely handsome like my Herbert, nor does he have that look of gentleness, but there is something about him that might be considered captivating. I am very stupid about explaining such things! And he does not seem to pay much heed to the women who cast their lures to him. Yet, the morning after his departure from Herbert's castle, my tiring women were full to bursting with the tale that Sir Roland had bedded some highborn woman that night. I was really quite shocked, for it could only have been— But I do not credit it! No, no, he is not at all like my Herbert."

I did not press her for more, for I saw that I would get no further description of this enigmatic man than how he measured up to—and fell short of—Alicia's beloved Herbert. "No," I conceded gravely, "but then you must admit that no other knight in the realm is as handsome or has as much address as your Herbert."

Alicia nodded at this, reflecting soberly on the truth of my statement for a few moments. Then her gray eyes lit with laughter. "Why, you—Grita! Ever the tease!"

I hugged her impulsively. "My love, I am delighted that you are so well pleased with Herbert. Why should it be otherwise? You have kind and wise parents to have married you so well."

Demoiselle Marie-Ange Dujarrie came upon us just then. She had apparently been parading in the gardens, obviously very well pleased that she was being squired by a somewhat rakish-looking knight, whose lively eyes alit first on Alicia and then on me.

"So there you are!" Marie-Ange exclaimed, thereby instantly disclosing the fact that she had been hunting us down, no doubt with the object of exhibiting the latest of her gallants.

"Were you looking for us, Marie-Ange?" I inquired politely.

"No—yes! That is, I had a recollection that I had seen you two once in the gardens at this hour."

"We come here every day, Marie-Ange," Alicia said matter-of-factly, and added guilelessly, "I thought you knew that."

"Oh, every day! Well! How fortunate to be such good friends!" She gave her very pretty head a toss. "But you have made me forget my manners. I have the honor of presenting Alicia Stafford and Marguerite Montcrief to Sir Robert FitzWarren."

Sir Robert executed an exquisite bow and bent a warm gaze on Alicia.

Marie-Ange was too experienced a fisherwoman to allow her catch to swim away so easily. "That is," she continued chattily, "Alicia Stafford soon to be Longchamps. You must know, Sir Robert, that Alicia is Herbert Longchamp's betrothed. The wedding is in August. I am part of the wedding party, and there is so much to do! We shall all of us be there a week early to help. I so much love weddings: the people, the ceremony, the dancing, oh, everything! The dancing especially. You will dance with me, Sir Robert?" She smiled up at him archly, paused, then added as an afterthought, "Marguerite will be there too, won't you, dearest?"

I nodded assent.

Sir Robert smiled smoothly through all this, and uttered vague but gracious words as to the connections between the FitzWarrens and the Longchamps, but his interest had been effectively diverted from Alicia. His eyes slid back to the original object of attraction. I had observed that Sir Robert seemed to have a turn for fashion, since he had taken an appreciative interest in the style of Marie-Ange's kirtle, the bodice being cut low and in the Provençal style. It was a daring creation, but she was petite and deep-bosomed and could carry it off to advantage, however inappropriate it may have been for such an early hour of the day. Marie-Ange could not have been unaware of her bait, for she hung delicately on Sir Robert's arm, angling for the precise tilt to cast her lure. Sir Robert's eyes rose to the fly, and once his attention was properly hooked, Marie-Ange turned to the real business of her visit.

"Alicia," she said, addressing both of us, "it seems that your wedding is not the only topic of conversation these days! I have just been hearing from Sir Robert about—"

"Can it be," I said, turning to Alicia, very much in a dampening spirit, "that Marie-Ange has just now heard of the scandal surrounding Isabelle Beauvais and Roland of Guimont?"

"So you have heard!" Marie-Ange cried in dismay, but recovered quickly. "Of course you have! I heard *yesterday* myself, but Sir Robert was just telling me the details, weren't you, Sir Robert?"

Sir Robert was not so behindhand as to miss his cue. "Most everyone has heard the general outlines of the story, but few know the inside facts."

"No, I am quite sure that I don't know the inside facts," I assured him.

Sir Robert belonged to those men who have the disconcerting habit of never looking a woman in the face but keep their eyes averted to a point somewhere between her neck and her navel. When Sir Robert pulled his eyes away from Marie-Ange's most interesting form, I had the distinction of being the one he addressed.

"For instance, did you know," he said with great consequence, "that Lady Isabelle was to come to Westminster but now finds herself in no condition to travel? You can imagine, I am sure, the delicate condition of her nerves at this time. Guimont, on the other hand, is on the premises, cool as ever."

"I have never met the Lady Isabelle, but I can well imagine her discomfort at this time," I said, feeling somehow compelled to speak. "You do know her, don't you?"

I may have been talking to Sir Robert, but Marie-Ange replied. "Oh, yes!" she chirped. "Sir Robert knows both of them, in fact, and quite well. Too well, one might say of

Guimont! Sir Robert says he drinks heavily, you know, and becomes violent . . . so you see? . . . I need hardly elaborate."

"I understand that his brother, Sir Roger, was also drinking heavily that night," I said.

Marie-Ange shot a quick look at her swain. "Perhaps! But that is just conjecture."

"Marie-Ange, this is all conjecture!" I countered. "How is one to decide which rumor to believe?"

Sir Robert came mercifully to her aid. He coughed delicately. "It helps—ah, Demoiselle Montcrief, I believe?—if one is acquainted with those involved. As Demoiselle Dujarrie says, I have the very dubious privilege of knowing Guimont. Let us say that he is a dangerous man."

"I should like to meet him, then, and decide for myself," I said bravely. "I wonder if I will have that, ah, dubious privilege this week at court."

Sir Robert smiled weakly. "No, I am afraid not. He has gone away this morning, I believe, to survey his new lands. The king, you see, has curiously given Guimont some territory. A gift, if you please!"

"The lands are in Wales, aren't they?" I said.

Sir Robert raised his eyes to mine. "Why, yes, I believe so," he said languidly.

Marie-Ange had had enough. "I have never known you to be so informed, Marguerite!"

I yielded to temptation. "So you see what happens when you don't meet Yvette and me in the afternoons to stitch. She told me everything yesterday, but that was when you heard too, wasn't it?"

"Yes, of course. So Yvette told you? Well, that is interesting, to be sure! Just look, Sir Robert, there are Charlotta and William. The very ones we were looking for! We must go now. Alicia, I hope to see you again before the wedding; and, Marguerite, dearest, I shall see you this afternoon—to stitch! I can't conceive why I missed it yesterday!"

"If that didn't take the wind out of her eye!" I said low to Alicia after they had gone.

"It was very bad of you, Grita, but I did enjoy it," she confessed. "How could you have done Yvette such an unfriendly turn, though? It is not like you!"

"What do you mean by unfriendly?" I asked mischievously.

"I fear that Marie-Ange and Yvette do not get along as well as they might, and now Yvette will have to answer to her."

"An understatement! But if I am there to act as a buffer between them, nothing will happen. Besides, Marie-Ange cannot now admit that she did not hear all about it yesterday."

"Yes, that's true, but I cannot like all this loose talk about Lady Isabelle and Sir Roland. I was only telling you, Marguerite, because it concerns you at Shrivenham."

"I appreciate it, too, but I believe there is nothing anyone can do to stop the talk. It is only natural."

Alicia sighed. "Herbert believes Guimont to be a *good* man, and I cannot help but think that the gossip will damage his reputation."

Her faith in Herbert's judgment was touching, and it would do no good to point out to her that perhaps she took more of an interest in Sir Roland's reputation than he did himself. "If he is in the right, the truth will prevail," I remarked.

"I am sure you are right. Nevertheless, Sir Robert certainly seems like a fine chevalier."

"Yes," I said, not bothering to argue so insignificant a point, "doesn't he?"

We turned our talk back to Alicia's forthcoming marriage and beguiled the rest of our hour in discussing the preparations to be done at Castle Burford in August. The gardens were hushed and drowsy, and a curious peace stole over me. I was forever to associate the perfume of roses in summer with Alicia, our quiet hours together, and the time before our lives really began, but I never once thought to link the dark and dangerous Roland, Earl of Guimont, to the rough, vital, wholly masculine man named Guy whom I had met the night before.

Chapter 2

Alicia's wedding was to provide me with a precious trove of memories that would sustain me during the uneventful days of autumn and winter that lay ahead. Certainly in size and magnificence I could not have imagined a grander occasion. Not that I was a judge in these matters, for I had not attended a social event in six years, and had never before that attended one with three hundred of the realm's peers. From the comments and reactions of the other guests, however, I knew it to have been opulent indeed. Even my father unwittingly contrived to make the wedding everything that was memorable, by falling victim to a colic that kept him at his bed. It was a sudden decision on his part, and he did not seem so very sick to me. I naturally did not persuade him to attend the wedding, for his absence relieved me of the burden of tending to his whims and capricious ill health. My enjoyment was only briefly marred by the unprovidential fact that I shared a plate with Charles Hartford at the bridal feast, but since I shrewdly suspected that Lady Constance had guided Fate's hand in seating me next to her son, I did not complain of that arrangement to Alicia.

In truth, I had no desire to cavil, for I was well satisfied with the rare freedom I enjoyed during those summer weeks. Upon my return to Shrivenham from London at the end of July, I had planned to begin what was needed for the coming harvests before I left for Alicia's wedding. However, when my father unexpectedly allowed me to go to Castle Burford for the entire week of wedding preparations and added that I might stay for the hunt if I liked, I mobilized the servants to hold household in one week rather than three. From cock's crow to vespers, my army besieged the castle. On the first day, I marshaled the blanchers to boil the linen and mend the inevitable rents, and I would not consider the job done in the laundry until the drains had afterward been unclogged. There was a leaky tub there to be patched, too, and while I was calling in the village carpenter, I summoned the wainwright as well to replace the rear axle of a wagon needed immediately for the haying. Bess, Gertrude, and the inside women forayed the sleeping quarters, turning out mattresses and pillows and leaving fresh, green rushes in their wake.

The next day dawned with a surprise attack on the undercroft where the grain baskets were cleaned and set aside for the imminent refilling, and the offal was sent to feed the swine. The argil crocks for pickling were scoured and aired, and the rancid oils were decanted and their flasks scalded in lime. A secondary force pillaged the weeds from the garden in the shelter of the parapet, and at day's end the beans were also restrung and the orchard was pruned. I swept through the dairy and brewhouse, and since they were in reasonable order, their management would have to await my return. The third day saw no respite for the ranks in the bakery, for refiring the ovens in the August heat was cruel punishment even for one's arch enemy. I discovered, then, one advantage to this frenzy of activity: I had no time to entertain the inevitable quarrels that arose, so that when Michael Armorer came to me with another complaint about Nan, I had to tell him that I was very sorry, but he would just have to suffer her vagaries, a prospect he considered with deep misgivings. I did catch a glimpse of John Cook brandishing a ladle and chasing his latest batter boy around the kitchens, but save for this minor skirmish within the ranks, the campaign went very well.

I spent the afternoon and evening attempting to balance my tally books. Although the rents and taxes would not fall due before the Michelmas, I could depend on neither my ciphering speed nor my accuracy to leave the entire task until my return. It was a long and tedious job at best and one that I would fain put off. I thanked my forethought the next day when I heard the jingle of the linen and woolen merchant's cart in the bailey.

Since I had a fair idea of how my accounts stood, I was able to make some advantageous purchases and indulged myself with five ells of blue sendal into the bargain. It was a bright day, one well suited for judging the fastness of the colors and the tightness of the weaves, although it caused Master Adam, the portly merchant, to wheeze slightly in the heat under the weight of his cart. I chose kendals and serges for the scullions and grooms, while preferring sarcenets, kerseymeres, and friezes for the knights and ladies, without forgetting to purchase the bodkins, threads, and silks for embroidery and braiding. We still received our linens and broadcloths from the village, so Master Adam knew better than to press me to purchase any from him. He knew me well, in fact, and after we had concluded the bulk of our trade and I humored him by buying some very pretty belts that I did not need, he mopped his brow and brought out a bale of material from the back of his cart. He unwound the canvas swaddling a bolt of homely homespun and offered me the entire cloth for a moderate sum. The weave was visibly irregular and the weft at an angle, but I knew the trick of boiling certain woolens to fasten the threads, countered him with a ridiculously low price, and finally met him in the middle. We parted, no doubt both satisfied that each had struck the best bargain. I was certainly pleased that I had enough material to provide winter capes for all the livery.

On the fifth day, I commanded my forces inside the castle. The stillroom off the hall gallery needed an airing, and I unlocked the wall cupboards for inspection. I was nothing loath to bundling my hair away in a plain kerchief, donning the white muslin smock required of all my inside women, and setting to cleaning. It was part of the duty of a chatelaine, I felt, to be able to *do* and not just to order. A mistress who did not know how to dress a joint to show the cook or set a stitch for the novice sempstress was like the field marshal who could sound the battle cry but not wield a mace, cock an arbalest, smite the enemy to the ground while remaining astride his destrier, or do any of the other things that knights seemed to consider diverting and devoted much time to perfecting. In this respect, I tried to live up to the motto of the late Lady Isolde, my predecessor and the seneschal's wife, from whose lips one would hear: "It is the bad mistress who cannot spin silk." I could, in a pinch, spin silk, but in all honesty I could not have earned my keep at the job in an exacting mistress's household. Rather, I tried to execute the spirit of that motto, and actually enjoyed many of the housewifely tasks that many another chatelaine shunned; dipping tallows, making soap, raising herbs, and preserving vegetables were part of my life, and I enjoyed it.

Thus, I did not dislike the rather prosaic occupation of taking stock of the preserves, spices, sugars, and dried fruits and nuts in the stillroom. I could not, of course, do everything, but depended on Dame Ellen, who was schooled in physic, to replenish the herbs and simples and to prepare the drugs and purges that were so necessary for the winter months. I also relied on Dame Ellen to oversee Shrivenham in the event that I was unable to do so. She was a masterful woman who liked to take charge; indeed, I had heard it from certain quarters that she was even a trifle overbearing. My women seemed to have a healthy respect for her tongue, and I did not know the man who would not submit to her orders, surely not her husband, Ian, our gameskeeper, whom she plainly kept in order, and not even my father, who gave her a wide berth. Thus she was a perfect surrogate for me, although I would hope not to be overbearing. From all reports, she had warmed to the job while I was at Westminster so that her cup was full to overflowing when I announced that I would be leaving shortly for Castle Burford. She swelled at the news but answered only with admirable restraint, "You may depend on me, my lady!"

We had reached the rows of preserved strawberries and I was receiving a crock from the hands of Hodierne when a sturdy young man, not much beyond his fourth summer, burst in upon us.

"Lady 'Garite! Lady 'Garite! You must come! It has happened!"

He ran up to me breathless and lifted his cherubic face, full of excitement, to mine.

"Master Thomas, I am in the dark! *What* has happened?" I responded, catching one of his chubby hands.

"Grenadine! She has whelped!" he answered with all the satisfaction of one who has the privilege to impart great news.

Thomas was the fruit of the autumn of Dame Ellen's child-bearing years and the apple of his father's eye. He was their first and only child, and as a result he was much indulged by his papa. Dame Ellen, who did not share her husband's weakness of spoiling the child, adjured him, "Stop plaguing the Lady Marguerite, Thomas! She has a flue-full of work to do and cannot be bothered with Grenadine's litter! Now, be gone with you, young man!"

Thomas, whose willful disposition rivaled his mama's, stood his ground. He turned to me with an artful mixture of wounded feelings and youthful expectation. "I am not plaguing you, am I? You told me to tell you when Grenadine had her pups, and now she has, and it's your—your duty to come see!"

I was not in the habit of conforming to others' ideas about my responsibilities. Neither was I in the habit of refusing Thomas anything.

"Very true, Thomas. I told you to fetch me, and it is right of you to have remembered and informed me of it. I am not so involved here that I cannot leave. Hodierne, would you continue with the preserves?"

Dame Ellen did not look pleased. I said to her in an aside, "It sets a very poor example to lie to children, don't you think? I told him very explicitly to tell me when Grenadine gave birth, and we are not so very busy that you and Hodierne cannot finish the inventory without me?"

Thomas tugged at my sleeve. "Come, Lady 'Garite. It won't wait!"

Dame Ellen showed signs of wavering. "Don't keep the Lady Marguerite gone too long," she said severely and shook her finger at her offspring. I could almost have taken it to have been directed at myself.

"Come along, then, Master Thomas," I commanded, and his face broke into a seraphic smile. "You must tell me where

Grenadine chose to have her pups," I said with slight trepidation.

"With Master Michael!" he said with a smile that boded no good for that trusted servant.

"And what of the litter?"

"Seven pups and not one died. That was because I was there to help! They are *all* healthy and strong—*every* one of them!"

"Well, I am sure they are if you say so," I said, wondering as we crossed the bailey why he had made such a point of their state of health, for it could only mean that some were perhaps sickly.

Although canine births were relatively tidy affairs, I knew that Michael would have just cause for annoyance. Indeed, this harassed smithy was glowering on the threshold of his large stall, which he always kept as neat as wax.

"I canna tell you, my lady," he said gloomily, "why she had to come here to whelp."

"Consider it a privilege, Michael!"

"She could easily have honored someone else," he said, "for instance, John Cook."

"But nowhere else is as clean and warm," I said as I crossed into the Vulcan realm. He accepted the compliment with a reluctant grace, for it was true: the dark glow of the fire radiated a warmth that was not unpleasant even in August and never failed to fascinate me, so that whenever I crossed before this door, I was obliged to stop for a moment or two to contemplate the flame; and Michael had swept the earthen floor until it was as smooth and hard as the polished wood in my bower. It was, in fact, a perfect place for a bitch to give birth. The humid and pungent odor of the birthing process assailed my nostrils from the corner where Grenadine, a large hound of indeterminate parentage, suckled her tumble of pups. I knelt beside her to stroke her orange-red coat, shiny with sweat, and she rolled tired but satisfied eyes to mine.

"There now, big girl, you've provided us with some useful animals. Thomas's papa will be pleased."

There were six healthy pups, eagerly nourishing themselves

at their mother's side, but there was one runt, who looked as if he would not live out the week. It seemed best to remove him immediately to provide extra food for the others.

"I suppose this one will have to be drowned," I muttered.

A gasp of dismay and disbelief escaped from my youthful companion. "Oh no, Lady 'Garite, you cannot mean it!"

"But I do mean it, love," I said as kindly as possible.

"Why, he is not as strong now as the others, but he will survive, I can tell!"

"Can you? Then tell me this: what am I to do with him? He is almost too weak to eat."

"Give him to me, I know just how to care for him. Remember the duckling that was so frail? I cared for him, and he grew up strong."

"Thomas, that duckling did not live beyond a month!"

"He got caught," Thomas said, ready with an answer.

"Yes," I corroborated. "Caught in the door to the undercroft where he did not belong!"

"*That* won't happen again. I promise! Besides, I am much older now."

"Much!"

Thomas looked up at me with an appeal in his eyes. It did not seem so terrible a thing to let him handle animals, especially if he was to follow in his father's post. "All right," I relented, "he is yours. But you cannot take him from his mother just yet. He still needs her."

Thomas beamed and reached for his new friend. At that moment the runt wriggled away from Grenadine, cracked open an eye, and surveyed us as if he knew he would soon be in Thomas's tender care.

I told him that he was a pitiful creature, a tribute that he acknowledged with a wet sneeze and a shiver that racked his scrawny body.

I sat back on my heels and laughed. "Now what will you name this poor little thing, Thomas?"

"Charger!" he responded with conviction.

Charger survived the next few days before I left for Castle

Burford, and, to give Thomas his due, the small creature was thriving. I saw the two of them the morning I left. The sun was cracking beyond the horizon when I went to the stables to see my horse Molly before the journey. Castle Burford was an honest day's ride from Shrivenham, and although I was no horsewoman and never rode for sport, I saw no need for a litter and instructed my groom to prepare my palfrey for the trip. Molly and I understood each other well, and I knew she would be good to me on this day's journey. Bess and Gertrude were to accompany me, and since I anticipated no obstacles in our trip, I reckoned that Master Ian and two of his men would provide ample escort for us.

Thomas, still foggy with sleep, came to see me as our small traveling party was gathering. He was holding Charger, who was wagging his tail and looking almost frisky.

"Now, Thomas, I hope to see a healthy puppy in two weeks when I return."

"Yes, my lady, and *he* won't get caught!"

I smiled and sent him back to his bed. In his retreat into the castle, he unfortunately met his mama, who scolded him for allowing the miserable runt to share his bed.

She had come to see me and her husband off on our journey. I did not have time to argue once again on the subject of Charger, so I decided to divert Dame Ellen's formidable energies into more productive channels. "Dame Ellen, I am confident that I may depend on your judgment and wise counsel while I am gone."

She assumed an attitude that improbably mixed humility and pride.

"And," I continued, "I would like you most particularly to keep your eye on Nan."

A martial light sparkled in her eye. Discretion and indignation struggled in her breast for supremacy, but only for the shortest moment; indignation won. "Adone-do, my lady! I surely know better than to burden you every time I come to learn of one of Nan's—ah—lapses. You have already overmuch work to do, being that you are called upon to do many of the duties of the seigneur, too!—and in addition, an unmarried maiden! These tales should not, in general, reach your ears! I have always thought it improper that your father allows, nay, forces upon you so many responsibilities, and I hope you won't think it a liberty if I tell you that it is most improper for you to know many of the things you do."

"Yes, yes," I said soothingly. "Very correct to express yourself. You have such a fine moral sense, which is why I look to you for guidance."

This mollified her somewhat, but her righteous anger was not slain. "That girl, that tavern slattern, that *hussy*, has caused a mort of trouble in the kitchen with manners more suitable to a camp follower than a Christian woman!"

This was strong censure indeed and could only mean that Nan had been caught red-handed.

"And now she has spread trouble into the dairy and the Lord only knows where else, teasing the men so that none can get any work done! I am surprised that she is not yet with child, but it has not come to that yet! But this is not fare for your plate!" Dame Ellen said, catching herself.

"I am aware of much of what goes on, Dame Ellen. No, don't be shocked! But I believe that reports of her behavior have been exaggerated by Sarah, don't you think?"

"Sarah is a good and honest woman!"

"I do not doubt that, but am I not correct that she has a decided preference for John Cook, who has been the latest victim of Nan's charms?"

"I do not know how you came by way of that knowledge," Dame Ellen said loftily, "but that would not prompt Sarah to lie."

I murmured some response.

"I do not know why you keep her!" Dame Ellen exclaimed.

"Sarah?" I said. "I have never known anyone to churn butter better than she!"

"No, Nan!" Dame Ellen pronounced with a spark of anger.

The statement was purely rhetorical, but I could not resist an answer. I was given more to practicality than morality and refused to turn her out, for Nan had her uses. "She does her job in any case, and does it well. Our breads have never been as good—"

Dame Ellen took instant exception to this, muttering darkly, "Food on the table, carrion in the soul."

"Nevertheless we must eat, and I prefer to eat well when I can. We all benefit."

"That may be! To be sure, I would not allow her such liberties under my rule!"

I was not going to enumerate the advantages of having at least one woman of her stamp in the community, but I said instead, "Which is why I am sure all will go well at Shrivenham while I am gone."

Dame Ellen had nothing to respond to my parting shot, while I mounted Molly and led our small party across the drawbridge, but a crusading spirit had clearly entered her massive bosom. I shuddered to think of the excesses of virtue that Shrivenham would enjoy in the days to come and preferred instead to contemplate the summer landscape, drowsy and peaceful in the August heat. I knew these hours to be the moment of calm before the tempest that awaited me in the days ahead. My wildest imaginings, however, were nothing to the frenetic reality that greeted me at Burford. The castle teemed with squires and pages, and the servants quarreled and fought and fell over one another in their numbers. The scullions washed and polished the plate, master bakers created confections to be admired but not eaten and spent four days concocting the bridal cake, a construction that stood some four feet high and six feet in diameter, while in the bailey a team of butchers was slaughtering the calves, lambs, baby boar, and deer for roasting. There were still thousands of candles to be dipped, garlands of flowers to be slung from beam to beam in the Great Hall, and fresh rushes to be strewn, as well as all manner of game and fowl to be plucked, farced, and replumed for display.

In the bower, the women escaped much of the noise from below but none of the frenzy, and our fingers fairly ached from plying the needle. Three days before the wedding we were far from finished. Alicia sat embroidering the neck of Herbert's wedding tunic, while Yvette was at the hem of it. As a needle-woman, I had not the artistry of Yvette, who was noted for her vivid designs, her eye for color, and her elegant stitchery, but I did boast a steady, even hand best suited for regular patterns. I had, therefore, insisted on the privilege of applying to Alicia's red silk dress the border of miniature pearls that would adorn the neckline and front panel, as well as the double row of beading that would grace her fine gazzatum veil. My efforts freed Alicia to lavish her skill and love on Herbert's raiment. Around us were gathered several handmaidens, all busy with bridal clothes, shirts, smocks, linens, and one sat cross-legged on a cushion finishing an altar piece. There was a hum of talk that broke off momentarily when Marie-Ange swept dramatically into the room, flung herself down on the seat in the window embrasure, and began flipping a striped pillow over and over.

She had clearly brought with her some news, but I was not going to gratify her by demanding outright what was about to burst forth from her lips.

"Marie-Ange," I said to her over my shoulder, "help me by holding the hem of the dress taut so that I may place the next row in a straight line."

She hesitated but came with something perilously close to a flounce and knelt facing me to catch and smooth out the lower half of the garment.

Yvette, apparently with less forbearance than I possessed, her fair head bent over her handiwork, said with a tone of resignation, "Well, Marie-Ange? What *is* it?"

From her kneeling position, Marie-Ange cast me a fulminating glance that read *So there!* and began, with one of her airy gestures that upset an entire row of pearls, "I have just seen Lady Henrietta's handmaiden who has a sister in attendance to the Princess Elisabeth, and she claims that Isabelle is back on the tip of every tongue at Westminster."

"But she never left it!" I interjected.

"Oh, *no*, Marie-Ange!" Alicia expostulated as she laid her sewing firmly in her lap. "Herbert strictly *forbade* me to talk about this subject. He assured me that Sir Roland never killed his brother and that the whole thing is just ugly rumor. And that is that!"

"But this has nothing to do with Sir Roland!" Marie-Ange replied.

Alicia pursed her lips and resumed her broderie.

"Really, Marie-Ange, we cannot credit the stories of hand-maidens—" Yvette ventured.

"But what better source?" The force of her argument being obvious to everyone, Marie-Ange continued uninterrupted, "And it is not rumor, ugly or otherwise, that Isabelle has made herself an important conquest: Hugh Falmouth!"

This intelligence had a startling effect on its audience. Yvette looked up sharply, and Alicia and I exchanged looks of dismay mingled with exasperation. Dismay because we knew that Yvette had conceived a decided preference for this handsome che-valier, exasperation because it was obvious that Marie-Ange knew it, too. I did not rate Marie-Ange's understanding above the most ordinary, but her ear for gossip and her intuitions about others' emotional affinities were unerring.

"Well!" said Alicia. "I am sure that is very interesting but I cannot know what you mean by it!"

"I mean precisely that there is talk of an imminent be-trothal."

"Oh!" Alicia uttered faintly. Yvette's blond head remained bent but her color was heightened.

"I can see that my sympathy for the poor Isabelle was wasted," I commented.

"Do you not perceive the cream of the matter?" asked Marie-Ange, visibly astonished.

"No," Yvette answered stiffly. "Pray, enlighten us."

"It is obvious! Hugh Falmouth and Roland of Guimont!" she pronounced somewhat obscurely.

"I *knew* it had something to do with Sir Roland," Alicia said crossly.

Marie-Ange looked around at our blank, expectant faces. "But they are the bitterest of enemies!"

I had met the handsome Hugh only once, a few weeks before at Westminster. He had paid me no heed for he was engaged

in a mild flirtation with Yvette. I had had little time to take
his measure, but his manners were smooth and refined, and I
could easily have succumbed to his charms myself. I could not
remember exactly what had been said about him, but it was
to the effect that although his fortune was not overlarge, he
was not without influence.

"Enemies?" Alicia said without guile. "But I have often
seen them together at court in the past month."

"Alicia, have you never heard of the lion sleeping with the
lamb?" Marie-Ange asked with a hint of sarcasm.

It was not to be clarified who the lion was and who the
lamb in this case, but we did learn Yvette's particular interpretation of the aphorism: "For my part, this Roland of Guimont
sounds like a wolf in sheep's clothing!"

For my part, I was becoming quite eager to meet the lovely
Isabelle.

"I cannot credit it," Alicia said, "for it is much too soon
for anything of that serious of a nature."

"I do not think," Marie-Ange said, "that it takes men any
time to fall in love with Isabelle."

"It seems that That Woman may have her pick of knights!"
Yvette said with unwonted asperity. "It is not inconceivable
that the rogue Guimont would instigate a vulgar brawl over
her with a man of honor like Sir Hugh and ruin the wedding!"

Yvette's apprehensions proved unfounded. From the wedding to the bedding when the women surrounded Alicia and
bore her off to the bridal chamber with laughter and much
jesting, nothing occurred to disturb the joyous day. The guests
began in the morning to flock to Burford's Norman church in
the village outside the castle walls, and by midday, when the
procession from the castle began, Alicia's father had to escort
her between the crowds that had spilled outside the church into
the square. Her hair was unbound and gleamed chestnut in the
sunlight, and her bejeweled train winked back at me as I, with
Yvette and Marie-Ange, carried its ponderous lengths. I had
never participated in such a grand event, and I knew that I was
flushed as much from the heat of the clear summer day as from
the ranks of staring eyes upon me. I schooled my face to conceal

my excitement, but it was quite impossible for me to keep my eyes demurely averted as we entered the church and I stole a glance ahead of me and saw Herbert, awaiting his bride by the altar steps, attended by his brother, Robert Longchamps, and several other lords whom I did not know. Close to the altar I caught a glimpse of Hugh Falmouth and next to him a woman of undeniable beauty. I did not have time to assess her features, but I knew from all descriptions that I had seen That Woman.

Brian, the bishop of Bath, performed the ceremony, throughout which four knights held a veil above Alicia's head, since she was a maiden.

After the marriage vows were exchanged and the blessing was bestowed, we crowned the wedded pair with flower circlets and proceeded back to the castle with much less decorum than we had left it. The atmosphere of the banquet was enlivened by mimes and tumblers and strolling minstrels. Pages scurried to and fro with flagons of wine, and before very long the men hailed the bridal couple in a shout, and three hundred cups and more were raised to them as they sat on a dais at the high table. On the heels of the tumblers came the jesters in their motley, and through these shuffled a muzzled bear led on a chain, with a tame monkey perched on its shoulders.

The meats were served on silver platters winking in the glow of a thousand candles that lit the Great Hall. There were haunches of English oxen roasted on the spit, no less than twenty boars' heads in aspic spiked with cloves, and venison in broth, along with the more delicately prepared swans, capons, and peacocks. One table that ran the width of the hall offered nothing but doves and larks in pastry shells latticed with braided dough and glazed, while another groaned under the weight of the sweetmeats, frumenty, marzipan, compotes of candied almonds, jellies, creams, and custards.

My appetite was, regrettably, diminished by the presence of Charles Hartford on my left. He, however, approached his fare with all the finesse of a swine to swill and made a very good meal. He soon became drunk into the bargain, which did not surprise me, for if he had been born with any other objective than to offend the sensibilities of those with a less crude nature,

I had yet to discover it. I glanced at him and marveled afresh how one who had only the first few wisps of hair on his chin could look so dissipated.

"I thirst!" he bellowed over his shoulder to no one in particular. "Refreshment! Here, you, page!"

A lad, not much younger than Charles, his tablier already badly stained, stopped obediently behind our chairs and poured freely into Charles's silver goblet until the wine spilled over onto the table. The page made a movement toward my goblet but I covered it with my hand. Charles wrapped his hand around the bottle, and the page bowed slightly and withdrew.

Charles immediately fortified himself with a deep drink.

"Will you not drink with me?" he asked in threatening tones.

"I have drunk my fill."

He cast off the rest of his wine in one gulp and said unsteadily, "You need not reproach me, you know."

"Did I do that?"

He shot me a bleary look as he refilled his vessel but ignored my comment. He picked up his goblet again and some of the wine spilled onto the table. He glared at it and placed the goblet back down with precision. "I suppose," he enunciated, "that you will tell my mother when next you see her."

"I cannot think, Charles, why I should go to Lady Constance bearing tales of your intemperance. Surely she knows what you are. And—"

"I expect that was meant as an insult, my dear Marguerite, knowing your surly disposition, but I will let it pass."

"—And indeed," I continued imprudently, "I cannot think why I should go to your mother at all."

This captured his weaving attention. Charles, whose features bore a creditable resemblance to those of a fish, turned to me and said, with as much life in his gaze as in the eye of a carp, "No? Now, I find that interesting. Am I to infer that you dislike my cherished mother? She will be sore upset."

"No, you are not. I like my Lady Constance very well," I replied with a fine disregard for veracity.

"You did not go see her at Westminster."

"What has that to say to anything?" A note of defensiveness

edged into my voice. I hoped he was too groggy to notice it, although by taking only moderate pains, he could speak with a remarkable coherence.

"I can only conclude that you do not like her. She mentioned it to me and regretted not having seen you. A poor widow! Why did you not pay her a visit?"

"She did not invite me, Charles."

"Our families do not stand on ceremony, dear Marguerite. You needed no invitation."

"Nevertheless, it is only proper to wait for one, or are you unaware of the courtly code?"

"It would be odd indeed," Charles responded with awesome deliberation, culling this expression from the phraseology of his parent, "if I were obliged to consult you on the observances of civility. But you have yet to explain why you did not visit my mother."

I suppose that it is the same for every man, for I can recall that whenever my father or his infrequent companions had been drinking and I had occasion to overhear their talk, they would take some notion into their heads, in general a very foolish one, and hold to it buckle and thong. Therefore, I was not alarmed by Charles's persistent question and answered at random, "Perhaps I had no reason to."

He lifted an eyebrow at that. "I assume that you mean to pay her one here."

"Of course," I said. I was to deliver yet another note from my father to Lady Constance at Alicia's wedding. It was no doubt a trivial message, and I could not like the role of messenger; but I was resolved to do penance for having forgotten my errand to her at Westminster.

Charles paused a moment as if to sort out a thought and asked with drunken logic, "If you had no reason to see my mother at Westminster, then why did your father allow you to go to court?"

"Because he wanted to hear the very latest gossip, of course!" I retorted with heavy sarcasm, tired of this very pointless argument.

Charles accepted this as a plausible explanation, although

he knew my father and his habits as well as I did. His mind then seized onto this fresh topic.

"Gossip, you say? Then you have heard of the coming union between Isabelle Beauvais and Hugh Falmouth?"

"And who has not?" I said. "I do not lend the story much credence."

"Then you are the only one who does not. It is a well-established liaison."

"Nothing is well established," I said, "until they are actually wed. I do not believe that he will go through with it."

"Oh? Are you so much in Hugh's confidence?" he asked with a suggestive leer.

"I do not think Sir Hugh is aware of my existence," I said.

Charles surveyed me with an assessing, insulting regard for the details of my person. "Not quite in his style, are you? But I can assure you, my dear, that he would not shun you if he found your form between his sheets some night."

Since I could think of few less-likely contingencies, I was not so much nauseated by his vulgarity as annoyed. "Charles! You have put my mind at ease! But now if you will excuse me—" and I rose to escape his company. The trestles at one end of the Great Hall were being removed and sets of dancers were forming.

His hand closed possessively over mine, and I instinctively withdrew from its clammy touch.

"We shall dance together," he commanded with that same menacing note in his voice as he had used earlier.

My evil genius prompted me to answer, "I can think of nothing more repugnant. Now release my hand!"

He was standing now, too, and his ample body swayed toward me. "We shall dance!" said the pot-valiant Charles. His voice boomed and several heads turned our way.

"Are you threatening me?" I said flippantly. "It would take rather something more than a swaggering coxcomb to make me cower in fear!"

"So you do not care to dance with me? Then I wonder how you shall fancy sharing the joys of our wedding bed? And that is no threat!"

I felt the blood drain from my face and looked straight into
his bloodshot eyes, which registered a hit. The triumph seemed
too genuine for me to believe that Charles was bluffing. I could
readily imagine, since Charles shared with his mother the same
venal turn of mind, that he would like to possess my rather
considerable lands to add to his smaller holdings. I could not,
on the other hand, imagine that my father would not have
informed me if such a marriage was imminent. I was momentarily ruffled by a sense of misgiving, too inchoate, however,
to be much more than a vague disquiet. I had merely been
caught off guard. With unsteady dignity, I placed my hand on
Charles's wrist and allowed him to lead me into the first set.

My apprehensions were forgotten with the first notes of the
lutes and pipes. Had I been told that I might be obliged to sit
among the young girls and the widows during a considerable
part of the evening, I would have accepted the warning perfectly placidly. I knew few men whom I could expect to ask
me to dance, and out of the scattered brief acquaintances I had
made at Westminster, I could think of none who cherished
anything warmer for me than friendship. To my surprise and
pleasure, then, I had no lack of partners from the moment that
Charles released my hand after the first round dance. I could
easily push to the back of my mind the words exchanged with
Charles, and I could even silently thank him for having led me
out for the first dance, for once in circulation, it was no difficult
thing to become an almost automatic part of the next dance.
King Henry's taste for Aquitanian culture extended to the savory Poitevin and Angevin dances with their lively rhythms
and intricate steps, and the musicians in the minstrel gallery
willingly bowed to this royal preference. The one disappointment in Alicia's wedding was that King Henry had at the last
moment been unable to attend because of the queen's early
lying-in. However, when it was learned that she had produced
another male heir to secure the succession, the sovereign's
absence was interpreted to be a good omen for Alicia's and
Herbert's union and contributed to the merriment. I caught that
gay mood and felt as spirited as the dances. I had convinced
myself that I was in my best looks, and met my new partners

with a certain measure of confidence. Alicia had encouraged my vanity when, a few days previous, as we were trying on our bride-maiden dresses, she exclaimed, "Dearest! You must always wear blue! The sky blue of Burford matches your eyes to perfection. I have always found life to be most unfair, and family colors are never so obliging as to become one's coloring. Our shade of blue has never pleased me, whereas the grays and greens of Shrivenham, which quite wash you out, would do very well for me!" Sir Robert apparently found my appearance to his liking, for he solicited my hand for two dances in succession, and although his eyes had an embarrassing tendency to wander, I found his attentions flattering.

So I danced and laughed and abandoned myself to the moment. I took delight in the rich variety of my dancing partners and hoped that they took pleasure in me. I did not believe that anyone would hail me as a beauty, but I was beginning to think that I passed myself off very well. My indulgent pretensions were dashed when I came face to face with the beautiful Isabelle.

At the end of a chaconne, I breathlessly declined the next offer to dance although my foot still tapped to the beat of the tambour. Courtesy obliged me to greet the Lady Constance before the evening passed. I crossed the room to where I had caught sight of her standing and found her deep in discussion with an elderly chevalier, one I recognized as having been once or twice at our castle. She broke off in midsentence when she saw me and directed a quelling eye at this knight. Before I could drop a curtsy, she waved her hand as if to dismiss the man, and he retired to another group of guests. If one had met her son first, one would have expected her to be a massive lady, with a hook nose and a commanding bosom. However, Charles resembled his mother only in his desire for wealth. Lady Constance was small and spare, with a short nose and a flat bosom. She had an air of fragility about her, which she emphasized with frequent reference to her ailments. She greeted me with a long-suffering smile as she held out her thin fingers to me.

We exchanged nothing more than cursory civilities. She

asked after my father's health, and had I enjoyed my visit at
Westminster? She expressed the hope that I would visit her on
the morrow, saying, "For you know, Marguerite, an odd thing
it would be if we found we had nothing to discuss!" Before
she could pinpoint me on the subject, however, there was a
small commotion near the doorway and all heads turned to
behold Isabelle, a striking vision in silver and gold. From her
dainty feet shod in slippers woven from silver threads to her
burnished gold tresses that held nothing of straw, she presented
a picture that took one's breath away. The chevalier next to
me was addressing a remark to the Lady Edwina; he broke off
in midsentence in awe of Isabelle's beauty, a response I could
well appreciate. She was petite, her slender form sheathed with
a kirtle woven from the same shining threads as her slippers,
over which a bliaut of white gauze trimmed with gilded braid
gently molded itself to her lithe curves. Her bearing was elegant, and a pair of large brown eyes set off her perfectly carved
features.

So absorbed was I in the drama of her entry that I almost
missed seeing Hugh Falmouth follow in her wake. I did not
pretend to know the male mind, but I could understand that a
man might overlook her lack of dowry if he wanted to possess
her exquisite loveliness. I could suppose that Isabelle's golden
beauty dimmed Yvette's blond charm and, quite possibly, diminished to insignificance the latter's vast, well-managed lands.
If I had had doubts about Falmouth's union with Isabelle before,
I had none now. She was a dazzling prize that would be, for
some men, more valuable than gold. I did not know where
Isabelle and Falmouth were coming from, other than the ramparts, for it seemed unusual to have left the feasting for any
reason, but I did not consider the question at length, for she
was coming straight toward us with her hand outstretched to
the Lady Constance.

"Lady Hartford!" Isabelle said in a light and pleasant voice.
"How good to see you!"

"Isabelle, my dear," Lady Constance replied in her failing
way. "I had hoped to see you before now."

"Yes, we had agreed to meet at Westminster some weeks

back." She paused for an almost imperceptible moment, gave her head a tiny shake as though to cast off a bad memory, and added with a fragile smile and a faint note of constraint, "But here we are now, and you must tell me how you go on. I hope your wretched insomnia has stopped plaguing you."

Lady Constance gave a moment's recital of the latest spell of sleepless nights, followed by a brief chapter on the inconveniences of a weak heart, with an animadversion on my own health, saying in soulful accents, "It is kind of you to ask. With your delicate nature you are naturally sensitive to my disorders. Marguerite, on the other hand, never concerns herself for another's ailments, but that is, I suppose, because she has never suffered a day's sickness. I do not know whose physical disposition you inherited, my dear—it is certainly not your father's!—but you have the constitution of a horse!"

It could not be flattering, in the presence of such a finished piece of femininity, to be compared to a horse, but Isabelle spared me embarrassment and a reply by coming smoothly into the gap. "You must be Marguerite Montcrief. I saw you, of course, in the bridal company. So lovely, all of you! I only wish I could wear blue the way you do! But I must tell you that I have heard so much about you from Marie-Ange."

Many replies hovered on my lips, but I said simply, "It is a pleasure to meet you."

She smiled and inquired after my connection with Alicia.

"We grew up in the same convent under the Abbess Catherine at Amesbury, so she is a very old childhood friend," I said, adding, "I could not be happier for Alicia, but I acknowledge freely that I am losing a good friend. I must be content with the reflection that one person's gain is another's loss."

"Just so," Isabelle murmured.

At that moment, Sir Hugh appeared noiselessly at Isabelle's side, and, as if by instinct, she slid her arm possessively through his. He was as dark as she was fair, and even their eyes, both brown, held little resemblance, hers being lustrous and almost amber, his liquid and darkly seductive. He possessed a singularly handsome countenance and the muscles of a knight trained long hours in combat. His tunic, of a costly burgundy velvet weighted with ornamentation, was cut according to the latest mode, for it was a half-length longer than the established fashion.

Sir Hugh needed no introduction to Lady Constance, and they exchanged the usual greetings. When Isabelle made him known to me, he raised my hand to his lips, which curved upward in a most charming and certainly winning way. But the smile did not reach his eyes, and I elected not to mention that we had met only four weeks previous. When he released my hand with a graceful flourish, the flickering lights caught the red fire of his heavy ruby ring, the mounting of which repeated the filigree pattern on his ruby pendant. I guessed the workmanship to have had an Italian origin, and its finery enhanced an ensemble that, to my judgment, was the most elegant at the banquet.

Constance and Isabelle fell to talking, leaving Sir Hugh to entertain me.

"Do you hunt on the morrow, Lady Marguerite?" he asked with a polite air of inquiry.

"No, my lord, I had not thought to be part of the hunting party. Alicia will need my help to arrange the day's feasting, so I am willing to forgo the pleasures of the fine hunting weather for her sake. And you, Sir Hugh?"

"Like you, I must also serve the Lady Alicia. My part will be to prevent the bridegroom from being gored by a boar before the marriage is brought to fruition. Longchamps has long been a favorite target of wild animals." I laughed at this mild joke, knowing the story of the encounter of a goat's head with Herbert's backside, before he continued, "Moreover, Lady Isabelle would feel herself poorly used if I were not there·to carry the burden of her catch. She loves the chase as no other and has a deadly aim."

"Yes, my dear Hugh, I do love the hunt!" Isabelle intervened, casting a brilliant smile on her suitor. "Marguerite must not think, however, that you accompany me only at my request. You are the best horseman I know, and the party will need you to lead us through the rugged moors of the Burford demesne."

She patted his arm fondly. "Lady Constance! You are leaving us? Well, we shall meet later."

"Marguerite, my dear," Lady Constance said for her valediction, "you will not fail to see me tomorrow, will you?"

"I look forward to it, my lady," I said, left with no other choice.

Then, turning to Isabelle, I said, "I admire your courage. I fear that after all the dancing, even if I had agreed to take part in the hunt, I would now have to cry off, pleading exhaustion!"

"I am sure that would normally be the case for me, too," she replied. Then, with a tiny crease between her finely arched brows, she said, "You see, I have not been dancing. It—it is so hot tonight, and Sir Hugh was kind enough to accompany me for a breath of fresh air. Added to that, after having traveled all the way from Northumberland these past few days, I need to conserve my forces so that I may be in good form tomorrow."

"Isabelle, my love, you should retire soon," Sir Hugh said solicitously. "But not before we have properly congratulated the bridal couple."

"To be sure, my Hugh never misses an opportunity!" Isabelle said to me with an arch look. "I promise you, dear Hugh, that I will felicitate the groom as warmly as you wish the bride happy!"

"It is to be hoped, Isabelle—" Hugh began in the same bantering tone.

I did not learn what, in Hugh's opinion, was to be hoped, for the arrival of Alicia and Herbert, flushed from the dancing and radiant with happiness, into our circle interrupted this lively nonsense.

"Isabelle and Sir Hugh!" Alicia cried. "You have not joined us in the dancing, and I feared we would not see you again."

Sir Hugh and Sir Herbert clasped hands, and Isabelle briefly hugged Alicia. "Now I shall steal your husband for a moment, Alicia," Isabelle said, "to claim a kiss, while you shall receive your bridal embrace from Hugh!"

"Lady Isabelle," said Herbert, a trifle flushed from Isabelle's attentions, "allow me to lead you out to one dance. There is an air starting now. Lady Marguerite has already done me that honor, so I know she will excuse me now."

"Indeed!" I said, smiling at Sir Herbert. "I have been longing for a few words with Alicia."

"Thank you, Sir Herbert," Isabelle replied, "but let us instead repair to those chairs—are you not tired?—and you may tell me about your forthcoming bride visits."

"In either case, I fear we will be leaving Falmouth in the impossible, but delightful, position of having two ladies vying for his favors! It won't be the first time, eh, Hugh?" Herbert quipped.

"On the contrary, Longchamps," Sir Hugh returned, "you leave me the impossible task of deciding which of the two exceedingly lovely ladies would deign dance with me."

I accorded this sally the tribute of a smile although I was not amused. I chanced at that instant to glance across the room and caught sight of the Unknown Guy. I had not entirely forgotten his existence, but he had intruded less and less into my thoughts since I had not seen him again at Westminster. I was fleetingly aware that I had been keeping half an eye out for him at the wedding, without really expecting him to be there. He was facing in my direction, but his attention was absorbed by a woman whose face I could not see, and I assumed that he had not yet noticed me. Being quite sure that I did not want to meet with him, I quickly weighed the consequences of leaving the dancing earlier than would normally have been the case. I judged the festivities to have already reached their liveliest pitch, and it would not have been deemed impolite if I were to take my leave at that point.

Alicia suggested, in response to Sir Hugh's dilemma, that all five of us sit down together at the nearby tables and refresh ourselves with wine. This afforded me an excellent opportunity to excuse myself, and I was on the point of bidding good eventide to the rest of the small party, when I found myself accosted by a tall, lanky youth whose red hair and freckles I instantly recognized. He was gazing at me with such an idiotic air of yearning that my heart went out to him and I momentarily forgot my impulse to flee.

He stammered and begged my pardon—and, with a deprecating glance around the group, everyone's—for having intruded.

I curtsied and bestowed my warmest smile upon the awkward boy.

"Allow—me to introduce myself, my lady, I know you—er—that is, you are the Lady Marguerite Montcrief."

"I am. Of course, I have seen you, too. At Westminster, wasn't it? I am delighted that you want to make yourself known to me."

His face brightened and at the same time turned an unbecoming shade of beet. "M-my name is Gavin McLaughlin, my lady. You saw me, n-no doubt, because I am the squire of—"

"My squire," came a deep voice from behind me. My heart lurched to my throat for an uncounted second, and even before I turned, I knew who stood there.

Chapter 3

Herbert was the first one to make a recover. "Well, Guy!" he exclaimed with brash affection after a split second's frozen silence. "Glad to see you—yes, very glad!"

"So you see, Longchamps, I have kept my promise after all," Guy replied with an almost lazy smile.

Herbert held his hand an instant longer, still shaking it. "We had quite given up on you!"

"My men and I encountered some bad terrain and even worse weather on our way from Wales. We were knee deep in mire from Paincastle to Gloucester." Guy withdrew his hand then and addressed the group in general. "Nevertheless, we have arrived—sodden and sharp-set, but of a piece, and in time to offer you and the Lady Alicia sincere felicitations." Then, perfectly at his ease, he glanced around our group and bowed perfunctorily. "Save you, Falmouth, and Lady Isabelle, you are looking well, as usual."

Sir Hugh returned the salutation with every appearance of composure, and even Isabelle, always the woman, managed to shape her rosebud lips into the words "Sir Guy."

Herbert quickly amended one obvious omission. "I believe, Guy, that you have not yet had the opportunity of meeting our good friend—"

Again he broke in. "Demoiselle Montcrief and I have already met. How do you do, Lady Marguerite?" he said. "I am happy to have this occasion of renewing our all too brief acquaintance."

My heart skipped a beat, but his words were spoken with such a bland courtesy, with no slightest hint of hidden meaning, that for a moment I doubted my own memory.

"Indeed, sir," I said, "a pleasure."

"I believe my squire was addressing his attentions to you. Now, Gavin, you may take yourself away and apply yourself to the meal and horn of ale that you have been yearning for these past three hours or more."

Without demur, Gavin immediately responded to this curt command, achieved a creditable bow, and retired from the circle with only the veriest glance in my direction.

Hugh turned to Guy. "You must tell us, coming fresh from the west, are the Welsh as troublesome as the roads you traveled over? Their ferocity is legendary, as is their thirst for Norman blood."

"The Welsh are much like other men," Guy said. "They chafe under the yoke and rebel against cruel masters, be they Norman, Saxon, Gael, or even their own clansmen."

"If you say so, Guy," was Sir Hugh's response.

"It is not I who say," Guy returned with a mirror image of Sir Hugh's thin smile. "I prefer to let the Welsh tribal leaders speak for themselves and will give them all the autonomy possible."

"Yet one cannot help but wonder at the kinds of 'gifts' the king bestows," Hugh pursued. "The lands entailed to you in Wales are hardly the kind of gift one can rejoice over."

"I waste little time in questioning the gifts of our sovereign and none at all in considering the grumblings of jealous lords." This he said with utmost cordiality, but an undercurrent of tension swirled around the circle, and Sir Hugh began to open his mouth to reply.

With nervous haste, Alicia interrupted this promising start to one of the interchanges she no doubt dreaded. "Sir Guy, do come sit with us. Surely you are tired."

"Thank you, no. You are very considerate, Lady Long-champs, but I prefer to stretch my legs after so many hours astride my destrier."

"I had quite forgotten your amazing stamina, Guy," said Isabelle. "Rumor has it that you have journeyed to Wales and back in two short weeks, or does rumor lie?"

"Rumor is never entirely unfounded," he said carelessly, "but it lends itself to exaggeration. The truth is that we made the journey in three weeks—not such an astonishing feat after all."

"Take a care," Sir Hugh said affably. "Eager young lords, in an attempt to impress, often overwork their vassals. Still, you had to set a strenuous pace to cover the distance in a mere three weeks."

"I will take care, but I am neither young nor entirely eager for the position I now occupy."

"No?" Hugh responded, making his incredulity apparent. "I wonder, is this lack of enthusiasm for your position shared by your vassals, or have you driven them to the bone so that they are too tired to protest?"

Sir Guy smiled then, and I would have thought it was genuine. "Lay your fears to rest, Falmouth," he said. "Even the devil himself would have been preferable to my men rather than the continued leadership of Roger. They hail me—for the moment!—as their deliverer and believe Roger's death to have been timely and even just, no matter what the circumstances surrounding it."

"Guy!" Herbert interjected. "You did not mean that the way it sounded!"

"My opinion of my brother's weaknesses and his mismanagement of our estate is a secret I have held from no one," Guy replied, "and I will not wrap his wasted life in clean linen."

"Such a model you set for forthrightness!" Sir Hugh exclaimed. "But are we also to understand that you believe any ends justify the means, when it comes to setting aright a poorly run estate?"

"To what purpose do you ask me a point of ethics? Do you contemplate eliminating your cousin in Northumbria in order to inherit his fat coffers to rebuild your impoverished lands in Lower Saxony?"

An angry flush stained Sir Hugh's cheeks; Isabelle stood by, eyes glittering. Alicia flung herself into the breach once again. "My lord," she said quickly to Guy, "you have arrived too late to join in the feasting—do but partake of the flesh and wine, if you hunger!—for the tables are still spread. And you have not yet been dancing."

"I myself was on the point of offering for one of the ladies. However, I will await your decision, for I would not like to steal from you the partner of your choice," Sir Hugh said, his voice as smooth as silk.

Sir Guy glanced down at Hugh from his slightly superior height, seemed to debate with himself whether this provoking remark was worth the trouble of a reply, and to decide that it was not, and turned back to Alicia.

"As to my not dancing, that may be instantly repaired," he said and unexpectedly turned to me. "Lady Marguerite, would you do me the honor?" he asked civilly, but with a hint of the bored demeanor of a guest doing his duty, and offered me his arm. "Let us join in the next set."

I laid my hand as delicately as I could on his wrist, afraid to touch him, and commanded my voice to articulate a "By your leave." I turned, almost too hastily, to go with him, but not before I apprehended a look of faint surprise on Falmouth's face.

But if Falmouth was surprised, I was wholly taken aback. I had little time to assess this man's bold behavior in directly confronting Sir Hugh and Lady Isabelle without a blush, nor could I speculate on the possibility that he had drawn me off to pique Isabelle. Even farther back in my mind was that night in July. I was, instead, directing all my powers to mastering my confusion.

How he contrived to find a way through the guests thronged at one end of the Great Hall was a mystery to me, for he certainly did not force our passage. He greeted many of the guests, most of whom were unknown to me, a brief handclasp with a knight, a bow and smile to a lady, and the thing was done. No one cut his acquaintance, although many of those whom he did not directly acknowledge regarded us with an ill-concealed curiosity.

As we sought our passage, I noted, too, the care with which he dressed. He chose simple kerseymeres, apparently shunning the rich velvets and silks that characterized Falmouth's fine raiment, which, by comparison, became almost vulgar in its extravagance, and I found myself revising my opinion of the standard for elegance. His bearing held both a challenge and a refined hauteur that I had not suspected on our first encounter, when my over-all impression of him had been one of loosely bridled power. His hair, cropped of its sun-lightened curls, was a crisp, dark brown, and contrasted with his eyes, which his gray tunic had muted to a stormy blue. His only adornment was the Guimont escutcheon he wore blazoned on his breast: an ebony eagle, wings spread, talons gripping a peregrine, against an écartelé field of blue and gold. He thus proclaimed his family's shield, and his right to it, with an insolent defiance for all to see.

Then, when the answer to my unspoken question finally came to me, I did not pause to consider the effect of my unweighed words on this rather terrifying personage, but said impulsively, "Guy from *Gui*mont, of course! How stupid of me not to have realized it before! I have been cudgeling my brain these past minutes trying to relate Sir Guy to the name Roland!"

He looked down at me with an unreadable expression.

"That is," I said quickly, "you *are* Sir Roland of Guimont, are you not?"

"Your servant, Demoiselle Montcrief," he said, his bow punctilious. The suspicion of mockery in that gesture was not lost on me.

"We were never formally introduced, you know!" I added defensively and quite unnecessarily. This point of etiquette, however, did not trouble me as deeply as another: I could not decide whether I was guilty of gross discourtesy or merely foolishness not to have known the most infamous person at court.

"I am aware of that, demoiselle," he replied dryly, and I flushed as the never sufficiently-to-be-regretted meeting in July flashed before my eyes. I thought I saw a glimmer of amusement light the depths of his otherwise cold blue eyes and so I was not entirely rebuffed.

A number of retorts, all of them unpleasant, rose to my lips, but fortunately, for a moment's reflection assured me that any one of them would have earned me a sharp set-down, Marie-Ange accosted us.

"Marguerite!" she exclaimed. "I have been having such a time! And—oh! to be sure, I did not notice your companion." This speech was accompanied with a roguish smile for my "companion." "Sir Guy, is it not? I had not looked to see you at the wedding. It's been so long since I've seen you!"

"Sir Roland has been in Wales these three weeks past," I said.

"But, Marguerite, dearest!" Marie-Ange said, rapping my knuckles playfully with her hand, "his *friends* call him Sir Guy!"

"Yes, so I am told," I said, sounding stiff even to my own ears.

"I am sure I don't know where he got his nickname, but it has always been so. Perhaps someday you will tell me, Sir Guy?"

I perceived that Sir Guy was making little effort to control what I guessed to be a growing mirth and saw my chance. "Now is the time, then!" I said. "Sir Roland has expressed his desire to dance, Marie-Ange, and I know how you love it so! In fact, I insist! And since Sir Roland has not yet had a chance to dance, the two of you can share the next set. After the exertions of the day, I am quite fatigued!"

"Sir Guy has only to ask," Marie-Ange said at her most coy.

"And yet," he interposed, addressing me, "must not Demoiselle Dujarrie be as exhausted as you?" Then he added, in response to my look of inquiry, "Having taken part in those same ceremonies?"

A tiny frown appeared between Marie-Ange's pretty pansy-brown eyes; she vaguely sensed an insult. A similar frown may have been on my forehead, for the thought flitted through my mind that not only had Sir Roland known my name, he had also known who had taken part in the bridal procession. Nothing seemed to escape this man, not even an insignificant detail, and I wondered what else he knew about me.

He took my arm again then and bowed to Marie-Ange, who looked, to put it mildly, surprised to see me walk away with her quarry. We were immediately absorbed by another mingling crowd. The musicians were taking a small break and the dancers had split off into smaller groups, which we maneuvered around. As my luck would have it, there would be no dancing for the next while. This prospect filled me with dismay, for I would have liefer danced with him than actually had to talk to him.

His next words indicated that he had read my mind.

"Since you were unable to pass me off on Demoiselle Dujarrie and there is no dancing, you will have to suffer my conversation for a few minutes at least. That is, unless you want to appear horribly rude." He looked at me with a very good semblance of offended outrage. "Disclaiming my friendship to Demoiselle Dujarrie . . . really, my lady, so uncivil!"

I gasped at such a direct attack. "Well! If we are talking of being rude—!"

"No," he said, "I would rather talk of you."

I looked up suddenly, and his smile disarmed me. I saw the laughter in his eyes that I had suspected moments before, and it transformed the harsh lines of his face, endowing it with an undeniable charm. There was an air about the man, I had to admit, that was no less effective for being indescribable. He was neither handsome like Sir Hugh nor polished like Sir Herbert, but I began to feel the effect of his spell.

"Wonderful idea! Such a fascinating life I lead!" I temporized. "But first I will take leave to tell you that I am now convinced: I collect that, in calling yourself Guy rather than Roland, you wish to avoid any association with your heroic namesake of song. The famous Roland was, as you may know, extremely courteous."

"Very good!" he replied politely, "but your Roland came to an untimely, albeit—as you say—heroic, end, and I have no desire to follow in his worthy path. And now you have told me something much more valuable about yourself: you were convent-bred."

"One does not hear 'La Chanson de Roland' sung by a *jongleur* in a convent!" I argued.

"True; however, knowing your father, you did not hear it at Shrivenham. In fact, I would be surprised if your sire allowed in a passing friar, much less a knight errant or a minstrel. So I conclude that you enjoyed the tutelage of the Abbess Catherine at Amesbury, whose tastes I am privileged to know very well."

My attitude of frank surprise affirmed his deduction.

"Was that a lucky guess, or did you ask Alicia about our girlhood together at Amesbury?" I recovered.

"I imagine," he said coolly, "that I could have asked Lady Alicia about you if I had needed to." His penetrating look assured me that I had been quite pretentious to presume that he would make inquiries about me. I felt two spots flame in my cheeks, and formed the resolve to break the habit of blushing in his presence. "But," he continued, "I did not need to, for you told me as much. I simply added two plus two and arrived, unerringly, at four."

"You must help me, then, my lord, for when I add a sum from the bottom up, and then again from the top down, the result is always different. How do you come to know the Abbess Catherine's tastes so intimately?"

"You can cipher, too? The Abbess Catherine has outdone herself!" His voice registered surprise and awe, but I would not fall for this gambit twice. I had a strong intuition that nothing surprised him and very few things awed him.

"It is helpful," I said with every effort at aplomb, "when the taxes fall due; someone must do the accounts after all. And now my question?"

"You mean you wonder that the Abbess Catherine would entertain such a questionable character as I and count me among her friends? I need not tell you that her tastes are entirely catholic, in the true sense of the word!"

I was provoked, and before I put a guard on my tongue I

heard myself say, "No, only that I am surprised to learn that your circle of acquaintances includes a learned and truly saintly person."

This shaft glanced off his armor, and with no loss of composure he responded immediately, "Admit that you think the better of me for it!"

There was no answer to this, so I returned none. He nodded then with a half-bow to a passing guest. He stopped abruptly and turned to me. His attitude seemed to convey more meaning than the message contained in his following words: "You have not yet told me if you enjoyed your visit at the royal castle."

I assured him that I had. I was slightly baffled, but determined not to show it, for I did not suppose that the question was posed in reference to our nocturnal encounter. However, with respect to that meeting, I could hardly tell him that my one adventure at court had proved to be a fine success in retrospect, for I could not have fallen in with a more dangerous adversary. I now possessed the identity of the man with the piercing blue gaze, the man who held the secret of my little indiscretion: Roland of Guimont, the practiced courtier, the heartless rake, the murderer. Yet, in his presence, I could not believe all the stories that had been told about him. I knew only that of all the men I had ever met, none had possessed so contradictory a nature.

An infinitesimal pause counseled me that I needed to elaborate, and I rushed into a tangle of words: "One meets so many people at court, and that is very exciting, for as you have said yourself, we have so few visitors at Shrivenham. How agreeable it is to see new faces, not just those of my tiring women, and hold real conversations, instead of merely acting on the complaints of the cook about the baker or resolving the petty squabbles that continually arise between the armorer and the farrier! That is very dull work, I assure you! The hours spent stitching—a man cannot imagine the tedium!—pass so much more quickly when in the company of my friends, of course, Alicia, Marie-Ange, and do you know Yvette Mortimer? How the time speeds by when we would gossip about—" Feeling the thin ice under my feet, I hurried on, "Well! All manner of things! Alicia's wedding, of course, and Yvette showed me a new stitch, for my broderie is really without distinction, and—But surely this women's talk cannot be of interest to you?" I ended on a note of inquiry, cursing my wretched tongue.

He ignored my question and my near blunder and seemed to be only idly listening. "I am surprised your father let you go," he said at last. These words uncomfortably echoed those that Charles Hartford had spoken earlier that evening.

"You seem to know much about my father," I said warily.

"It is my business," he returned. "One must look to one's lands and know one's neighbors. It is only reasonable, do you not agree?"

"I should think so, but I have no experience in these matters. My father, however, apparently is not of the same mind as you, my lord. He concerns himself very little for his neighbors, or for any other matter of interest outside our castle walls."

"Indeed?" He held my eyes with a steady gaze. "Surely your father has friends."

"Yes, of course. I saw a gentleman just this evening whom I have seen several times at Shrivenham. Oddly, though, I have never been introduced to him, so I could not call him by name. Then there is of course the Lady Constance Hartford. Are you acquainted with her?"

"Yes, I know her," he said as if it were no great privilege. "In fact, I believe that she was in residence at Westminster when you were. Is that not so?"

"Why, yes, she—"

"As one of your few acquaintances at court, you must have seen her often and privately."

I regarded him with suspicion, but his startling blue eyes gave back my image and no more. I thought for a moment that I was looking into a pool of water on a sunny day that would reflect a passing cloud or the flight of a bird, but would keep its depths hidden. There was, too, an indefinable quality in his voice that alerted me to danger. Yet I could not perceive in what direction the danger lurked. The man was a sorcerer; not only could he cast spells, he could peer into one's thoughts. I sensed that he somehow associated my movements that night in July with the Lady Constance, and yet no word of my intention to see her at that time had passed my lips.

"No," I said, stating only the truth, "I did not happen to see her at all during my stay at court."

"Then you must not be the dutiful daughter I had thought, for you apparently did not feel any compulsion to pay a visit to a family friend."

"My father did bid me to see her, if that's what you mean, although I cannot conceive that that is of the slightest interest. Simply, I have a sad habit of putting off disagreeable tasks, and I delayed this one until it was too late."

"I can understand your wish to avoid her company."

"Or anyone's wish!" I said, forgetting myself. "Her conversation centers on her physical disorders, and if that is not bad enough, she delivers the recital of her ailments in a voice that sometimes whines and sometimes accuses. The only person more unpleasant than Lady Constance is her son, Charles!" I stopped suddenly. "That was very unkind of me to say. She is, after all, a widow in poor health, and Charles is really a very innocuous creature."

"Do not underrate Charles. Nevertheless, I imagine, since Lady Constance stands on ceremony, that you will be treated to a fine discourse for your failure to see her at Westminster."

"There was no harm done." I shrugged. "She is perfectly willing to see me on the morrow."

"Then you do not hunt?"

I shook my head. I hesitated to give him the same excuse I had given to Sir Hugh. I bit my lower lip; he noticed my constraint.

"No, you will not hunt," he said. "You are debating with yourself, whether to tell me all of the plans you have made that prevent you from participating, when in reality you are reluctant to admit that you are no enthusiastic horsewoman and do not display to best advantage on a docile mare in the midst of a vigorous chase."

A chuckle betrayed me.

"How *could* you know that? Are you a mind-reader, or are you merely doing sums?"

"A little of both. I have never seen you riding on your lands; in fact, I would venture that you are not certain of the boundary markers between our two demesnes. I, on the other hand, have spent considerable hours in the saddle overseeing my lands. That I added to my observation that you are too delicate to control a hunting horse."

I was absurdly flattered. "Although I have recently been compared to one!" I said. Not desiring a confirmation, nor really fishing for a denial of that statement, I added quickly, "You have the truth of it, though, I am no horsewoman."

"Then I am spared an account of the bruising rides you have had, the game you have bagged, and the many hedges you have cleared when your companions were bullfinched!"

"Exactly so, sir!" I said with an involuntary laugh. "My most memorable hunt must have been all of six or seven years ago, at any rate, before the seneschal's wife died. My mare had a perverse habit of bolting after the game, which was daunting enough, but suddenly, in the midst of the action, she was frightened when a cock pheasant exploded out of the woods. She came to a dead halt, and I was thrown headlong into a stream. I received an ignominious dunking in front of the entire hunting party, and it is not my ambition to find myself seated up to my waist in river mud here for the amusement of the wedding guests!"

"That I would like to have seen," he said with an appreciative laugh.

"I do not scruple to tell you, my lord, that unlike your namesake, you have not an ounce of chivalry!"

"Not an ounce," he agreed cheerfully. His eyes were warm with laughter and something else that made my pulses race. I no longer had to guess what it was that made him fatally attractive. Had I been asked at that moment if this man was capable of murder, I would have laughed and said that the dark Earl of Guimont might easily have seduced a score or two of gentlewomen, but kill his own brother he could not.

"Do you hunt on the morrow?" I asked.

"I would not miss it for the kingdom."

I would have given a kingdom just then to have been able

to ride out with the hunting party, but one was not at my disposal, and it was just as well: I did not understand the forces that governed Sir Roland's world and perceived little value in trying to thrust myself into a domain where men's passions and desires were sovereign. My life existed in a mundane realm ruled by domestic need and regulated by the earth's rhythm of providing. I had no turn for politics and thought myself not wise enough in the ways of this other world to survive in it. Although I rebelled on occasion against the strictures imposed on me by my role as a woman whose lot it was to keep the cycle of castle life in motion, I had no intention of defying my fate and pursuing a life that held the promise of excitement and adventure but the threat of failure and exposure. In this way, the hunt had come to epitomize for me the whole of this other world. Being in the presence of Sir Roland, the thought had danced through my head that it would be very grand to be a part of it, but my practical self prevented me from risking the comfort and security of the castle for the freedom and exhilaration of the chase.

I noticed that Lady Edwina, a kind, motherly woman, full of good humor, was gathering the womenfolk to assist in the bedding ceremony. The conversation with Sir Roland had turned to indifferent topics and bore the signs that our interview had come to an end. Thus, when I saw Lady Edwina approach, I thanked him for his company, to which he answered, "You are still in my debt for a dance, if you recall. I will collect on it at the next opportunity, although I expect you will try to persuade me that your dancing, like your horsemanship, is really unremarkable."

"No such thing!" I replied with a laugh, and derived confidence from the belief that a second occasion would never arise. "In truth, I judge myself to be very light on my feet and dance with great pleasure!"

He smiled and fell into conversation with another knight. Lady Edwina took my arm and we crossed the Great Hall to the broad newel stair leading to the tower.

"I am persuaded, Marguerite," she said in a confiding tone, "that you are too sensible a young woman to be taken in by the new Earl of Guimont! I know how difficult it is for you, without any feminine guidance at Shrivenham. And—no, no! —I do not count Constance Hartford as a counselor. A devoted mother she is, and as proof she has no thought for anything save her Charles, which is witness to the fact that a mother's love is blind! That, however, is of no moment—I know I have only to drop a word in your ear, and you will not take offense! Sir Guy is a dangerous man."

"Lady Edwina, I know it is the strangest quirk in me, but until it is clear that Guimont is guilty of his brother's death, I feel that one should acquit him of the crime," I replied.

"My dear, it is the oldest story in the world! The king cannot punish him, of course, without firm proof. A fine thing it would be for King Henry to indiscriminately prosecute his lords. There is nothing at all he can do under the circumstances. But you will see that Sir Guy is not well received in the time to come. Indeed, I applaud Isabelle's courage in breaking with Guimont, even though her family stood to benefit from that union now that he has come into the estate. I own, I had always thought her a bit vain—heaven knows, I can understand why!— and interested only in finery and extravagance. In the end, however, she has demonstrated her fine moral sense, and I am not the only one who has a better opinion of her for it! And what a handsome couple she and Hugh Falmouth make! A preux chevalier, that one!" She sighed and patted my hand. "His family coffers may be to let, but he will come about again. Here I am prattling and not at all to the purpose. It is not *him* that I need to warn you about. Why, some ten years ago—that was before your time—I remember that Mathilda Chester made a perfect goose out of herself over Sir Guy. She had just been widowed, too! His attentions to her could not have been more particular for as long as a six-month, but nothing came of it. It was generally supposed that he finally got what he wanted from her and lost interest—well! I mean, she went into a rapid decline after that and ended by marrying a John Kent, who was a fourth son! So you see! Only—and I will not bother you again with such talk, my dear—do not add to the ranks of Sir Guy's discarded loves."

"I should hope, Lady Edwina," I said, "that I am getting too old and have too much common sense to succumb to what can be described as nothing more than a very mild flirtation. Besides, I cannot imagine that he will make me the object of his attention for any length of time."

She scanned my face for a moment. "Do not be too sure of that!" she said, and ushered us into the antechamber where Alicia was to be disrobed.

It was of no use telling her that I was an unlikely candidate for either a courtship or a seduction. Sir Roland's taste in gentlewomen ran to great beauties; I had heard of Mathilda's legendary face from Lady Ellen when I was a girl, and Isabelle was breathtaking. Into the second category fell either married noblewomen in search of adventure or those women of questionable background and virtue who could be found in any court. On either score, then, there seemed little danger of him distinguishing me with his favors.

A dozen or more women had circled around Alicia, laughing and untying the bindings down her back and loosening the lacets from her elbow to her wrist. Yvette and I removed from her hair the golden circlet, and we groomed her loose tresses while several other women, including Isabelle, removed her hose and slippers. I could not help but wonder what Isabelle's feelings toward Roland had been and what he had felt for her. She glanced up at me from her kneeling position and met my look with a sweet, secret smile, as if to say, "Let us be friends." Perhaps she, too, had been beguiled by his smile, only to be undeceived by the cold murder of his brother. She came to stand next to me as we pulled the thin shift over Alicia's head. Alicia was smiling and flushed, a shy but eager bride. She shivered slightly in the cold , and with her small, high breasts, slim waist, and narrow hips, she looked unable to withstand the tide of Herbert's passion. A wave of fear passed over me as the significance of Alicia's undressing bored in on me. I stepped back from her almost involuntarily, a movement that Isabelle correctly interpreted.

"Thinking of your own wedding night?" she whispered to me.

"Yes," I laughed shakily, "but fortunately it is not imminent."

"Are you not betrothed?"

"Not as yet. And you?"

"Soon, I hope," she answered. I could not see in the candlelight if her color rose, but her voice was shy and maidenly. "Perhaps it is as the more experienced women say, that it is not so terrible a thing when one is in love."

"I hope that is right. Alicia does not look at all terrified."

"Then we shall take that as a good sign," she said as she pressed my hand reassuringly. She smiled at me again, and I returned it this time to seal the bond that existed between us as unmarried women and to acknowledge our fragile, new friendship. She looked very beautiful in the flickering shadows, and I chastised myself for my initial, unnamed reaction to her, attributing it to the Eve-old feelings that are stirred when one woman comes face to face with her exceedingly handsome sister.

We wrapped Alicia in a sendal robe and pushed her gently into the next chamber where a large bed and her husband, seconded by a gathering of the men, awaited her. "Take heart, my child!" called one woman. Another thrust into her hand a steaming cup of hot wine mixed with honey and spiced with the rare cinnamon. "An aphrodisiac for your husband, in case he needs one!" whispered another, but loud enough so that the men on the other side of the room could hear. This sally inaugurated a series of jests and jibes that volleyed between the women and the men. Alicia and Herbert seemed to take it all in good part, but I began to wish myself otherwhere and kept my eyes self-consciously averted from the scene. Finally, the men removed Herbert's chausses, accompanied by another round of witticisms, while the women removed Alicia's robe amid answering giggles. The bridal pair was placed between the sheets that we would be called upon to display in the morning, the bed curtains were drawn shut, and we withdrew.

I mingled with the women for only a few moments in the antechamber, restoring Alicia's clothes to order, and then hurried to my room in the guest quarters. I was thankful that I had given Bess and Gertrude their *congé* until the next morning, for I wanted to be alone. I divested myself of my clothing, donned by sleeping shift, and sank gratefully into the soft mattress. I pulled the eiderdown up to my ears without first snuffing the candle. My eyes closed so quickly that I had not the time to tell myself: "I am falling asleep." An hour later— so I reckoned from the reduced size of the candle and the puddle of wax drippings around its base— the thought that I had forgotten to reflect upon something before going to sleep woke me up, and I was surprised to find around me the dim aureole of light from the candle. I extinguished its tiny flame between my thumb and finger and listened for a moment to the few distant, muffled sounds of the castle before I remembered that what had disturbed my sleep was the vague but persistent impression that all was not as it seemed and that I still had very much to learn about human nature.

In the event, I learned the next morning the lesson that a mother's love has no bounds, and I was offered that evening an insight into the depths of jealousy and rivalry.

I arose the day after the wedding later than my wont, feeling aimless and with an ill-defined sense of dissatisfaction, but Bess forbore to reprove me, a circumstance I attributed more to her preoccupation with the splendid wedding celebrations than to a feeling for tact. My early morning lethargy, intensified by the prospect of an interview with Lady Constance, went virtually ignored, and I washed and dressed under a pelter of observations, remarks, and questions that required no answers. There was scarcely any person whom I would not have preferred to confront that morning than Lady Constance, but remembering my words of the evening before that I often put off a disagreeable task until it was too late, I resolved to mend that fault on the instant. Yet, Bess's cheerfulness had insensibly lifted the vague stirrings of disappointment I felt in not riding out with the chase, so that by the time I left my chambers I was able to stride to meet my fate with composure and even to deliver myself of two healthy raps on Constance's chamber door. A discreet moment passed before it swung back cautiously to reveal the gaunt form of Agnes, whose faded eyes gazed back at me with the frailest flicker of recognition. If one were to say anything about Agnes—that is if one were to notice her at all—it must be that she was the most self-effacing person imaginable. She nodded a greeting and bowed me into the antechamber where Constance sat before a low fire, wrapped in a linsey shawl, eyes closed and holding a cloth at her temples. Her lids fluttered open at the sound of my step, an act that sent Agnes flitting to the windows, where she averted the shutters against the sunlight.

"Thank you, Agnes. You may go," my reclining hostess said in a thin thread of a voice, and Agnes skittered out of the room, just as a shadow will vanish when the sun darts behind a cloud.

Lady Constance did not greet me, the effort apparently being too great. Instead she shifted uneasily in her chair, wincing exquisitely with the exertion. "I have not slept a minute since I have been at Burford," she said at last with all the weariness of one who has not slept for a week. "And it is useless to complain that I have been given the draftiest chambers in the castle."

The dictates of civility supplied me with an answer. "However, you looked very well last night, my lady. I would never have guessed that you had been bothered by insomnia."

"One tries to put forth a bold face in public," she sighed, "for nothing is more fatiguing than a conversation about one's ailments."

I recognized in her tone the signs that she was about to embark on such a discourse. This, I suspected, was her way of gently punishing me for not having visited her at Westminster. I saw no reason to submit to it and indulged instead in a mild counterattack. "Yes," I agreed, "and I particularly admire your ability to rise to the effort, no matter how fatigued you are."

A fleeting pause suggested that she was momentarily disarmed. She allowed her lips to relax into an infinitesimal smile, observing, "Dearest Marguerite, it has been so long since you and I have had a quiet talk together."

Since this was, to my recollection, the very first time we had ever faced each other alone, woman to woman, I was safe in responding, with an air of innocent inquiry, "Yes, when *was* the last time?"

She opened her eyes a little wider at that, and sat up a fraction in her chair. "My dear, I am sure that I do not know, but there is no need for you to be standing about! Pray, be seated."

Thus adjured, I disposed myself in a chair opposite her, arranged my skirts for a moment, and waited.

She leaned forward slightly and subjected me to a squinting scrutiny. "Have you been out in the sun?"

"No," I replied, "I have been far too busy here even to take a walk on the parapet. Whatever could make you think so?"

She eased herself back into the chair and shut her eyes again, as if the sight of me gave her pain. "Your cheeks are blooming," she said in a way that not even the most inveterate optimist would have mistaken for a compliment.

I thanked her nonetheless. "I am merely enjoying my customary good health, my lady."

"Perhaps it is the attention you have been drawing from certain male quarters."

"Perhaps!" I said. "I enjoyed the dancing greatly last night and can only imagine that the attention accorded me was due to my position in the bridal procession. You know, I have not had occasion to go much amongst—"

"I was referring to the Earl of Guimont," she interrupted with a hint of impatience.

So! She had decided on a direct approach; I opted for diversionary tactics. "Did he favor me with attention? Ah, yes! It must have been after you had retired for the evening."

She responded with a metallic laugh. "But that does not mean that I did not hear all about it this morning. Rest assured that you are a much-discussed pair today!"

"Do you mean to warn me about him, too?"

"Warn you? You are not my daughter!" she said, and continued, seemingly oblivious to the inherent contradiction, "Besides, as a mother, I know only too well that to forbid a child an object only serves to make that object all the more desirable."

"No doubt," I laughed, "but I am relieved to hear that you will not read me a catechism."

"As if I would," she replied, "or would need to! I have too much faith in your intelligence, Marguerite, to tell you what is good for you or to alert you to danger. I am sure that it is unnecessary for me to point out to you that pursuing an association with Guimont is as unwise as it is pointless."

"Then you *are* warning me. What harm can he do me?"

"Dear me, no. He can do you no harm. He has all he wants now—or, at least, almost all. We were only discussing how ineligible he is."

"Oh? How ineligible is he?"

"Very." She sighed, and paused a moment to put the cloth back at her temples. "You know, I am in Isabelle's confidence, and, although I would never betray it, I can tell you that she is relieved to be free of Guimont."

"I cannot believe that it was so distasteful to be betrothed to him," I said in perfect honesty.

"He can be charming, I am sure, but you must know that Isabelle's affections have been engaged elsewhere for quite some time. She did not find it at all agreeable to be subjected to his jealous fits. He has—shall we say?—a violent temper at times and began at last to recognize a rival in Falmouth. And now poor Isabelle must feel the guilt of Roger's death. She cannot help but think that she was indirectly responsible for his precipitous flight down the stairs."

As it appeared that Lady Constance was not going to elaborate on this provocative statement, I was obliged to press her for more. "Indirectly?" I asked.

She looked mildly surprised. "Of course. I thought everyone knew that Isabelle went to Hungerford with the intention of asking Guimont to release her from the betrothal. But she could not know that when she did he would fly into one of his uncontrollable rages." My face no doubt registered a greater surprise than she had felt. "Well," she continued, "I can see that I have said too much. I merely thought . . . But the harm is done now! I must ask you not to divulge this, for it will surely increase Isabelle's pain for this fact to be generally known."

"Yes," I said, "I will certainly respect Isabelle's feelings in the matter. But how unusual for her to have undertaken such a mission. It does not seem to have been wise to have directly addressed Sir Roland without the intervention of her father."

"Of course not, in retrospect. But her father was—*is*—ill. He suffers from rheum, you know. So painful! They say it has become so that Beauvais cannot sit astride a horse." She had become almost animated, and I feared a long digression, but this did not come to pass, for she recollected herself. "Not that he is any worse off than your dear father, but we shall come to him directly. Needless to say, Beauvais was not able to undertake Isabelle's errand, and she, being a bit willful, thought that it might be best for her to approach Guimont herself. He had only just returned to England—"

"Yes, but was not Guimont's reaction a strange one? Should not his victim have been Falmouth instead of his own brother?"

"My dear, I cannot know the mind of a man in the grip of a violent and destructive passion. Guimont always loathed his elder brother and his spleen spilled itself on the nearest object of hatred. Perhaps he thought in gaining the Guimont lands he would win Isabelle back. Instead, it provided the means of her release. And that, Marguerite, must be another of life's little ironies."

"To be sure!" I responded, unable to find fault with the explanation. "But for a man of such a violent cast, I must say he can conduct himself with remarkable nonchalance. He greeted Hugh and Isabelle last night quite dispassionately."

"I never said he was a fool. His displays of temper have never occurred for the edification of the general public. And although it is my belief that he will always love Isabelle, he is not so lost to reason as to forget that he must establish himself with a marriage and a legitimate heir—and quickly."

"You mean he has some illegitimate ones?" I asked with unmaidenly interest.

Lady Constance did not look gratified. "All men do!" she snapped. "What I said was merely a manner of speaking."

"But why the rush for marriage and a son? He is not yet in his dotage."

An odd look crossed Constances's pinched features. I could have imagined it, but somehow she became more guarded in her conversation with me and seemed anxious to put aside the subject of Guimont. She twitched her shawl tighter around her shoulders. "No, but he is no longer young, either. My dear, would you be so kind as to stir the embers a bit? I have felt a chill ever since you came in. So many questions about the fascinating Guimont. Am I to infer that you are interested in the man?"

I rose and went to the hearth, saying, as I handled the poker, "I beg pardon. I merely pursued the topic that you initiated."

"Then I shall terminate it. Guimont will probably marry Joan of Shrewsbury before the year is out. Are you now satisfied? She is a little young but very lovely, as you know, and her lands in the west will complement Guimont's new Welsh holdings. Her father, in spite of everything, seems to favor the match."

"Poor Joan," I said, recalling her delicate features. "Very pretty, but a poor second to Isabelle."

"She is to be pitied," Lady Constance sighed, "but not in relation to how she measures up to Isabelle. It is my belief that her heart lies elsewhere." Constance paused a dramatic moment before she added, "She seems quite taken with my Charles."

I was lucky at that moment to have been on my knees facing the fire, for only the bronze bears' heads capping the andirons could have caught my amusement, and I fancied for a split, unbalanced moment that they shared the humor, their eyes winking with laughter. If my initial feeling was one of mirth, my second one was of disbelief, for I could not credit my ears. Both reactions were followed quickly by a third, more fantastic suspicion that what I had heard was neither a jest nor a misunderstanding. I stared into the fire a moment longer, arrested by a blinding realization. I quickly busied myself with stirring the embers, while I gave myself time to consider the possibility I had previously dismissed as unthinkable.

"And does Charles reciprocate that regard?" I asked, my back to her still.

"He does not seem indifferent to her, let us say," she replied.

"Can you be considering a marriage between Charles and Joan?" I said, unable to keep a horrified undertone from my voice as I pictured the slender Joan being mauled by Charles's fat hands.

Constance was alive to my tone and made her own interpretation. "No, Marguerite, do not worry yourself. I am persuaded that Charles, although he has many good qualities, needs someone a bit more *mature*, more responsible, one who has had experience running a castle. Joan has not."

Her expressive tone caused a quiver of alarm to run through my breast.

"Such a fine figure he cuts, too!" she continued. "Lucky is the woman who will wed him. And I need not tell you that his lands, although they are not as big as those dowered to you, are quite handsome."

"I am sure the right person will come along when Charles is of age," I said with admirable calm.

"Of age? Why, he is practically a man! I have come to depend on him so. His years may number only fourteen, but he has a wisdom that springs, no doubt, from the early demise of his father and the subsequent responsibilities that have fallen on his shoulders. Don't you agree?"

This maternal confidence in Charles's maturity found no echo in my heart, but I managed to answer in sufficient agreement without totally compromising my honesty. "Yes, one has only to look at Charles to know him for what he is."

"There now! I knew you would agree with me. But now you must tell me how your father goes on."

That decided the matter for me. As incredible as it seemed, I now surmised that my father, actually deluded into believing he was doing me a favor, could hand me over to Charles. I now saw my father planning this visit to Lady Constance as an occasion for me to become better acquainted with my future mother-in-law. I now guessed that the note nestled in the pocket of my sleeve carried my father's blessings on the union between Charles and me.

The parchment suddenly itched my arm past bearing. I could not be rid of it fast enough. The opportunity was there. I would be a fool not to avail myself of it. Thus, I quickly, unobtrusively slid the note out of the pocket and placed it on the hungry flames. With a vast, perhaps misplaced, relief, I saw it curl and vanish into ash.

"Tolerably well, my lady," I replied immediately, rising and turning, "but this latest indisposition came on very suddenly."

"Yes, I know, but it could not be helped, I am sure. Did he give you any message for me?"

I had not disposed of the note any too soon. "No," I lied, "he did not."

"No?" she repeated hollowly and became a little agitated. "Then that can only mean one thing . . ." she said, as if to herself.

I was determined to misinterpret her agitation. "My lady! It is not as grave as that! I do not think my father's health is in any real danger!"

This seemed to restore her calm, and I wondered momentarily whether I had done the right thing. She summoned a thin smile. "I am sure you are right. It's just that—that I was alarmed for an instant. And now I will ask you to bear a verbal message from me back to your father. Pray tell him that I shall be happy to receive him at Downton when he is better."

"You will receive him at Downton," I said, committing this to memory. "I shall certainly tell him."

"I know I can depend on you. Your father persuaded me that you were such a dutiful girl."

"Did he? Then I must thank you for confirming what I could only suspect. Women are such helpless creatures in this world that I have always thought it best to give the appearance of complaisance. Our only weapon lies in bending our men to our wishes, while making them believe all along that it was their wish from the start. I believe the woman's mind must run society."

"Yes," she said and smiled in a way that was designed to show me how well she understood my courageous attitude for mere bravado. "But it is the man's hand that signs all the contracts. Come, embrace me as your mother. I am so glad that we have had this chance to become better acquainted."

Any doubts I might have felt about the rightness of my action were instantly dispelled. I knew that the break in communication between my father and Lady Constance could be instantly repaired if they chose. I knew as well that I could ultimately do nothing if my father was determined that I marry Charles. To have burned the note, then, was only to have forestalled the inevitable. But I would have been a helpless creature indeed had I met my awful fate without one small gesture of defiance.

I was nettled throughout the day and was unable to rid myself of my disquiet as easily as I had the evening before. Nevertheless, I was not so preoccupied that I was not infected by the spirit of the posthunt feast. The evening began on an animated and noisy note and gained nothing in dignity as the night wore on. I happened to have been present in the Great Hall, aiding Lady Stafford with last-minute instructions to the understaff, when a little girl's shriek warned of impending disaster. Before anyone knew what had happened, the monkey of the night before scampered into the Great Hall, gibbered at the sight of the many guests then assembling for the feast, and swarmed up an arras covering a wall and alit on one of the points of a cornice over a door leading to a gallery. A storm of gleeful children followed immediately in the monkey's wake. An extensive search to find the culprit among them was undertaken by a young woman, no doubt a mother with wide experience in similar situations. The investigation produced the criminal, a chubby youngster named Geoffrey, who had reportedly teased the monkey out of his cage when his trainer was not attending, but finding the culprit did not help remove the monkey from his perch. Geoffrey was pulled out of the

hall by his ear. The monkey remained where he was, hurling
insults down on his amused audience.

"Come down from there!" cried one of the pages, who had
fetched a long-handled broom and was using it to pound the
wall on either side of the doorway.

The monkey's reply to this, though voluble, was incom-
prehensible. His attitude, however, was clearly unconciliatory,
so that everyone was surprised when, upon a soft voice's command for everyone to disperse followed by that same voice's
firm command to the monkey, he began to descend the arras.
Excited cries from some of the children caused a slight setback,
but the youth then requested his audience to refrain from making any noise or sudden movements, and again commanded
the monkey to come down. He seemed to descend almost
reluctantly, but allowed himself at last to be seized by the
redheaded lad.

"You have a new friend, Gavin McLaughlin!" called a spec-
tator, in response to which the monkey clasped both skinny
arms around Gavin's neck, causing a ripple of laughter from
the onlookers.

In swift succession, a swarthy man whose voice scanned of
Spanish rhythms emerged from the nether regions of the castle
calling anxiously, "Jacko! My Jacko! Where are you, *mio mo-
nito?*"

He burst through the circle of people, accosting Gavin with
profuse apologies and lavish thanks, whereupon Gavin detached Jacko and handed him to his trainer.

It was not to be supposed that the man whose livelihood
depended on the indulgences of his audience would not profit
from such a ready-made situation. Without the benefit of the
customary tambour, he stomped his foot on the floor and clapped
his hands, murmuring Spanish endearments, and the monkey
obliged him by performing a series of somersaults and flips to
the delight of all gathered. They were rewarded for their efforts
by an offering of coins, which the trainer stowed in his hat,
saying, in the dusky accents of the Mediterranean, as he left
that he must return to his bear before any mischief could be
perpetrated on that hapless animal.

The crowd dispersed, and I found the opportunity to talk to Gavin. "That was a very neat piece of work," I said. "I wish you would tell me the trick that makes an animal trust you. Or perhaps it is some inborn quality that you are lucky to possess?"

Gavin flushed slightly but seemed pleased by the compliment. "Lady Montcrief, it is good of you to say so. It is neither a trick nor an inborn quality, though. Everything I know about handling animals I have learned from Sir Guy. Sir Guy says that the secret lies in not alarming an already frightened animal."

"Does he? Then I feel sure that you are right. I am afraid, however, that it is I, and not the animal, who would be frightened."

A smile swept his face. "No, my lady, there is nothing to be afraid of. A poor monkey cannot hurt anyone."

"Well, in all events, he did not, and that was due to your skill. Nevertheless, I imagine that he could bite and do all manner of horrid things to a person, in spite of what you say. I can see that it is in my interest to stay close by you in case that bear, who does not look at all tame, should be let loose!"

"Th-the tables are just now being set up, my lady. Would you—do you think that you might dine with me? That is, unless you are already bespoken."

I hesitated, but only for a moment, for the difference in our stations would have prevented such a pairing in a more formal environment. However, the feasting this evening was much less ceremonious than the night before, and there was open seating, except at the head table on the dais and above the salt. I had made no plans for an eating partner but had loosely arranged with Yvette and Marie-Ange, as well as Demoiselles Hariette, Helvie, and Leah, whom I knew from Westminster, that we should make up a table. I thought that I should enjoy myself very much to share a plate with such a well-mannered young man, so I bade him choose a table, not a section of one of the long trestles forming an L on either side of the head table, but one of the smaller tables set off by itself, where we could face our dinner companions. I set about to gather the women, coming last upon Marie-Ange flirting outrageously with a young knight, Sir Bruce Huxley, and thus it was no difficult matter to include him at our table. Sir Robert somehow joined the group, and in the end we numbered twelve, an even pairing of ladies and men, divided in an agreeable mixture between three squires and three knights. We sat down, after Alicia and Herbert gave the signal, to a very entertaining meal.

As it happened, it was not the bear but a merlin that later swooped down on the assembled company, and it was not Gavin but the falconer who finally retrieved it. It was already well into an evening not distinguished by its temperance when some reveler, whose taste one might doubt but whose drunken condition one could not, let loose in the Great Hall a large falcon who reacted quite naturally by shrieking angrily and circling madly in the vaulting. Since the wine had flowed freely at our table, too, much discussion was necessary before it was decided just exactly which species of falcon was threatening to disrupt the entire banquet.

Sir Robert was the first to become aware of the disturbance. "Hell's teeth!" he exclaimed suddenly. "Look at that!"

Gavin, Sir Nigel on my right, and I followed Sir Robert's pointing finger. "A harrier!" Sir Nigel confirmed as the bird swooped down among the tables not far from us, eliciting delightful cries of sheer fright from the ladies seated there.

Sir Robert regarded it a moment before answering, "I am sure I do not know whose idea of a prank this is, but are you sure it's a harrier, Stockbridge?"

Sir Nigel insisted. "A harrier. I prefer them to all other falcons."

Sir Bruce, who had been regaling Marie-Ange with an apparently very droll story, had imbibed a great quantity of spirits. He was not, I was later told, known for his hard head, but there were others at our table who were at that hour even more intoxicated than he. He had not been paying the slightest attention to anything or anyone but Marie-Ange and so had missed the first passage of discussion. "God's wounds!" he cried, as the great bird's wings threatened to overturn the candles of the central chandelier. "It's a hawk!"

Sir Nigel took instant exception to this. "I never said it wasn't, Huxley!"

"I have no idea or interest in what you said, Stockbridge, but there is a peregrine circling the room!"

"Not a peregrine, you drunken fool, a harrier!" Sir Nigel returned belligerently.

"I may be drunk," he responded with dignity, "but I am no fool. I can certainly distinguish a peregrine from a harrier, no matter what my condition!"

"I say it's a harrier!" Sir Nigel said, rising and reaching across the table to grab Sir Bruce.

"I don't care what the devil it is," said Godfrey, who happened to be Sir Herbert's squire and a bosom friend of Gavin's, "but just because it's creating havoc in the hall, that is no reason to start a brawl at our table!"

At this, John, a young squire on the verge of knighthood, raised his head. "A brawl, you say?" he said with interest, if somewhat thickly. "A brawl!"

"Go soak you head, Langdon!" Godfrey recommended. "We're discussing hawks. See, at that table over there."

The identification of hawks with tables engendered a false notion, which he was thereafter unable to shake, that the hawk was going to be consumed. "Someone is eating hawk?" John said, alarmed.

"Of course not!" Sir Nigel said, momentarily diverted from lunging at Sir Bruce.

"I should hope not!" John said in accents of outrage.

"If you would but pause a moment from your drink," Godfrey said, "you would discover that there is one flying around the room!"

Thus commanded, John looked up. "So there is!" confirmed this aspirant to the golden spurs. "But why would anyone want to eat a goshawk?"

This unfortunate remark renewed and intensified the original point of contention, Sir Nigel stating caustically that there was no need for John to soak his head for Langdon's sodden wits had already gone a-swimming and had drowned and was, therefore, not to be heeded; any fool could see, he said contentiously, that it was a harrier, to which Sir Bruce replied in sarcastic tones that of course only a fool would see it as such for it was a peregrine. John demanded to know why he should soak his head and informed us that he had no intention of doing so but thought instead that the one in need of having his head washed was the one who ate hawk. Godfrey wanted to know where John got the idea that anyone would want to eat a hawk, and John replied reasonably, "We're at a banquet, aren't we?" Meanwhile, the bird made another pass across the width of the hall and dove down among some of the serving tables at one end.

Sir Robert recalled the bickering men to their surroundings. "Would you not expect," he said with a smile for each of the ladies in turn, "that the chevaliers Stockbridge and Huxley, not to mention Movrey, although I can't count Langdon, who can hardly focus his eyes, but would you not expect them to display more chivalrous behavior in the presence of such refined demoiselles?"

The hawk shrieked again.

"No," Gavin said flatly, who had been studying the hawk in its flight with narrowed eyes.

"No *what?*" Sir Nigel challenged, suddenly eyeing Gavin in the light of his next victim.

"Not a harrier, a peregrine, or a goshawk," he said simply. "It's a merlin!"

"A merlin doesn't have a white beak," Sir Nigel said with disgust for Gavin's simplicity.

"It's not a white beak. He's carrying a piece of bread," Gavin said.

The others took a moment to investigate this claim. "Bread?" John moaned, past understanding the conversation. "Goshawks with bread? I think I am going to be ill!"

"I believe you're right, McLaughlin," Godfrey said, ignoring John and his imminent malady. "Damn good eyes you've got."

"But it still doesn't make it a merlin," Sir Nigel protested.

"No, but look at the wingspread and the plumage," Gavin said matter-of-factly. "You can always tell a merlin by the blue-black sheen on the underside of the wings."

The bird obligingly hovered a moment not far from us before swooping down once more.

"Believe you're right, McLaughlin. There it is, the blue-black sheen," said Sir Bruce, who, satisfied with the bird's identity, turned back to Marie-Ange. Sir Robert seconded this and Godfrey agreed. Only Sir Nigel remained argumentative.

"That may well be a merlin," he said, not ready to abandon the joust, "but I keep only harriers. Much superior for tracking small game."

"If you keep so many of them, then why can't you identify one?" Godfrey said, reopening the rift that Gavin had mended.

Sir Nigel looked menacing, but Gavin averted disaster again by agreeing that the harrier was a superior gaming hawk and won for his efforts an approving nod from Sir Nigel; by the time the respective merits of the harrier, peregrine, merlin, tiercel, goshawk, and accipiter had been sufficiently argued out, the falconer had handily retrieved his charge by laying a small titmouse on the heavy gauntlet on his left hand and, as the falcon alit, by quickly latching a thick chain onto the bird's collar. The man and his noble bird then left the hall to the cheers of the audience, the merlin straining against the chain, squawking furiously, and flapping his powerful wings futilely. "And a good thing, too," John piped in, "that the falconer got him before the cook could."

The meal had opened on an equally lively subject, that of the day's hunt, and except for the brief flight into the realm of gaming hawks and falconry, the conversation did not stray far from this fertile topic for the duration of the meal. I did not, as I might have expected, feel left out of a discussion that focused on events I knew nothing about, for Gavin addressed most of his comments to me, and Sir Robert was kind enough to clarify the more obscure points for my benefit and that of Hariette, Helvie, and Leah, who had also not been part of the hunting party. Marie-Ange, an accomplished horsewoman, was riding on her high horse in the account of the hunt, but Yvette, an equally enthusiastic equestrienne, was unusually silent and offered few comments. She kept her mask, however, firmly in place and performed her role by smiling at every comment directed to her by Sir Robert and Godfrey on either side. I did not have to strain my powers of imagination to guess the reason for her subdued spirits. The reason possessed a sensually curved mouth and a pair of liquid brown eyes. These eyes, I noted, had come to rest from time to time on me during the course of the evening. The first time I caught Sir Hugh gazing intently at me, I was sure I had been mistaken, but a second time, I was less apt to mistrust my perceptions, and a third time, it was impossible to misinterpret a warm, seductive look that hinted of intimacy. I was neither flattered nor embarrassed, and I certainly was not impressed by Sir Hugh's tactics. I might have been even vaguely amused, had it not been for the look of pain in the eyes that pierced Yvette's mask of smiles. Yvette's only hope now, I reckoned, was that Sir Roland would turn his attention to her. This interest would, no doubt, draw Sir Hugh to Yvette more quickly than a *routier* to the spoils of battle. I thought, as I glanced at her, that I never wanted to be as hopelessly in love with someone as Yvette was with Sir Hugh. I also had no interest in becoming a pawn in the rivalry between Sir Hugh and Sir Roland.

The various and often simultaneous accounts of the hunt produced a vivid tapestry—however loosely woven at times —with bright threads of detail and splashes of color, mostly red. I pieced together the broad swatches of the chase: how Sir Herbert had sounded the horn, how the thong restraining the greyhounds was cut, freeing the sleek beasts to ferret out the boar, how the cry *"Au sanglier!"* rose to spur the hunters on, how the lyam-hounds and alauns on the scent led the party through forest and bush. Sir Nigel proudly displayed how a low-hanging branch had slashed his neck, and was not to be outdone by Sir Bruce, who was almost gored by the boar's crazed rush before death. Confused was the end, when the hunters circled around their quarry, frenzied from exertion and the many spears riddling his hide, the men and women whooping and darting from the boar's path. Only one clear pattern emerged here: Sir Roland had delivered the coup de grace. Then Sir Herbert had blown the mort.

Sir Robert smiled and said smoothly, "Who would doubt that Guimont would kill the boar. They say he never misses his prey," and paused for emphasis, "animal or man."

Gavin, with an unlooked-for nonchalance, turned Sir Robert's statement to good account. "Accurate, FitzWarren, and typical Guimont style. He threw his boar spear for all to see and stabbed the boar right between the eyes. He was never one to approach his prey from behind."

Sir Robert was effectively silenced, and the conversation turned down different paths.

At the end of the meal, Gavin did not ask to stand up with me for the dancing, but instead we merely turned ourselves away from the table, remaining seated on the bench, facing out into the hall where we could see all the activity. I had encouraged him to instruct me in the differences among the various hunting hounds, for, as I told him with a laugh, I was as unable to distinguish a lyam-hound from a brach as I was to tell a merlin from a peregrine or goshawk. He did so with pleasure, noting with simple pride that even very good hunters could not always do so.

We remained there for some time before Sir Roland approached us. He greeted me with proper distance and informed Gavin that they would be departing before daybreak on the morrow. This had the effect of causing Gavin to go in search of the others of his patrol, leaving Sir Roland at my side.

"My squire edifying you with more details of the hunt? I admire your forbearance, for you did not look at all bored when I came up," he said, a smile lighting his eyes.

"I find Gavin very well informed and a charming dinner companion. And to prove my fortitude, I will beg you to tell me more of your role as boar slayer! How was the chase?"

He was not going to sing his own praise, but said merely, "No doubt more enjoyable than your interview with the Lady Constance, but perhaps not as interesting."

"No doubt more enjoyable! But if you consider a hymn to

Charles to be interesting, grant me leave to tell you that you have very strange notions, my lord!"

"Then, let us say, informative."

I considered this for a moment and said slowly, "Indeed, it was informative."

"Do not be so quick in the future to show your surprise! I do not number myself among those who have ears only for her ailments. In fact, I have a high regard for Constance's acumen."

"It is my belief that she holds you in equally high esteem."

"She should, demoiselle, but do not try to convince me that there is any love lost between us." He glanced down at me, the blue of his eyes as cool and clear as a mountain stream. "Yet she suffers from one flaw. She has a way of underestimating her opponents and overestimating her allies."

I did not pretend to understand that remark but knew that he meant to convey something to me. "Yes, it is possible."

He bowed briefly as he said, "Please pay your father my respects, and tell him that I shall come round to visit him very soon."

I told him that I would do so gladly, and he turned on his heels and strode out of the room.

Chapter 4

I stood high above the Shrivenham lands, surveying the fields and forests spread before me and savoring the fading warmth of the twilight on the last day of September. Ever since I could remember, I had enjoyed occasional walks on the parapets of Shrivenham. Whenever I had a moment to myself, usually after the evening repast, I would climb, summer or winter, to the highest battlement protecting our fortress from the north, where I could steal precious time to myself. I perched myself in one of the crenels to reflect on my problems, dream my dreams, or clear my head of the quarrels among the servants that never ceased to fill my days. Below in the castle during the day, I felt isolated amidst all my retainers; here I was alone but never lonely. Below I was in truth no freer than the lowliest kitchen maid; here I was, or could create the illusion of being, my own mistress. I loved this vantage point, for from it my sight could embrace the untrammeled view of the vast, rolling countryside. As I turned north and east I fancied my eye could touch the lands of Guimont, while to the north and west lay the Burford demesne. Aye, I loved the lands and knew them well. And yet, no matter how perfectly I held the placement of every bosk and every row of hedges in my mind, Sir Roland had the right of it: I could not have said where our lands stopped and his began. From here I knew the contour of every hill and every stream and could travel with my eye across the land without obstacle. However, had I been astride Molly, exploring those same lands from the ground, I would no doubt have become hopelessly lost in the tangle of trees. I had had until now neither the inclination nor the freedom to ride out into our domain, but suddenly I felt the stirrings of a desire to saddle my palfrey and ride with the wind in my face to the crest of the most distant hill.

I had the leisure this eventide to polish my memories of Alicia's wedding, a luxury I had not had since my return four weeks previous. I recalled, sometimes with pleasure and sometimes with puzzlement, the various incidents that had occurred during those full two weeks of excitement, which came so rarely into my life. I was feeling more optimistic, too, as each day passed with no news of a betrothal between me and Charles, and so I held fast to the hope that I had imagined everything. Thus, on this unusually balmy and dreamy September eve, I not only looked back, I looked forward, too, to the morrow, when I was to receive Alicia—the new Lady Longchamps, I thought with a pang—for what would be an extended stay.

I had not seen Alicia since the wedding at Burford, for she and Sir Herbert had departed for their bride visits immediately after the week of hunts, and I had had, understandably, little chance to converse with her during the celebrations. It was difficult to realize that she had been married more than a month, and I was eager to learn of her new status. I admitted to myself a selfish pleasure that Alicia would be visiting me alone. The week before, Sir Herbert had been unexpectedly called away to some unspecified service for the king, and his absence provided the excuse for Alicia's visit to me. My brief stay at the royal court and my subsequent experiences at Alicia's wedding had introduced me into the mysterious world of politics and subterfuge. I was a novice, but still not so green as to have missed the swirling currents and crosscurrents of deceit that had seemed to be flowing throughout the assembled peers at Burford Castle. I could not determine precisely who was directly involved in the episode, but I had noted significant lapses in conversation when one or another knight entered a group, and the expressive glances then exchanged. There had seemed at times to be an air of expectation hanging over the week of the hunt, like a shadowy presence of some awaited event. I suspected that Alicia's Herbert had been summoned with regard to this unknown and unnamed crisis, and I could only guess at its proportions, my imagination having an unruly life of its own. I planned to discuss the whole with Alicia, for I did not doubt that as Sir Herbert's wife she would now be privy to his political leanings.

I wondered briefly who was involved in the (imagined) plotting and almost felt relief for Sir Roland's sake that he had left when he did and so could not be implicated in the shapeless mass of intrigue that seemed to be slowly taking form. I had seen no more of Sir Roland after our brief exchange on the first evening of the hunt. I had, however, seen more and more of Sir Hugh in the following days, and he was clearly involved in an intrigue of his own making. We had frequently encountered each other in odd places, and I was never entirely convinced that the encounters were accidental. One afternoon, for instance, when I would have supposed all men to be participating in the stag hunt, Yvette and I were carrying fresh linens from the laundry to the pressing room. We turned a corner and literally bumped into Sir Hugh.

"Such a picture this makes!" he said with a grand gesture as he took a step back from us. After a brief glance and greeting to Yvette, he explained his rather odd exclamation to me. "You carry your burden so tenderly as if it were a babe at your breast. I can tell that you were born into the gentle role of a mother."

I was slightly annoyed by this remark. It was no doubt calculated only to throw me into maidenly confusion, and the fact that it did to a certain extent achieve that goal irritated me all the more. I answered him somewhat at random and not without feeling my color rise.

He then expressed the warm hope that I would dance with him that evening. I replied civilly; he bowed and continued purposefully in the opposite direction without another look at Yvette. I cast her a furtive glance and noted that in her attempt to hide her mortification she looked suddenly tired. I said nothing, for there were no words to ease her aching heart, and as she did not mention the encounter, I felt it best to try to divert her attention. My observations on Marie-Ange's latest flirt drew from her a reluctant smile, but she responded somewhat mechanically.

I nourished the hope that Sir Hugh would not ask me to dance, but it was as short-lived as it was faint. Early into the festivities, he sought my hand for a dance and was not content to release it after the music had ended. Instead, he managed to draw me off into the recesses of the Great Hall where he told me that I was a rare and fragile flower and compared my eyes to smoldering sapphires. No woman could be completely impervious to such flattery, but I derived little satisfaction from his marked attentions. If Lady Constance was to be believed, many people had discussed the fact that Sir Roland had singled me out at the wedding feast, and these same people had linked my colorless name to his black one. I found this mildly amusing, given the reason for his interest in me. It was completely natural for Sir Roland to have been curious about a person he had first met under such unusual circumstances, and his curiosity could only have been intensified when he somehow learned that I was the daughter of his nearest neighbor. I was sure, however, that after our conversation he had satisfied himself that I was really a very unremarkable person. Sir Hugh, misunderstanding Sir Roland's attentions, wanted only to lay claim to another of Sir Roland's women. Strange, too, was Isabelle's reaction to her prospective bridegroom's "pursuit" of me. Although she certainly did not encourage Sir Hugh, she did not seem to discourage his particular attentions to me. No one knew better than I that she had no cause to be jealous of me, yet I found it noteworthy that she held her reins on him so loosely. It occurred to me on more than one occasion that her lack of possessiveness mayhap kept Sir Hugh interested in her. It was not difficult to perceive that Sir Hugh had no interest in Yvette, who wore her heart in her eyes. Isabelle also did not employ another of Yvette's tactics—which involved Yvette's cutting of Isabelle's acquaintance— because the friendship between Isabelle and me prospered that week, and Isabelle spoke to me openly and frequently of Sir Hugh, extolling his fine qualities and stressing the fortune he could expect when his ailing cousin in Northumbria died.

Whatever the reason, I could not say that it was a disagreeable thing to be sought after. Nevertheless, I would have pre-

ferred not to be the object of Sir Hugh's practiced courtesies.
I would not in anyone's eyes be considered a serious rival of
Isabelle, and however little attached I was to Sir Hugh, I was
concerned that I would end looking the fool.

The day was sinking rapidly as I sat in my lofty perch.
Everything was veiled in a thin blue haze of heat. I inhaled
deeply the familiar scent of fresh-cut hay that rose up from the
scene I knew so well. Yet something was different now. This
evening the fields seemed as fluid and inaccessible as I imagined the oceans to be. The days, now becoming shorter, transformed the dusty roads into ocean waves behind which the fine
point of a distant spire passed for the topsail of a far-off vessel.
The clouds and breezes signaled a shift in atmosphere and a
welcome, if unpredictable, change in mood.

My reflections were halted by the sound of heavy footsteps
on the spiral stairs leading from my solar to the battlement.
The sight of Dame Ellen approaching brought me instantly to
my feet.

"My lady!" she called, breathless. "I have found you at
last!"

Everyone in the castle knew that I took these solitary walks.
They generally respected my privacy and bothered me only for
emergencies. I knew, therefore, that something was wrong and
strove to maintain my customary calm. "Yes, Dame Ellen?" I
said, shaking out my skirts. "I was just about to come down.
Is something amiss?"

"They are carrying on down below to raise the dead!" she
exclaimed. "I've never heard the like nor shall I, if I live to
be a hundred! I had not thought at first to call you, but I saw
that it was getting out of control and I knew that there was
nothing for it but to fetch you. Not that it is proper for you to
intervene in such circumstances! Indeed, it is most *improper*,
and so I told Master Ian, who was there, too. He bade me find
you at once, to which I replied, 'You may depend on it, husband, that I go straightaway to the Lady Marguerite!' *That*
silenced him—as if do not know my duty!—which I am proud
to say I do, for a crowd has begun to gather, and, knowing as

I do how you feel about airing the dirty linen in public, I felt you would want perhaps to dispel the crowd of vulgar spectators. But, as for the other matter—!"

At this juncture, we reached the bottom of the spiral stair, which left Dame Ellen gasping as much from indignation as from the labor of her descent. We turned down a short communicating hallway to my solar.

"Yes, Dame Ellen," I said while she caught her breath. "I may always depend on you to know what you are about and do just the right thing."

Her bosom swelled. "Then, my lady, please inform Nan of that. She was so bold-faced as to disclaim my authority—not that she phrased it in such a genteel way!"

"I see," I replied, not totally convinced that Nan was in the wrong on that score.

"How she does carry on! To let that—that *bawd* continue in an honest keep is—well, it is not my place to say, after all! It is just that you cannot realize the extent to which she has turned everything topsy-turvy. And now she is extending the influence of her positively lewd behavior—there is no other word for it—to some of the younger serving maidens. We must have a stop to it!"

"Am I to collect that Nan is at the center of this present drama?" I asked.

"As if there would be anyone else a-stirring up a witches' brew!" she responded with feeling.

When we turned into my solar, I began to get the impression that whatever was going on downstairs was reaching immense proportions. In the center of the room, around the cushions, lay a heap of needlework hastily abandoned, while at the windows—not the ones overlooking my garden, but the ones that gave onto the courtyard and that featured a view of the stables—stood all of my tiring women, giggling, gossiping, and gaping at some very interesting scene below. Only Gertrude hung a little back from the crowd and took no part in the excitement. I sharply called my women to order and motioned to Gertrude to shoo them away from the windows. I issued several directives to them before I swept out of the room and had no doubts that under Gertrude's eagle-eye stare they would comply.

Dame Ellen, who had had enough sense to say nothing in front of my women, retrieved the reins of the conversation and briefly sketched what awaited me. As we made our way through the castle by the back route, crossing the servants' quarters, I allowed Ellen to expound on the iniquities of Nan's behavior and Sarah's virtue, but silently withheld judgment until I could decide for myself. There was clearly mischief afoot, but of whose making I was not sure. I hoped only that it was nothing that I could not deal with; and as one of Lady Isolde's maxims came to mind: "Make haste slowly," I quickened my step but preserved my dignity.

For the remainder of our descent into the back bailey I was treated to Dame Ellen's sweeping and magnificently censorious opinion of Nan in particular, licentious women in general, and the fates they might expect, which she summarized in one grand condemnation: "On the Judgment Day, the Heavenly Father shall excoriate those who lustfully place the flesh before the soul and send them to burn in the everlasting flames of the Inferno!" She quite ruined her effect, however, in the next moment by adding, anticlimactically, "But that is of no moment now! If only your *earthly* father had not gone away at this time!"

The confidence that my father would be at all helpful in a domestic crisis of any proportion was, at best, misplaced and sparked my often-inconvenient sense of the ridiculous, for the scene that rose to my mind of my father caught between the flying feathers of Nan, Sarah, and Dame Ellen was funny to the point of being ludicrous. I compelled myself to swallow the laughter that welled inside me and responded, so I thought, with a convincing ring of authority, "We have no need for Sir Maurice. I am mistress here and will handle this incident in his stead. Let us not make a gargantua out of a gargoyle!"

These words, once said, were instantly regretted and the humor gone the moment we emerged into the yard. The prospect that greeted me verged on the overwhelming. "Holy

Mother!" I murmured, as I took in the size of the throng that filled that large space. Practically the whole rank and file of Shrivenham keep had assembled in the courtyard, and those who were not down in the yard were hanging out the windows of the manor house, and the entire bailey was buzzing with conversation. I did not mistake the matter: I knew that the enmity between Nan and Sarah had been growing over the past weeks and had captured the fancy of Shrivenham. I had no doubts that there had been wagers laid on when and how the matter would come to a head and who would win: It was only luck that had brought things to a point on this warm September eve, providing good sport and a pleasant diversion for (almost) everyone concerned. Much the atmosphere of a summer fair reigned, and a better part of the folk seemed only mildly interested in the central drama being enacted in the far stables. There were several young mothers on the outer ring, comparing their infants and exchanging advice; nearby was an older group of my indoor women idly gossiping; in the corner, young boys were playing with a hoop, while their older counterparts stood in a circle casting dice. On the benches by the trough, some men, including Master Ian, were engaged in a noisy and apparently very satisfying discussion, Hodierne was flirting madly with Michel Armorer, and it spoke volumes for the universality of the occasion that Sir Reynauld, our ancient seneschal, had come out to see what all the disturbance was about.

I plunged into the first group milling about and asked them to return to their stations. Dame Ellen followed my lead. It was growing late, and the first current of excitement had run its course, so it was only with a small show of reluctance that I was able to disperse some of the people. I eventually came upon Bess, freely airing her opinions with her half-sister, Avice, and enlisted her aid in breaking up the crowds. She was glad to be of service, so she said, but warned as I pressed closer to the heart of the action that Nan was in a fighting mood.

I finally arrived at the door of the stable but did not enter. Dame Ellen checked her step behind me. I wanted to get a clearer grasp of the issues before meting out any justice, and

I felt it wise to let Nan and Sarah vent their feelings as they were, at the moment, unabashedly doing. In addition to the two central figures stood one of our new young grooms (Edric I believed his name to be) looking embarrassed but defiant, and next to him was John Cook, whose naturally rubicund countenance was suffused with an alarming shade of red, and these two stood slightly behind Nan. In the other camp, behind Sarah, was ranged Halbert, the head groom, looking every bit as murderous as Sarah was herself. The feelings and voices were running high, but the words were superfluous to what was revealed on the faces and in the attitudes of the five people gathered there: Nan had—how should I put it?—taken a roll in the hay with Edric, and Sarah had either accidentally or purposely caught them in the act and had gone in search of John Cook in order to discredit Nan in his eyes. Halbert had had the fortune, or misfortune, to have been near enough on hand to become involved, and suddenly, through no design of her own making, Sarah had been able to promote this incident to a full-scale scandal, buttressed by a wall of witnesses. Sarah had put me in a very difficult position, for there would be no way to keep the story quiet; this did not endear her to me, and she would not emerge from the evening unchastised. It was Sarah's words that I made out first.

"I reckon that we all have your full measure now, you bawdy house mistress!" she hurled at Nan in a shrill, grating way.

"You don't reckon naught!" Nan answered, in a fine rage of her own.

"A bawdy house is t' only place filthy enough to house the likes of you."

"Where is the filth on me, Mistress Sarah? T' only filth is in your mind!"

"We've eyes and can see what you've been about!"

"I've eyes too, blind Sarah, and have seen you try your luck on occasion."

"You slanderous liar! A bawdy house is too good for you! I'll have you in t' stocks!"

"I won't be pilloried for the crime of your jealousy!"

"Jealousy?" Sarah echoed at her most shrill.

"Aye," Nan said with satisfaction. "That I'm in the kitchen with your John Cook, while you're in the dairy with that gaumless creature Harry, and even he has too much wit to tumble to your scrawny body!"

"You leave John Cook out of this!" Sarah said and shook a bony fist in Nan's face. She was, truth to tell, rather thin, but not as thin as Gertrude.

"*You* brought him in," Nan responded, with a brief glance at that chagrined man, and then added, without further regard for his presence, "and he'll still prefer me on the morrow."

"Because I don't behave with your sinful ways."

"My only sin is my success."

"Success! Mary Mother! As if I wouldn't share the same, if I hawked my wares the way you do," Sarah said, goaded into unwise retort.

"But your basket's empty and mine is full!"

Sarah, the daughter of a Saxon dairy farmer, had something to say to that. I had observed how her normally sweet disposition had been curdling over the past few months as Nan had claimed John Cook's attention, and it had now completely soured at the sight of Nan's open bodice, displaying both her ripe curves and the truth of her statement. "Shiftless slut!" Sarah cried.

"Silly trollop!" Nan spat back.

"Have done!" I said with finality and stepped through the low door.

All heads turned toward me.

"Now we shall see!" Sarah said triumphantly and smiled maliciously.

"Yes, indeed we shall," I said, "and I have seen quite enough —from both of you!"

It was Nan's turn to smile, but she did not avail herself of it.

The stable was almost completely cloaked in darkness now. To relieve some of the tension, I bade John Cook fetch a lantern. I then excused Halbert, who took his dismissal with mixed feelings. As he stood on the threshold to go, he ventured to speak.

"If I may say so, my lady—" he began.

"No, you may not, Halbert," I said, hoping to strike a firm but gentle note, "but I shall certainly consult you in the morning. I prefer to speak alone with Sarah and Nan now."

When John Cook returned, I desired him to please escort Dame Ellen back to the hall, and I specifically did not turn around to see how Dame Ellen received her dismissal. She could not have been happy, but I could not feel that her presence would aid in my search for objectivity.

I looked slowly from Sarah to Nan and finally to Edric, and Nan was the only one of the three who did not shift uncomfortably or look away. She did not edge closer to Edric for support, as I might have thought a woman in her position would do, but stood straight and independent. Bess had been right: Nan was clearly in a fighting mood, as Sarah had found out to her cost. My best course was to dispose of Sarah as quickly as possible and deal with her later.

"I have gathered the broad outlines of what has happened here," I said, "but there are still one or two points that have me puzzled. I am sure, however, that they will speedily be clarified to my satisfaction." I turned toward Sarah, who instantly betrayed herself with her guilty mien. "What, may I ask you, Sarah, were you doing in the stable this evening?"

"I was only doing my duty," she answered.

"And since when has your duty taken you into these quarters? The dairy stands at the other end of the keep. Now, tell me in plainer terms what brought you in here."

She eyed me with dislike. I was unmoved. "I saw them go in, " she said with a rough gesture toward Nan and Edric.

"And how came John Cook into the stable?"

"I don't ken."

"Yes, you do." I paused. "Shall I tell you? Very well, then. You brought John Cook in order to show him that Nan is unfaithful, isn't that right?"

Sarah's eyes were unwisely blazing anger at me. "He belongs to me!"

"No, he does not," I said.

"You are welcome to him, Sarah," Nan said derisively. "I don't want him, nor ever have, but no matter what I do, he'll never have you, so your actions were wasted! You with yer yaller head and skinny—"

"Enough, Nan!" I intervened. Nan had the truth of it; Sarah had acted on a false premise and caused me more trouble than she knew, but it was not Nan's place to speak. "Your turn will come soon enough, but don't be looking forward to it! Now, Sarah, explain why Halbert was drawn into this as well as the rest of Shrivenham."

"Everyone must know of her ways!"

"Everyone does know now, thanks to you. You should have come to me first, rather than alerting the whole castle."

"She should be turned out!" Sarah whined.

My anger rose. "If she is, it won't be on your authority! And I have less patience with your ill-judged actions than with Nan. Let that be very plain! Are you aware of what you have done? Are you aware that through your spite, you have created an intolerable and irreparable situation? Your purposes would have been better served had you come to me discreetly! But now . . . ! You should be turned out without further notice, but I am not so inclined, for that would only condone Nan's behavior, and my sense of justice will not permit me to turn out the both of you. Nan has not caused me a moment's trouble, but let it be known, Sarah, that your liabilities far outweigh your merits, and you will have to walk a thin line from now on!"

Sarah, past rational thought, lost no time in stepping off that line. "You'll defend a whore afore you defend a seemly maid?"

"I will take no more moralizing from you, Sarah! You are excused!"

At that inauspicious moment, an unwelcome diversion presented itself. Thomas and Charger inexplicably appeared at the door, and at least one of them looked mischievous.

Sarah, who was on the point of leaving, said majestically, "Out of my way!"

Either Sarah's tone, or the dog's natural antipathy to her, provoked Charger into uttering a subdued growl.

This proved too much for Sarah's exacerbated dignity. "Stupid cur!" she snapped and made as if to kick him.

Without another thought, Charger lunged forth and bit her forearm. A dizzy moment of pandemonium passed before Thomas subdued Charger and Sarah recovered a measure of control.

Nan seized on this occurrence to make a further point. "They say a dog can always tell!" she crowed.

"Thomas, remove this untrained dog from here at once!" I commanded.

"He is gen'rally well behaved, Lady 'Garite!" Thomas assured me, oblivious, as only a child can be, of the strain in the atmosphere. "I have nearly trained him not to kill chickens, or chase sheep, and if only he does not meet any other dogs — or people who attack him," Thomas said with a reproachful glance at Sarah, "I do not have the least trouble with him!"

"Thomas! Out!"

Thomas and Charger departed, leaving Sarah trembling in anger. She had suffered only a flesh wound on her arm, but her dignity had been dealt a mortal blow. She flung herself out of the stable.

"Hold!" I called in a voice that brought her to a halt with a snap. "You shall be waiting for me outside my solar when I am finished here, and I recommend that you exchange not a word of this with anyone, *do you understand?* Now be gone!"

I squared my shoulders and faced Nan and Edric. We stood there for a few moments, each appraising the other, while I considered how best to handle this predicament. I knew that I could not justifiably send Nan away. Not that I doubted that she was guilty of intimacy with Edric, but to dismiss her for that—and Edric too, for that matter, because he was not blameless—would be as senseless as punishing someone for something as natural as eating in between meals, if that person was hungry. Society could dictate only so far how a person was to regulate his body, and after that point, I asked only for discretion. Their dismissal would also deprive me of two hands —a loss I could ill afford. Another of Lady Isolde's sayings came unbidden to mind: "A beautiful woman within the keep is a curse; a beautiful woman outside its walls is e'en worse." The curious thing about Lady Isolde's maxims, I noted wryly, was that they were always open to interpretation. This one seemed to suggest that men would always have urges, and, if given a choice, the chatelaine might prefer that the men satisfy their appetites where they could get into the least trouble. It certainly seemed reasonable to me to keep the men entertained within the castle walls, for village inns were, more often than not, verminous and dangerous places. Our gateman, Odo, had lost his left eye in a tavern brawl not too many years ago. And Nan was certainly a toothsome young woman a man would stay inside a castle for: she had thick auburn hair, wide-set eyes, a straight nose with only the slightest bump, and a comely smile that was marred by the fact that she was slightly gap-toothed. She carried herself well, but not with any height in her manner, and it was easy for me to see why she had the success she so readily acknowledged, because her curves were such—although I was certainly no judge—that would excite a man's imagination. I did not know if I could call her beautiful. She was not beautiful in the way that, for instance, Isabelle was. A delicate, ethereal beauty was Isabelle's; Nan's was earthy and sensual. Nan would certainly arouse a man's passion; Isabelle might torment a man's soul. Moreover, Nan was well kempt and clean. I valued this above all, especially for a kitchen post, and she set a standard for the other serving maids. I admired Nan's particular beauty and admitted the tiniest, most wicked wish to trade stations with her for a day.

"I will come presently to the situation at hand," I said, addressing both Edric and Nan, "but there is a more general matter that needs must be discussed first. Nan, I must ask you how things stand between you and John Cook."

"There's naught that stands between us. He's a swaggering oaf, and I'll have no part o' him."

"I've heard about it now for some time."

"That's Sarah's mischief."

"All that I hear has not come from Sarah—or Dame Ellen," I added as I saw that she was about to speak. "Michel Armorer has suggested that you have been a little, ah, free in your ways, too."

Nan's features took on a knowing look. "Well, I'll admit that Big Cook likes to put his paws on me all right, and I'm to suffer it, being as how my job depends on him, but Michel Armorer's got reason to complain only since Edric here came to t' stables."

I was beginning to see Michel's interest, but that still did not argue Nan's innocence.

"Are you suggesting that the stories about you are unfounded?" I asked.

"I'll surely say that there is them that just don't like my person," she replied. She could have added that they were either the women who were not as pretty as she or the men who did not turn her head, but she didn't.

"Did John Cook force himself on you?"

"Only once, and that's when I turned to the Armorer."

"To what purpose?"

"A girl must look to herself."

I took this cryptic statement to mean that since Nan did not welcome John Cook's advances, she turned for protection to the strongest male most to her liking. John Cook, with his soft, doughy body, would be unlikely to challenge Michel's iron-thewed muscles forged from the many hours spent at the bellows and anvil. Still, the image I conjured up of Nan the victim of men's desires did not coincide with the Nan who stood before me, although I knew that she had not remained a maid much past her first flowering, through no fault of her own. Edric's presence remained unexplained.

"And Edric?"

"That was for my pleasure," she answered, without a blink.

Well, she was honest, in all events! But I supposed that was the answer I was expecting, or some version of it, for I did not think that she would cling to a story of outraged virtue. Or perhaps she sensed my weak point that I preferred pound dealing. "Then I must tell you that your pleasure will cost you this time, very dearly, and you, Edric, will have to pay too," I said, at last turning to him.

Edric was a handsome, virile young man, almost a lad, not to my taste precisely, although I could not have qualified it, but certainly more appealing than Michel, who was as ugly as he was strong. Edric would do very well for Nan, I thought.

"Where do you come from, Edric?"

"From ower Shrivenham Hill, my lady, the next hamlet, Bird-in-Hand," he said, betraying slightly his nervousness.

"And when did you come?"

"After the midsummer."

"And how came you here?"

"My aunt is Master Halbert's sister-in-law."

"Do you have a family? Brothers and sisters?"

"Aye, my lady. Me widowed mother, an older sister already wed, three younger brothers, and two younger sisters."

That decided the matter for me. "Would they be sorely circumstanced if you were turned out of here?"

He gulped. "Aye, my lady."

"Do you think they would be very surprised if they heard you were to be married?"

"That they would," he said. "A certainty!"

"Then you may inform them of it when next you see them."

"My lady?" he said, his widened eyes indicating that he was not quick to grasp my meaning.

I glanced at Nan and saw that she understood. "I can think of no other solution that will answer," I said. "The whole of Shrivenham knows of what went on here tonight. I can neither wink at your intimacy nor allow it to pass without action. I recommend, therefore, that you be married within the month. Understand that I do not view this as punishment! But I must maintain a certain standard of conduct within the castle, and your marriage will be the only condition under which you two can remain here." I looked to Nan at that moment. She remained impassive, neither happy nor unhappy, as if long inured to the vagaries of fortune; she accepted her fate without question or comment. "Consider yourselves betrothed, then. Friar

Helm will wed you at the next moon. Edric, you may go now and give the news to Master Halbert. Nan, you may stay a moment."

Edric left. Nan and I stood alone in the flickering, yellow lantern light. I had to be sure we understood each other.

"How old are you, Nan?" I asked.

"Seventeen—almost eighteen."

Certainly not too old for marriage. "How have you escaped marriage thus far?"

"Just good fortune, I suppose," she said with the shadow of a laugh.

"Your luck just ran out," I observed.

"Edric's no' so bad," she replied, and I guessed this was her way of telling me that I had dealt with her fairly.

"You will not go near Sarah for the next month—or any other man of questionable reputation. No matter how you have been victimized here, you have undoubtedly left yourself open to attack. Your actions tonight have been indiscreet and a shame on our house. I will have no more of it from you. Have I made myself understood?"

"No use carping on what's best forgotten," she said simply.

"I agree and consider the matter finished. You may return to the house."

She nodded and I preceded her out of the stables. The air was fresh and the moon was full. A perfect night for love, I thought with an ironic sniff. Love, how tiresome a human emotion! And still I was not finished with the repercussions of this night's love tangle.

I would have been happy to have regained my solar and enjoyed there the luxury of a few moments' private reflection. They were not to be mine, for my solar hummed with the excited whisperings of my women who had been eagerly anticipating my arrival for news. I decided they would just have to await the morning light to learn of my decisions, and so I dismissed them without comment. I took a turn or two around the room before the sound of wooden clogs on stone signaled Sarah's arrival.

"Enter!" I commanded before she had had a chance to knock.

Sarah peered around the door with painful humility. The time she had just spent alone had apparently provided her with a sense of the enormity of her actions.

I did not sit down but stood regarding her sternly for a space of time that was not calculated to put her at ease. She clearly was not, for she shifted her weight several times, eyed a flag with interest, and made an unsuccessful attempt to clear her throat.

I closed the space between us by a step. "Your behavior this evening, Sarah, is past comment. On the morrow we are to receive Lady Longchamps. Instead of preparing for her arrival, Shrivenham amused itself at a spectacle of your making. The waves of what has happened will not be calmed by tomorrow, yet welcome Lady Longchamps we must, and I will not be proud to have her come into a castle more anxious to gossip about the evening's diversions than to please a guest! For that I have you to thank, and that is only the first of your misdeeds! You may also take credit for the betrothal of Nan and Edric." Sarah's eyes flew to my face, astonished. "No, I shan't dismiss her, as you would like. She has served me well, and she needs only the benefit of a religious blessing over her relationship with Edric to make her an honest maid." I mentally crossed myself for the lie, planning to repent it at my prie-dieu before retiring. "You may have the honor of informing your comrades of this wedding. It will take place next month. Dame Ellen will be informed by me. You will stay out of Nan's way, and if *any* comments cross your lips concerning Nan, you will be instantly dismissed without discussion. You are not to entertain any comments about her either. Do you think that you can abide by this?"

"Yes, my lady," she replied meekly.

"You are not to plague John Cook anymore. You may take the thought to bed with you tonight that you have probably given him a hearty disgust of you!"

"Yes, my lady."

"What could have prompted you to such action, Sarah?" I said on a gentler note.

"It was Nan! It's not fair! She has bedeviled all the men!"

"She has obviously bedeviled you, too, but I will not allow her to be the cause of your misbehavior!"

Sarah sought for words to express her hopeless anguish and fell back on the age-old cry of youth and the lovelorn. "You do not understand!" she moaned, but instantly realized the impropriety of her speech.

She was more right than she knew, but that was of no moment. "You may ascribe my indulgence in not summarily turning you out to the fact that I do sympathize with your plight. But nothing will save you now from your gross impertinence and continued insolence! Henceforth, you will exchange sleeping quarters with Hodierne. She has been deserving of a promotion. And you may spend the rest of the time until Nan's and Edric's wedding with the laundry chores. There will be a replacement for you in the dairy on the morrow. I am persuaded that you are not at present in a frame to discuss this further. You may well say something more that will get you into further trouble. So, to avert that undesirable pass, I desire you to seek Hodierne's pallet, and think well on your future here at Shrivenham!"

Sarah left, thoroughly crushed, but I could do nothing less and still exact obedience from my retainers. I did not relish having to issue reprimands and wished my father would exercise his authority in these matters. But that would be wishing for the moon, and so I retired to my chambers satisfied that I had dealt justice with as even a hand as I could balance. Dame Ellen corroborated my intuitions about the wisdom of my decisions the next morning by uncharacteristically saying nothing to my announcement that Nan and Edric were to be married, thus solving the problem. She looked momentarily taken aback and then nodded her approval. I committed a tactical error, however, by reiterating the belief that marriage was all that was needed to make Nan into an honest woman. She was not in the least diverted by this and responded somewhat acidly by saying that Edric would be a lucky man if the first bairn Nan carried was his own. I let this pass and requested her instead to keep her eye on Sarah.

I left Dame Ellen to her own devices in the kitchen and found my way to the stables. The morning sun's weak rays were straining to burn the autumn haze off of the harvest-stubbled fields, and I knew that the weather had taken a decisive turn away from the long summer. I went around to the back of the stables, which had been built to accommodate many more horses than now stood in the stalls, and passed a short row of shut doors before I turned in. Near one of the stalls stood Halbert, a middle-aged Shrivenham man of stocky build and dour countenance, who, as last evening had demonstrated, had little stomach for Nan's behavior. He was vigorously oiling a saddle that was slung over the middle rail and apparently did not hear me approach, for my greeting surprised him.

"Good morrow to ye, my lady!" he said as he nearly overset his work, causing the big bay in the contiguous stall to snort and stomp with agitation. Herbert deftly gentled him with some soothing, unintelligible noises.

"Excuse me, Master Halbert! I have made you lose your concentration. Am I interrupting you inconveniently?"

"Nay then, my lady! At-after I' finished wi' t' settle, I' bahn to take t' gray to the smithy: he's got a shoe loose. Happen t' Armorer'll fix him up right and tight."

"Indeed," I said, my attention momentarily diverted by a fresh problem. I stretched out a tentative hand to stroke the calmed animal. "This is Rufus, isn't it?"

"Aye, my lady."

I considered him a moment. "Would you say—what is the expression?—that Rufus might be a bit short in the back?"

Halbert rubbed his nose. "Chance it happens, a trifle, my lady."

"And the next horse, how is he called?" I asked, pointing to a strawberry roan.

"That is Medor."

"A prime blood?"

"A prime 'un? No, I canna say so, God's truth."

"What is wrong with him, in a horseman's terms?"

"Naught, my lady."

"Come, Halbert! You may tell me! But I shall put it to you this way: if you were being offered to buy this horse and you declined, what would be your reasons?"

His stolid features sketched a smile. "He's big, he's strong, but high in flesh."

"Ah," I said knowledgeably. "Shall I go on to the next?" Halbert shrugged. "No, I think not. I have the idea. Would you say our stables are in need of replenishing?"

"I canna say," came the cautious response.

"Well, you should! I can see that I have neglected this area of our castle for too long! You should have come to me long ago!"

"You're mortal busy, my lady."

"Not too busy for something so important. It's just that I know so little about horses." Then, as my gaze swept the glories of our cattle, I added, "And my father apparently does not, either."

"Sir Maurice leaves me tend t' stables to my suit. I ha' no call to complain."

"Thank you, Master Halbert, but I shall turn my energies here immediately after the soap making next week. Well, all in all, perhaps the contretemps of last evening has not been a complete loss, since it's brought me to a sense of my reprehensible disregard for the maintenance of our stable." I suppressed the sigh that rose to my lips.

A dark look crossed Halbert's face. "I ha' ne'r seen afore what gaes on here wi' that lass. A slamtrash wi' her ways!"

I felt compelled to speak. "Nan cannot take all the blame for last night. Sarah must shoulder some of that burden, too."

I surprised a queer expression on his face and formed the suspicion that he was sweet on Sarah. That might provide a partial solution to Sarah's troubles, but I could not bend my efforts to matchmaking just now. "Nevertheless, I seek your advice, Master Halbert. Can you tell me how old Edric is?"

"No' above a score, my lady. I reckon nine-and-ten."

"That's a comfort," I replied, "because he looks much younger."

"He's just a randy stallion, that one, a-feeling his oats."

"Well then, what do you think of a match between Edric and Nan?"

He rubbed his nose meditatively. "He'll settle to t' harness onct he's wed," he responded impassively after a few moments.

"Good! I will take that as approval. I must tell you that they are now betrothed, and their wedding will take place in a month. I consider the incident finished and hope that its resolution is to your satisfaction."

He received this news dispassionately. "Aye, my lady," he said, betraying nothing.

"Perhaps you could help me, too," I pursued. "It would be well if you, as Edric's superior, were to lend your support— in a quiet way!— to the marriage. It might smooth things over, if you see what I mean. But no concerted efforts or obvious displays. Just a word from you, a respected figure at Shrivenham, from time to time, for I know the incident will be discussed."

"It mun be now-and-now, choose how."

"Yes, and about Sarah. Perhaps you could keep an eye on her for me. She shall be in the laundry for a spell, just around the corner from you, and in her case, I think the wisest course is: 'The least said, the soonest mended,' don't you?"

"I'd be fain to be shut o' t' matter and'll keep my tongue between my teeth."

"Then we are in agreement. I depend on you. Now, we must direct our attention to the future—the immediate future. Please prepare six stalls for the party of Lady Longchamps. She will be accompanied by two women and escorted by at least three grooms, although I believe the grooms will not be staying for any length. They will arrive sometime today, and I shall assume that you have everything you need, and if not, do not hesitate to seek me."

I turned to go and caught sight of my father's horse. "What is Sim doing here, Halbert? Did my father not ride out on him last week?"

Halbert looked uneasy. "Nay, my lady. Sim is getting old and has his problems."

"You need not tell me! He has a terrible tendency to throw

out splints. But what else is to be expected? And my resolve to put our cattle in order has been strengthened. Faith! Has my father gone abroad on an even lesser mount than Sim? We shall be disgraced!"

"He's respectable mounted," Halbert assured me with the rarest of smiles.

"Then I won't worry myself on that head, and I shall not fail you, Halbert! Thank you!"

I left on Halbert's firm command to a dawdling stableboy to bustle about, and wondered yet again what had taken my father away with such haste and mystery. He had left giving no destination or reason, saying only that he would be away for a fortnight. I assumed that he was going to Downton, for he had said that he would return with Lady Constance, a prospect that filled me with dismay and slight alarm and made me all the happier that Alicia would be coming to act as a buffer. The problem of my father's whereabouts did not exercise my mind long, for while crossing the bailey, Charger loped up to me as if nothing in the world had happened.

"Naughty animal!" I said, eyeing him malevolently, and remembered too late that Sarah had said much the same thing just before he bit her. But Charger, so far from biting me, greeted me as a benefactress from whom he had been parted for years. He was yet a gangly, awkward creature who bore all the signs that, far from remaining a sickly runt, he would grow into a brute. Prancing along with me as I walked through the courtyard, he had the manner of a dog who had things well in hand, and cocked his ears at me expectantly. As I turned to go indoors, he growled once again, making it clear that he thought poorly of my taste in choosing not to be outdoors on such a fine, crisp morning. I told him that I had too much to do to prepare for Alicia's arrival to go off jauntering about the castle grounds with him and called to Thomas to take Charger for a walk. Adjuring them both to avoid chickens, sheep, other dogs, and, above all, Mistress Sarah, I entered the main portals in search of Dame Ellen, Bess, and Gertrude to finish the preparations for my guest.

Chapter 5

It was Charger, in fact, who heralded Alicia's arrival late that afternoon. He and Thomas had been bounding around on the ramparts, without permission, and as soon as the travelers came into view, Charger began to hail their arrival in an enthusiastic, puppyish way. Thomas had not yet the trick of calling him to order, so that the canine greeting endured long after we had been alerted to the visitors' advent and any slumbering servants had been aroused, and caused Michel Armorer to hope that Charger would "yap his fool head off."

Alicia's actual welcome, once the small party had crossed the drawbridge, was a good deal more orderly than Charger's reaction had foreboded. I was already outside when they entered the bailey, and I let Alicia's groom help her dismount before I rushed to embrace her.

"Alicia! God save you and welcome!" I said, gathering her in my arms.

"Grita! It has been so long!"

"So long?" I queried as I stepped back a pace and regarded her. "But it has been little more than a month, my dear!"

"Is that all? It seems like so much more!" she responded with a laugh and pushed back the marten-lined hood of her mantle.

"Pray do not tell me the moment of your arrival that your marriage is so disagreeable that the time drags! *That* confidence must wait until we have supped and can linger together in your antechamber over a goblet of wine. Only in private will I entertain your complaints, which I am sure are many!" I chided her with mock severity.

Alicia smiled and flushed. "No, Grita! You are too bad! It

is just that—that it seems that Herbert and I have been married for so long, and yet the time has flown by! I cannot explain it, nor will I try, for you are just teasing me!"

"Exactly! And I think I understand. When something is so right and so natural, you cannot conceive of ever having existed apart from him and have found your other half, is that it?"

"Yes! I knew you would understand!" she said, peeling off her gloves. "You have always been able to put your experience into words better than I."

"If you think I have experienced something similar, you are sadly out, Alicia! I know only what I have been told or can imagine. But I am glad, at least, that it is experience for you."

"It will be for you too, my dear," she said.

"No doubt!" I answered, chuckling at the patronizing tone in the voice of the wise matron. "But why are we standing about in the courtyard? Come! I know that you will want to remove your travel stains before the meal. I hope that between me, John Cook, and Dame Ellen, we will contrive to find dishes that will tempt your palate. You are not a robust eater, you know. Quite the despair of John Cook, in fact!"

As we entered the hall, leaving Dame Ellen and Bess to attend to the details of the welcome arrangements, Alicia would have it that she had been gaining weight since her marriage, so well did they eat at Luxley. Her appetite that evening, however, was even less hearty than usual, but that was easily due to her fatigue and did nothing to lessen my enjoyment of the meal and the gaiety that pervaded it. Alicia's spirits were high, and the conversation never lagged, with the topic of her wedding so fresh, and seemed to interest those nearest to the head table who could hear us.

Meals were generally a problem at Shrivenham when my father was present, which was most of the time. He had no boon companions whom he could elevate to the head table, and unless any guests were in residence, I could seat above the salt only myself, my father, Sir Reynauld, Friar Helm, who boasted a noble heritage, and two of my father's vassals, both of indifferent countenance and personality, as well as their wives. The conversation was usually as sparse as the company. Although the Abbess Catherine had trained me well in the duties of the lady of a manor, I saw no need to exercise my ingenuity at introducing topics and maintaining a flow of talk if I was not in the mood, for neither my father nor his vassals were inclined to communicate. Friar Helm, on the other hand, loved to debate. He had once had scholarly aspirations, I believed, and I did try on occasion to accommodate his interests. I had no such scholarly pretensions, but we had been allowed rare intellectual freedom under Abbess Catherine, so that I could discuss with Friar Helm some of the doctrinary explanations of the Church's position on the *esse* of material things. But when he would introduce the *modi significandi* or discuss the finer points in the long-running debates between the great Saint Thomas Aquinas and other masters in Paris, I was carried far beyond my depths. My father usually put an end to such discussions by saying that hearing such gibble-gabble at mealtime was in a fair way to maudling his insides. Sir Reynauld, our seneschal, could also be counted on to converse, but as he was getting very old and was slightly deaf, he could be depended on only to befuddle whatever topic was at hand or to doze off before the meal ended.

Sir Reynauld was a kindly man, though, and I liked him very well. It saddened me to see how he had gone into a decline after the Lady Isolde's death years ago. I remembered him as a vibrant, erect man of decision, but he had been losing flesh now for some years and had acquired a dreamy, almost foggy gaze, seeing only with his inner eye of memories. He seemed also to have a rather looser grasp on the happenings in the castle than a bailiff should. For instance, just before Alicia's arrival, Master Ian had told me, with a disregard for the respect due his superiors, that he had encountered Sir Reynauld still shaking his head over what had happened the night before. Sir Reynauld informed him, apparently having misinterpreted the explanation of the events that took place in the stables between Nan and Sarah, that never had he heard of a dog and a pullet fighting with the pullet coming out the winner. I bit my lower lip, for I could readily imagine in what terms things had been described to him, but I could think of no suitable response. Ian merely grinned, adding, "No need to scold me, my lady, for I knew you would appreciate the joke!"

This evening I had placed Alicia between me and Sir Reynauld, Friar Helm on my left, and the two vassals and their wives flanking either end of the head table. Below the salt sat our company of fifty or so retainers, and I made sure that Dame Ellen, who had a real fondness for Alicia, and Master Ian were high up. She was storing up our descriptions of the wedding for later reflection. Friar Helm was visibly impressed that Brian of Bath had performed the holy ceremony and lauded that fact, adding the rider that he had met Brian once at Lincoln Abbey and would never have thought that he had the spiritual fabric of a bishop, and muttering something about his own talents being wasted on sanctifying such vulgar unions as between harlots and their servicemen. I rejoined that God and the Archbishop of Canterbury cared more for saving souls than for worldly rank, a facile argument with which I could always score points. Friar Helm nobly ignored my remark and inquired instead after Bishop Brian's itinerary. Alicia was not precisely certain, but she believed that he might have been on his way to Salisbury.

At this point, Sir Reynauld, who had formed a very imperfect impression of what had been said, nodded and confided to Alicia in the overloud voice of the deaf, "You should have been there, my lady! A dog fighting a pullet—or was it a cock, now?—and the cock winning! By the Holy Rood, have you ever heard of such?"

I hastily claimed Alicia's attention. "The stockfish is nothing out of the ordinary, I admit, Alicia, but you have not touched your mortrewe!"

My intervention was wholly unnecessary. Alicia, perceiving from the suppressed chuckles of those nearby that Sir Reynauld had wandered into questionable territory, knew just how to handle him. After taking a bite of the stew, she surprised him by saying, "I have heard something similar, I believe, a story told to me by the Lady Isolde, your lovely wife, whom I loved dearly, as did we all—"

"You knew Lady Isolde?" Sir Reynauld asked, now diverted. He had probably asked Alicia that same question at least a half-dozen times in as many years, but I was grateful for the change of topic. I noticed that Dame Ellen approved of Alicia's tactics, too.

"Yes," said Alicia. "Do you remember that I met her when I was used to visit Shrivenham on holy days when Marguerite and I would come home from Amesbury? You and Lady Isolde would meet me and always make me feel at home. I have never forgotten!"

"Aye, she was a fine woman, my Isolde. Little Marguerite depended on her so. She was wise in the ways of Shrivenham. Knew everyone in the castle and everything about it. Was like a mother to little Marguerite, who lost hers when she was born."

"Then it was doubly fortunate that you had Lady Isolde, wasn't it, Grita?"

"You have no idea!" I responded. "Alicia knows that a day does not go by but that I call to mind some piece of advice your wife gave me as I was growing up. She lives with me still!"

After dinner as we strolled outside in the garden below my solar, I thanked Alicia for her efforts toward Sir Reynauld at dinner.

"After you have caught your breath, Alicia," I suggested, "perhaps the day after tomorrow, shall we ride out together?"

"I should like that very much. But only a gentle ride, mind you."

"Alicia!" I said, much shocked. "You above all people should know that if you ride with me you would be very lucky to get anything more strenuous than a gentle ride! But I have tired you out. Let us retire."

I had appointed Dame Ellen to attend Alicia, a task she considered a privilege. I was seeking my own chambers, having issued the instructions for the morrow, when I passed Dame

Ellen on the stair. She was in raptures over our guest and apostrophized Alicia as "an angel! Nothing could make that girl—a *married woman* now!—dearer to me!"

Contrary to Dame Ellen's pronouncement, a circumstance was to arise that would further endear Alicia to her. We became aware of it on the evening after our ride. We had set forth on the second afternoon of Alicia's visit into the crisp October air, and I felt my spirits rise with the flight of a curlew I spied on the horizon. We mounted the first hill to the east of Shrivenham's main flanking tower and paused at the summit to gaze about us.

"Grita, I fear that there are no words left to thank you for everything you did at my wedding."

"You don't know how glad I am to hear that! Between you, your mother, and Lady Longchamps, your thanks tired me far more than any small effort I made in the preparations. I enjoyed myself thoroughly, and did nothing to be thanked for!"

"Did you enjoy yourself?" she asked earnestly. "I could not be certain."

"Your attention was otherwise, I imagine!" I said teasingly.

"But not so far removed from my guests that I did not notice the attention that the Earl of Guimont paid you. He singled you out in a very marked way!"

I flushed slightly. "I could hardly say that he singled me out."

"Yet he talked with no other woman at length."

"Perhaps not, but that was because he stayed only one night and did not have a chance."

"So you see, he passed the greater part of his one evening with you," she countered. I shrugged and acknowledged defeat on that score. "You did not tell me that you knew him. I had the impression that you did not."

"Oh, a fleeting encounter! I must have forgotten it."

"He did not."

"That is because he is very polite."

"He is not! I did not find him very polite to Sir Hugh, and I am beginning to think that Marie-Ange was right. He and Sir Hugh are not very friendly to each other."

"So it seems. And the reason was standing right there!"

She did not immediately catch my meaning. "Oh, you mean Isabelle. But he's not betrothed to her any longer."

"Exactly, and he drew me off just to annoy her."

"I don't know about that, but I knew he was interested in you."

"That was different," I said.

"I said very much the same thing when Herbert was first courting me."

"There is no talk of his, or anyone's, courting me. That really *was* different," I said firmly.

"So *I* too was convinced!" She laughed. "But have it your own way: he found no pleasure in your company."

Since I could not convince her that his interest was more curious than amorous without also divulging our first encounter, I let this pass. "Besides," I said, "he is going to marry Joan of Shrewsbury."

"Is he?" she said, considering this. "I had heard that she was to marry Joscelin Godefry."

"Well, I do not know for certain, and she did not confide in me, at any rate," I replied, happy for any turn in conversation. "And just another example of how unreliable gossip is! But that puts me in mind of something. I have been meaning to ask you why Sir Herbert was called by the king."

"A council meeting, I believe. Why do you ask?"

"Simply the strong suspicion that there were undercurrents of intrigue during the wedding festivities at Burford," I replied. "I had thought perhaps the summons was somehow related to whatever is toward. Maybe an uprising in Aquitania—there was one there last year, you know—or a—a plot against the king's life!"

Alicia laughed. "Grita! Your imagination runs away with you!" She added more sympathetically when she saw the corners of my mouth pull down, "Are you terribly disappointed that it is only a very routine meeting?"

"But are you sure that is all it is?"

"Why, yes, dearest!" she said. "Herbert explained it to me very explicitly before he left Luxley. Oh, do not ask me the particulars! He said it had something to do with taxes and unhappy barons, but then the barons are always unhappy, aren't they?"

"I was so *sure,*" I complained. "The air seemed so full of mystery and plotting."

"Well, there are always plots brewing," she admitted, "for I did not live at court a year and not learn that! Not that I understood how one can know that a plot is brewing exactly—"

"Ah, but there is meaning in even the most innocent phrase and hidden significance in every sidelong glance, my dear!"

"Grita! You exaggerate shamefully!"

"No, I have that on best authority: Sir Hugh!"

"Then leave the conspiring to the men! Sir Hugh may understand such things, but I do not! If I were to tell you how badly Marie-Ange muddles every scrap of gossip—well! We have been over that road before, although it proves my point that these matters are better left to men. It is not for us! I am persuaded that you agree with me!"

"I will agree that it is not for *us,* in all events," I conceded, "but still, if there *were* something political going on, would Herbert confide in you?"

"Why, I believe so, but the opportunity has not yet arisen."

I saw the slight frown marking her forehead and thought that I might have offended her. "Of course! I did not mean to doubt you—or your relationship with Sir Herbert. I am just too fanciful, as you say! I suppose that what I am asking is more general. That is, does Herbert confide in you?"

"We have always told each other everything, but I fail to—"

"I am making a mull of it, I can see! I mean, what do you and Herbert find to talk about?"

"All manner of things," she said, surprised by the question.

"Have patience with me, my dear. My imagination is not fertile enough to imagine what married people talk about. I have always thought that, after a time, the conversation must run out!"

"No." She laughed again. "That is impossible, but I cannot

tell you exactly what we do find to talk about, but I assure you that it is endless. For instance, you and I never lack for topics of discussion."

"But that is not at all the same thing!" I objected.

"No, it isn't," she said, and blushed slightly. "But, in another way, it is very similar."

Inquisitiveness got the better of me. "Tell me, Alicia: what *is* it like to be married?"

"How can one answer such a question?" she protested. "It is impossible to put into words. You are asking the strangest things, my love!"

"Forgive me," I said. "I won't tease you further." We had reined in to let our mounts graze in a meadow. I was still not satisfied, and turned the matter over in my mind. I realized in a flash of honesty that I was asking her something quite different. Alicia was my dearest, truest friend, and I thought that I could ask her what I wanted to know without embarrassment. We had never ventured into this territory in our conversations before, but I had no one else to consult about such matters who had any experience.

"Alicia," I said after a moment and turned to her, "I suppose that what I want to know is something far simpler—or perhaps more complex! To say the word with no bark on it: what was it like on your wedding night?"

Her blush deepened. "Oh, I see!" she said, and met my eyes fleetingly. "I am sure it is very natural you should want to know, and I will do my best." She was clearly groping for the words to express herself in an acceptable manner and finding none.

"I know," I said at length. "It is not easy. But perhaps you can tell me if you were—afraid on your wedding night. I was certainly afraid for you!"

"Afraid? On the wedding night, no," she said after a momentary pause. "But you must understand that Herbert and I— well, he thought it would go better for me, what with all the excitement and exhaustion of the wedding day itself, if—!"

"If?" I prodded in blankest incomprehension.

"That is, I tell you in the strictest confidence—!"

"How can you doubt me, Alicia?" I cried, my curiosity strained to the limit.

"Herbert and I consummated the marriage before the ceremony," she said simply.

Alicia had clearly overestimated my worldliness in this confidence, for I was astounded. Such a thought would never have occurred to me. Of course, I knew all there was to know about the world of Nan and Edric, or so I thought, but for the women of my order, I unquestioningly applied another set of rules. And this was my Alicia speaking! I studied the point between Molly's ears, trying to digest this.

"I have shocked you, Grita," Alicia said quietly.

"Yes, a little," I said shakily, "but I have been advised against showing my surprise so readily. However, now you have an entirely captive audience, and I wish, if I am not trespassing, you would tell me what it is all about."

"Gladly, in the hope that it will all become clear! Do not misunderstand! We did not have a relationship long before the actual wedding. You see, three days before the wedding, Herbert arrived, as you know. He said that sometimes it does not go well with a woman on her first time and that it might be better for me if I were more relaxed, and I think he was a little eager, too, so we took a walk in the gardens, and—well, it was not as if the marriage were not going through, after all! It was but three days before. Is that better?"

"Much!" I responded, a little relieved. "I think I can understand, but is that common practice?" I thought that such behavior might reflect court ways, for I had never heard of such a thing.

"I would not say that it is common, but neither is it entirely uncommon, I think. I have overheard other ladies make references to that effect."

"But what of the marriage sheets the next day?" I asked, diverted by this practical thought.

She did not immediately respond.

"Oh!" I said at last in a little-girl voice, feeling somewhat naive. I did not really want clarification on that point, and Alicia did not seem inclined to elaborate.

"The answer to your original question is, however, that I was not afraid. Maybe a little, but Herbert made everything all right. When you are in love, there is nothing to fear. It is very natural. So I hope that I have answered your question and relieved your mind."

She certainly had not relieved my mind, whatever else she may have done. I felt distinctly uneasy and firmly repressed all thought of Charles. "Three days before the wedding, you say? Herbert was indeed the eager bridegroom. I perfectly understand, and I thank you for being so honest."

"And no one will really be counting if the baby is three days early," she said in a shy voice.

I whirled around to her. "The *baby?*" I exclaimed. "No! Alicia!"

She smiled her answer. "Yes, I am to be a mother!"

"My love, I am delighted. Nay, I am *thrilled!* But we must go back immediately. You should not be out riding. It might be harmful to you."

"No, really, Grita," she protested, "I am sure that it is perfectly safe for me to ride as we have done. I had such a craving for the out-of-doors today! You certainly do not expect me to lie abed for nine months, for I am not ill! And just think how demoralizing that would be for me!"

"But why didn't you tell me?"

"I just did, goose!"

"I realize that," I said, torn between amusement, surprise, and exasperation, "but you have been here already two days, and I would have thought that— Does Herbert know?" I asked suddenly.

"No, and that is what I am trying to tell you," she said. "I only became certain of it this morning, although I have had my suspicions for several weeks. It is still a little early to be sure that it will last, but when I woke up I felt so sick—and so pregnant!—that I thought I could tell you. I believed that you might have guessed: my lack of energy, my failing appetite . . ."

"I had not the least suspicion! I am very want-witted, for all my imagination, as you can see! We must go back and tell

everyone. Dame Ellen will be delighted! And then we shall
send a courier to Herbert, and—"

"You go too fast for me," Alicia interposed, stemming the
tide of my plans. "Please, not all this fuss! Women have children every day, and you know that I really cannot like being
the center of attention."

"Very true, and I shall do my best to curb my enthusiasm
and to treat you in a normal fashion, but if you do not want a
fuss," I said with a touch of wry humor, "then we must keep
it from Dame Ellen!"

I proved a prophet. The fortunate circumstances of Alicia's
pregnancy turned her merely pleasant visit, in Dame Ellen's
eyes, into a high treat for her. Needless to say, I had been a
sad disappointment to Dame Ellen's maternal proclivities. It
was past time for me to have married and started filling my
household with children. She had been blessed with only one
child, Thomas, and I did not doubt that she had hoped to fill
the gaps with mine. Thus, when Alicia imparted the joyful
news to Dame Ellen, she saw at once the deeply satisfying
prospect of expanding her mothering genius on Alicia, and
although her Thomas had only five summers behind him, Dame
Ellen instantly warmed to a role that had more of the char-
acteristics of a grandmother than a mother. It was determined
over the next few days, based on Alicia's increasing nausea in
both the mornings and the evenings, that she must be somewhere in the sixth week of her term. Dame Ellen practiced
some cumbersome calculations and finally, with a sudden light
dawning in her eye, said, "By the Grace of God, my lady!
Yours is truly a blessed union to have conceived on your wedding night!"

I winked broadly at Alicia and let the comment pass with
no further teasing.

Then came the inevitable predictions. From the severity of
Alicia's sicknesses, Dame Ellen announced that it would be a
boy, and had many long conversations on the subject of male
names. It would be a braw lad, and strong like his sire, despite
the fact that Dame Ellen had never laid eyes on Sir Herbert,
and he would inherit the coloring of his mother. He would

be born under the heavens of the Twins, too, a good sign. Dame Ellen tirelessly applied her energies to the comfort of our breeding guest, which proved both a blessing and a curse for me. I was, on one hand, relieved that Alicia was receiving the best of care during this crucial period—far better than I could have offered her—but, on the other hand, I was deprived of much of her company and had to expend an extra effort to temper some of Dame Ellen's fanatical excesses.

On the whole, however, I enjoyed myself in the week that followed. To be sure, these quiet days spent with Alicia could not begin to compare to the excitement and magnificence of her wedding or to the diversions of the court, but this was something unique, and I appreciated our time together. I had much on my mind during that season, with the harvest, the laying up of the fruits, nuts, and grains, the brewing of the new ale, and the pickling of the vegetables. I could not, therefore, devote myself exclusively to her entertainment. However, that suited Alicia's constitution, for she had never been a robust person and found that she was obliged to lie abed quite late in the mornings and take at least one rest a day. Her stamina could not carry her through the evenings, so after the last meal, we made a habit of going to her rooms and sitting until she could relax into sleep. The weather had turned suddenly cool with a sharp undercurrent, so we curtailed our walks in the gardens. I felt curiously withdrawn during those days, but not because of Alicia's pregnancy, although I did openly admit my envy of her condition. My restlessness, however, was temporarily dormant, and so I did not question my mood. Sometimes one senses something, too vaguely perhaps to be even conscious of it, and retreats into some inner space where one can rest. But one should also recognize that those apparent calms are much like the weather and presage the coming storms.

Lady Stafford, Alicia's mother, came over from Castle Burford for several days to attend to her daughter. She was very welcome company and approved so heartily of Dame Ellen that I believed she would have whisked that woman out of my service and into hers on the instant if I had offered. I did not. It was decided that Alicia was not to be removed from Shrivenham until the worst days of nausea were over, and any riding, gentle or otherwise, was strictly prohibited. Lady Stafford did not offer any medical reasons for this stricture, but she said in a challenging and protective tone that everyone knew it was simply bad luck for a pregnant woman to mount a horse, and just as you would never think of eating juniper berries on the thirteenth of the month or invoking the Virgin Mary on Saint Agnes's Day, so a pregnant woman did not ride. She clinched her statements with a line from the Scriptures about the women of Judea and the plague among the horses, which did not exactly fit the argument, but as Dame Ellen looked much struck, I naturally kept my own counsel and agreed in a very docile way to see that Alicia took her exercise by walking. Lady Stafford was unable to stay more than a couple of days, since her two youngest sons had thrown out spots. It was nothing but a childhood illness, but since Alicia's two brothers were a little older than normal to have contracted it, Lady Stafford felt her first duty was at her own keep, and she was entirely satisfied with the care Alicia was receiving at Dame Ellen's tender hands. Lady Stafford, upon taking her leave, did not doubt that Alicia would be able to travel to Burford within the fortnight, and it was there that Herbert would come to fetch her.

Alicia had suffered a severe nausea the day after her mother's departure and so sought her bed even before the evening meal. I relinquished Alicia to the care of Dame Ellen, having no fears that my guest would languish abed without supper. As I closed the door to her chambers, I had to smile as I heard Dame Ellen's voice, with its own mixture of coaxing and severity, gently scold, "Never mind whether you're hungry, my lady! You've two to feed now, and you'll do just as Ellen says and no nonsense! Now, do you take some bites of the egg posset I have prepared for you just the way you like it with spiced wine!"

I visited the slightly browbeaten but well-fed invalid later, only briefly. Since she was drawn and slightly peevish and more in need of sleep than of my company, I did not hesitate to leave her after only a few minutes, for I had already set that evening aside to begin the twice-yearly soap making. Leaving Alicia's door, I headed for the outside stairs that led to the yard in front of the laundry. I rarely used that flight of steps and so surprised two milkmaids sitting idly on the bottom step, gossiping in Saxon. When they heard someone descend and turned around to look up at me, they stopped their talk abruptly, and began again, this time in their version of Norman, with two somewhat dissonant topics. I had a reasonably fluent understanding of Saxon, but even if I had not understood one word of that peasant tongue, I would not have supposed the subject of their first conversation was either Marthe's sister's new baby boy or Runegild's broken toe. It did confirm my suspicions, however, that the interest surrounding the tangled affairs of Nan, Edric, Sarah, and John Cook had not palled, a fact that did not disturb me as much as the news, if I had grasped the gist of their comments correctly, that several of the men who championed Sarah seemed to be baiting Nan for sport. I liked to think that Nan would be circumspect—if not for my sake, at least for her own—but nothing could save her or my authority if she was discovered in another compromising situation, even if it was not of her own making. I depended more than I would care to admit on just such encounters as this to feel the pulse of my keep, and as chatelaine I maintained a high visibility and kept in circulation. It would be easy enough to drop some hints in the next few days about the fate of any man who might be found consorting with Nan.

"If you find yourselves so idle, Marthe and Runegild," I said in French, for I never spoke English, "you may accompany me to the laundry. Tonight we are boiling the fat for soap and candles, and you will want to participate. To be sure, Runegild, I am sorry to hear about your toe, and you may assist Gertrude and Hodierne with dipping the tallows, where you may remain seated. But you must learn to keep your feet out from under Margot, especially now when she is ready to calf!"

Marthe and Runegild exchanged rueful glances and reluctantly followed me. I had not originally intended to enlist their aid in the task, but it would do no harm for them to know that I had perfectly understood their conversation.

Late in the afternoon I had had several boys set up a dozen caldrons in the yard, and so by the time I arrived on the scene, the fat had already been boiling in the water for over an hour. I had established the rhythm of attending to the soap making in the fall and spring, and on clear evenings, when the heat of the caldrons would not be unpleasant. This particular evening looked to be excellent. The products of this evenings's endeavors, however, were not for immediate consumption; I prided myself in my well-ordered household and planned my provisions so that they would last a six-month, for I had discovered that soap, like wine, improved with age. It was a messy task, in sooth, but I savored in a homely way how it was that the simple waste products of animal fat and wood ash would combine almost like magic with water to render such useful items as soap and candles, as well as the whitewash for the castle walls. It was Lady Isolde's favorite example of "something out of nothing," and seeing the honey-thick mixture being poured into the molds always brought me a satisfaction comparable only to a clear conscience or a becoming kirtle.

Bess, who shared my curious enthusiasm for soap making, was already in the yard, as were Gertrude, Hodierne, the laundry maids, a group of younger pages for fetching and stirring, and several older boys who stood ready to hoist the caldrons off the fire when the time came. Bess handed me a white linen smock that I tied over my working kirtle, and I had her procure two more for the disinclined newcomers. I had already exchanged my coif for a plain kerchief, and so was ready to begin managing the process of sieving the wood ash into the boiling water and fat.

Ever since my return to Shrivenham from my girlhood convent and especially since the death of Lady Isolde, I had had a growing interest in tinkering with fragrances. Under the eaves of the laundry sat an ancient al-ambic that had belonged to Lady Isolde's predecessor and had been part of the exotic and ill-assorted booty brought back from the crusade of Boniface II of Montferrat to the Holy Land and had made its way in some mysterious fashion to our keep. No one quite knew how it got there, but its presence was long established, and it was commonly referred to as the Infidel's Arm, most likely because of the tall, coiling tube that cooled whatever essence was being distilled. What had sparked my interest in the more esoteric realm of essences was a chance reference in a letter from the Abbess Catherine. I did try to correspond with her as frequently as my father and my time permitted such an extravagance, as much out of respect for her as from a desire to practice my script, which had never been anything more than passable, and in one letter I had mentioned the Infidel's Arm. The abbess responded to me in time, and noted in passing that she had learned that alcohol of late had been introduced to perfumery in the Orient. This idea intrigued me, so at the next soap making I substituted some alcohol for the fat base in mixing my perfumes. My alchemy was a success, and although I produced no gold, I did discover that alcohol gave to perfumes a vehicle in which they could be conveniently stored, a substance that would dissolve them without leaving a heavy odor, and that furthermore was not greasy and would not stain. I experimented with animals oils and resins in this alcohol base but infinitely preferred flower oils, and fancied I made a fine attar of rose, a bottle of which I had presented to Alicia some Christmases before. She assured me it was a rare treat and praised my efforts until I promised her a steady supply. For Dame Ellen I distilled the rare eucalyptus whose medicinal value was fabled, and for myself, always hydrangea. I had had the idea once to make essence of Marguerite, because of my name, but that had proved a dismal failure. My father had sniffed rudely at dinner the first time I applied it, and even Dame Ellen mustered all her tact to tell me that pressing the lowly daisy for its oil was below my station. The several bottles I had of it made their way to the kitchen, where it was discovered after a while that essence of Marguerite was infallible as a means of clearing mold and mildew from basketry and rushes. Despite this worthy application, I never made it again.

Bent over my task, I was at first unaware that Charger had trotted into the yard with Thomas in tow and was sniffing expectantly at the caldrons, apparently under the mistaken impression that there was flesh therein and that he had only to growl in the manner of a starving waif who had not eaten for days to be thrown a meaty bone. Since no such treat was forthcoming, Charger took exception to the boy who was tending the farthest caldron from me and started nipping at his leg. The noisy result of this action brought my attention around in a hurry. My intervention in the matter was entirely unnecessary, for Thomas had quickly cowed the boy, some five years his senior, into thinking that he was lucky to have suffered from the teeth of so fierce a brute nothing more than torn breeks. I did not know what Thomas was about not being in bed at such an hour. I could only assume that Dame Ellen was preoccupied with Alicia, but it was well past vespers and surely time for Thomas to be asleep. I gazed up momentarily at the milky spill of stars across the sky and judged it even to be past the compline, but owing to the fact that this canonical hour was never observed at Shrivenham when we were engaged in soap making, I could not have said exactly the lateness of the evening.

I had just finished the first distillation of my hydrangea, and Rannulf had signaled that the mixtures had saponified and were ready to be poured into the firkins, when Dame Ellen steamed into the yard and announced breathlessly that the Earl of Guimont and a small company of men had entered the portals of our keep and would momentarily await my welcome in the main hall.

Chapter 6

"The Earl of Guimont?" I repeated blankly.

"I believe it is indeed the *new* earl," she clarified with an expression of disapproval.

I wiped my hands absently on my smock. "Yes, of course," I said, trying to order my wits, "but it is so—unforeseen! He sent no message, no word as to when— But it is only to be expected when I am in the midst of the— *How* did they enter the keep without our hearing the lowering of the *pont-levis?*"

Dame Ellen assumed an attitude of righteous indignation. "It is my belief," she said with awful dignity, "that the gate-keeper drank his dinner, as the saying goes, in the widow's inn and was, therefore, remiss in his duties. The bridge was never drawn up, nor the portcullis lowered, and this is not the first time he has left the castle open to attack from any passing band of adventurers!"

"Nothing so disastrous has happened, in all events," I said firmly, "and I cannot now address myself to Odo's habits, although I assure you that I am aware of the problem."

"If I were mistress here—"

"But you are not!" I snapped. "Turn your outrage into more productive channels and help me contrive how we may best offer Sir Roland and his men a suitable welcome."

"It hardly seems appropriate to receive them without your father here," she pointed out.

"Then we will just have to settle for it being inappropriate! Would you have me send them away?" I was suddenly harassed—at the situation, at Dame Ellen, and at myself for having allowed her so much license. In general she was helpful, but at the moment I could have throttled her. "After all, Sir Roland could not have known that Sir Maurice would not be here, for he so rarely leaves! But his absence, just when I need him, is only typical! I cannot waste my time discussing this. I must hurry to change these clothes. I am hardly presentable!"

"I think," Dame Ellen said more contritely, "that you had best go straight away to the hall. The earl seemed desirous of being received immediately, for he and his men looked as if they had ridden a long way, and it is late. Perhaps he will not notice your clothes."

I saw that she probably had the right of it. To keep tired men waiting with no one to receive them seemed less hospitable than to receive them in working clothes. "Oh, the *devil!*" I muttered in exasperation, startling all the women within earshot and causing Dame Ellen to bridle slightly. "Very well, I shall go to him now. Hodierne, give me your kerchief. I do not even have time to fetch a fresh coif, and yours is the cleaner. Your smock, Adela! I simply cannot present myself in this plain kirtle. Come, we must greet our guests."

I bade half the women stay to complete the soap and candle making; the other half were to join me and Dame Ellen in the welcome party. I could not have imagined a worse moment to receive visitors, especially Sir Roland. My father was gone, I was unkempt and in no mood to act the gracious hostess, Alicia was already abed, and I hesitated sending for Sir Reynauld, for I feared that his presence would not be helpful. There would be no one besides myself of a station to properly welcome a neighboring earl on his first visit. The fires were already banked, the candles doused, and the trestles stacked against the walls. There would be no signs of welcome for a group of tired and hungry men. It seemed, somehow, beside the point that Sir Roland's visit was unannounced. I would have liked to have been in his eyes equal to any unexpected situation, although I wanted to think that he would understand the lack of the usual courtesies. I roused several sleepy pages on my way to the hall and commanded them to lay out the tables immediately and to relight the wall sconces, singling out the quickest among them to alert John Cook to start preparing whatever fresh food was at hand and not to skimp on the flesh.

We entered the hall from the portal opposite the main entry from the bailey. I glanced across the dim expanse to see Sir Roland and his men penetrate the arched stone entry and lowered my eyes again, as much from cowardice as from propriety, filled with an inexplicable sense of doom. So awkward and defenseless did I feel that I was put forcibly in mind of the cheerless altarpiece at the convent in Amesbury, which I had spent many an hour contemplating in my youth and whose center panel portrayed a bedraggled and downtrodden assortment of Christians defending a hideously bloodied Saint Agatha from the Roman mob. My women were certainly not as ragged as those depicted on the panel, and they were ranged behind me, rather than protecting me, and Sir Roland's company could hardly have been described as an angry mob, for there were only five or six of them, and they looked rather travel-worn. Neither were they garbed in the long robes of the ancients but wore the familiar mail of warriors, which should have comforted me. Nevertheless, as our two forces advanced toward each other, I thought that I would soon know Saint Agatha's fate. I had to give myself a mental shake: Sir Roland was not carrying any stones, and I was certainly not cast in the martyr's mold; my imagination had plainly got the better of me again.

We halted in the center of the hall, which was rapidly being lit, and at a respectful distance one from the other. When I looked up, I saw that Sir Roland had pushed back the hood of his hauberk and was looking at me through coolly distant eyes, his dark face inscrutable. For the space while one might say an Ave, there fell a silence as though everyone had suspended breathing, and all eyes fell on Sir Roland and me.

I curtsied with as much dignity as a slightly wrinkled smock and a crumpled kerchief would allow and opened my mouth to speak.

Before any words came out, whatever solemnity attended the occasion was suddenly shattered and the assembled company thrown into confusion by Charger, who, having found the diversion he desired, bounded into the hall, yapping incessantly, scrambling through the tangle of legs, snapping playfully at skirts and chausses, until he came to the center, where he began to jump up alternately between Sir Roland and me. It needed only Charger to assault our guest for the welcome to be a complete disaster. In the din was heard the thin thread of Thomas's high-pitched voice, crying, "Charger! Charger!" Despite my efforts to quiet the ungainly beast, I was powerless to stem the tide of either the barking or the commotion. Finally, Sir Roland took command.

"Heel!" The unmistakable note of the master struck in Sir Roland's voice. In one swift moment, Charger learned his lesson on the supremacy of man. He suddenly became quiet, sat down, and cocked his head up at the commanding person above him, whimpering in obeisance. Under Sir Roland's quelling eye, even Charger's tail ceased thumping, and he sat at rigid attention.

Once again a second of silence reigned, but it was not broken by my welcome, as I would have liked, but this time by Thomas, who had just then found his way to his unruly animal and immediately began chastising him, heedless of our visitors. I was obliged to call Thomas to his surroundings and to desire him with all the authority I could summon to remove himself and Charger from the premises and to do so immediately.

Thomas looked up anxiously, never having heard so stern a command from me, but instead of either obeying me or protesting, he exclaimed with a burst of youthful candor and in high, carrying tones, "Lady 'Garite! There's a smudge on your nose!"

Mentally hurling curses down on his head and devoutly wishing that Charger had been drowned at birth, I wondered briefly if one could die of mortification. I was not to be afforded the luxury of this convenient escape. Only by the strongest resolution was I able not to demean myself by trying to wipe the offending blemish from my face. I was unable to meet Sir Roland's eye, but I noticed that several of the men seconding him, among whom stood a surprised and slightly pale Gavin McLaughlin, had taken on the aspect of being stuffed. My

women were not so well controlled, however, for several of
them behind me were betrayed into nervous laughter that hastily
turned into convulsed fits of coughing. Urged by my strong
sense of the ridiculous, I would have been sorely tempted
myself to laugh at the extreme absurdity of the situation, had
not one glance at Sir Roland's cool blue eyes slain any amusement I might have felt.

"God save you, and well come to Shrivenham Keep, my
lord," I said at last, beyond any hope of repairing Sir Roland's
opinion of me.

"God save you, my lady," he responded, and added dryly,
"I had hoped that my coming would be met with a modicum
of pleasure, but I naturally did not flatter myself that it would
cause a riot."

"It is, of course, a pleasure to—"

Thomas, who, unmindful of his dismissal, was looking up
at Sir Roland with round eyes, drinking in the obvious, if dusty,
magnificence of a knight who so easily bore the weight of his
coat and mail and the heavy broadsword resting in its scabbard,
seemed to recognize in Sir Roland a model of manhood that
was otherwise in absence at Shrivenham. Thomas did not hesitate to endow the scene that he and his miserable animal had
created with the grandeur that Sir Roland's presence apparently
evoked in his mind. "No, not a riot, sir, a *melee*! You see,
Charger is going to be a *tourney* hound!"

Sir Roland tapped the leather gauntlets he held in one hand
against a muscled thigh. "Has not your tutor at arms taught
you that the melee comes only after a victor has been declared?"

"I do not have an arms tutor," Thomas confessed.

"So I had thought," Sir Roland replied blandly, and turned
back to me.

The moment was not to be mine, for Dame Ellen came
forward to claim it. She, unlike her son, did not find in Sir
Roland an object of admiration. She had doubtless heard all
the dark stories cloaking this ill-famed visitor and did not find
the sight of him at variance with his black reputation. Unfortunately, she shared with her son a domineering disposition
and a singular want of finesse. "Thomas," she informed our

formidable visitor, "is a high-spirited boy who has shown a remarkable aptitude for handling animals, and shall follow in the footsteps of his father, Master Ian, the gameskeeper. Although he is not born into the highest orders, there is nothing to blush for his birth, and he shall soon have an arms tutor, as Lady Marguerite will be happy to tell you—"

"You must forgive me, madame," Sir Roland interrupted politely, but there was steel in his voice that cut cleanly across Dame Ellen's, "but this is my first visit to Shrivenham, and I believe I haven't the pleasure of your acquaintance. Lady Marguerite, before you tell me about Thomas's arms tutor, pray introduce me."

I felt ready to sink and performed a most inadequate introduction. If Sir Roland's object was to show me that I had hopelessly lost control, he succeeded far too well, and if I had had little experience in receiving visitors, there was still no excuse for this pitiful example of hospitality. The situation seemed far past the point where one could turn it off with a jest, and I did not think Sir Roland would care to be edified with excuses for this lamentable welcome or explanations about my retainers whose rank clearly did not warrant their conduct. Instead, I suggested that Dame Ellen remove Thomas and Charger from the hall so that I could attend to the wants of the company, and, thankfully, she deferred to my command with only the slightest pinching of her features, although I suspected that her withdrawal was due more to a dislike, and perhaps fear, of Sir Roland than to a yielding to my authority.

"How may I serve you?" I said when they had gone.

"You are aware, no doubt, that I am come to see Sir Maurice," he said.

"My father is not here, my lord," I answered.

He looked at me keenly. I had only told the truth, and yet, that feeling of impending doom weighed me down again. "I see."

"You are very welcome here, nevertheless," I said quickly, trying to imagine what Lady Isolde might have said in these circumstances. "I am sure that my father would want me to act in his stead and to offer you everything to make your visit comfortable. I perceive that you have traveled a long way, perhaps not from Hungerford?"

"We are this moment come from London."

"Then you must decide if you prefer to bathe first or to sup. Both can be ready on the instant, but you must tell me which you will be most comfortable having first."

"Such unlooked-for hospitality," he murmured and cast his eye briefly over his men. "Since we have ridden such a long way, I believe that we must eat first. That is, if you will not be offended by our setting to table in all of our dirt."

"Certainly not," I returned, "but I am afraid that you will have to sit alone. I am sorry! But our seneschal is—he is not well, and I must look to the preparation of your chambers, you understand."

"Perfectly; and it is no trouble to accommodate us?" he asked, as if daring me to contradict him.

"Not at all!" I replied with unnecessary emphasis. "I must only see that the chambers are swept and fresh linens provided." The hall was lit by now and the tables set up. The men would not have long to wait. "Shall I have Wulfric draw you some ale before you are seated?"

"Very well," he said, and I thought I detected a weary note in his voice, but his face remained guarded and closed.

"There are six of you, including yourself," I said, gesturing to Wulfric, who stood in readiness not far from me, "and since Lady Alicia is here with me, I will have two of your men occupy one chamber. She is staying in one of the double guest chambers." I thought this piece of news might bring him pleasure and me more credibility as a hostess.

"Lady Longchamps is here?" He favored me with another of his searching looks.

"Why, yes," I responded. "Perhaps you saw Sir Herbert at court, and he made you aware of her visit to me?"

"I did see him," he acknowledged, "but since I did not happen to mention to him my object or destination, he did not inform me of his wife's movements."

I supposed, rather childishly, that men had better things to speak of than women when they were together. "She has been

here for a week now," I said, "since my father left. I am sure
that you will want to pay her your respects on the morrow."

"I will be most happy to do so. And my compliments," he
said with a slight bow. "It is a pleasant surprise."

"Yes," I said cautiously, as I worked his words over in my
mind and tried to decide whether it was safe to take them as
they stood or if I had better turn them over and look behind
them. I judged it wisest to let them pass, saying only, "I will
have a page show you to your chambers, where a bath will
await you when you have finished. Ah, here is Wulfric with
the ale."

He bowed again and motioned to his men. I left the hall
then and went in search of John Cook, my heart fluttering
uncomfortably. I took the opportunity to remove the smudge
that my fingers had itched to wipe off, but I could not rid
myself of the clinging notion that something was amiss, although there was nothing precisely in Sir Roland's manner to
indicate that. But then again, I reflected, he gave very little
away. Perhaps it was more the look on Gavin's face that warned
me of something, and yet, the strain on his face could have
easily been due to fatigue. These thoughts chased me into the
kitchens, where they were given a new turn when I thankfully
spied a large platter of smoked eels flanked by two loaves of
fresh bread that were intended for consumption the next day.
I ordered John Cook to serve these up, readily approved of his
choice of viand royal garnished with salsify fried in butter, and
asked if there was any neat's tongue in supply. He assured me
that he would do his possible for the late arrivals, and confident
that Sir Roland and his men would have naught to complain
for their meal, I was about to leave those quarters when inspiration visited me.

It was my notion of a clever stroke to send Nan to attend
to Sir Roland's bath. I had originally thought of Wulfric for
the honor, since the custom of the lady of the manor attending
to the washing of male guests of highborn rank was little
practiced nowadays, but it was still perfectly acceptable—and
in this circumstance, even strategic—to send a woman for the
task. If reports on Sir Roland's reputation were true, and I did

not doubt that they were, he could certainly not object to finding himself ministered to by a comely lass who knew just what to do.

I found Nan in a far corner of the kitchen. She stood over a kneading trough, her sleeves rolled up, with something like a scowl on her face. It seemed far too late in the day to be engaged in such labor, but I immediately understood the reason when I saw a stableboy, who had always struck me as having a rather bold look in his eye, hovering behind Nan in the shadows. I chose to read her absorption in the task as a way of hinting the young man away, but he seemed impervious to the fact that her back was toward him and she was not responding to his taunts.

"Adam, how fortunate it is that I find you here," I said easily. "Master Herbert has been wondering why you are not helping him stall to rub down the guests' mounts."

His flush, visible even in the dim light, rose to the roots of his hair, and he slid away, murmuring apologies.

I turned to Nan and smiled. She stood back from her work and dusted her arms and skirts. I might almost have thought she meant to thank me for the intervention, but she did not. She merely wished me good eventide and asked me, in her forthright way, what she could do for me.

"Put on a fresh kirtle, if you please," I replied, "and go to the easterly double guest chambers, where you will attend to the Earl of Guimont when he ascends for his bath. And this is not the moment to think of Edric or any of the moral precepts that Dame Ellen and I have been advocating this week past."

She made no reply, but nodded her understanding with a speculative gleam. I assumed that Sir Roland's reputation preceded him here.

I turned to go, saying over my shoulder as I left, "One warning: no boasting afterward!"

I was satisfied that I had done the best I was able on such short notice. To Bess's surprise, I dismissed her before she had a chance to help me with the evening's toilette. She reported only that the soap making was at an end for the day and withdrew. I needed the time alone to sponge myself clean, brush and bind my hair, and mull over the unexpected visitors.

Much later, Nan burst without ceremony into my chambers and would have fallen sobbing into my arms had I not checked her.

"Go! Go to him now, my lady!" She caught her breath between a whimper and a sob and stared up at me with frightened eyes. I had never seen the composed Nan so discomposed, and never had she behaved with such rudeness, and her state alarmed me.

"Nan!" I called to her sharply, and I was strongly tempted to slap her in order to avert a fit of hysterics, but she seemed to get herself under some control. "What is all this nonsense? Why are you not serving Sir Roland?"

"He—he—" She faltered. "Oh, my lady! Go to him!"

I could not imagine that Nan was out of countenance because Sir Roland had made improper advances to her. Perhaps he had offered her violence, but she did not look bruised, nor were her clothes torn or in any way disheveled.

"Go!" she pleaded once again when I did not immediately respond.

"I am sure that it will be all right, my dear. Go seek your pallet, and I shall take care of everything," I said with a conviction I was far from feeling.

I sent her on her way, while my feet carried me automatically in the direction of Sir Roland's chambers. For the second time in as many hours, I would be appearing before Sir Roland at less than my best. I could not say that I did not care about presenting myself in an old, comfortable kirtle that I reserved for my private chambers, with no girdle, and with worn slippers and a coif that I had hardly had time to arrange. I did care, but somehow my concern for my appearance got lost in my anxiety of the moment. I arrived at his door, my heart thudding at a sickening tempo, and I took a deep breath to steady myself before stepping through it.

What I saw before me held me motionless with surprise on the threshold. I had expected to behold either the remnants of wild debauch or the aftermath of violence. Instead, the room presented a picture of calm repose. There was not a chair overturned, not a piece of furniture out of place; the fire was soughing quietly and casting warm, flickering shadows across the swollen and aged wood of the bathing tub squatting next to the hearth. Limp curls of steam rose steadily from its waters and beckoned immersion. In the center of the room was Sir Roland, fully clothed, and leaning, somewhat insolently, I thought, against the broad table that dominated the chamber. He had been quietly contemplating the fire, his thumbs in the belt slung at his waist, but at the sound of my footfall at the door, he turned his regard slowly and focused on me.

He continued to regard me with penetrating eyes, and a faint, sardonic look of humor played at the corners of his hard mouth. My skin rose in bumps. I did not have any indication of what had sent Nan flying into my arms, nor did he give me any, but I knew that something was gravely amiss and that I could no longer dismiss it as my imagination.

"Good eventide, my lord," I said. I was displeased to hear a tremor in my voice, and was obliged to clear my throat. "My woman said that you—requested my presence. What may I do for you?"

"Yes," he corroborated, "I desire my bath." He gestured toward the steaming tub and smiled with chilling civility.

I was relieved and oddly disturbed at the same time. There had apparently been some misunderstanding. "Yes, of course. Perhaps I did not make this very clear to my woman, although Nan is not slow of wit."

"She does not seem to be," he agreed.

"Then shall I send for her again?" I inquired. I was vaguely aware that I had offended him.

"No."

I raised my brow in question. "But I sent her here specifically to tend to you."

"I know exactly why you sent her here," he replied.

His glance stripped me naked. I gasped, but with real effort I was able to suppress the instinct to retreat a pace and shield my very properly clad body with my hands.

"You forget," he continued, his eyes resting on me, "that I have seen, shall we say, more of your charms than that trollop's, and I must say that from what I have witnessed, you are more to my taste than she."

A tide of color flooded my cheeks. This reference to our first meeting threw me off my stride. "I did not think that—"

"That I would be so unchivalrous as to mention that ill-fated night?" he supplied helpfully. "It would have gone so very much better for you if we had not met! Nevertheless, I thought we were agreed that I am not afflicted by chivalry. So, then, I prefer you to your whore." His eyes narrowed dangerously, but that disconcerting look of amusement did not leave his face. "My bath!"

The color in my cheeks ebbed with his words and must have blended with the whiteness of my coif. Lady Isolde had never, to my knowledge, personally bathed a visitor.

"'Tis not meet—" I began, but the rest of the words rose stillborn to my lips. A flicker that was not quite violent lit the depths of his deep, blue eyes. He looked ready to strike me into submission if I refused to obey him, and I began to feel the effect of the force that had reduced the solid Nan to a trembling blancmange.

"Do you think to inform me that the custom obliging the lady of the manor to bathe her well-born guests has fallen into disuse? Let me assure you that, although the last few years have taken me at long absences from the kingdom and recent events have made me, ah, unwelcome in certain houses, I am still conversant with the usages of castle ways." He straightened up and moved away from the table. He looked very tall and forbidding and loomed above me as on the first night we met, his voice sounding as it had then, with no smooth finish of charm or amusement now, possessing a hard ring, as if Michel Armorer were pounding out iron on his anvil. "Now, unless I very much mistake the matter, you are the lady of the manor. I desire my bath and have called you here, and I shall be accorded this service!"

He sat down on the stool next to the tub and waited to be undressed.

I did not need further words to know that in seeking to mollify him with a pretty wench, I had blundered badly. Yet,

I did not think that my presumption was the source of his barely concealed anger. I felt that I was, in his eyes, guilty of some rather more serious wrongdoing, but its nature was no clearer or more substantial to me than the innuendoes he had made that night in July.

I lifted my chin and said clearly, "Yes, of course. Let us not delay, lest the water grow cold."

And to show him that I was not afraid, I shut the door to the chamber, stating that his death from a draft would not be laid at my address. He laughed at that and threw my already precarious dignity a little off balance, so it was with fumbling fingers that I drew his tunic over his head. Fortunately, he had already shed his heavy hauberk, and I assumed that it was in the care of the Armorer to be examined for repairs. I folded the plain tunic slowly, trying desperately to avoid the inevitable, and laid it on the table. I unlaced the linen shirt, now stiff with travel stains and perspiration, but its fineness was still apparent, and it had obviously been chosen with care, as had all of his clothes. As I placed the shirt on top of the tunic, I carefully avoided looking at his torso and knelt circumspectly to unfasten his shoes and cross-garters. Since I had had little practice undressing men and my hands would not obey me, the task took rather longer than I would have liked for the sake of appearances, but I had just completed it when Sir Roland's hand stretched out and plucked the coif from my head, causing my hastily bound hair to come tumbling down in disarray over my shoulders, and dropped it carelessly at my feet, where it was absorbed by a small puddle. I rose swiftly to my feet, my cheeks washed with a fresh wave of color, and stood staring blankly at the crisp material as it crumpled and melted into a spineless and bedraggled square of cloth.

"That is much better," he said.

"Pray, what are you about, my lord?" I asked indignantly.

"Your coif was askew," he replied.

"I had very little opportunity to prepare myself," I said angrily, stung into hasty retort. "I am very sorry that my appearance does not meet with your approval, but I would have been most happy to have righted the wrong myself."

"You should have been here in the first place," he said, "and besides, Nan was not wearing one."

"Do you think to compare me to Nan?" I trembled with anger.

"No," he replied calmly. "I have already established that I hold you higher than her in at least one respect."

I preserved a stony silence.

"You know," he said, keeping a maddeningly even tone, "I cannot think that our welcome here was of the most cordial. It would be interesting to know why."

I was happy to have this opening to offer explanation. "We were engaged in the soap making, my lord. It is a messy job at best and accounts for why I received you in my working clothes. I assure you that you could not have come at a more inopportune moment!"

"Did you think that it would serve?" was all he said.

"I do not perfectly understand you," I said stiffly after a moment.

One mobile brow shot up, but he did not trouble himself with a reply, and said only as he stood to his full height, "My chausses!"

I held his gaze steadily for the briefest second before turning my back to him. I could not work with my hair unbound, for it would be in my way and made me feel like a wanton. I was going to have to roll back my sleeves in any case, so I slid the lacing out of one wrist to tie back my hair and used that moment to try to compose my face. I do not think I was very successful, because when I turned to face him again, he looked distinctly amused and knew that he had me at a disadvantage.

There was no honorable escape. I went to him to unhitch his chausses, my face flaming, and kept my eyes fixed in a darkened corner of the room until I heard the water swallow the lower half of his body.

He sat back in the tub, obviously soothed by the warmth enveloping his strained muscles. I was able to busy myself at first with the washing of his hair and dug my fingers into his scalp, reasoning that to treat him roughly would rob the touching of its intimacy. So far from seeming to mind my vigor, he visibly relaxed and allowed his head to follow the motion of my fingertips. I rinsed off the lather with two buckets of water provided for that purpose and then turned to the tray of soap placed next to a pile of washing cloths and drying linens on the floor by the tub. In my distraction, I chose a white soap that I had concocted last year, thinking it to be an unscented variety, and began to scrub his neck and shoulders. An unnatural silence, which Sir Roland did nothing to break, soon fell, and I groped for a topic of discussion.

"What news do you bring from London?" I asked at last, striking what I thought to be neutral territory.

"I was hoping that you would tell me," he returned without hesitation.

"How should I be able to tell you, my lord?" I asked lightly.

"How indeed?" he replied. "But I will not press you for an answer! At least not while I am at your mercy in the bath. Perhaps you have heard that the chief of Fortesque's vassals died recently in a hunting accident."

"Oh," I said, trying to inject a knowledgeable note, but honesty compelled me to add, "I am very sorry to hear it, but I did not know the man. Nor do I know the Earl of Fortesque, for that matter."

"He is a Baron Ware," he corrected politely. "Then you are no doubt more interested in the news that Louis of France is on the brink of defeat at Mansura. Indeed, he has probably lost all by now and has fled."

I thought I could do better on this one. "Does that mean he will have lost Jerusalem too?"

"Mansura is in Egypt."

"Well!" I said bracingly. "I am afraid my head is made only for women's gossip."

"Ah! Allow me to inform you that Demoiselle Dujarrie— you are acquainted with her, are you not?—has almost accomplished the impossible. She has Huxley firmly in tow without having let FitzWarren off his leash."

"You seem to be up to every move on the board," I observed with a laugh.

He did not respond to that. "Tell me what you scent your

soap with. It is a charming fragrance, but not, I fear, one that I am accustomed to using."

"I beg pardon!" I exclaimed hastily, realizing that I had chosen a rosewater soap. "I am sure you would prefer a plain soap. Yes! I have one right here!" I resumed where I had left off.

"Are you aware, my lady," he said, looking around at me with a look I had learned to be wary of, "that this is the third time you have washed my back?"

I was now embarrassed, humiliated, and not just a little provoked, and so better counsel could not prevail with me. I plunked the soap into the water and got up off my knees.

"I shall call Wulfric to attend to you," I said, hardly suppressing my irritation, and headed for the door.

Scarcely had the meaning behind the sound of swooshing water penetrated my brain before I was grabbed brusquely by my forearms and was whirled around to face Sir Roland, his eyes snapping with anger. They did not waver from my face, and I, for obvious reasons, could not afford to lower my eyes to spare myself from the intensity of his wrath. I felt the moisture from his wet hands seep into my bodice until it became so thoroughly wet that it clung immodestly to my figure. He did not notice, nor did he seem to care.

"I would not do that," he warned me. "I am in no mood for anymore of your games. I own that I am surprised at your tricks, although why I should be has me in a puzzle! And I came thinking to spare you some pain. But take a care, my girl, for now that I am here, you shall have some answers for me, and I am not so easily gulled by wiles. Now, I have demanded a courtesy of you, and if you are unwilling to give it freely, I shall exact it from you!"

I was thoroughly baffled now, and my composure was dissolving in rapid waves. To my horror, I felt tears prick behind my eyes, but before I could thoroughly disgrace myself before him, he got back into the tub and left me to pull myself together. I went blindly to him and picked up the bar of soap bobbing elusively on the water's murky surface.

Then came an imperious knock at the door before it was

flung portentously open. My salvation stood on the threshold in the form of the stocky man who had been with Sir Roland on the infamous night in July.

"Guy! Guy!" he said breathlessly as he rushed into the room. "John Potter has been found—beaten almost to death!"

Sir Roland said nothing immediately, but his face was set in grim lines. My stocky savior became aware of my presence, snatched his cap off his head, and bade me a respectful good eventide. He did not give me any reason to believe that he had seen me before and in a circumstance that did not show him off to advantage.

Sir Roland quickly ascertained where and when John Potter had been attacked and clues to possible assailants and did not hesitate to learn the worst. "Shall he die, Will?"

"I think not," Will replied, mitigating the initial impression he had created, but added with relish, "however, his face is a bloody mess, and I think he may ha' broken an arm."

"What more do you know about it?"

"Not much, for I came posthaste to you. But perhaps this will explain it. I have brought a message from—"

"I know who it is from," Sir Roland interrupted impatiently, as he took the folded parchment and turned it over.

He broke the seal, spread out the single crackling sheet, taking care not to get any moisture on it, and ran his eye down the missive. He easily mastered its contents.

He folded the letter very deliberately, as if giving himself time to think, and handed it back to Will.

"Burn it."

Will was then commanded to find Gavin, and he bowed and withdrew. Sir Roland eyed me briefly.

"You may await me in the next chamber," he said curtly.

He had dismissed me in my own house as he would one of his servants, but I did not dare disobey him. Before leaving him, I found a page waiting in the hall and sent him to fetch a pitcher of ale, two drinking horns, and a bowl of walnuts. I then went to the next room to wait, and was pleased that the chamber women who had prepared the room had thought to light a fire here. I stood on the hearth and shook out my skirts and bodice, allowing them to dry. The page came and left the tray with refreshments on a low table; I remained staring into the depths of the fire, breathing deeply until I was thinking rationally again and not just feeling. When I had myself under control, I sat down on the hearth bench, clasping and unclasping my hands in anticipation of the forthcoming interview.

I did not have long to wait.

Sir Roland entered the room, looking clean and in command, but grave. His crisp curls were already beginning to dry, and he was wearing a fresh tunic of slate blue with no ornamentation.

"It seems that I must acquit you of one crime," he said coolly, and before sitting down in a large chair opposite me, he poured both of us some ale.

"That is a relief, in all events," I said, accepting the potation. "Which one?"

"It seems probable that you never received my message informing you of my visit."

"No; indeed I thought it odd that you would come with no forewarning. John Potter?"

He nodded. "When I learned that it would be, ah, necessary to come to Shrivenham, I sent him off from London a few days ahead of me and my men. He did not make it more than fifty miles."

"I am happy that he shall not lose his life over it. And my crime?" I asked.

"Under normal circumstances, which these apparently are not, the welcome you accorded my party could have been interpreted as an open insult."

"It—it was quite beyond my control!"

"Quite," he agreed unhandsomely.

"But I have explained that I was off in the laundry and busy with the candles and soaps."

"So you led me to believe," he said pleasantly.

"Led you to believe!" I echoed in astonishment.

"Do you really expect me to believe that you were engaged in a task that is so easily left to the servants?"

My honor was at stake. "I do not delegate authority," I said with dignity, "for so important a task."

"I am chastened," he said.

"My soaps and candles are something that I take great— But there is no point arguing with you, for I am sure that I do not care what you may or may not believe!"

"There is no reason why you should. And it is of little consequence. Tell me instead if you are aware of your father's whereabouts."

"He left about nine days ago, I believe."

"That is not my question," he said. "I assume that when he left, he informed you of his destination."

"No, he did not."

Sir Roland appeared not to credit this, so I added with some hesitation, "However, it is my belief that he will eventually present himself at Downton—Lady Constance's estate."

"I know," he said flatly.

I felt oddly compelled to speak and offered as much information as I could. "He said that he would be back within the fortnight with Lady Constance, but I do not know more. I— Is something wrong?"

The chill in his blue eyes did not promise good news. "I feel sure that you know something is. In fact, I would say that your plans are entirely overset. Your father will not be returning."

I laughed nervously. "What can you mean by that?"

"Your father is dead."

The words had no meaning for me. I said the first thing that came to mind: "I do not believe you."

"I assure you—he is dead."

"But how can you know this?"

"The message I received minutes ago from London apprised me of it. I would have preferred you to learn of it in another way, but you and I have too much to discuss now in light of that fact."

"But—London! Surely there is some mistake. He had no business in going to London. You are jesting!"

"Come now. You know very well his business, as you put it, in London. And I did not come here to indulge in jests. We will get on very much better if you will be a little more honest."

I took a sip of ale to ease the ache in my throat, but I was not able to raise my voice above a hoarse whisper. "I am at sea. I do not know what you are talking about."

"Very well, I shall be explicit, so that we may put an end to this profitless sparring. Yes, my lady, I am aware that he was at the head of a plot on the king's life, but it went sadly awry. As you can imagine, I have been aware of it for some time and have put forth efforts to avert it. The purpose of my visit here, in fact, was to tell your father to give up, that he had been found out. It is always so much better for internal peace in the realm to scotch these unpleasant plots before they surface! I had reason to believe that he would not be making his move for several weeks, but his plans changed—to his cost! Nevertheless, Henry and I had already discussed the affair at length before I left for Shrivenham, so that when your father and Gervase Frant were discovered in the royal bedchamber armed with knives, few questions were asked. I need not tell you that our sovereign deals a swift justice in these matters, but I will spare you the details. I can assure you that your father's death was merciful."

I felt nauseated.

It was entirely fantastic. My father the recluse, the man least interested in politics that I knew, at the head of a plot on the king's life! And for what? It was equally difficult to believe, however, that Sir Roland was on a flight of fancy.

"Who is Gervase Frant?" I asked.

Sir Roland's countenance became unpleasant. "There is no need to affect ignorance. You referred to him yourself at Lady Longchamps's wedding as a man you had seen on occasion here. I believe that you also encountered him speaking with Lady Constance."

The image of an aging knight came to mind, but the pieces had not quite fallen into place for me yet, and I was still struggling to comprehend. I had nothing to respond.

"Do not think that I do not appreciate your calm at this time," he said, "and I feel sure that we shall come to understand each other before very long."

I supposed that he expected tears or some other display of emotion, but I was still too much in the grip of shock to react. Thus, I was too dazed to prevent myself from saying simply, "I was never close to my father. I have no tears for him."

"But surely you have some regrets for the failure of such a neat plan. There was much to be gained."

I swallowed hard. "You have said that you would be explicit," I said, "and I beg you to continue."

"Very wise to plumb the depths of my knowledge before committing yourself!" he retorted with biting force. "You will discover that there is very little about it that I do not know. It would gratify me to learn, however, where it went wrong. Just to satisfy my curiosity, of course! All in all, I was impressed by the excellence of the plan, the purity of the motives, and the stunning gains to be won, although I cannot give your father full credit for having planned and executed it. Constance's part in all this is not negligible, and I credit her with being a very clever woman. She may well prove the cleverest of them all."

"Lady Constance?" I exclaimed in question and surprise.

"I have told you," Sir Roland said in the manner of a man whose patience was being tried, "that I have very nearly the full sum of it."

"Yes, but—"

"Do not bother to protest her innocence," he said matter-of-factly. "It is entirely unnecessary, for she has covered her tracks well. I suspect that somewhere along the way communication between her and your father broke down and caused the plan to fail. But Constance prepared for such an eventuality and is committed to nothing. I had thought that your father would go to Downton before London, but their signals must have crossed somewhere, and your father expected her to be at Westminster this week to fulfill her end of the matter."

Something began to nag at me, but until I discovered the

object in checkmating the king, I could not understand the other moves of the game. "But a plot against the king's life! That is somewhat extreme!"

"But not at all unusual in recent history! And do not tell me that you had no knowledge of which way the wind was blowing, for that would be carrying innocence to an extreme, my lady," he said without heat. "Only a child could have stayed at Burford for two weeks of wedding celebrations without being any the wiser. After only one day, I knew that it was about to break open and that I would have to act fast. Would it surprise you if I told you I knew that the original plan was to kill the king at Burford? A clever stroke that would have provided so many suspects! But, of course, that plan was foiled by the queen's poor planning to give birth when she did. I did not know, of course, until I arrived there that Henry had stayed in London, and the knowledge that there was a plot against his life caused me a bad moment or two on my way to Burford from Wales."

If what Sir Roland had said was true, my father's sudden decision to stay at Shrivenham for the wedding began to make sense. My flush told Sir Roland that I did indeed know something, but it was useless to try to convince him that I had never suspected anything so enormous as a plot to kill the king, nor that my father—of all people!—and Lady Constance had any roles, much less the central ones, to play in it. So, I had my intrigue—in full measure. I derived no satisfaction now from having my suspicions confirmed.

"However, if, as you say," I began slowly, choosing my words with care, "my—my father wished to kill the king in the midst of a large gathering to provide a variety of suspects for the crime, there must be many people who have a motive for killing him."

"Very good," he said, and cast me a look of cool appraisal. "Yet, do not forget that I possess the pieces of the larger picture, too. Who stands next in line to the throne?"

"The king's uncle—Beauclerc," I responded.

"I know of his relationship with Constance," he said baldly. I did not know, nor did I want to know, any more on that score. I perceived that I was in far over my head and registered a mental oath never to become involved in politics.

"Shall I go on?" he continued smoothly into the silence. "But the primary object was not power—that is, royal power—but land. There is something about land that a person will kill for."

These words, uttered dispassionately, even reflectively, sent a cold shiver down my spine. "Land?" I repeated stupidly.

"My land," he said flatly. "So you want me to bare all? It is really very ugly, but I know about that, too. My death was planned first, as you no doubt know. I find myself in the enviable position of having any number of people ready to draw my blood; thus, again, there would be a variety of people on whom to pin suspicion. There would even be some who would say that my death was divine justice, and leave it at that. So, as reluctant as I am to admit it, I do not think a great fuss would be made if I were to meet a violent end. Then, there would be the small problem of what to do with my land."

"Escheat," I said softly, as the perfection of the plan as he had laid it out dawned on me.

"Aye. It is as you say. I am the last of the Guimonts, and my lands would have reverted to the overlord by default of heir. Your father would exact payment of my land for the installation of Beauclerc on the throne, and no one could have pointed a finger directly at him. Your father would have been exceptionally land rich in the kingdom—and you a well-dowered woman."

I had to have this one point out with him.

"Are you suggesting," I asked cautiously, "that I am involved in the planning of your death?"

"My dear," he said as if explaining a simple story to a little girl, "you seem to be forgetting one circumstance."

I knew that we were at the heart of the matter, but still it eluded me. I said evenly, "I knew nothing of what you have just revealed to me, and although I find it—difficult to believe, I can think of several instances that make what you say ring true, but as for planning your death—well! It is something I could neither contemplate nor have a hand in doing."

Sir Roland looked almost contemptuous. "You shall learn not to underrate me," he said coldly and left the room abruptly. Before I had a chance to collect my wits, he returned with a leather pouch, from which he abstracted a thin sheaf of papers. He dropped these into my lap, and with a leap of my heart I recognized instantly the kind of parchment and the peculiar way my father had of folding his letters. It was just such a note that I had been carrying to Lady Constance when I first met Sir Roland. I remembered with painful clarity how the note had fallen from my sleeve, how Sir Roland had picked it up seeming somehow to know what it was, and how I had taken it from him, freely acknowledging it as my own.

I looked up at him looming above me. The firelight was playing on the hard, implacable planes of his face, and his eyes were glittering with something I could not define.

"These are your father's instructions to Frant," he said conversationally. "You are at liberty to read them—and do not think to convince me that you are not lettered."

It came to me all at once and with such impact that I could scarce credit my stupidity. If I had not quite believed Sir Roland's incredible tale up until this point, I believed him now and with all the conviction of a convert to a new faith. From thinking my father to be the least interesting and least complex man of my acquaintance, I now pictured him as the perfect plotter. He was so colorless that no one save Sir Roland had guessed how deep were his dealings. With the reality of his death, his already pale image faded a shade in my mind: his face I remembered as parchment, with thin, bloodless lips, and eyes of a shallow, washed-out blue; and even his hair was of an indeterminate hue, between sand and gray. He had never been a talker, and when he listened, mostly without comment, it was always without expression. He was a man who had concealed himself perfectly behind a faceless mask.

I, who had wanted adventure, had found more than I had bargained for. There were no words to explain to Sir Roland that I was innocent, that I had not read the note my father had written to Lady Constance, that I had not even delivered it, and that I was, ironically, the one responsible for the demise of their perfect plot, for at the wedding I had burned my father's note to Lady Constance that no doubt informed her of the altered plans. No, I was too implicated in all of this. It was too clear what my role must have been. I would not cavil, would not lower my dignity.

"You of all people," I said at last, raising my eyes bravely to his, "should realize how damaging—and perhaps misleading—circumstantial evidence can be."

Something in his face changed, and he looked almost pleased. He sat back down and took the horn of ale in his hand.

I wanted to know my fate right away. "Had you already decided what you were going to do with me before coming here?" I asked quietly.

"No, I had not," he said, then drained his liquid and reached for a walnut. "I wanted first to hear what you would have to say for yourself. I had also expected to find Sir Maurice here, but circumstances have now changed."

"Yes, they have," I agreed.

He cracked a walnut between his long fingers and looked up briefly, considering me. "Not all of them! One part of the plan, at least, is still intact, and I believe that Constance is holding those cards."

I had not yet dared examine Constance's motives for aiding my father in securing the Guimont lands, but now that my father was dead and Sir Roland very much alive, I failed to see where she could make any gains. I raised my brows in inquiry.

He gave me a crooked smile and his voice had a note of sympathy in it. "I wondered how that aspect of it would sit with you. Was your father less than honest with you about your future? Or do you always turn your face away and hide from unpleasant prospects?"

"If I have avoided the truth in the past weeks," I said evenly, "I have learned the folly of it this night. Perhaps you rate my—my intelligence low, but you need not explain to me now, and indeed, I have known for quite some time and see it all very vividly, that Lady Constance and Sir Maurice intended my hand in marriage to Charles." It was difficult to pronounce his name without an acrid taste of disgust. I understood now that Charles had known about everything, too, and I did not know which I thought the baser of the two forms of humanity: a mother who would willfully involve her son, a mere child, in such an ignoble scheme, or the son, already wasted and rotting, licking his loose, wet lips in anticipation of possessing the spoils of the scheme.

"But now that you have foiled their plan," I said, "will Lady Constance be permitted to continue—that is, to remain free?"

"I told you that Constance has left no traces, and she never soiled her own hands. You see there only your father's correspondence with Frant—but I have no concrete proof of Constance's participation. She is far too sly to put herself on paper."

"Then how do you know she is involved?"

"You might be able to answer that better than I."

I did not respond to that but said impulsively, "You are close to the king!" and immediately realized my mistake. "That is— so I am led to believe! Do you not intend to tell him about it and bring Lady Constance to justice?"

"He knows everything that I do," he acknowledged, "but on what charge shall she be arrested? She has, to my knowledge, committed no crime. He cannot prosecute the well-born willy-nilly. It is unjust and very bad for morale."

I seemed to recall having heard a similar statement made in the context of Sir Roland's own case.

He must have seen the shadow cross my face, for he added ruthlessly, "I have only to bring the case into open court for Constance to deny everything. It would then be her word against mine, and since my credit is not high in the world at this time, it would hardly be politic for the king to do me too many favors. Constance calculated well, and has depended on just that fact."

"Can't it be done quietly?" I argued naively.

"There are no plots or intrigues that are quiet in the end, and Constance would have the right to demand an open trial. The laws have changed here, you know, and for the better! No, I would not request even an open trial in any case. It is bad enough that there are two dead men to account for, although I have reason to believe that their deaths will cause little stir. Forgive me for such bluntness at this time, but as little as your father circulated and as well as he guarded himself, he also protected the king's interests. Few people will miss him, and Constance can hardly afford to publicly mourn his passing. You should know that it is an object with me—with the king— to keep at least a surface appearance of peace and well-being, and that perception, in politics, is worth more than reality. Indeed, it becomes reality."

"Nevertheless, what can Lady Constance hope to gain now?"

"Your lands are not insignificant, and although she does not have within her grasp the rich prize she had hoped for, I doubt she has abandoned her quest. She was never one to lose sight of the main chance. There is still much time for her to try for a new plan." His voice was cool and composed, and I marveled that a person could speak so calmly of a plot against himself and of his own death.

"She cannot force me to marry him now that my father is dead!" I protested, holding out the flimsiest of hopes.

"It is my belief," he said with conviction, "that a marriage settlement between you and Charles has already been drawn up and signed by your father, and is in Constance's possession. She left nothing to chance."

I was struck dumb and a cold weight gripped my stomach. There seemed no escape from it now. My father had given his blessing, Lady Constance was off free, and the king could hardly refuse to honor the marriage document without also exposing the plot against his life.

"How can you know?" I managed weakly, hoping that he was bluffing.

"Charles has a way of talking when he has had a bit to drink," he said in a way that suggested that he thought very little of the swaggering, bragging boy. "He has always been the weak link in Constance's plans. He should never have let that information slip, but I am not complaining."

"I thought you told me once not to underrate Charles."

A smile hovered around the corners of his mouth. "Did I?

Perhaps that was in response to your opinion that Charles was harmless. I think him very stupid but not incapable of violence. Does that clarify the matter?"

"Yes," I said dully, for it hardly made it better to have to marry a stupid, violent person than just a plain stupid one.

"Did you not know of the settlement?" he asked at length.

"No—yes! That is, enough hints have been dropped lately for me to believe that you are right."

He paused, as if assessing the truth of my words, and said, "I can offer you an alternative."

Prison? Death? These alternatives were almost preferable to the prospect of marrying Charles. Perhaps Sir Roland would call on me to testify against Lady Constance as a way of exonerating myself for any part I might have taken. I was heartily sorry in that moment that I had so thoughtlessly disposed of the letters my father had written to Lady Constance, for they had no doubt contained much incriminating evidence. What a fool my father must have thought me to have entrusted them to my care!

"I am open to suggestions," I said with little hope that he could help me.

"You can marry me," he said.

I blinked and looked straight into Sir Roland's eyes. I suddenly saw that it had been his object almost from the start of our conversation to make me an offer. I had been very blind not to have realized it, and my patent surprise once again attested to my stupidity and visibly amused my very remarkable guest.

"But the marriage settlement!" I said.

"You told me that you know nothing of it, and how should I?" he answered reasonably.

"Are you not engaged yourself?" I blurted without thinking.

"My betrothal has been terminated," he replied without hesitation and without the slightest trace of embarrassment.

It was I who was embarrassed. "I beg your pardon! You must think me very foolish!"

"Not at all."

"Well, I am sure everyone must know about it! It—" I broke off, mortified that I was only making things worse.

"I am sure they must," he answered, unshaken.

"But, Joan of Shrewsbury! You are not engaged to her?" I demanded, thinking to amend my hideous blunder.

"Not that I am aware of," he said.

And then it came to me that I had received this piece of news from Lady Constance. "Well, then, she is free to follow her heart and marry Charles!" I said roundly, but this statement did not seem to make much sense to Sir Roland.

"Have I misunderstood something?" he asked politely.

"No, nothing!" I answered hastily, and asked instead when a thought occurred to me, "How do I know that Lady Constance has any such marriage settlement signed by my father?"

"You do not," he said, "and that is the chance you must take."

I opened my mouth to speak, thought better of it, and bit my lip.

"I shall not demand an answer from you at this moment," he continued. "You will want time to consider my offer."

"Yes, yes, I shall," I said, very much unsure of myself.

"I am afraid, however, that I cannot give you much time. I must have the answer by tomorrow morning."

I looked down at my hands clasped in my lap and told him that I thought I could give him one by then. I foresaw a sleepless night before me considering the various sides of the issue. I had a strong desire to ask him why he wished this marriage, but an even stronger feminine instinct advised me not to. I would not like the answer, and Sir Roland would not like being brought to the sticking point in such a blunt fashion. It was not necessary for one to be well versed in the ways of the world to realize that the Guimont and Montcrief estates together would be vast and powerful. That vision was, after all, what had inspired my father's and Lady Constance's plottings. And it was equally obvious that Sir Roland would hardly be comfortable with my lands allied to the Hartford family, were I to wed Charles.

"One thing you must understand," he said after a prolonged silence. "My brother left the estate in very poor straits. My resources at the moment are low, the lands have been wastefully farmed, and so the harvests are not plentiful. The serfs are in rags and my vassals are not much better off. It will take much time, effort, and gold to rebuild. You are no doubt aware of this, but I want no misunderstandings on that head."

"I did not know, and I thank you for informing me. But that is not what bothers me."

As soon as the words were out, I wished them unsaid. I searched desperately for something else to say but could think of nothing. These hasty, unweighed words hung in the air and became like a vulture-eaten corpse until Sir Roland finally cut them down without mercy.

His words chilled my soul and raised the hairs on the nape of my neck in a thrill of horror. "Do not think that I will comfort you by assuring you that I did not kill my brother. I will tell you nothing of the kind."

I made some inarticulate sounds of protest, but I was flustered past saving. My cheeks burned. I looked up at him, and I must have looked very wretched, for he took pity on me.

"Have you had enough for one night?" he asked quietly. His voice was still hard, but amusement was there again, too.

I nodded, not trusting myself to speak, for I could not be sure that I would not blunder again. I even tried to smile.

"I think it best that we both retire," he recommended. "It is very late, and you shall want your privacy and leisure to consider your future."

"And you will want to rest after your strenuous journey."

"Perhaps. May I ask how close you stand to Lady Longchamps?"

I was mildly surprised. "Alicia and I are very close. I consider her my sister."

"It would be best not to discuss with her any of the particulars of our conversation."

I flushed painfully. "I do not think I shall feel the slightest inclination to do so."

"Well, then," he said lightly, "you are the one woman of

my acquaintance who does not share all her confidences with her closest friend."

I smiled then genuinely, if a little ruefully. "No, in truth I am no exception. However, in this case, I feel sure that you are right. Alicia need not be burdened by the story of my father's infamy and his—death. It would be very upsetting to her at this time. I shall keep my own counsel."

I was thankful that he did not inquire more closely into Alicia's condition. "That is very wise. Does Lady Longchamps make a long visit with you?"

"She has been here this sennight and will probably depart within the next when Sir Herbert comes."

He commented briefly about Alicia, Herbert, the wedding, and their families. I was grateful to him for easing the tension and all the discomfort of our interview, and I tried to respond in kind. The conversation came to its natural conclusion, and I rose to go to the door. He stood up with me and took a few steps in my direction.

"I shall see you on the morrow, then," he said.

"I arise daily at cock-crow and shall meet with you in the hall at your earliest convenience. We can be private in Sir Maurice's receiving chamber."

"Very well. You need not fear that I shall not honor whatever decision you reach."

"I understand," I said.

He held out his hand. Without ado I took it, and I saw nothing incongruous about sealing our bargain with such a plainly masculine gesture. My hair was in disarray, I was wearing an old kirtle and chamber shoes, and I reflected that few women had entertained a marriage proposal such as this. In the brief moment that our hands made contact, I detected the faint scent of rosewater on him. He had a way, I had noted, of wearing his clothes so that each article became an intimate part of himself, uniquely his, and possessed a part of him in the wearing. So it was with the fragrance of rosewater, which no longer smelled the way I remembered, but took on a new personality all its own. That sensation accompanied me to my chambers.

There I immediately stripped down to my linen shift and kicked off my shoes. I ignored my unbound hair and consigned the problem to Bess's care in the morning. Stung by the sharp cold of the floor, I scurried to my bed and curled into its comfortable warmth, while my conscience and several of the more mischievous saints came and sat on the footboard of my bed and leered at me with mocking eyes.

"Holy Mother," I murmured, "I am in the devil of a hobble now."

Chapter 7

It was not, after all, a difficult decision. For the same reasons that Sir Roland made me an offer of marriage, I saw the wisdom in accepting. It would be better for both of us if our lands marched together in peace rather than against each other in war. It had disturbed me profoundly that Sir Roland had all but admitted killing his brother, for I had not really believed the stories until last night; but if Sir Roland's reading of Charles's character as both violent and stupid was accurate, then it seemed better to go with the man who was admittedly violent but at least not stupid. Sir Roland had never, at any rate, treated me in the disgusting manner in which Charles had. Furthermore, to refuse Sir Roland would be gambling against bad odds: Constance might very well have a legal document signing my independence over to her son, and then I would have both a loathsome husband in Charles and a fearsome and deadly enemy just across my border in Roland. And if Sir Roland could not be sure, from his point of view, that I would not involve myself in another plot, then that was just the chance that he was prepared to take. Perhaps he thought it better to have me under his eye where he could surveil my movements. I only hoped that I would do nothing more to awaken the cold anger in him that he let me glimpse last night. I was sure that I never wanted to be there when he lost control of it, as he must have done the night his brother died.

I awoke betimes from a troubled, uneasy sleep, prodded to consciousness by a prick of anxiety. I immediately called Bess to dress me with care and all the decorum befitting the lady of the manor. I found Sir Roland in the hall with one leg swinging over the corner of the main table, laughing with his men over some jest. He looked fit and rested and without a care. He had also, mysteriously, established his authority in my household, for there were several pages running to his commands, and sirloin and ale were already laid out for his men to break their fast. When he saw me enter, he crossed immediately to my side, and I led him down a hallway I rarely traveled to my father's receiving chamber. I told him in a brief, practiced speech that I had considered his kind offer of marriage and was pleased to accept it.

His manner displayed neither triumph nor relief. He simply took my hand and, in an uncharacteristically gallant gesture, kissed it. "I am honored," he said.

"I shall try to be a—a dutiful wife, my lord," I said unsteadily, "and fulfill all my obligations."

"And I hope to make you a suitable husband," he replied with cool civility. "The new bond between our two houses will be of mutual benefit."

I had prepared a few chosen words on the subject of my father's plot against his life, but Sir Roland dismissed the problem with one short, clipped phrase: "And whatever the relationship between the Montcriefs and the Guimonts has been in the past, we can regard this as a new beginning. Do you have a suitable red dress?" he asked, abruptly changing the subject.

"I shall certainly make one for the wedding," I replied, wondering why he would bother with such a feminine detail.

"Will it be ready by tomorrow?"

"Tomorrow, my lord?"

"Since we shall be married on the morrow," he said, "I thought you might like the traditional attire."

"I had no idea that you intended the ceremony immediately!" I exclaimed.

"It would have been presumptuous of me to mention it while the marriage itself was in question," he replied reasonably.

"But, tomorrow! It is too soon!" I protested.

"Another day may be too late," he answered. "I have every confidence in Constance's channels of information, and I do not doubt that the first place she will come is Shrivenham. She could be here in as soon as three days, and by then I should like already to be on my way."

I was irritated both by his high-handedness and by my lack of foresight. "I understand perfectly," I said, a little on edge. "It was just that I was taken by surprise. I am sure I can be ready whenever you wish."

"Then we are agreed it shall be tomorrow—unless you would prefer it today?"

"No!" I said, a bit alarmed.

"Very well, you shall have the day to make whatever preparations you deem necessary, and I shall ride out with my men. We will not be returning until the evening meal."

"You will want to meet my father's vassals sometime soon, I imagine?"

"Yes, but first I should like to discuss a few things with your man of God before riding out."

"Our man of God?" I said quickly.

"Certainly. A marriage is usually performed by a priest, is it not? Friar Obersman from Hungerford has been informed to be prepared to come here at my summons, but I thought you might prefer your own, for the sake of appearances."

In the face of this piece of information, I abandoned my first cowardly impulse to say that our holy man had recently been carried away by the flux. "Friar Helm can usually be found in the church in Shrivenham Village at this hour," I replied.

Sir Roland smiled faintly. "Very wise," he commented, with the uncanny perspicacity that must have made him so valuable to the king. "I would be unlikely to believe that Shrivenham had no man of God or that he was not on the premises at the moment."

I colored in spite of myself. "I was thinking rather that you might find him reluctant to perform such a hasty ceremony."

"So I should think," he agreed, "and that is precisely why I want to see him. I think some explanations may be in order."

"What do you propose to tell him?"

"I have sent a message with Will to London. I think we can

arrange for a story to be put about that your father died of
some ailment. He was known to suffer some digestive disorder,
was he not?"

He looked at me briefly, and I nodded assent. "Your father
was carried away by an attack of the stomach, then, several
days ago, but before he died, he summoned me to his side,
and we struck our bargain. I came here to fulfill his dying
wish. That is all that need be said at this point. Does this meet
with your approval?"

"Yes," I said, perfectly aware that my approval had very
little to do with it, "but it may appear to some people a bit
strange."

"How so, my lady? What father could desire more than to
see his lands doubled through the marriage of his daughter?"

"True, but the suddenness of it all!"

He loomed above me. "You are alone now, and there is
nothing to prevent the marriage from taking place. You may
mourn your father as easily being a married woman as being
a maid. He would have wanted it that way." There was a certain
finality in his voice, and I wondered idly what he would have
said and done had I refused his offer of marriage.

His explanation, however, was plausible, and it would have
to do. "I don't think Lady Constance will like this," I remarked.

"I do not think so," he said, the glint in his eye more
pronounced, warning me.

"However, she may decide to come forward with her document to contest our marriage," I suggested.

"I do not think her such a fool," he said curtly. "She will
just have to acknowledge defeat—for now." He paused and
looked down at me. "She will not know that I am aware of
the marriage settlement, unless, of course, someone tells her.
Charles is unlikely to admit to having divulged so interesting
a piece of information." My eyes did not waver from his. "So,
coming forward with her document will serve no better purpose
than to put me on my guard, since there will be nothing she
can legally do to nullify our marriage."

He had planned it all, and I could hardly cavil since he was
protecting my name and giving our marriage the varnish of

parental approval. "You leave me with nothing to say," I replied.

"Good." He inclined his head. "I shall beg to take my leave of you. Pray give my respects to Lady Longchamps and tell her that I shall be looking forward to hearing how she goes on this evening."

I told him that I would do so, we exchanged the usual courtesies, and he exited, leaving me to fight a rising panic. During the night, I had come to terms with the idea of marriage and, in particular, marriage to Sir Roland, but it would have been a far more difficult decision to make had I known the immediacy of his intentions. I guessed that for a man, marriage was a relatively easy affair, as simple and direct as any business transaction; but for a woman, and one as unused to male company as I, it was complicated past verbalization. I did not doubt that Sir Roland somehow suspected this. He must have known that once I had agreed to the marriage, there would be no cogent reason to back out just because it would take place on the morrow, instead of in some distant, unreal future as it had seemed when I had considered the matter. In fact, there were all too many good reasons, which I should have thought of myself, for tying the knot early.

I hardly knew where to turn first in the face of the spate of tasks that preceded a wedding celebration, and it was that very overwhelming number that made me quickly realize that there was actually very little to be done, that could be done. My marriage ceremony and feast were not to be the usual ones, and no one would expect them to be so, least of all the bridegroom, and if I could find an appropriate dress to alter by the time I would meet Sir Roland in the aisle of our small church, I could count myself lucky.

On one count, I considered myself already fortunate: Alicia was here, and it was toward her chambers that I turned my steps first. The food, the wines and ales, the cleaning, and all my retainers could wait; I would talk to Alicia before all else.

I found her propped up in bed, sipping a hot posset and looking more herself than she had in a week.

I greeted her and complimented her on her color.

"Good morrow, Grita," she said with a smile. "I have discovered a wonderful thing today."

"And what may that be, my dear?"

"My appetite! Last night I could hardly touch my food, but this morning Dame Ellen—the dear!—came with another spiced milk and it smelled, well, delicious. I vow, I have not been so hungry in two weeks!"

"I am very glad. I am told that the sickness lasts only a short time, and then one takes on color, as you have," I said. "So, you have already seen Dame Ellen this morning?"

"Yes," she said with a mischievous twinkle, "and I think you are the slyest thing in nature."

"Oh?"

"I am told that you received visitors last night."

"The Earl of Guimont," I said, adding, "But it is not what you think!"

"How should you know what I think?" she asked roguishly.

"Sir Roland came with bad news," I said, not mincing matters.

Alicia put down her cup on the side table. "I should not have teased you, my dear. I am sorry! Tell me what it is."

"It seems that my father—died from an attack of the stomach," I said, and, to my surprise, I felt my lower lip begin to tremble, "a few days ago in London. Sir Roland was—kind enough to convey the news without delay."

"My dear," Alicia said with ready sympathy, "this is so unexpected for you. How sad for you—for us all! Here, I have a mouchoir handy."

I was not going to cry, but my composure, so tightly held during the last hours, deserted me in the telling of my misfortunes. I took the linen from Alicia's hand and blew my nose ineffectually. She soothed me with comforting words, until finally I broke her off. "No, I am being stupid. My father and I were never close. He was not like Lord Stafford, that is—"

"I have an unusual father, I admit," she said and placed an understanding hand on my arm, "but I know your father cared for you, although he was not demonstrative. Many men are not, but that does not mean he did not care for you deeply."

I thought it useless to argue.

"When will the funeral take place? I am so glad to be with you in your time of need!"

"He has already been buried—quietly, in London," I said, improvising rapidly, for I did not imagine that the king would bother to provide my father with a proper burial. "Sir Maurice wanted his passing to go—unnoticed. Instead, there is to be a wedding here."

Alicia demanded to know better what I was talking about.

"I am still in my senses, I can assure you, my dear! Sir Roland and—my father had decided, before my father was— attacked, that I was to marry Sir Roland. You might call it a deathbed wish. Sir Roland has come to honor it."

She smiled with satisfaction. "There! You see! I *knew* your father had your interests at heart. He must have known that his hours were limited, and yet he took it upon himself— despite his pain!—to make an alliance that would suit you. If that is not a demonstration of a father's love, then I do not know what is!" she said, never able to see but good in a person's actions or character.

"How can you say so? His decision to ally me with the Guimonts had nothing to do with *my* wishes."

Her eyes instantly lit up. "I think it probable that your father yielded to Sir Guy's wishes."

"But he does not *wish* to marry me!"

"Now, Grita," she said in a reproving tone, "you are being obstinate. You can be, you know, when you don't want to admit to something. I know you well enough to realize that you carry your modesty—as becoming as it is—to an extreme sometimes. It is quite clear to me that when the Earl of Guimont could have his pick of almost any woman in the kingdom, and he chooses you, then there must be a strong attraction there."

I was astonished. "Surely you cannot be implying that he is in—has conceived a—a romantic attachment to me!"

"Why, yes," she replied simply.

I had a few words to say on carrying naïveté to an extreme, but hoped I was better bred than to hurt Alicia's feelings, especially when she was so patently trying to help and did not know the whole story. "You are too flattering, Alicia, I assure you! Sir Roland has not laid eyes on me above three times! But perhaps that is to my advantage, after all."

"Only three times?" she said, somewhat surprised.

"Well, four," I admitted reluctantly, if one wanted to count the fact that I had seen him on two separate occasions at Alicia's wedding.

"That is of no consequence," she said, dismissing the matter. "He strikes me as a man of decision"—with that I could agree— "and I suspect that the moment he saw you, he was instantly struck by your beauty and character."

This genuinely amused me. "Ho! That same beauty and character had half the men at court languishing at my feet. I am sure it was apparent to everyone!"

"Everyone but you," she said. "You had many admirers, Grita."

"Really? I must commend their discretion, then!" I said, laughing. "But do pray tell me, Alicia, how likely is it for a man like Sir Roland to—to fall in love at first sight?"

She did not answer me directly. "I was forgetting," she said, maintaining her teasing manner, "*you* think it more likely that plots are brewing."

I tried to school my features and said hastily, "No, I think it much more likely that he has fallen in love with my land! Need I point out that our two estates together make an impressive expanse?"

"That is true!" she said, much struck. "The marriage could not have been better arranged, my love. I am so happy for you."

With that, she leaned over to hug me.

The battle against her was hopeless. "How can I gainsay you when you are so determined that I shall be happy?"

"And why should you not be happy with such a union?"

I frowned slightly, but held my tongue.

"No, Grita!" Alicia cried on a note of genuine distress. "*That* ugly rumor has surely been laid to rest! Sir Guy most certainly did not kill his brother!"

I, too, wanted to put the topic firmly aside, for I was reluctant to divulge my worst fears, even to Alicia. "It's not just that," I said. "He's so—unpredictable. Why, you even told me yourself once that you were afraid of him."

"But I am not at all like you," she argued, and then added on a note of triumph, "And besides, you told me once that you feared your father would marry you off to Charles Hartford—you must now realize the folly of that notion!—and you will admit that however forbidding Sir Guy may be, he will make a far superior husband to Charles!"

I had to admit he would.

"And I also recall saying that Sir Guy has a certain charm," she continued, pressing her advantage. "So you see, my dear, you could do very much worse than to marry the Earl of Guimont. In fact, I have thought ever since seeing the two of you together at my wedding that you would suit each other perfectly!"

"Your optimism positively overwhelms me, and I can only attribute it to your restored spirits, for which I am very pleased. But do not carry your sanguine prospects for my forthcoming marriage too far. Do not think to model it after your own perfect marriage!"

"How should I?" she said, laughing. "I have already said that you and I are not the same, and, after all, Sir Guy is not very much like my Herbert, now, is he?"

"We hardly need emphasize *that!*"

A knock fell on the door at that moment, and the next brought Dame Ellen into the chamber. She began immediately to cosset and cluck, an activity, I noted, that did not seem to disturb Alicia's composure one hair. I observed, too, that Alicia's tiring women were, mysteriously, not visible. I had no doubt that they could be found on the other side of the castle on an errand of Dame Ellen's contrivance.

I interrupted Dame Ellen's ministering offices long enough to discover whether Sir Roland's company had had their needs attended to. She assured me that while I was in conference with the Earl of Guimont, his men had broken their fast and then repaired to the stables to prepare for their patrol of the lands and the day's hunt, but she offered no hints that she knew what was toward.

Alicia was quickly dressed and coiffed, and she lacked only her shoes. Dame Ellen grunted to her knees.

"No, I thank you, dearest Ellen!" Alicia protested. "I am surely able to buckle my own shoes. I insist that you allow one of my women to do it—where are they now, I wonder?—well, I own! It is doubly fortunate that you are here!"

The task done, Dame Ellen puffed back up to her feet and said with a perfectly serious face, "Aye, my lady, you are far too kind a mistress and allow your women to grow lazy in serving you. But Ellen is with you for as long as you are at Shrivenham, and you need have no worries here about being neglected."

Alicia apostrophized my sly retainer as her True and Faithful Ellen and settled the matter with a smile and the following words: "Never mind that! We have much more important things to discuss, don't we, Grita?"

Dame Ellen turned to me with a look of inquiry in her eyes that widened with genuine surprise when I informed her, "Yes, I am to be married."

So, she had not heard, she who caught the breath of every rumor within these walls! It seemed that Sir Roland and his men had been very discreet and had properly left to me the task of informing my own retainers of my change in status. An expansive vision of the grandeur of this long-awaited wedding celebration immediately spread across Dame Ellen's face, to be swept away an instant later as it dawned on her whom I would be marrying.

"Need I ask who your consort is to be?" she asked cautiously.

"I do not think it will surprise you to know that the Earl of Guimont—the *new* earl," I said, quoting wickedly, "has offered for my hand, and I have accepted it."

"Yes! Is it not wonderful?" interjected Alicia, before there was time for a response.

I could have hugged her, for Dame Ellen, fair bursting with disapproval, could only agree. She did, however, detect a flaw in the marriage proposal. "*You* have accepted his hand, Lady Marguerite? What of Sir Maurice? I find this highly irregular!"

Alicia and I exchanged pained glances. "My father blessed this marriage," I said, "just before he died."

Dame Ellen gasped, crossed herself, and clasped her hands over her heart. "Sir Maurice! The Lord bless him and comfort him! How did it happen?"

"An attack of the stomach," I said, and described briefly the story that was intended for public consumption.

Put off her guard, Dame Ellen muttered in a moment of rare insight, "Who would have thought that his stomach pains were real? Bless my soul!" She digested the thought and crossed herself again. "We must observe the strictest mourning immediately."

Now we had come to the ticklish part, the one Sir Roland had left to me. I depended entirely on Dame Ellen to see that the tone I set was followed throughout the household. I needed to convince her of the need for a speedy marriage, for, whatever else happened, Shrivenham would have to present a united front in its acceptance of the circumstances of my marriage, in the event that Lady Constance came and asked questions.

"It seems," I said, "that Sir Maurice and Sir Roland settled the details of the marriage proposal shortly before my father's death. It was decided then that the mourning should wait until after the wedding."

"But, my dear, when is the marriage to be?" Alicia demanded.

I knew a feeling of trepidation but said firmly, "Tomorrow."

Alicia was struck silent. Dame Ellen experienced no similar difficulty. "That is impossible!" she stated categorically.

"It is hardly past the prime," I said, deliberately misinterpreting her objection, "and we have ample time to prepare the food, air the chambers, and make all ready. No one will expect this to be an elegant celebration, but we have enough on hand to provide in a seemly manner, I think."

Dame Ellen majestically ignored my impertinence. "I have never heard of such! A marriage in the midst of mourning! It is not proper! This is plainly the Earl of Guimont's doing!"

That was true, but there was more at stake than mere protocol. Dame Ellen and I could have argued at length on the proprieties of such a scheme, but Alicia came to my rescue again.

"Well," she said slowly, a furrow marking her forehead, "it is not what one would choose, to be sure, but one must think of Sir Maurice's motives. We must suppose that he fell ill and called the earl to his side. Of course, it is fortunate that Sir Guy was in London at the time! Sir Maurice must have known that he was dying and did not want to leave his daughter without a protector. Thus, the insistence on a swift union."

"It is possible," Dame Ellen replied, somewhat unconvinced.

"Why, yes!" Alicia said. "I can see that you agree! Marguerite has no uncles, no brothers, no man to turn to now, and I think that Sir Reynauld is not, shall we say, dependable?"

Dame Ellen looked inclined to relent a little. "Our seneschal is— Well, perhaps you are right, but—"

"Sir Maurice was never one to leave things to hazard, was he?" Alicia continued in persuasive tones. "I laud him as a parent, for putting the safety of his child before any thought of mourning, the sign of respect customarily and rightfully due him. His wish indicates the kind of selfless love that only a father can give a daughter, and we should honor his wish by making Marguerite's wedding a fitting occasion for her, tempered necessarily by the shadow of Sir Maurice's death."

Dame Ellen was persuaded by this gentle eloquence, and I threw a grateful glance to my entirely capable friend.

"But the Earl of Guimont—" Dame Ellen began.

"Will make Marguerite an excellent husband," Alicia finished. "There is no doubt but that Sir Maurice had both Marguerite's happiness and fortune in mind when he contracted the union. Sir Guy can only be commended for having come so readily to fulfill Sir Maurice's fondest wish."

Dame Ellen looked strongly inclined to disagree on several of Alicia's points, but there was nothing tangible in her argument to take issue with. I reserved for myself the observation that Lady Longchamps had her own special way of dealing with delicate situations, and decided that she had no slightest need of help when it came to handling retainers.

"Well," Dame Ellen said at last, addressing me, "I suppose you will want Friar Helm to perform the ceremony, but I strongly doubt that he will consent to such an irregular arrangement."

Dame Ellen and Friar Helm were well known for not agreeing on anything, except that the conventions must be observed at all cost. I, too, doubted that Sir Roland would be able to persuade Friar Helm to deviate so grossly from the norm by sanctioning our marriage and was curious as to the outcome of their interview. Of course, I did not mention any of this to Dame Ellen, but merely presented her with Sir Roland's counterargument. "If Friar Helm is unwilling, then Friar Obersman from Hungerford will be summoned."

Dame Ellen, once beaten on all points, rapidly adjusted to the situation. "I suppose, nevertheless, that the castle must be informed of the lord's death?"

"By all means," I said. "I shall ask you, however, not to mention it just yet. I have been thinking that perhaps an announcement should be made this evening at dinner when the earl and his men return. As Sir Roland will soon be the legal head of this household, I think it appropriate that he impart the news of my father's death, and perhaps we can maneuver Sir Reynauld into announcing the wedding, for the sake of form."

Alicia assented readily to this plan, and various strategies were discussed for achieving the best wedding celebration on such short notice that would still observe a muted mourning atmosphere. Alicia very quietly took control of the situation and bade me look for a wedding dress while she and Dame Ellen planned the menu. I went first to Lady Isolde's wardrobe, which I had locked away in a storeroom, as the most likely place to find a suitable dress to alter, for she had been almost as tall as I and a thought on the stout side. My instinct proved correct: I found what must have been Lady Isolde's wedding dress with a minimum of searching. It was truly a lovely garment, fragile with age and of a costly baudekin, with a warp of gold thread woven against a woof of red silk. The sleeves were no longer in fashion, being cut close to the wrist, but I did not think it would be of much importance for a ceremonial dress, and I rather liked the tressed beading that ornamented the sleeves. I held the dress up to me and was satisfied that a few tucks could fit the lines to my figure, for Lady Isolde had apparently been somewhat slimmer in her youth.

By the time I returned to Alicia's chambers, a menu had been contrived of viands and poultry and pigs, mullet and shad pasties and fritters, smoked trout, quenelles, peas and beans with onions and saffron, jellies, custards, compotes, stewed fruits, and almonds. No sauces or creams would be served; music, dancing, and wines and ales would be kept to a minimum. I naturally approved of this program, and Alicia took up her needle to reset the seams of my dress.

On the surface, the day passed much as any other, except for the additional organizing. No one in the castle, save Alicia, Dame Ellen, and myself, was aware that we were planning anything other than a banquet on the morrow for the Guimont company. I tried hard not to think about my immediate future, and the strain of it tired me. I remembered later very little of that day, and before I knew it, dusk had seeped across the sky. I was in the back bailey overseeing the erection of the spits when I heard the general din in the direction of the main bailey. I saw to completion the mounting and lighting of one spit spearing four suckling pigs and then excused myself to attend to the Guimont men. I emerged into the front yard in time to see six of them dominate the scene, their horses snorting and stamping in the crisp evening air, with all manner of game slung across their rumps. I spotted Sir Roland astride a huge, rawboned brute, who chose at that moment to curvet across the bailey, having taken exception to a castle dog, but he seemed to know his master and responded to a slight movement of Sir Roland's hand on the bridle. Halbert had come out to lead them to the stalls, and behind Sir Roland fell Gavin McLaughlin and the other men, whose names I had learned were Peter, Geoff, Gaston, and Hedrick.

Some minutes later, Sir Roland appeared and came toward me, with Thomas and Charger, who had obviously been lying in wait for him, at his heels. Thomas was clearly awed but singularly not overwhelmed by our formidable visitor, for he was pelting Sir Roland with questions. Charger, on the other hand, was prancing along beside them, on his best behavior. I could not hear what was being said, but it was obvious that Thomas was pleading some case, and I judged that Sir Roland was not annoyed, by the looks that he bestowed on the youth, which were softened with amusement.

Sir Roland greeted me and bowed over my hand.

"Lady 'Garite," Thomas piped up, "tell Sir Guy that he must show me how to teach Charger some tricks!"

"I do not think the Earl of Guimont has the least desire to do so, my love," I said, "and there is some doubt that your dog is capable of obeying even the simplest commands."

"Oh, no!" Thomas objected. "He surely knows *heel!*"

"Indeed, I should hope!" I retorted roundly.

"Gavin has told me," Thomas continued, "that Sir Guy knows some very good tricks and—"

"Then we must give Gavin the privilege of training him," Sir Roland interpolated.

"But it would be so much better for *you* to do it!" Thomas cried.

"Better for whom?" Sir Roland demanded.

"Me!" Thomas replied with disarming frankness.

"We shall see if there is time," Sir Roland said. "Get thee gone now, tiresome chub, and take that ill-mannered animal with you, or I shall tell Gavin to loose the both of you in the forest!"

Thomas scampered off immediately, with Charger in tow, and I observed with some relief that Sir Roland seemed in a mood of tolerant good humor. It seemed, too, that the day's activities, instead of tiring him, had invigorated him.

I found myself alone with Sir Roland, and we took a few steps together toward the main portal of the hall.

"I see that you have brought back the game for the wedding feast tomorrow," I said, throwing out my leader.

"Yes, Master Ian showed us the hunting in Montcrief forests, and we made ourselves good sport of it while we met some of the landsmen. There are mostly boar and deer, but we did not shun rabbit and hare," he returned easily.

"That is to say, then, that there is to be a wedding feast tomorrow?" I pursued.

"Did you doubt it?" he countered with a satirical glint in his eye.

I looked away quickly. "It did cross my mind that you might have encountered opposition from Friar Helm."

"I found him very willing to comply with my request," he said. "Does that surprise you?"

"Yes," I admitted, "it does. He stands on very high form. He has always been somewhat of a high stickler when it comes to the proprieties."

"So, too, did he strike me," he agreed pleasantly.

"Then how did you do it?" I demanded bluntly, my curiosity getting the better of me.

Sir Roland slowed the pace and looked down at me in his disquieting way. He paused a moment before saying, "Perhaps because Friar Helm and I share the same opinions on Siger of Brabant."

I had to admit to myself that I was nonplussed. "Who?"

"The new rebel master in Paris who bids to challenge Thomas of Aquinas in the interpretation of Church doctrine."

I blinked in disbelief.

"I find that the Abbess Catherine has left a gap in your education after all!" he responded to my silence. "When I encountered the good friar this morning, he was poring over his parchments and grappling with Siger's assertion about the eternity of the world."

"You are not going to try to tell me that this has anything to do with the object of your errand to him!"

"Not at all," he obliged me. "But you must see that the question is of prime importance."

I considered the matter. It was hard for me to believe that anyone could seriously question the belief that God created the world, thereby making it impossible to posit an eternity prior to Him, but apparently there were people who thought about such things, and that realization gave me pause. "The eternity of the world?" I said. "The notion is heretical."

"It is," he said. "We—Friar Helm and I—agreed that Siger would have to soften his position if he wanted to stay outside of prison and within the Church, but on the whole, we felt that the challenger had scored significantly with his arguments."

"How is it you know so much about this man, Siger of Brabant?"

"I suppose I have a taste for heretics," he said carelessly.

"How fortunate that you came upon Friar Helm at just that moment! But how did you obtain his willingness to perform the ceremony?"

"By an ignoble strategem: once I got within his outer walls by siding with Siger, it was easy enough to storm his fortifications with the most dangerous weapon of all, the Evangel."

"You did not try quoting the Bible for Friar Helm, I hope!" I said, much shocked.

"I do not see why not. I outlined the situation confronting Shrivenham, diplomatically reviewing the alternatives, and armed myself with the passage: *The house of mourning and the house of feasting are one, for in the tears of sorrow are the tears of joy, and in death, life.*"

"What was his response?"

"The only obvious one: that the devil can misuse the Holy Writ to his purpose."

"But he complied," I pointed out.

"He complied."

This was clever talking, in sooth, but there was something more behind what he said. "Who would have thought," I said, casting Sir Roland a sideward glance, "that you had been educated in the cloister and destined for the Church?"

The metallic gleam in his eyes vanished in a smile of genuine amusement. "No one," he said, sharing the joke, "and, least of all, you."

I looked up at him and saw the amusement that I knew lurked behind his cool exterior, and in his smile the glimmer of his mercurial charm.

The horn blew just then to herald the evening meal, and so we parted company to wash our hands and clean up for the table. It was just that sort of exchange, I reflected in the interim, that made Sir Roland, to my mind, so incalculable. He was at once cool and forbidding, compelling and attractive, and he seemed to control both contradictory moods, as if what I saw of him constituted only that part that he allowed me to glimpse. Fortunately for the success of the evening, his more accessible mood lasted throughout the meal.

Sir Roland unquestioningly occupied my father's chair, and when he sat down I heard murmurs ripple through my retainers. His own men paid little heed, apparently accepting his authority on all occasions. Sir Roland and I shared manchet and wine, so that it was he who broke the bread, cut the meat, and passed the cup. To his right sat Alicia, and beyond her Sir Reynauld, for I knew that she, if anyone, could manage him. To my left I placed Friar Helm, and during a moment when Alicia had claimed Sir Roland's attention, I was able to exchange a few words with "the good friar" on the subject of Sir Roland.

"He speaks like a resonable man," Friar Helm told me, and added after a moment's reflection, "although his ideas on free will do not suit mine. For his other sins, it is not for me to judge."

So lenient a view seemed uncharacteristic of Friar Helm. "He must be very reasonable indeed to have won you over so easily," I said.

He looked momentarily austere. "Let us just say that, unlike his views on free will, Sir Guy's arguments for your marriage were—very cogent."

At least my suspicions were confirmed that Sir Roland's ultimate success with Friar Helm was due to tactics somewhat less subtle than those he had related to me.

"Your blessing on our marriage will surely come as a surprise to Dame Ellen," I remarked.

His lips drew together in what one might loosely interpret as a smile. "Yes." This hollow monosyllable resonated with satisfaction. He did not pursue the topic, however, but seemed more inclined to draw my attention to the pitfalls that one commonly encounters when discussing free will, followed by more extended comments on the notions of eternity. I was naturally not behindhand in observing that Siger of Brabant had advanced some interesting views on that very subject.

While Friar Helm was instructing me that the strength of Siger's arguments derived from his postulation of the unity of the intellect, I was able to overhear some of the conversation that flowed between Alicia and Sir Roland. At no time, I noted, did Sir Roland allow the subject to focus on himself, and he deftly deflected all of her mild openings onto his life.

She seemed determined to overcome her shyness of him, and I suspected that she was exerting herself with him for my benefit. "Is it not so that only this summer you returned from an extended sojourn in Aquitania?" I heard her ask him.

"Yes, my lady," he replied, "I spent over a twelve-month there."

"One knows so little about what you do," she said when he did not elaborate, and then paused as if in embarrassment. "That is, one must believe that you were in the service of the king."

"Yes, I was on a very important mission," he said gravely, "but it was no secret, Lady Longchamps, as your husband can tell you. I was there to make sure that Aquitania remained under Henry's rule in order to keep the Bordeaux wines flowing into England. I hardly need emphasize how important good wine is to peace in the realm!"

"I see!" Alicia said with a chuckle when she realized he was taking a light tack. "And perhaps it is most true at court?"

"Especially there, my lady. Wines produced in climates less temperate than Aquitania easily turn sour and moldy. I have seen, even at court, the lords served with wine so muddy that a man must needs filter the stuff rather than drink it." On such a neutral topic, Sir Roland did not hesitate to expatiate on the different aspects of viniculture that were practiced in Gascony, quipping that "King Henry long ago noticed the correlation between inferior wine and general discontent among his peers.

Supplying his lords with excellent beverages may not be politics at its most refined, but it is uncommonly effective!"

"You are something of an expert on wines, I perceive," Alicia commented.

"A diplomatic necessity in Aquitania!" he said. "On the whole, however, I prefer ale—English ale."

"Herbert almost never drinks ale," she said.

"Perhaps he has not tasted the Shrivenham brew. It is excellent."

Not for nothing had I hired a good ale-wife, even if she was a widow who ran an inn of dubious reputation, which received comprehensive disapproval from Dame Ellen, but she produced a fine barley brew and was worth every pence I paid her for her skills.

"Shall I call for another jug?" Alicia asked.

Sir Roland invited her to do so, saying that he never refused good drink.

Contrary to his comments, Sir Roland's own drinking at the meal was temperate, even abstemious, and his men took their cue from him. In general, the atmosphere in the hall was subdued. Meals at Shrivenham, when my father was present, had never been boisterous occasions, but this evening the as-yet-unexplained presence of the Guimont men held my retainers in suspense.

When the tables were cleared save the goblets, I gave the signal for the servants to come with the ewers of water, basins, and towels. Sir Roland and I exchanged no intimate words and maintained our distance by discussing such indifferent topics as the ingenious construction of the barbican at Castle Kenilworth. Our conversation soon came to its conclusion. He pushed his chair back from the table but did not rise. He lifted the tankard he had reserved for his ale and drained the contents, and that one, understated gesture somehow commanded the attention of all eyes.

Sir Roland paused and scanned the hall when all was quiet. "King Henry of England, Anjou, and Aquitania," he began, as if it were entirely natural that he should address my company in such a fashion, "has charged me with the sad office of

informing Castle Shrivenham of the death of Sir Maurice Montcrief, your lord and master." There rose an instant buzz that
just as quickly died. Sir Roland continued, dispassionate and
brief, "Death claimed Sir Maurice suddenly, but perhaps not
unexpectedly for those who knew of his ailments, three days
ago in London. At his own request, Sir Maurice has been laid
to rest in an anonymous grave and desired no public or prolonged mourning. Friar Helm shall pronounce the eulogy now."

Friar Helm rose to his feet. My father had not been a beloved
lord, but neither had he been hated; just as there were no tears
shed over him this evening, neither was there any cause for
rejoicing. Friar Helm's certainly uninspired words were therefore fitting to the occasion, and, more significantly, they were
concise. I surmised that Sir Roland intended this series of
announcements to be as swift and clean as the justice dealt my
father and his cohort when they were discovered in the royal
bedchamber.

To this end, Sir Roland wanted the announcement of our
wedding to follow immediately, before any of the vassals could
organize among themselves and challenge Sir Roland's right
to marry me. I had informed him that Sir Reynauld would
publicly approve of our union after Friar Helm's speech. But
when the latter sat down, Sir Reynauld's attention had apparently been wandering, so that Alicia had to nudge him gently
to his feet and remind him discreetly of his task.

Sir Reynauld opened on one of Lady Isolde's favorite aphorisms, and that was to be the last appropriate phrase he uttered.
"'When the Almighty closes a door, he often leaves a window
open,'" he quoted. "He, in his Divine wisdom, has seen fit to
close the door on Sir Maurice's life, but has opened the window
onto the marriage between"—he looked over at me—"your
mistress, the Lady Marguerite Montcrief, and—" He looked
at Sir Roland, furrowed his brow, and stopped. It became
apparent that he had simply forgotten the name of my bridegroom. Such a lapse, even for Sir Reynauld, was outrageous,
but, so far from seeming embarrassed, Sir Reynauld merely
looked blank.

"Roland of Guimont."

Into the awkward silence Sir Roland supplied his own name. This he did quietly and clearly, betraying neither anger nor resentment at the obvious, if unintended, insult. I could not bring myself to look at Sir Roland's face and instead stole a look at Gavin to gauge his reaction. The squire looked distinctly apprehensive.

"Guimont—yes, of course!" Sir Reynauld said with a vague smile and repeated the name under his breath several times, as if trying to conjure a memory. "Guimont. The name tells me something."

"We are neighbors," Sir Roland replied.

"For about five leagues on the northeast border," Sir Reynauld informed him knowledgeably, and since there was not a person present in the room who did not know that fact as well as his own name, I saw with dismay the shock on people's faces dissolve into a kind of horrified amusement.

"No, no, there's something else there," Sir Reynauld insisted.

"Your wife and my mother were second cousins," Sir Roland said calmly.

"From the Senlis branch?" Sir Reynauld queried.

Sir Roland nodded.

"Excellent family, that!" Sir Reynauld said with obvious approbation. The next moment, however, he looked dubious. "But are you not the second son?"

My heart sank to my stomach. Sir Roland could have easily been offended by this public questioning; he chose not to be, and actually, incredibly, turned the possible disaster to good account.

"I have recently come into the property, sir." This he said with much the humble but expectant demeanor of the greenest of suitors applying to a stern father, and the incongruity of the situation drew some suppressed snorts of laughter.

Sir Reynauld's brow cleared. "Well, this is better than I could have expected for my little Marguerite!" he said as if to himself, and then looked up to embrace the hall as a whole. "I have the honor and pleasure to announce to you the marriage of Lady Marguerite Montcrief and Sir Roland of Guimont."

Now there was open laughter, some scattered applause for the entertaining performance, and even a "Bravo, Reynauld!"

"And when is the marriage to be, my dear?" Sir Reynauld asked me, clearly pleased with himself for his adroitness.

"Tomorrow," I said hastily.

"The sooner the better." Sir Reynauld nodded sagely and then dismissed everyone to bowls and dicing, but outlawed betting for the evening "in deference to Sir Maurice's untimely passing."

Sir Roland asked to see me immediately in my father's receiving chambers. If the events of the last minutes had not already dispelled his elusive good humor, what happened next most certainly did.

"Shall I apologize now or later for Sir Reynauld?" I asked when we were alone.

He looked at me briefly before sitting down at my father's large oak table. "It went better than anticipated," he said curtly, but I knew that he did not relish the role of buffoon. I did not judge it wise to pursue the topic.

Neither had he any intention of expanding on it. He bade me sit down and came immediately to the point. "To prevent any future legal misunderstandings, I should like before tomorrow to come to an agreement about the settlements, your marriage portion and the dower I am to bestow on you. Under normal circumstances I would not apply directly to you, but we are agreed, I believe, that these are not normal circumstances, and I do not wish others present. I am persuaded that you do not, either. A perhaps distasteful, but necessary, precaution." He did not explain the need for a precaution in so routine a matter.

When I did not immediately respond, he said, "You once told me that you do the accounts. Is that not so?"

"Yes. I record the taxes paid and the rents received. I know that it is Sir Reynauld who should do so, but I think I need hardly explain—"

"Hardly," he interrupted dryly. "I see no need for his, or anyone else's, presence."

"Of course not," I said. "Then let us get started. I always

keep my tally books on the table here. By your right hand.
The top book is the most recent."

Sir Roland opened them and ran his eyes down page after
page of my painstakingly neat figures. I had spent hours filling
those pages and was rather proud of myself. "Yes, we shall
go by these for the legal basis. That will simplify things," he
said.

I found this statement extremely odd, but forgot about it
momentarily in the ensuing discussion. I appreciated that he
did not insult my intelligence with unnecessary explanations,
but, on the other hand, the way he had of depersonalizing the
matter was somehow disturbing. He was right, of course, but
some feeling in me—surely a silly feminine caprice—balked
at the fact that he did not see me, Marguerite, across the table,
but an accountant of reasonable understanding.

I could do little but agree with him when he named ap-
proximately one-third of the Guimont estate and listed the
specific lands that would become mine if he predeceased me.
This was standard procedure. But when he named a very modest sum for my marriage portion, I made some protest. He
glanced up at me, ignored my comment, and continued making
the list that would be read before the church on the following
day. I did not open my mouth to speak again.

"It is agreed," he said and shut my ledgers with finality. He
then leaned back in the chair, his strong hands spread on the
table top.

"Now, I would like the second set of books, if you please."

Once again I felt myself floundering in waters beyond my
depth. "I—I beg your pardon," I faltered at last.

"Certainly. I would like to see the parallel accounts."

"I know nothing of what you say," I said in a constricted
voice.

His eyes flicked over my face. "Let us find them together,
then," he said with a disquieting note of mockery. "Your father
was a master of the inconspicuous, was he not? And what is
more unobtrusive than a large table in his very own chambers?"
He rapped the table top with his knuckles, as if testing for
hollowness in the massive planks, and then slid his hands

beneath the table to search for catches. Presently I saw his eyebrows raise in discovery, and then I heard a click and the sliding of wood against wood. "There. That was very easy," he said, and I could only stare wide-eyed as he produced a large tome, scrawled, I saw when he opened it, with long, black columns of figures drawn by a very different hand from my own.

I tried very hard to swallow my bewilderment and surprise. "Is that what you were looking for?"

"Yes."

"Can I assume that these parallel accounts are illegal?"

"Very."

"How has it been possible for him to maintain two sets of accounts without my knowledge?" I asked, unwilling to accept without a fight his tacit condemnation of my participation in my father's schemes.

He focused his blue gaze on me, chilling me. "You are clever with ciphers," he said grimly, "and can make some guesses on your own. I have no intention of enlightening you myself."

A frown gathered over Sir Roland's eyes as he turned the pages. My heart thudded sickeningly. "There is a great deal of money at stake here," he said quietly, after pausing to figure and refigure one column.

"I wonder what he has done with all of it," I said.

Sir Roland did not answer that; he did not even look up. "You have been of sufficient help to me here," he said, "and I do not think I require your presence further. If you have duties to attend to, or desire your rest, feel free to excuse yourself."

I rose to go. He did not spare me a final insult. "There will be no need for you to come back for this," he said, his voice devoid of emotion, "for it shall be in my possession."

I believed that he deemed the precaution of privacy to have been justified.

I bade him good night and found my chambers, unable to face Dame Ellen, Alicia, or anyone else. I was angry, I was scared, but worse, I was confused. I was caught in a trap I did not understand, and I felt certain that I would remain there, confused, as long as Sir Roland believed in my guilt.

I could not turn my thoughts from the morrow, when everything in my life would change and my confusion would be compounded with unfamiliarity. Only one thing was a certainty: when Alicia spoke of my happiness with this man, she had grossly oversimplified the matter.

Chapter 8

Huddled on a stool next to the mullioned window in my room, I witnessed the day of my wedding dawn gray and overcast. Not only in the weather did my wedding day offer a contrast to Alicia's; our marriage celebrations differed as dramatically as, well, Sir Roland and Sir Herbert. First of all and most obviously, my wedding could not compare with Alicia's in size and magnificence, not that I would necessarily have wanted it that way, and, on a less tangible level, my father's death dampened the merrymaking at my celebration, just as the news of King Henry's infant son had enlivened the atmosphere at Alicia's. It was not, it is useless to repeat, the usual marriage: there were few guests from outside Shrivenham Castle and Village, there were even fewer preparations, and there was no time for a true feeling of a celebration as only a period of anticipation can produce. Perhaps for these reasons, the day of my marriage had no more reality for me than did Sir Maurice's death.

Nevertheless, although the celebration was small, it was not nondescript, and while it was without pomp, it was not without drama. I would come to know that Sir Roland did few things in a bland fashion, that few places remained unchanged after his passing, and the lesson that Sir Roland would continually surprise me I learned before we entered the church.

The most important part of the marriage service took place before the church door. Here Sir Roland named the dower that we had decided upon the evening before in my father's chambers. In token of it, he presented me with a ring that represented a pledge, what I knew the Saxons called a *wed*, and we exchanged vows. There was nothing in this to startle the crowd that hardly filled the churchyard. Sir Roland's next words, however, invested this ritual with something out of the ordinary.

"The Lady Marguerite Montcrief," he said, "does me great honor by accepting my hand in marriage. To acknowledge my humble gratitude and, indeed, pleasure, I present to her this gift."

He then produced a large velvet pouch from inside his tunic and withdrew a magnificent emerald necklace and bracelet. He clasped these around my neck and wrist so deftly that I could not but suppose that he was in the habit of adorning women with jewels. I was not so foolish as to believe that he was also in the habit of *giving* such gifts; that would have been impossible, even for the king himself, for in the brief moments that I glanced down to see the dazzling green fire lying against my white skin, I judged by the size of the stones and by the cunningly wrought settings that the set was well worth more than the dower lands he had already put in my name. By this public presentation, he meant these jewels to belong to me, not to be just mine to wear in the name of Guimont. They represented both his respect for me and an added security should anything happen to him. It was a grand gesture, and one that was greeted with murmurs of approval from the sparse gathering. I noted that Alicia clasped her hands together at the compliment Sir Roland paid me; the Guimont men looked pleased with their master's generosity. I thanked him as graciously as I was able, and we then moved into the church itself, where Friar Helm celebrated the long nuptial Mass.

Inside, the church was dim with antiquity; and, even at midday, the sun's gray light could barely filter through the small windows oppressed by the heavy Roman arches. Shrivenham Church did not boast the modern arched vaulting whose construction allowed high, light windows; and it was cold. Throughout the ceremony, Sir Roland held my hand in his, the light pressure of his warm fingers and the weight of the gems at my throat and wrist being my only links with reality. Try as I might, I could not keep my mind on the heavy Latin phrases tumbling from Friar Helm's mouth. I could think only of Sir

Roland's gift to me, and it was quite some time before I realized that it was just as well that Sir Roland gave me the precious family heirlooms, for if anything did happen to him before I conceived an heir, they would revert back to the crown and could fall into anybody's hands, perhaps even Lady Constance's. These reflections carried me far, so, consequently, when the service was over and we kissed, I was unprepared for the feel of his mouth on mine. I was momentarily dizzy, and my sense of unreality deepened.

I looked up at my husband. He did not look displeased and, in truth, had all the appearance of one not attempting to conceal what might be interpreted as satisfaction. Back at the hall, his mood was unchanged. The feasting was simple but ample, the drink visible but not flowing. Yet, for all appearances again, Sir Roland seemed to be enjoying himself heartily, although since we shared plate and cup, as we would from then on whenever we would eat together, I could tell that he consumed in extreme moderation. His attitude was one of restrained ease, if such a contradiction is possible, and it did not perturb him one wit that his wedding feast was not all that one joining our two houses should have been. At the appropriate time, he reminded me with a straight face that I stood in his debt one dance. At his command, the lutes and pipes struck up a stately tune, lively airs having been banned for the day. We took the floor, and another of Lady Isolde's aphorisms sprang to mind: "Dance at your wedding, and you shall not have another. Sit the dance out, and you shall find yourself a lover." This couplet was, of course, open to much speculation, and I found no interpretation of it that was satisfying, save for the belief that by dancing, I hoped I would not be subjected to a second marriage. That is not to say that my mind was on dancing; it was not, and no doubt my movements suffered for it, causing my execution to fall short of my vaguely remembered boast to Sir Roland of being light on my feet. When the tune was done, other couples joined in, and we were able to leave off dancing and parted company to circulate among our well-wishers. Alicia was plainly delighted by everything, as was Sir Reynauld, but for different reasons; Dame Ellen condescended to accept the union but did not trouble to hide her disapproval; Friar Helm acknowledged a kind of tight-lipped pleasure; most of my retainers seemed relieved to be assured of protection no matter what the source; and I noted in passing that if Nan had any thoughts on the subject, she was not displaying them on her face. Bess and Gertrude, to my dismay, were more inclined to console me than congratulate me.

I took my seat again and refused all dances. I spoke at some length with Gavin, who seemed oddly withdrawn, although his felicitations were warm and sincere, as were those of all the other Guimont men.

The sun had set. The celebration advanced but remained always decorous under Sir Roland's watchful but unobtrusive eye. He made it his particular duty to meet and talk with all of Shrivenham and engaged Alicia for a period. Eventually he found his seat next to mine, but he did not ask me for a second dance. Instead he filled our cup, and we commented on various aspects of the wedding celebration. I thanked him now privately for the extraordinary gift. He inclined his head in acknowledgment.

Finally he turned to me. "It is time," he said with unmistakable meaning.

"I warrant so," I said, meeting his eye and trying to match his assurance.

I rose from the table, steadied only by the belief that this was not really happening, and signed to Alicia and Dame Ellen. They stepped quickly to my side, and I was whisked away to a lilting tune on the pipes and fancied that it was mocking me.

Bess and Gertrude came to help me. I had refused all other female aid. We had made ready the master's chambers for Sir Roland and me, chambers that my father had never used in my lifetime, and I was in the room my mother had kept long before I was born. Sir Roland left with his men to prepare himself in the room long ago occupied by my father.

Dame Ellen lost no time in venting her feelings against my marriage. This she did not do in a direct manner. Even she was not so tactless as that. Instead, she took after Friar Helm, whose smug satisfaction at her disapproval had nettled her almost as much as had the marriage itself. She found fault with almost every aspect of Friar Helm's demeanor and dwelled most particularly on the length of the service. She continued in this style for several minutes before Alicia interjected, "Well, dear Ellen, he certainly seemed so very—so very *spiritual!*"

"Lady Longchamps, you found him infused with spirit? Permit me to say that I would have rather thought it was wind!"

"I am unable to unclasp the necklace," I said, ignoring this exchange. I was becoming anxious at the prospect of what lay before me, and Dame Ellen was beginning to irritate me as she had never done before. I wished that her opinions could have then afforded me amusement, as they so often did, but I was too nervous to maintain my sense of humor.

"My dear, let me help you," said Alicia, "and it is a most exquisite necklace and bracelet."

Dame Ellen sniffed.

"It is a magnificent set," I acknowledged, cradling the ice-cold jewels in my hands after Alicia had released them and handed them to my care.

"He is a generous man, Grita," she continued, and dealt with Dame Ellen's reflections on the less savory side of Sir Roland's nature by suggesting that perhaps the new Lady Guimont—a name I had difficulty in relating to myself—needed a few moments alone.

I was grateful for the hint, which Dame Ellen reluctantly took. Bess and Gertrude were also thereby obliged to leave. Alicia began to brush my hair, which had been left unbound.

"You look very beautiful," she said after a moment.

"Red is not my color."

Alicia did not respond to that, true as it was. "It is a very lovely dress, and the emeralds were set off to perfection."

I was silent.

"And do not tell me that green is not your color, either," she said, laughing.

"I won't," I said, and laughed shakily in return. "It was a most—generous gift, although I am sure that Sir Roland had his reasons."

"I call it reason enough, my dear, to honor you."

I could not think about the jewels, his reasons, the honor, or anything else, except the scene that would soon take place in the adjoining room. "I am so frightened!"

"There is nothing to be frightened of, Grita," she said soothingly.

"No? Then how is it that I find myself nearly out of my wits?"

"You are merely excited."

"I am simply afraid," I insisted.

"There is nothing to be afraid of," she said, "when you are in love."

"Love? How can I be in love with him? I barely know him!" I cried in exasperation. I feared my tone was a thought too sharp, for Alicia recoiled, hurt, and begged pardon.

"Nay, it is I who must beg your pardon," I said, sorry that I had offended my best friend.

Alicia recovered and smiled. "You may not be sure of your love, but I can tell you that he is in love with you. You shall see. Everything shall go well."

This was goodness to the point of imbecility. I had a mind to tell her that he was a good actor, but refrained. I could also have pointed out that it was not in his best interest not to look pleased at our wedding, given the circumstances, but such an observation would have required explanation.

I could say nothing in reply that would not possibly upset her, and somehow I did not, at that moment, appreciate being in the role of comforter. I wanted, rather, to be comforted.

Alicia interpreted my lack of response to mean that she had relieved my anxiety. "There, now," she said softly, "it is as I say. All will go well, and you are a very lucky woman. How all the women will envy you, to be sure, when they hear about your wedding!" She continued in this vein as she undressed me and wrapped a warm robe about my shivering form. She led me into the bedchamber, where the men were already assembled. It occurred to me, irrelevantly, that it took men less time to undress than women, for they were not hampered by so many hooks and laces.

I did not look up, and it seemed only a matter of seconds before Sir Roland dismissed his men.

"Don't leave me!" I breathed into Alicia's ear, now very much afraid. I think I clutched her arm.

"You have nothing to fear, my dearest," she whispered, and I believed, although I had never known Alicia to be so perverse, that she was amused. She gave me a final hug, took my hand from her arm, drew my chamber gown off my shoulders, and pushed me gently into the bed.

I heard the doors click shut, and I knew that my last support had been removed. I lay rigid under the covers, conflicting fears chasing one another in my mind, fears all the more intense for their irrationality. At last the fantastic veil that had hung around the events of the past two days drew back to expose a hard, tangible reality that sat like a cold lump in the pit of my stomach.

The sound of my husband's easy laughter at the jokes over his obvious eagerness as a bridegroom still echoed in my ears. The voices behind the doors trailed off one by one, and then I heard only the sough of the warm fire inside and the shutters rattling in the wind outside. I knew at last that we were completely alone. Then I felt his weight on the mattress and heard the rustling of bedclothes as loud as thunder in the silence, but my heart bid fair to outstrip them in noise. Since Lady Isolde's wisdom and Alicia's encouragement went only as far as the bed, I was left with only the instincts of a frightened animal.

I bolted up and swung my legs over the side of the bed. I sat on its edge with my back toward my husband and tugged the covers around as much of my limbs as possible. The light from the candles on the low tables at either side of the bed played tricks with my overwrought senses. My own tremulous form was cast against the far wall, distorted and in ominous proportion to my own looming fears. I realized suddenly how little I had slept the past two nights. At the moment, however, I was so far from tired that my taut wakefulness was on the point of snapping.

I heard a rearranging of the sheets behind me and felt a shift in weight as Sir Roland must have propped up on one elbow. I felt his eyes on my back.

"Your hair is very beautiful, my lady," he said, "but it is hardly sufficient covering for you."

I did not know how to take that ambiguous comment and so elected not to respond to it. I kept my eyes fixed on the bleak shadows before me, determined to suppress the chill invading my bones.

With a lithe movement, Sir Roland was seated next to me on the edge of the bed before I had a chance to move away. I was unnerved by his body close to mine and averted my eyes so as not to see the candlelight glittering in his fair eyes, the hard, angular planes of his face thrown into relief by the firelight, and his powerful thighs and shoulders, which could bend me to his will in a moment. I tried to ignore the fact that I myself was naked save for the flimsy pool of linen sheet that spilled from my lap to the floor.

"How old are you, my lady?" he asked unexpectedly, in a quiet, conversational tone.

"I shall be one-and-twenty in another month, my lord," I replied with effort.

If he was surprised, it was not for the reasons I had fashioned for myself.

"I had feared you were younger." He laughed softly and took my unresisting hand in his. "Having almost arrived at the ancient age of one-and-twenty, has no one ever told you the way it is for a woman on her wedding night?"

"My mother died in childbirth," I offered by way of explanation, and then immediately wished I had not said as much to him.

He offered no conventional sympathy and did not appear to feel any great pity for the motherless child soon to become a wife. He kept only to the practical matter at hand.

"Your father took no steps to educate you? No suitors?"

I shook my head slightly, blushing at such a suggestion from this man, my husband.

"And your women friends?"

"Dame Ellen—does not speak of such things, and Alicia and I, we—" It was too difficult to explain. "No, my lord."

"So it was left to your husband to show you the way of it," he said softly.

I regarded him for a fraction of a second and saw his hard mouth curve into a smile. "I am not totally ignorant of the ways of the world," I said, trying hard to cover the fear that he was mocking me. But I succeeded only in sounding foolish, even to my own ears. I felt compelled to explain myself. "Surely you understand, my lord, that this has all happened so quickly! I had no time to prepare myself or to think about . . ." My words trailed off.

The idea, left unsaid, dangled in the air. Sir Roland gave it a body. "I doubt that it is helpful to a woman to think about her wedding night," he said. "In fact, it would have been foolhardy on my part to have given you more time—had it been mine to give."

There was no mockery in his tone. Rather, I detected an urgency about him that I thought had nothing to do with my father's death, Lady Constance, Charles, the marriage contract, or any other factor that lay outside the room.

"Now, come, my lady," he cajoled. "There is no dishonor here. It is marriage."

His hands, which I imagined were so accustomed to violence, were oddly gentle on me when they gripped my shoulders and pushed me back down into the pillows. I lay back in mute horror as he spread the covers over both of us. Out of the corner of my eyes I saw him prop his head casually against a raised arm, and I was reassured by the regular rise and fall of his chest.

As he seemed in no particular hurry to make any movements in my direction, I gradually relaxed and regained a measure of ability to breathe normally. The room grew still and curiously peaceful. The fire burned low, crackling and hissing its opinion of my predicament.

I, in my naïveté, did not quite understand how he could go through with the bedding, and I held out a faint hope that I could somehow talk him out of it. The thought that he had no intention of consummating the marriage occurred to me only to be banished from my mind for its obvious absurdity. The marriage act would be his most valuable safeguard to the legal binding of the marriage ceremony. Whatever else I did not understand about the situation, it was clear that men and women regarded the matter in widely divergent lights.

My deep sigh broke the silence, but the man next to me did not stir, nor did he look in my direction.

"You need not fear me," he said at last. "I have no wish to harm you, but it will not be easy for you, and nothing will make it so."

I bit my lip and felt frightened tears well up inside me. "You told me once," I said, making a shaky attempt at best to delay the inevitable, "that you cared little for women who—" I did not know how to finish the thought.

"Who—?" he pressed.

I sensed rather than saw that he was curiously amused. "That you want nothing to do with women who—who plot and contrive," was all I could think of to say.

"That is correct."

"Then, why this?"

"I do not always find myself married to them," he replied easily.

"You do not understand—" I began in protest.

"My lady," he said, barely concealing now an amusement that perplexed me, "now is not the time either to confess or to exculpate yourself."

"But it makes a difference!"

"At the moment, I can think of few things of less consequence."

It was I who did not understand and thought I never would. "If it is so important to me," I said, "how can you ignore it?"

"That is the difference between us."

"But why must it be like this?" I blurted out with the petulance of a child.

As if he could see through my question to the workings of my mind, he did not insult me by enumerating all the reasons why our houses needed to be united in a bond of blood, and he spared me the observation that this was as much an un-looked-for marriage on his part as on mine. Instead, he rolled over on his side to face me, and I made the mistake of looking into his eyes. They glinted with something I had never seen in a man's eyes before.

"Because you are a woman," he said, "and you have given me reason to believe this evening that you are a chaste one, at that."

"You could not have thought otherwise!" I exclaimed incredulously.

His silence replied unequivocally to my unguarded outburst.

"No, I won't go through with it," I said, feeling the trap close about me. "It is not fair!"

"Unfortunately for you, wife, that is the nature of a cruel world," he said.

I opened my mouth to speak again, but his voice sliced evenly across mine.

"I am done with words," he said.

Then, with a slow, deliberate movement, he turned around to douse the candle behind him, stretched across me to extinguish the small flame just beyond my side of the bed, and closed the bed curtains. As he moved over me, I did not flinch, but in withdrawing to his original position, his knee grazed the inside of my thigh and his broad chest brushed my breasts. All thoughts fled at his touch. His hands, strong and ungentle, commanded all sensations, bruising my softness, and the heavy thud of his heart drummed mine to insignificance. Just as his mouth came down on mine, silencing all further objections, his powerful body against mine obliterated the world where I existed as an individual. I had but one response—for it could not be called a choice—and that was to give in to his ruthless demand.

I was frightened at first, and struggled against hot tears when he took me, my innocence, breaking my painful chastity with the violence of his passion. I derived no comfort from the dimly recognized insight that such must be the experience for every woman when she first knows a man, to feel herself flounder and drown in his strength. I felt as helpless as a tired swimmer in an ocean tide swelling to an almost unbearable intensity, carried by a selfish wave that had no regard for my person, knowing only that it was crashing slowly to an unknown shore, taking me with it, until, finally, I was deposited awash on the strand, feeling exhausted and violated.

It was easy to discern that what had been a shattering experience for me had been for him nothing more than the mere act of possession, of me, of my lands, and of everything I owned. He had possessed me thoroughly, asserting an authority whose selfish and savage pleasure was completely justified in the eyes of society. I could only begin to understand the laws that bound men and women; I would not know until much later how little freedom I had from him once he had made me his, how I would depend on him for much more than protection and shelter. In the brief moments afterward, I sensed only that there was something more to the physical bonds between a man and a woman than pain, and that it could lead to inexplicable joy or unbearable torment of the soul.

I did not, however, pause at length to ponder these weighty matters or the effects of the profound changes that had occurred in my life. If the past minutes had disrupted my life through cataclysm, the next hours provided comfort through a more prosaic action: I simply fell asleep.

I awoke some time later. It was not morning, but something had awakened me. I was disoriented, curiously heavy in body and spirit, and unable to clear my mind.

"What is it?" I said involuntarily through the groggy mist, for I was still sluggish from sleep. I then remembered where I was and who was with me. In another moment, I understood the nature of his intentions, but I still had no control over my speech and blurted out, "Oh, no, not again."

"So soon the wife," he commented low, into my neck, "already protesting."

"It's not that," I said, making an unsuccessful attempt to untangle myself from him.

"It never is," he said, and effectively cut off conversation by placing his imperative lips on mine. I discovered then that, for a woman, pain rapidly gives way to ache, but I did not think that Sir Roland's intention in those limitless hours of the night was to assure me that he had already done his worst. Nor did I flatter myself that I inspired in him an uncontrollable lust. Rather, I judged him a very thorough man. In the morning there would be no question, least of all from me, to whom I belonged. I suspected my husband of as much caution as passion when he made me his wife again.

The next thing I knew, it was full daylight. I awoke with a start. It took me only the briefest second to determine that I was alone, a fact that caused me to sink back into the pillows with relief. I did not have long, however, to savor my solitude. Presently, as many women from the castle as could fit into the room came to rouse and dress me, as custom required, and to examine the sheets. There came laughter and jokes and all the embarrassment that I had wanted to avoid last night and that had gratefully been spared me at the bedding. I imagined that Alicia was the author of the present ceremony, no doubt acting on the premise that at least some aspect of the wedding should conform to practice.

"My dearest friend!" she exclaimed upon seeing me. "The Lady Guimont! How well the title befits you, love! You really must get up at once. The day has come and your husband awaits you!"

The talk ran merrily in this vein for quite a while, as I was being dressed. I was in the fortunate position of not having to say too much, and neither did I have much time to wonder what had become of my husband.

I was soon to discover that he was seen to have broken his fast and was already belowstairs in the stables issuing orders to his men.

"He is leaving?" I asked Alicia.

"Why, yes!" she said with a suspiciously determined cheerfulness. "I believe it is on urgent business—not to be put off!"

"Who would think otherwise?" I said. "Am I to go, too?"

She looked away and thought perhaps not. This was the first time I had seen Alicia betray any indication that she thought all might not be perfect. There was no use trying to convince her of it, and I was in no mood to hear her interpret in the most flattering light possible every glaring blemish in my relationship to Sir Roland. Nor could I see any use in my dwelling on it in my own thoughts, either.

I consequently gave the conversation a turn toward Alicia's own plans for the days ahead, and we managed to finish my toilette and descend to the hall, with a gaggle of women in our wake, in discussing only the most trivial topics.

It was past the prime, but no one was at his usual station. Everyone was gathered in the main bailey to witness the departure of the Earl of Guimont, the uncontested lord and master of Shrivenham. I was actually relieved that my first meeting with Sir Roland, now that we were truly married, would take place in such a public way, so as to obviate the need for any intimate speech.

Upon my appearance on the step at the main portal outside the hall, Sir Roland looked up from the task of lashing saddle straps and gear, smiled at me with pleasure, and crossed to my side. He took my hand and bowed low over it, kissed it, and held it a moment longer than necessary before releasing it. It was gracefully done, and not at all ostentatious, but there were probably few who witnessed the greeting without thinking that Sir Roland was a very satisfied husband.

I am sure I imagined it, but it seemed as if people moved closer to us to hear what we said. Sir Roland did not raise his voice, but he spoke in a clear tone that could be heard by the interested.

"Good morrow, madam wife," he said. "We are on the point of departure, as you see."

I returned the civility and asked with reasonable poise, "Are you bound for Hungerford?"

"No, my lady," he returned, but he did not specify his destination. "I cannot now predict, but we will be gone at least five days. Perhaps it will be a sennight, but I will make every effort to return to you in haste."

I am quite certain that I blushed, and I was incapable of making an appropriate reply.

"I leave, however, knowing that at least one Shrivenham man is willing to follow my command blindly."

"I am sure there is more than one, my lord," I replied, having found my voice again. "But, tell me, of whose loyalty are you so certain?"

"Halbert," he said, "was ready to lay his best saddle down at my feet when he first clapped eyes on my horse. I believe he has conceived a fondness for Morocco." Sir Roland nodded in the direction of his stallion, whose bridle Master Halbert was reverently holding. "And I have taken the liberty of ordering a restocking of your stables here. Just a piece of stewardship, you understand, for Halbert stands too idle at present."

I appreciated his tactful dismissal of our broken-down cattle. "An excellent notion," I said. I glanced at the black brute who was the object of Halbert's affection, and he just then reared his head. "I can understand Halbert's appreciation. He is most beautiful, and one cannot help but admire him."

"An Arabian," he said with a measure of pride.

"And did you indeed acquire him in Morocco?" I asked.

"Yes," he answered. Instead of elaborating on this unexpected aspect of his life, he chose to tease me. "He is a noble destrier, but not, I fear, the animal for your hand."

"Not at all!" I agreed readily, returning his smile. "I am quite comfortable with my Molly. She may lack spirit, but she has very polite manners."

"Well, now," he said, "you will learn what an overbearing husband I mean to be, for I have already sent Gaston to Hungerford to fetch you the bay mare that I think will be just the horse for you."

I smiled and thanked him and wondered to myself if he would think my Molly would not do his wife credit.

"Whatever else Roger was incapable of doing," Sir Roland continued, with a rare allusion to his brother, "he had a fine eye for horseflesh. I shall be sending some of our horses here within the next few days. I hope you will approve of Starfire. She's playful, but there's no vice, and she, too, is a polite young lady."

I longed to ask him if he had chosen Starfire for me before he came to Shrivenham, but refrained. "I hope, then, that I shall have a chance to ride her and become acquainted with her soon," was all I had the courage to say.

"It shall be very soon, in fact, for she shall arrive this evening with Gaston," he said. Then, looking down at me with one of his inscrutable gazes, "My men and I are leaving on the moment, but do not think I expect you also to leave Shrivenham so immediately. You may need to attend to things here before going to Hungerford."

"I have very little to do here now that the wedding is over," I responded in perfect honesty, thinking that I could prepare to leave within the week, if need be, and meet Sir Roland there when he returned.

"Nevertheless, I am sure there are things you want to do the day before your definitive departure. You shall thank me for the respite tomorrow."

I was becoming inured to his compressed view of time. "Shall I not be returning to Shrivenham anytime soon?" I asked cautiously.

"I do not think your presence is needed here above four times a year," he said smoothly.

So I was to reside with him on a regular basis—or at least at Hungerford, since I did not know how much time he intended to spend there. "Do I understand that I am to leave for Hungerford on the day after tomorrow?"

"Yes," he said. "If you leave not too long past dawn, you can make the journey in one day. It is tiring, but I see no other solution. I am leaving Gavin behind to escort you, and, of course, there will be Gaston."

"And my women," I said.

"I would rather say 'woman.'"

"My lord?"

"How, now!" he said easily with his dangerously charming smile. "Do not tell me when it is too late that you require a retinue of no less than twenty with trunks and boxes on litters that stretch for a mile! But I am just a man and do not see the need for more than one woman to accompany you."

This was very glib. "I always travel with at least Bess and Gertrude, my two tiring women who have been with me since my girlhood," I said lightly.

"Were they with you in London?" he inquired with seeming politeness, but I at once caught the meaning of his question and his reason for allowing only one attendant.

"Yes, they were," I said, not bothering to lie on so obvious a point.

"Then I do not suggest that you choose either of them," he said. "I am sure you will find someone who will serve you well enough."

My eye scanned the company and came to rest briefly on Dame Ellen, who had kept her distance from Sir Roland.

"Need I mention," he said, following the direction of my regard, "that Shrivenham will need someone to oversee it during your extended absences? I simply cannot spare a woman from Hungerford for the duty."

I was, in spite of myself, somewhat relieved. "I repose every confidence in Dame Ellen for that position," I said. "She has stood in my stead several times and proved equal to every situation. She, of course, has many ties here, her son, her husband, and would be reluctant to leave, in any case."

"Of course," he replied dryly.

As I was speaking, I had noted Sir Roland's eyes moving over my retainers. When they stopped, I was slightly taken aback to find him looking at Nan. At first I thought he was testing me, teasing me, but as he continued to look at her, I began to fear that he was in earnest.

Nan was standing alone at the far end of the bailey, leaning against the corner, staring at nothing in particular, wrapped in her peculiar dignity, and with her hands thrust into the bodice of her apron at the waist. She seemed to become aware of our scrutiny. Her countenance did not change, except perhaps that her customary wary look became more pronounced.

"I will have to consider the problem at some length," I said. "I really cannot think of anyone who could fill the position."

"Can you not?" he said and transferred his gaze to me. "Then may I make a suggestion?"

"Perhaps you mean for me to choose Nan?" I asked. There was little point in evasion.

"Is that her name?" he said and paused, as if to consider the matter. "Yes. I should think she would serve you excellently."

"But she is a kitchen maid," I pointed out, "and has no experience in attending ladies."

"Then she shall learn. I believe you told me that her understanding was sufficient. Put the proper clothes on her, and she shall look the part, too."

I searched for other objections and said before thinking the matter through, "I would not like to take her from Shrivenham. She is betrothed to a young man here, and was to be married within a fortnight."

Sir Roland's interest in this fact was lively. "What a charming bride she would have made!" he exclaimed. "And an exceptionally lucky groom!"

"I believe they have an understanding," I said, reddening, but unwilling to relent.

"So I should hope!" he said and, as so often happened, cut straight to the core of things. "An understanding. Is it of your making, perhaps?"

I dropped my gaze. "Perhaps."

"Then I believe your purpose was served," he said, "and now we may use her to mine."

"I would have thought," I said, unwilling to compromise when it came to subalterns, "that she would continue to serve my purpose at Hungerford."

"By all means," he said coolly, "she is to be your personal maid."

I had to be satisfied with that, although all my better judgment warned me of trouble. I would have enough to do and learn as Sir Roland's wife and the new mistress of Hungerford without the additional burden of controlling Nan's behavior.

"I shall be happy to inform her of her new post immediately," I said. "I am sure she will be thrilled at the prospect."

My irony left Sir Roland unmoved. "It is always, is it not," he responded, "the main object of the chatelaine to match the position and the person as they fit into a particular castle's ways. You cannot now determine, but I think you shall find that she will do well for herself at Hungerford."

That was, depending on how one interpreted it, a safe statement. But not very encouraging, from my point of view. "By the time you return to Hungerford, I hope you will find both of us getting along with no trouble," I said.

"My lady," he said, bowing over my hand to take his leave, "I look forward to finding you well established in my household."

A new husband must say something of the sort, I supposed, especially when he was quitting his wife of less than a day, but still, it put me to the blush.

Before he left, I had to clear one topic. "And if Lady Constance should come to Hungerford before your return, what am I to tell her?" I asked.

His face closed against me, almost imperceptibly. "I would not presume to dictate to you what to tell her," he said. "You shall have to decide that depending on what course your interview takes."

I nodded and dropped the subject. "I bid you Godspeed, my lord," I said.

He bowed again over my hand and paid it a parting tribute. He wished me health and a safe journey. It was a spare minute after he had mounted his warhorse and thrown several directives over his shoulder when the hooves on the drawbridge thundered a valediction.

I turned to impart the news of my impending departure. I gestured for all to disperse and get about their duties before I approached Dame Ellen and Alicia.

"I shall be meeting Sir Roland at Hungerford," I said. "He has left on business, and I myself shall be leaving Shrivenham the day after tomorrow."

"Not until then!" Alicia cried.

"So soon!" Dame Ellen expostulated in unison with Alicia.

"I had thought that Sir Roland originally had some reason for wanting me to leave Shrivenham immediately," I said, "but apparently he has changed his mind. He did make it plain, however, that I am to leave on the day after tomorrow. I think

I shall be grateful for the time to collect my thoughts and my things."

"And when does the earl return to Hungerford?" Alicia asked.

"Next week," I said.

Alicia made no response.

Dame Ellen looked at me and, forming an idea, said after a moment, "Well! It is very fine, I suppose, but I do not know what he is about leaving you behind like this. Not even a wedding hunt! And I am sure my Ian would have provided a merry chase for you, Lady Marguerite! Not that you would have wanted to be careering around the countryside after your wedding night, or even following your husband to heaven knows where! It would have been extremely uncomfortable for you astride a horse, although I am sure we cannot credit the Earl of Guimont with such—such—"

Words failed her. I did not think Sir Roland entirely incapable of so delicate a consideration; in any case, it was to remain a moot point, since I had no intention of asking him if such had been his motive for keeping me behind a day.

"Be that as it may!" she continued, "how shall we contrive to get you and your tiring women off by the day after tomorrow? That is something I am sure the earl did not pause to consider!"

"There will be only one woman besides myself," I said.

"Only one?" Dame Ellen echoed. I noticed that Alicia had fallen silent.

"Yes. I am taking Nan."

Dame Ellen swelled with indignation. "This latest maneuver," she pronounced, "is of a piece with the rest! To take that—that *person* to Hungerford!—and as your personal maid!"

"Had you rather she stayed here, Dame Ellen?" I asked.

She did not honor my pert question with a response. "Her ways will surely, upon my soul, corrupt your new household, if—and that is a strong *if*—that is possible. You will not know how to deal with her, and she will bring your household down," she predicted mournfully.

"I am well aware of her ways, and I know how to manage her," I said. "You forget that I am a married woman now."

That was all that was needed to set her off.

"You, my lady," she said, airing all the seething annoyance that had been welling up inside her in the past days, "are as innocent as a lamb! Nay! Do not attempt to convince me otherwise. No, indeed! I saw you for the first time the day after you were born—as you well know, for I have never kept that fact from you, for it is the essence of what I have to say to you—and watched you grow up—not that I occupied the position *then* that I do now—until you were sent to Amesbury, and then when you came back. You were but a thin, gangling stripling who did not know the undercroft from the garderobe—upon my soul, if that wasn't the case! And although you've filled out better than anyone would have suspected, you have not lost all your girlish ways. And do not think to interrupt!"

I had no intention, and indeed no power, to stem this apparently very salutary flow, however embarrassing it was to me.

"Thank the Lord above that when you returned the Lady Isolde was still alive to take you under her wing for several years and show you how to go on, for you would have been a sorry case if she had not been there at the beginning! I am not saying that you are not a clever housewife. Never think it! For no one knows better than I how you have wrapped Master Adam around your little finger to get all your woolens at *such* prices. And he has never paid *me* the least consideration and would cheat me blind on a bobbin of thread if I permitted it. *I* am not the one to fatten his purse, which seems, in God's own truth, to be only too full already. Every time I see the man, he has been obliged to loosen his belt a notch, and he will presently become enormous! *That* is what comes from eating too much pork—and whoever heard of a woolen merchant being so rich that he is able to afford to eat pork more than once in a fortnight? It is as I say, however, that you owe much to the Lady Isolde. May she rest in peace, and may Sir Reynauld be delivered to her soon! The poor man's wits have wandered so far that he will never find them again. Imagine forgetting the name of Guimont! I have never heard the like! But I suppose we had no choice but to assign to Sir Reynauld the honor of announcing your marriage. If only your father had been there! That would never have happened. And, come to think on it, perhaps the entire marriage would never have happened, although he did give his approval to it. Why he did, I shall never know! I can say only that it was extremely unwise of your father to have died just before your marriage—just when he could have been of so much *use!*"

I was unwise enough at this juncture to observe that my father had, in life, never been present when I had need of him, so I saw nothing unusual in this circumstance.

Dame Ellen wasted no time in wading into a morass of contradictions, and I thereafter held my tongue and allowed her to speak her mind, which seemed to want to give vent to almost any topic or side topic that occurred to her fertile brain. Truth to tell, I stood a little in awe of her ability to digress in almost every direction, and seemingly simultaneously, while never altogether losing the main thread.

"You speak as if he died on purpose, and nothing could be farther from the truth! He was eccentric, to be sure, but never odd, whatever his friends may have been! It can be attributed only to your mother's tragic death, but at least Sir Maurice did not go into the decline that Sir Reynauld has experienced. Your father's grief took another course: he shunned society and left the management of such a large enterprise as Shrivenham to you. He seemed to care not a wit about what was happening about him, yet we must credit him with having appointed me to stand in Lady Isolde's position after that dear lady's death. *I* take no credit if the castle is well run. You know I do not! Nevertheless, Sir Maurice made a good decision in placing you under my care. There were some who said that I rose above myself. Need I tell you that such was not the case? My birth (but I have never been one to boast!) is of the most respectable. No one knows that better than Friar Helm, and yet he was moved to say some of the most unkind things to me shortly after Lady Isolde's death. I cannot call him un-Christian. Indeed, how could I? For I am sure that he is as pious as the day is long, but if we are to talk about someone rising above himself—! But we are not, and I never considered myself anything other than your chief stewardess, upon my soul, never! But I can say, with all due respect, that I have guided you and helped you in every way that I knew, with the result that you have become a very fine chatelaine. But you are not, whatever you may think, *not* as experienced as is necessary for your coming position. It is one thing to run a castle that you have known your entire life, and quite another to step into another as its chatelaine! I know that for a fact— *I* have never personally experienced such, for you know that I am not a grandam—but it is only common sense that tells me that you have a large task ahead of you! Little though you may think it!"

I nodded my head at the appropriate times and shook it at others, never knowing if she wanted me to agree or disagree, sure only that it was important for her to talk.

"And then *he* comes here, as calm as you please, behaving as if he were lord and master here, although he is now, but when he came he wasn't! It is beyond everything! It all happened so fast that it leaves me breathless. How Sir Maurice came to countenance this match is a riddle whose answer he has taken to his grave. I am sure that I do not know whom you should have married otherwise. Even a simpleton can see the advantages to be gained in your lands. Why, Sir Reynauld remarked on it immediately! But there is a price to be paid for everything, and I am not convinced that your father was not pressured into accepting the earl's suit. It is rumored that he was going to have a very difficult time finding a bride, for no father would want to stain his name with an alliance to the Guimonts. You wonder how I come by such information? There is nothing to wonder, for I am sure everyone knows it. But, you see, he has made himself a fine marriage after all. One might say that he could not have married to better advantage! *I* should say so, in all events, and who shall be surprised if the particulars of your marriage become generally known? I think it happened so fast that no one had a chance to object. I shall own myself surprised if that wasn't his strategy. And then to ride off the next day, leaving his bride behind, to say *nothing* of the fact that he chooses the most disreputable woman at Shrivenham to be your personal maid. *That* says it all, for I am sure that I have nothing to say on that subject—or on any other!"

Dame Ellen was far from spent and stopped in mid-career only by an unconscious reaction to Alicia's laying a restraining hand on her arm.

Even Alicia seemed a little dubious of the course of events, and I was remotely amused to see her, during Dame Ellen's discourse, work out on her face the problem of my husband's hasty departure and his appointment of my new attendant. She struggled visibly. At Dame Ellen's momentary silence, Alicia summarized her thoughts in one insightful phrase:

"Sir Guy is a strange sort of man."

I could do naught but agree.

"And you are just the wife to understand him," she said.

"Am I to thank you for the implication?" I said, teasing.

Her face dawned with amusement. "Pray, Grita, be serious!"

"I am only too serious, Alicia!"

She tapped my arm playfully. "You know me better than that!"

"I know you well enough," I said, "to know that you say exactly what you mean. But let us not argue! We have other matters to consider. I find myself in a peculiar situation as your hostess: what am I to do with you now that I am leaving?"

"You need not worry. Dame Ellen and I have already decided what is best."

"Ah!"

Dame Ellen then proceeded to outline the plans for Alicia's immediate future. I discovered that those plans had not altered. She was to stay out the week in Dame Ellen's care, as originally foreseen, and await Sir Herbert.

There was nothing for me to do but inform Nan of her new position, the news of which she received with equanimity. "I could ha' done worse for myself," she said with a touch of fugitive humor. I determined from the very start that I would take very little with me. It was an easy enough thing to send someone to fetch an item from Shrivenham that was not in use at Hungerford. I saw no reason, therefore, to take my spinning wheel, for instance. There were a few essentials, and I consulted with Gavin on the best methods for packing my trunks of clothing, my toilette articles, my sewing equipment, including the box of pins, needles, shears, threads, the lengths of cloth purchased for my clothing, the countless tambours, and my cutting board (which I would not leave without), my personal gardening tools, several vials of essences, sachets of dried herbs, my Bible, Missal, and Book of Hours, the quills I was accustomed to, and all the rolls of parchment that Friar Helm had so generously cut, dried, and lined for me from last year's sheepskins. It was a modest array of items, and Gavin foresaw no difficulty in transporting them with us.

I do not know to this day how I managed to get through the day after my wedding and the next. I was tired and strained, uncustomarily weak and confused. The afternoon of the first day, I was finally obliged to seek my chambers and lie down to compose myself. I even wept a little—but only from exhaustion. The little rest had its desired effect, and I was able to descend to the evening repast in possession of myself and made a fairly tidy meal.

Absolutely no one—besides Dame Ellen, and she did so only once—breathed a word to me about the inordinate elevation in Nan's status. Her new position at Hungerford Castle was generally known, I believed, within the half-hour after Sir Roland's departure. I learned, furthermore, through the usual sources, that the odds were running dead even in the two camps favoring opposing explanations: the one group held, and there would be no persuading them otherwise, that the new master had an eye for Nan himself, and the reports on his character (which few, by this time, doubted, and which had earned for Sir Roland a respect at Shrivenham bordering on awe) as well as his own masterful disposition gave little room for any alternative interpretation of so extraordinary a move; the other group thought it more likely and maintained that since I had always had a liking for Nan, which recent events had highlighted, I, although not usually given to caprice (I hoped), had chosen incalculably to do her this favor. Nan was not in general well liked, and so the prospect of her removal from Shrivenham was not met unfavorably. Edric did not seem too abashed; Sarah had the good sense not to display too much satisfaction upon our leaving.

I was gratified, nevertheless, that all of Shrivenham gathered to see us off in the predawn cold. It was a sad occasion. Bess had tears in her eyes, as did Hodierne and some of the other inside women. Sir Reynauld was there, but the significance of the assembly seemed to have escaped him; Friar Helm looked merely pious, although I could not imagine why; and John Cook, Michel Armorer, and Master Ian were frank in their repeated assertions that I would be missed. I decided against any general speech, but tried to press everyone's hand. It was finally time to go.

Thomas and his faithful canine loped up and tugged at my skirts. I picked Thomas up and ruffled Charger's coat for the last time.

"Are you really Sir Guy's lady now?" Thomas asked wide-eyed as I deposited him on the ground.

"Yes, I am, Thomas."

"But you don't look any different!" he said, disappointed. It seemed probable that Thomas had envisioned a much grander lady for his hero, or at least one not as familiar to him as I was.

"I am not any different," I replied.

Alicia then hugged me with the assurance that all was for the best. "You shall see, Grita, how soon you shall feel yourself mistress of the castle. You are such a fine housekeeper! And so organized! I wonder that you do it all!" she said with her reassuring smile, and then gave me the following advice: "Just follow the principles you have laid down here, and everyone will love you there as they do here. Just look how they all mourn your departure."

I found myself incapable of speech. She bridged the silence. "I shall visit you soon at Hungerford, my dearest! I look forward to it already!"

Dame Ellen was the last to draw me aside. I was shocked to see her tears.

"My lady," she said, "have a care what you are about. It is

a strange place, is Hungerford Castle—and well you know it!
You've a wit—as innocent as you are!—and I trust you'll use
it. It is a strange place, as I say, and I want to hear of no harm
coming to you there."

For my final act as Marguerite Montcrief, I unhooked my
trousseau of keys and handed them to Dame Ellen. She spoke
no further words, a fact that told its own tale.

Chapter 9

It was a tiring journey and long. The day was clear and cold, the kind one likes to spend at the hearth, contemplating a roaring fire, an embroidery lying idle on one's lap.

Gaston rode out ahead of us and maintained a distance of several lengths throughout. He had arrived at Shrivenham with Starfire late the evening before, but he seemed to think nothing of rising before dawn the next day and returning to Hungerford — typical Guimont style. He was a man of few words, dark, his cold granite eyes doing nothing to relieve the stark look about him. I judged him to be several years younger than Sir Roland and guessed that he had possessed for many years the rough and rugged aspect that characterized all the Guimont men. Gavin stood out as the exception, being lanky rather than muscle-bound, his face open and entirely readable. Sir Roland's squire rode beside me the entire way and left me with no doubt that his master had instructed him on the pace of the ride, on the exact number and places of rest stops and meals, and even, I suspected, on the general tenor of the conversation with which he was to entertain me during the ten-hour ride. Gavin, in an unguarded moment, referred to Gaston as "the bastard." When I questioned him more closely, he flushed — being cursed with the translucent skin of redheads — and explained that Gaston merely recognized no family name but that of Guimont, assuring me, however, that Gaston was no blood kin. Observing the dot of horse and rider on the horizon, I thought it appropriate that Gaston should be so alone in the world.

Nan rode close behind us. She said not a word the entire day, uttered no complaint of cold or hunger. I had procured for her a new kirtle and hooded cloak. She was not entitled to gloves, so I had released the cuffs on the coat sleeves and told her to turn the flaps over her hands to protect them. She could not have had many opportunities to ride a horse, and never for so long a stretch. It was clear that she would have to lie abed for several days to recover from the punishment her body received with each mile.

I was a little better off, although I, too, would have to pamper myself on the morrow. Thoughts of the morrow frightened me, so instead I reflected on Shrivenham and on all that I had left behind, in short, everything familiar and comfortable. Dame Ellen had been right: my authority at Shrivenham had derived in large measure from an assurance that only familiarity could offer. I knew all the manor's inhabitants and everything about them, from their families to their adversaries, from their best qualities to their worst faults, and even their preferences in foods. Shrivenham had been mine because I knew it so thoroughly. I was afraid of the unknown—what reasonable human being was not?—and then chided myself a moment later for my lack of spirit. Even my mount was new and unknown to me. I terribly regretted not having my Molly on this ride. Dependable, predictable, spiritless Molly. How I longed for her!

In the midst of these reflections, Starfire, sensing my insecurity, reared up as though to unseat so unworthy a mistress, but Gavin, who kept an almost unnerving watch over me, bent swiftly forward and caught the mare's bridle close to the bit before I had a chance to try to bring her under control. Starfire was brought down easily by Gavin's hand, and hung her head to repent her bad behavior at Gavin's stern reprimand.

"I thank you, Gavin," I said, a little shaken. "I am afraid that she's a bit too much horse for me."

"Starfire?" he said, his disbelief patent that this mare could be too much for anyone.

"I am not much of a horsewoman," I confessed.

"Oh, no, my lady!" he said and colored again. "I mean, she is fresh, that is all, and has tricksy manners. When I found out the master had chosen her for you, I thought she was too tame, and still do. I have no doubt that you shall very soon want to choose another mount. Our stables are the best." This, with simple pride.

It was apparent from his tone that he greatly overestimated my abilities. I was grateful, at least, that Sir Roland had not done so, else I could have ended up with a much more spirited horse. As it was, I guessed that Starfire was the tamest of their lot. While she was gentle, I still would have been happier to be on Molly.

However little I liked to ride, I was not ill disposed to the subject of horses and thought it a suitable topic with which to draw Gavin out. I was not wrong. He spoke passionately about horses in general, Hungerford's in particular, and lost some of his self-consciousness. I heard him out, finding him, as I had on other occasions, interesting and well informed. It was as pleasant a topic as any, I supposed, to pass the miles of autumn-bare scenery. All at once, though, he caught himself up and turned beet red.

"This can—hardly be of—interest to you, my lady," he faltered. "So stupid of me to have carried on so! You have already told me you are not a horsewoman—but you have a fine seat and steady hand!—and I can talk of other things, you know!"

He looked so eager to please me that I could not help but smile. "Do not apologize, I pray!" I said. "I have much to learn about cattle. I shall tell you a secret that Shrivenham suffered in this arena." I could see from his face that it was no secret to him. "And I shall call you my friend if you will conduct me personally through Hungerford's stables *first thing* and instruct me on the qualities of excellent horseflesh. No, on second thought, *not* first thing! I shall have to recover from this ride before I shall have any desire to so much as look at another horse!"

He smiled appreciatively and stammered his delight at such an honor. In high good humor, and no doubt with a sense of courtesy, he then plied me with questions about the management of a castle, the answers to which could hardly have bored him more. Nevertheless, he kept his eyes pinned on me, and

I was relieved when at last he recollected himself and took an all-absorbing interest in the point between his horse's ears.

So the day passed.

When the sun was sinking into a gray west striped with amber, Gaston galloped back to inform us that he had already ordered the lowering of the drawbridge. The sun behind us now, I presently saw in the distance only part of the great, isolated castle that crowned a rugged, rising slope, the eastern half being enveloped in a vast, cold shadow. Hungerford looked to be older than Shrivenham, and it was bigger, more imposing, and certainly a great deal more forbidding, although I was too saddle weary to feel more than a vague apprehension as we approached it. If I was merely weary, Nan must have been numb from fatigue.

The hollow ring of our horses' hooves on the planks of the drawbridge revived me a little, my spirits encouraged further by the torchlight already flaring at the other end of the entry's tunnel. We were led through a large, cobbled bailey to the stables, warm and close with the smell of animal flesh. With Gavin's help, I dismounted, every bone creaking, and shook out my skirts and limbs. Nan did not move. Nor did she speak. Her face was rigid with painful discomfort. It took me a moment or two to realize that she was unable to dismount. I mentioned to the stablemaster that my maidservant needed help. Gaston went wordlessly to her side and ungently yanked her from the horse. She crumpled in his arms. He frowned a little and put her down gruffly before striding out of the stables, looking for all the world as if he had just come in from a pleasure ride.

Nan gathered her forces and came to my side when summoned. We were led into the hall. I could not say that we were officially welcomed, but there was a kind of disunified group in the hall apparently come to look over their new mistress. I could not determine from their faces if they were surprised, shocked, disappointed, or in any other way moved by my presence. The impassive faces before me, my husband's absence, and my own feelings of unsureness and hesitation so befitted every other aspect of my marriage thus far that I would have deemed any reception more cordial or formal to be entirely inappropriate.

One large form detached itself from the group, adjuring the curious, in his words, to bustle about and stop gawking. He was a great, burly bear of a man, with a slight limp, his arm in a sling, and a probably unhandsome but amiable countenance rendered hideous by a swollen cheek and black-and-blue eye. I guessed this to be John Potter. His introduction bore out the truth of my deduction.

"I heard about the attack on your life, Master John," I said, when we had exhausted the topics of the weather and the ride, "and I am glad that you suffered no more than a broken arm and a few bumps and bruises, but nothing that won't heal with time."

He grinned, the shiny flesh of his cheek stretched grotesquely over a large lump. "Call me John!" he invited. "I was never a pretty face, my lady, but you can imagine that mortal crestfallen I was when I saw my Josie—that's my wife, and you'll be meeting her tomorrow—and she noticed nothing amiss wi' my face!" He paused to enjoy a hearty laugh.

"I am sure she was just glad to see you alive," I said, not sure how best to manage so much self-deprecatory good humor.

"When I returned yesterday," he said, "I don't think she had heard how I was set to."

"You came back only yesterday?" I inquired. "I am sure that from the way Will described it you must have had a slow recovery."

"It were so, my lady," he said cheerfully. "It took me a full day and a half before I was on my feet again. Then another two to make it back here. God's blood! (if you'll pardon my Latin), mortal put out I were, and so I say, with such an important message I was carrying for the master. But I am a hard cove to snuff and can think of one man who may never walk again because of it. That's what happens when you tangle with John Potter!"

I was astounded. I had forgotten that John's attack must have come only five or six days before. My father's death had occurred not above a week ago, and I had been an unmarried girl but the day before. It seemed a lifetime ago.

"Although the important message never reached Shrivenham," I said, "you may console yourself that your unfortunate accident did not have a lasting adverse effect on the course of events. That is, if you consider the rather sudden and unexpected appearance of myself in your keep as a permanent ill, it was through no fault of the message not being delivered!"

"We'll just have to see, my lady, if you're a permanent ill or no'," he said with a mischievous twinkle, and I thought for all the world that he was going to nudge me humorously. I braced myself, but the attack did not come. I let out my breath slowly, relieved, for I could not have withstood at that moment physical contact from the bear, playful or otherwise.

"But as for being surprised," he continued, "never think it! I knew he was up to something when last I saw him, which is no cause for amusement, for the master is always in it thicker than flies." This he said with such bluff good nature that I did not believe he meant any evil by it. "And married, too! I could not be gladder of it. My Josie—my wife!—though her real name is Josette—has been needing some help around here, and if she is not here to give you good-eventide tonight, it's because she's assisting at a lying-in. God's throat (excuse me!), busy she is and will be fain to see you, for Hungerford's been without a lady three months or more."

I cast a swift glance about me. I was dead tired, but my homemaking instinct, which is inoperative only when I am asleep, told me that John had spoken the truth. The hall was not precisely unkempt, but the rushes were not newly laid, and from the appearance of this main room, I judged that Hungerford lacked nothing more than a woman's hand to make it presentable.

John remarked that we must be tired after the journey and offered to show us to our chambers, saying that we had likely never been received at a castle by a man who could carry both lady and servant to their chambers with one arm in a sling. I assured him I had not and doubted privately that it would add to my consequence to have him prove the boast. I made all haste to demonstrate that I was in no need of such assistance. I motioned to Nan to follow behind me, just in case she had any ideas about taking him up on his offer.

We arrived at the chambers where John assured us that he would have food and drink brought up to us "in an ant's foot." Off my private chamber was a small room for Nan, and I was cheered to find fires lit in both rooms. Nan looked too tired to eat or drink, so when I personally undressed her and put her to bed, she was unable to raise a hand or utter a word in protest.

My first impression of Hungerford as a masculine stronghold remained and even deepened on the days that followed my arrival. I now understood that Sir Roland had not overstated the case when he had said he could spare no woman from Hungerford to oversee Shrivenham. There were very few women in residence at Hungerford, and no one among them who was the acknowledged leader. Josette, perhaps, had acquired that position by default, and she reacted to my presence with something resembling relief. She was a gentlewoman whose birth was better than her husband's, but she was clearly under his thumb, and was as meek as he was outgoing. I also had the impression that she was afraid of me for some reason. I thought that with time I could win her over. As was expected, there were several women in the laundry and dairy, but none at all in the kitchen, and few to speak of in the house. As a consequence, most of the rooms were simply shut up and not used. I could assume only that the late earl, Roger, had done no receiving, and perhaps Sir Roland's father had had no use for guest rooms, either. I dropped many a hint to Josette that I would like to know how the castle had been run in the past generation, but she volunteered no information.

I took Nan with me everywhere. I was pleased that she had the good sense to expose none of her ignorance. She merely watched and listened and seemed quick to grasp the ways of a lady's maidservant. I was hopeful that she would become someone of importance to me in this otherwise unresponsive castle. When it came time for Gavin to take me on the extensive

tour of the stables, I mercifully spared Nan this painful reminder. I was still no expert at the end of the tour, but it did
not require a trained eye to recognize that the Guimont horses
were fine beauties. In fact, everything at Hungerford that touched
on hunting bespoke excellence. Gavin was proud to show me
the kennels where there were blooded hounds of all breeds,
most of which we did not have at Shrivenham. My interest,
however, was captivated by the falcons, and to satisfy my
curiosity, Gavin turned me over to the care of Master Thomas,
the falconer. One of the best-kept buildings in Hungerford's
courtyard, upon the master's orders, I was informed, was the
mews where the hawks roosted and where they took refuge
during molting season. This mews must have been a model
for others, and it surely put Shrivenham's to shame: it was
spacious enough to allow limited flight, had two windows, and
had a door large enough for the falconer to pass through with
a bird on his wrist. The floor was covered with gravel, which
Master Thomas changed at regular intervals. In the semidark-
ness inside, Master Thomas instructed me on the different birds
on the various perches. There were true falcons, or long-winged
hawks, including the gerfalcon, the peregrine, the saker, and
the lanner, contrasted with the short-winged hawks of the spar-
row variety. I found myself fascinated with falconry and would
often pause, in the weeks to come, to observe a falcon weath-
ering on one of the low stone blocks outside the mews whenever
I crossed the bailey. I would also come to know well Master
Thomas, who, like his hawks, was proud, fierce, and tem-
peramental, which was probably why I liked him so much.

I hesitated beginning any project while Sir Roland was in
absence. The Michaelmas had come and gone while I was at
Shrivenham, and with it the beginning of the castle's fiscal
year, which I had recorded. In my set of tally books at any
rate. I doubted that Sir Roland would ask me to keep the
accounts at Hungerford. The fields had already been harvested,
so there was little in that area for me to manage. We had come
to the slaughter time, what the Saxons called, with reason, the
blood month. I did not think I was taking too much upon myself
to see to the smoking and salting of the meats for the winter.

Saint Martin's Day was upon us, and still Sir Roland had not returned. I thought it only appropriate to celebrate the Martinmas with the traditional cakes, pasties, and frumenty. I set aside several days to put the hall to rights, and borrowed several women from the laundry to help: I was happy to have had the foresight to bring smock and kerchief for myself as well as Nan and ordered the making of these linen cleaning clothes for five other women. I simply did not like to see inside women scrubbing and washing in plain kirtles. We laid new rushes, dusted and oiled the furniture, washed the windows, and cleaned out the two wide fireplaces that faced each other across the wide expanse of the wood-vaulted room. There was surprise to a person, including Gavin, to see me working alongside my women, but none so great as when I ordered the lowering of the Guimont coat-of-arms from above one of the fireplaces for a thorough cleansing. It took four men to get it down and several hours to remove the crust of many years. It was a massive but finely crafted escutcheon; I watched with satisfaction during the cleaning process how its dusty and tarnished magnificence was restored to its original brilliance. It was an impressive seal and when cleaned became instantly a focal point of the hall: its huge eagle in flight, gripping a peregrine hawk, against the four alternating squares, two gold, two blue, underlined by the Latin words, I PREVAIL etched on a gilded scroll, could not fail to catch the eyes of all who entered.

In the evenings, Nan and I would stitch in my antechamber. She was, in all honesty, a miserable seamstress. It was such a waste to have her at my side, where I had to reset almost every seam she made, not to mention having to remove the little drops of blood from the material that would result from endless needle pricks, instead of having her work the dough in the kitchens. I tried to think of ways to get her where she belonged, but nothing occurred to me, so for now we were condemned to each other's company. It took an amazingly long time, but eventually we achieved some suitable clothes for ourselves in the Guimont colors of blue and gold.

I filled the idle hours exploring the castle grounds and manor house. One afternoon, when I had been at Hungerford for over

a sennight, I put Nan to good use in the kitchens and invested
her with the task of showing three or four of the boys there
how to achieve a light pastry crust. I then went adventuring.
I wandered down an unused wing of the house and came upon
a very curious wooden door. My pulse quickened unaccountably. I tried the handle and ascertained that it was locked. Some
fumbling with the heavy ring of keys, which Josette had speedily given me and which now hung at my belt, produced one
that looked likely to fit the little lock. I jiggled the key gently
and eventually heard the bolt slide rustily from the catch. The
door creaked protest against my curiosity, but opened at my
persistence onto a room that charmed me almost as much as
it intrigued me.

It was a funny, angular room and very small, suggesting
that the builder of this wing of the manor house, discovering
that he had miscalculated in joining the wing to the main part
of the house, decided, whimsically, to create a nook, a little
wrinkle in the line of the building, and then had put a wall
and a door around it and claimed it as a room. It was a charming
space, and one that had apparently been put to some use. That
must have been years ago, however, for the dust had settled,
glazing over the memories, and the room was now a fairyland
of cobwebs. The light was dim and made dimmer by the years
of dirt covering the little leaded window. I tried several times
to pry it open, and just as I was on the point of giving up it
swung noisily on its hinges, and I was surprised to look down
over a small, oddly shaped pleasance, somehow in consonance
with the little room where I stood. The garden seemed to exist
solely for the benefit of the view from this window, for no
others looked down upon it. A cock pheasant, pacing across
the garden, disturbed momentarily by my prying eyes, froze
into an instant's immobility, and then, as though he knew
himself safe from me, resumed his stately progress. He was
threatened from no other quarter, for it was a private place
with a high wall that had access through only one closed gate
and which, when I had mentally weeded it, promised beauty.

I turned against the window and took stock of the little
room. There were two large settles, never covered, several side

tables, a small trunk, something resembling a desk, and out of a cranny even a fireplace had been conjured. It gaped now cold and silent, yet with my mind's eye I saw it stoked and blazing gaily, making the room cozy and warm. I went to the desk and rummaged through its drawers, without bothering to chide myself for prying. In one of them I found a delicately illuminated Book of Hours, far more exquisite than my own, depicting the tranquil castle life as it must be lived in someone's mind where the sky is never gray, and then below it a bestiary, wildly and colorfully illuminated. I instantly fell in love with the artist's imagination, which did not stop at lions, tigers, and monkeys but went on to illustrate basilisks and unicorns and all manner of exotic animals to which I could assign no names, each sensually, almost lovingly, represented. I did not think that Friar Helm, whose dry imagination governed an austere sense of aesthetics, would have approved. In another drawer I discovered a tiny, polished pewter hand mirror, with a thin but sturdy ribbon attached to its handle. I had never owned one myself, but I had seen women at court carry such from their belts and keep them hidden in the folds of their skirts. I could not resist picking it up and studying my image. A startled face looked back at me. I was incapable of judging whether the blue of my eyes was as pale as my father's had been. It seemed a trivial point, so I put the mirror gingerly back in its place and closed the drawer. I did not know which lady's sitting and sewing room this had been; I knew only that I wanted to make it mine. Before leaving, I locked the door again against other trespassers.

The first week grew into two, bringing no sign of my husband. There came no word from him, either. No one betrayed the slightest alarm at his prolonged absence and silence, least of all Gavin, who had a touching, boyish faith in Sir Roland's infallibility; no one seemed to question Sir Roland's authority at Hungerford, even in absentia, or his right to it, and, above all, no one responded to my queries, be they never so subtle, about the night in July when Sir Roger fell down the wide stone stairs leading to the hall. It was hard, every time I used those stairs, which was often, not to think of Sir Roger's death, Sir Roland, Isabelle, and how their lives had become entwined with mine.

As the events of that fateful evening when Roger fell to his death began to preoccupy me more and more, the less I was able to elicit any information from the Hungerford folk. One evening while Nan and I were stitching by the fire in my antechamber, I asked her, ever so casually, if she knew anything about the incident. She was hardly deceived by my tactics and broke into one of her rare smiles. It made her look as youthful as her seventeen years.

"I don't think it's a matter that will be answered," she said, "at least not to your satisfaction."

She likely was right. Nevertheless, I pursued into the opening. "If you do hear anything, I would appreciate it if you would tell me—however unsatisfying it might prove to me."

"I don't hear much that you don't," she said simply, and then added reflectively, "I'm not in circulation much."

"Do you think I have tied you to my skirts?" I said, laughing. "For all of our combined frustrations at the evenings we spend together sewing—and you must believe that I suffer every bit as much as you do!—at least I have the peace of mind of knowing how and where you spend your time."

She took this mild reproof in good part. "There's naught to tempt me here," she said with her own wry humor.

I wondered if this referred to my husband's absence, but then realized later that this comment was merely her way of letting me know that she would not risk disgracing herself or me.

"Do you pine for your Edric, Nan?"

She smiled again, this time with less confidence. "Let us just say that I do," she said. "But I don't despair."

"I'm glad," I said, and left it at that. We both bent our heads over our work again.

A week after that, I was descending the main stairs well before the horn was to blow to bring everyone to the evening table. Something prompted me to stop at the bottom of the stairs and to scrutinize the floor for some sign of foul play. There was, of course, no trace of anything, but I stared for more than a brief moment, lost in abstraction.

"This is not the place," I heard a voice say behind me.

I gave a start and whirled around to face an old woman I had seen before, perhaps in the laundry. I could not remember her name. "Pardon me?" I said.

"This is not the place," the old woman repeated.

"I am afraid I do not understand you," I said, making every effort to sound genuinely confused, but my heart thudded uncontrollably, and I must have looked nervous. I tried my best, however, to look back at her as steadily as she measured me. She had been pretty once, I thought, but now her beauty was blurred by the harsh lines of age and something else again. Sadness? Bitterness? Whatever marred her face had not also blinded her. Her eyes were the sharpest I had ever seen, much like those of the gerfalcon Master Thomas had told me was used to hunt small game hidden in brush and swamp.

"You were looking at the foot of the stairs," she said. "It has been cleaned up by now and the dead buried, as you might expect, although there was no mess to begin with, you see. There never is when someone falls. But these were not the stairs."

"I know I have met you before," I said, steadfastly ignoring her comments, "but your name escapes me."

"Gunhild. My name is Gunhild," she said.

I came one step further toward my goal of learning every retainer's name before Sir Roland's return. I was not now likely to forget Gunhild's.

She did not move on. Her watchful eye made me suddenly self-conscious. I searched for a plausible explanation for my interest in this spot.

"I stopped here to look for one of my rings that I seem to have lost," I said. "I thought I might have dropped it here."

"You never wear aught but your wedding band," she said.

I was rendered speechless for a moment or two. Her eyes were sharper than I had thought. "I am glad to know, then, that these stairs are not dangerous," I said at last, "and that one need not fear a fall."

I should have dismissed her then. Perhaps I should have continued on my way, but I could not command myself to leave just when I was so close to learning something.

A smile not calculated to warm my heart displayed a set of even, white teeth. She must have been beautiful once. "These stairs could serve the purpose, so cold and hard," she said when she was sure of my attention. "Never doubt it! But he died on the wooden stairs that lead to the back bailey."

The dead man had, as yet, remained unnamed. "Sir Roger?"

"Aye."

"Could the stairs be rickety and perhaps treacherous?"

"Perhaps."

"So it could have been an accidental fall," I said, hoping to end the matter.

There came no response.

"Did you see it happen?" I tried again.

Her falcon's eyes flickered. "No," she said, "I did not have to."

"Do you know the truth about what happened that night?"

"I know what I know," came the reply.

"Then pray tell me what you know." I had become bold indeed.

She paused momentarily. "Sir Guy's ways are strange," she said, "but he always has a reason."

She, with her keen eyes, must have seen flash across my face the pain in my breast.

She shook a crooked finger at me. "If you don't like the answers you should not ask questions," she said.

It seemed undignified to point out to her that she had not precisely answered my question.

"Sir Roger—was—a bad lord?" The words came thickly from my throat. I swallowed hard.

"Few mourned his passing," she said. "In sooth, I know of only one man who grieved, and even he was not likely to have shed a tear."

I longed to discover the identity of this lone mourner, but I did not think she would tell me. She seemed to be teasing me, tantalizing me, and I did not know if I could trust her. Instead, I asked in a voice barely above a whisper, "Are you saying that Sir Roger's death was justified?"

She did not answer that; it deserved no answer, for it was a silly question, and I could have answered it myself.

"You are not mistress here," she said suddenly, in rather ominous tones.

Such a remark did not increase my self-confidence. One of Lady Isolde's maxims came happily to mind: "Authority is for those who use it," and I had every intention of using mine. "I feel compelled to inform you," I said evenly, "that I am indeed mistress here."

"Another woman rules in your place," she said, ignoring my assertion.

"We hardly need argue the point," I said, "for I am Sir Roland's lawful wife."

"I know the law," she said, "and hope it brings you comfort in the future. But you are not like her, you are not like the other Guimont women."

"Since there are so few women here," I said, "it is hard to say what the Guimont women are like."

"One does not have to bear the name Guimont to belong here," she said. "You are not like them, and if you do not know it now, you shall soon discover it."

"I am a Guimont now," I insisted, "and I carry the name. You would do well to remember it."

"Have it as you wish," she said, "for it is as you say: you are the master's lawful wife. I bid you good eventide, but you shall get no rest this night."

At these words, I, who had had every intention of bringing her insolence to a summary end, irrationally wanted her to stay and explain herself. Short of physically detaining her, however, there was nothing I could do to keep her at my side. She vanished the next moment, almost before my eyes. I had to give myself a mental shake: Gunhild was just an old woman, not a sorceress commanding mystic powers of perception, and

I was a prosaic creature, when all was said, one not given to superstition or dark reflection on cryptic utterances. "You are not mistress here," and, "Another woman rules in your place," she had said, but these phrases, without her presence before me, rang with empty drama. There was no place for two mistresses in the daily workings of the castle, and not one retainer had, to date, shown any reluctance to obey any of my commands. Gunhild had not, at any rate, questioned the legality of my marriage, but I was not so naive that I had not also considered that she might have been referring to other women in Sir Roland's life. I knew nothing about that aspect of his life and was unlikely to learn about it soon. Faceless, nameless women who had had a hold on my husband for no more than a night could not trouble my sleep. I thought it far more likely, upon second thought, that Gunhild's "other woman" referred to some mistress past, one of Sir Roger's wives, perhaps, or even Sir Roland's mother, whom Gunhild must have served in her youth. I wasted no further thought on the problem, for I was my own mistress and knew how to manage as well as anyone. The knowledge that one man had grieved for Sir Roger did bother me. Was that a warning that someone within the castle walls was unsympathetic to Sir Roland's lordship? I immediately discounted Gavin and John Potter as possible rebels, and Gaston was too much like his master to be anything but one with him.

Gunhild had not witnessed Sir Roger's fall—that much I believed—but she had a clear idea that it had been murder, and she was not alone in pointing the finger at Sir Roland. She was not all-seeing, nor was she a sorceress, but I had a feeling that she was not telling me all she knew. My dislike of her implications made them no less true. The truth is not a pliable thing, and I could not shape it to suit my taste.

Morbid curiosity sent me in the direction of the wooden stairs, but before I reached the back bailey, Josette bustled up to me and announced in fearful accents that I was receiving visitors.

When I regained the hall, I was not entirely surprised to see Lady Constance coming forward to greet me with a smile as sour as the rind of lemons. In her train came Charles, coached to silence.

"My dearest child. Marguerite!" she said in her faint, plaintive voice. "How I am torn between the joy at your marriage and the sorrow at your father's death!"

Despite this comment, her opening remarks did not concern themselves with the particulars of my life; rather, she found the breath, though it came with difficulty at times, to describe in detail the extreme fragility of her health, which *recent news* had dealt several severe blows, and through it all she led me to believe that she had borne with noble fortitude all the trials that had beset her. Her only consolation was, she told me in the manner of a fair merchant mournfully demonstrating the superiorities of his product over the one a hapless shopper misguidedly bought at another booth, that Charles enjoyed such an excellent constitution.

"Nevertheless, my dear," she continued, "am I truly the first to wish you health and happiness, as I so hoped I would be?"

"I had well-wishers among the wedding party at Shrivenham, and Alicia Longchamps was there," I said, "but you are my first visitors at Hungerford."

This seemed to please her. "Your first visitors? Well! You must tell me all about it! I cannot help but think that the wedding was rather sudden. Did you have many guests? I cannot think that you did, else we would have been invited, but perhaps in your grief you forgot how close we Hartfords have always stood to your family. That is, you did learn of your dear father's death *before* the wedding, did you not? That is the story circulating, I feel it my duty to inform you!"

I affirmed that I had learned the news of his death two days before the wedding and explained the irregularity by mentioning how, on his deathbed, my father had summoned Sir Roland to his side and offered him my hand. Sir Roland had graciously agreed to the arrangement, attracted, I told her in a confidential tone, by the Montcrief lands, which, when joined to the Guimont estate, made a pretty piece of property.

"I had heard something of your father's—unusual request," she said in a fading voice, which I admired for its affectation of disinterest, "and I also heard—my dear child!—that your husband left you almost the moment after you were wedded! Is this true? And is he here with you now? I would so love to congratulate him."

"Yes, he did leave almost immediately, and no, he is not here now."

"Surely he did not depart so quickly as to leave you a wife in name only?" she said in her sweetly acidic voice.

"Lady Constance, you did not travel all these miles to discover whether my husband and I had our wedding night!"

"My, dear, *dear* Marguerite, how you do take one up on things. I asked you to tell me all about it! You need not be so modest. That has always been your way with me," she complained. "You do not answer my questions."

"Then I shall answer this question by asking another," I said. "How likely is it that Sir Roland did not consummate the marriage?"

She acknowledged that with a tight smile and tried another tack. She stood back and beheld me. "My dear, *what* have you done to your hair?"

"Do you like it?" I said. "I do not usually circulate without a coif as I am now, but I saw women at court knot their hair at the nape of the neck and liked it very well. I have knitted this net with silver thread and pearls to offer a contrast with my hair."

"It is very becoming," she said, "and makes you look so— much older, which is your object, is it not, my child? And your dress. It is so—blue!"

"For Guimont," I said. "I chose to trim it in gray, for I thought black too mournful for a new bride, despite my bereavement."

"Times have changed," she sighed, "but you look charming. Is it not cut rather full about the waist—perhaps to accommodate a growing figure? Or do I only imagine it?"

She only imagined it. This very morning, just as I had suspected, I had received confirmation that I was not breeding. I had never dared hope to be as lucky as Alicia, so I was not downcast. Lady Constance did not need to know my barren state; it could only bring her joy, for the possibility of an heir would seriously complicate her plans. One look at Charles was all the resolution I needed to keep Lady Constance guessing.

I assumed the demeanor of modest confusion. "It is too early to tell," I said, eyes cast down, "so I took the precaution of cutting all my dresses a little larger."

She surveyed me once again critically, murmured, "What foresight!" and then decided, after all, that the apparent fullness of the dress was due rather to a weight loss. "For it is only natural, my dear, that you should look slightly pale and not at all robust with the shock of your father's death still so fresh."

"It did come as a shock to me," I said in all honesty. "I would never have thought his stomach ailment would prove fatal! But there you have it! Sir Roland informed me of both Sir Maurice's death and his dying request, although Sir Roland tactfully spared me the details of my father's suffering."

"Oh, indeed!" She shuddered delicately. "I am sure that his end was quite, *quite* horrible. But I, unlike you, was not surprised. No, do not look at me so! Few understand what a person of ill health must endure!"

"Pray excuse my bad manners, my lady," I said, interrupting a promising start to an instructive discourse on the inconveniences of every ailment known to man, "for I am sure you would like to refresh yourself before the evening meal after so tiring a journey. And Charles—"

I turned to him, but his fond mother spared him the necessity of any direct conversation with me.

"Charles, pay your respects to Lady Marguerite," she said in a way that reminded me of a tone that Dame Ellen might have taken with Thomas in a moment of good humor, "and run along. Why don't you go see to our horses? Yes, that is an excellent idea. Go to the stables and make sure they are being well attended to. Now, what is that boy's name whose hair is so very red? Well, I am sure I have forgotten, but he would be honored if you condescended to talk to him. You have always been so clever with horses, my dear, and perhaps you could give him some advice."

Charles's hesitation indicated that he might have had other ideas about how he wanted to spend his time.

"Charles—" she said in a light manner darkened with impatience, "do as your mama tells you."

Her obedient offspring took my hand and bowed over it. Before releasing it, he looked up at me and achieved an expression between a pout and a leer, a combination I had not seen on a human face before.

I could not resist saying, "I think it more likely that you will find Gavin in the back yard practicing with the quintain. Perhaps you can persuade him to let you tilt at it, too."

"Such a comfort he is to me at this time," Lady Constance said with a sigh at his retreating bulk.

"How sad it will be for you when he marries," I commented. "Shall I show you to your chambers?"

"There is no talk of marriage, my dear," she replied, following in my wake.

"Oh?" I said with every appearance of mistaken surprise. "I had thought that you had begun to look on Joan of Shrewsbury as a daughter."

"Joan of Shrewsbury?"

"You are not looking toward an alliance with her house?"

"The Shrewsburys are very well, but I cannot yet bear to part with the dear child," she said. "These stairs are very steep, my dear, and could prove dangerous. Mark my word! But Charles is still far too young to be contracted in marriage— as many opportunities as he has had! What is the hurry, after all? The times are so uncertain. So much can happen. Just think what has changed in the course of the last moon. In your life, for instance."

"Would you like to pause for breath after the climb? No? Then turn to your right, and your room is not far from the landing. Well situated, I think," I said. "It was a trying time for me at first, I admit, but all has settled down, and I am comfortably settled into my role as a married woman."

"You shall bring on one of my spasms with all this talk of marriage," she said. "My heart is not well, not well at all.

How I have suffered since hearing about the loss of my dear friend, your father!" She dabbed her eyes with a thoroughly wrung hand linen that she withdrew from her sleeve. "Maurice was such a companion to me—and a faithful correspondent. How I shall miss him! I do so already. I could only wonder when I received no word from him this summer. And then nothing from him at Alicia's wedding!"

"Perhaps he was too sick to write you," I suggested helpfully.

"He was never too sick to write!" she said. "It always seemed to ease the pain so. I feared the worst after I received nothing in August. Are you quite sure he gave you no message for me?"

"Quite sure," I lied, and bent to fit a key into the lock on one of the chamber doors.

"Come now, dear! In the rush of the wedding preparations, the excitement, was there not something you have forgotten?"

I paused with my fingers on the handle. "My memory is not so short," I said. "Here we are. I think you will find that since the wind comes from the north, the chimneys in this wing of the house do not smoke. I shall place Charles next door."

"Thank you. The room is quite tolerable," she said. "Came you across nothing addressed to me in your father's personal papers?"

"I did not think to look," I responded. "How very careless of me! But what should there be?"

"I do not know, my dear, but perhaps only something to remind a suffering woman of a dear friend. I should so love to have a look at his correspondence. He had such an excellent writing style, and a fine hand for letters!"

"Then I invite you to go to Shrivenham and see for yourself," I said. "I do not know, of course, what documents of my father's may be in Sir Roland's possession. I do know, however, that he spent some time in my father's receiving chambers going over my tally books."

She dropped the matter abruptly and backed off from the questioning at such close range. She sank into a chair. "Two blows at once," she said, sobbing into her handkerchief. "It has been so difficult for me the past weeks."

I pulled up a chair next to her and sat down. "Two?"

"Yes, my dear," she said, trying to master her grief. "A second of my friends is gone now. Right after your father— passed on—I learned the news of this other death. It was enough to carry me away that very evening! My heart fluttered so violently—! But I do not speak of that—you know I do not!"

"My dear lady, I am so sorry for you! Who was this second friend?"

"Gervase Frant. A fine man, so distinguished! So dependable!"

"I do not think I was acquainted with him. The name does not even sound familiar. I am naturally grieved for you, dear lady, since I do not know the Frants and cannot grieve with them."

"Perhaps you never met him. Did your husband not inform you of his death?"

"If the gentleman died after my father, it is probable that Sir Roland knew nothing about it, for he was already at Shrivenham, or at least on his way."

She nodded her head mournfully and murmured that that must have been why Sir Roland had not informed me of it.

"How did he die?" I asked. "Was he ailing, too?"

"A hunting accident," she said and shuddered eloquently. "His body was found lying under a bush in the woods not far from Canterbury—gored! It is said that a wild boar must have attacked him, but I believe there was foul play, for it is also said that he seemed to have been dead for several days."

"How does that suggest foul play?"

"All his money was gone." She moaned. "I believe he was carrying a certain amount of gold on his person. He owed me several thou— But it is not the money! He was robbed, there is no doubt about it. There is treachery everywhere in the kingdom. It has become so that one now fears to travel abroad!"

I had nothing to respond.

"So much bad news," she continued after a moment. "But life goes on, and I find, to my sadness, that it is a frivolous world we live in. One pauses to mourn the passing of two such fine men as your father and Sir Gervase only until the next news scuttles through the court. Such an idle, vain world! The news of your wedding reduced all other—shall we call it gossip?—all other gossip, then, to insignificance."

"Did you hear of my marriage at court, then?"

"Why, yes, my dear. I go there now and now. I arrived in London a couple of weeks ago to discover that your father had died the week before! O Unlucky Star that I should have missed seeing him by so short a space! Need I repeat that it grieved me terribly? No, for you see how I am affected! Then I heard the news of Sir Gervase, and then came your marriage. Everyone was reeling under impact of so much news. Your marriage, of course, became the instant topic of conversation, as you can imagine."

"Holy Mother, news travels fast!" I said, in spite of myself. "We could have been married scarcely a day or two when you heard."

"In your case, of course, it was quite understandable, for your husband was seen at court. *I* did not deign to—that is, I did not see him, but I was told he was there. No doubt with the express purpose of announcing it. But then you knew he was going there."

"Naturally," I said.

"But you have had no other visitors?" she inquired again. "No bride-visits?"

I reiterated that she had indeed the honor of being first. "I have not been idle, however, nor do I languish without company. There has been so much to learn about my new home. I can scarce believe that it has almost been a month already! The Holy Season shall be upon us before long, which quite takes my breath away. I do not think Sir Roland and I shall make bride-visits upon his return, for it is too cold now to travel long distances, and as for visitors, I should not like to receive large numbers when he is not here with me."

"You must await your husband's return! Of course, you must

wait until he is at home before you receive large numbers of visitors. That is, naturally, why everyone is waiting to pay you visits. I am quite different, however, and do not consider myself a visitor. No, I am one of the family, and thus can tell you to take a care and do what is proper. There are so many other irregularities that attend your marriage that it is . . . Well—!"

An awkward second of silence fell.

"Since I have had no other visitors, you must, of course, tell me all the latest news—besides my marriage," I said calmly, for she was not able to throw me off my stride so easily.

She paused in thoughtful consideration. "News! I have no news! My mind was wholly taken up with the dual tragedies of your father and Sir Gervase. Such sadness! Did I also mention that the Frant emeralds seem to have disappeared just before his body was discovered? I tell you, there was foul play!"

"The Frant emeralds?" I echoed. My heart began to beat irregularly.

"Why, yes! A beautiful necklace-and-bracelet set. Sir Gervase was used to boast about them. *That* is what killed him! The rumors have become quite garbled as to what actually happened to them, but I believe he had brought them to court to pay off his debts—the poor man had so many debts! he was literally crushed by them!—and then he was robbed and beaten to death. Oh, the injustice of it has kept me awake for weeks! I suffer so from insomnia, you know."

"This is a coincidence," I said, very unsure of myself. "Do not the Guimonts have emeralds, too?"

"The Guimonts have rubies, my dear," she said matter-of-factly.

I should have been ready. I had rehearsed a dozen times with myself in the weeks past all the various angles from which she might attack me, and I should have been ready for anything from her, but these disclosures caught me off guard.

"I did not know it," I said, unable to think of anything else to say.

"But—" she broke off artistically and pinned on a fading smile. "Of course, there is no particular reason why you should have known that. It is early days yet, and as you have said, you have much to learn about your new home. You know, I had tried to warn you against— But when has youth listened to the wisdom of age?" She sighed in mournful reflection on this verity.

Her arrows had struck home, as she must have known they would. Knowing that she was aiming her poisonous shafts at me did not in any way alleviate their sting.

"When does your husband return, my dear?" she asked. "Surely he has been keeping you informed of his movements."

"Any day now he could return," I replied, entirely distracted.

Scarcely had the words left my mouth than I heard a general commotion belowstairs, some masculine shouts in the bailey, and movement in the hall. It would have been too good to be true if it were Sir Roland returning home. Then the horn blew for the evening meal.

"I must leave you now, Lady Constance. I hope you will join us shortly."

"My dearest Marguerite," she said as I was about to leave, "my faithful Agnes was unable to make the journey with me, so I am completely without a maidservant. Would you please have one of your women come up and lay the fire here? It has turned so very cold and my bones ache so."

I left her then, thoughts jostling one another in my brain as I descended the stairs. A visceral intuition informed me that Sir Roland had come back, and my confusion over the dreadful emeralds was exacerbated by the guilt I felt at having received Lady Constance without Sir Roland's knowledge. He could not know that I had not sent for her; he did know, since he had not written me one missive since his departure from Shrivenham, that I had no idea of his date of return. It would be easy enough for him to assume that he had, by good fortune, tumbled onto our scheming.

I emerged into the hall just in time to see Sir Roland stride through the main portal, two great hunting hounds flanking his sides. He looked lean and hard and in command of himself; his presence immediately filled the hall and brought it to life.

I fancied, erratically, that the flames in both fireplaces blazed brighter at his entrance, that the room grew suddenly warmer, more alive and vibrant. I blinked in disbelief that flesh and blood could so tangibly transform the inanimate, but the impression remained: he had brought with him his urgency and vitality, the essence of his being, and the very room breathed with him.

Sir Roland snapped his fingers and his two *lévriers* left him to stretch luxuriously on the hearth, their gray coats gleaming in the firelight; now that their master was home again, they were obviously content to take up sentry at what must have been their accustomed posts.

In the next moment he was at my side. He took my hand and brought it to his lips before gathering me into his arms and kissing me in full view of all interested eyes. I momentarily forgot where I was. I had the oddest sensation of suffering a shock, I even felt a trifle dizzy and it was several moments after he had released me before I could focus on anything but his tunic. It was his customary gray, travel-worn but clean. He smelled of the out-of-doors.

When I finally did look up, he was regarding me with a half-smile flirting at the corners of his mouth. "The five days grew into a week, and the one week grew into several," he said. His words did not have the ring of apology. "I trust you go on well."

I could not scold him, and it took some resolution to refrain from asking him where he had been. "Very well, my lord," I replied. "I have devoted all my energies to becoming adjusted to Hungerford."

He cast his eyes around the room, registered approval, and then dropped them on me, where they lingered. "All is in order here," he said. "Have you encountered any problems?"

"No," I assured him quickly and proceeded to babble a little. "None! I have learned almost everyone's name. Your—our people have been most cooperative, but I hesitated starting any grand projects until your return. I could not guess if you would like anything changed here. There are a few things I would like to do, although everything was most satisfactory when I arrived!"

"You do not need my permission for anything you choose to do," he said curtly. "You are mistress here."

"Oh, yes! Of course!" I said, and without further preamble I rushed headlong into the matter most on my mind. "But we have visitors! Lady Constance and Charles are come!"

"I am aware of this circumstance."

"They arrived but an hour ago—nay, a spare half-hour ago! Most unexpected!"

"Then it is too bad that I did not return a few days later and avoid their company completely," he said easily.

"You do not mind?" I asked cautiously.

He put my hand on his arm and led me to the head table. "You might say that I am not altogether displeased. What is for dinner? I am heartily sick of dried meat and Will's cooking."

The meals at Hungerford were attended with much less formality and more conviviality than I was used to. There was an easy camaraderie floating throughout the hall, with Sir Roland comfortable in the lord's chair, and I chanced to look up once and see even Gaston smiling. I had never seen Sir Roland so much at repose, but then I had never seen the lion in his own den before. Even the presence of Lady Constance on his right had no power to alter his mood. Unfortunately, I could not say that I was equally undisturbed by Charles on my left, but the knowledge that my husband was present greatly eased my mind.

I did my best to swallow my disgust for Charles and tried to maintain decent conversation with him. It was impossible, however, and the talk soon degenerated, on his part, to veiled insults, a mild threat or two, and culminated in the wholly incredible observation: "What an odd thing I find your wedding, little Grita, and here I was telling everybody how hot you were after Hugh Falmouth!"

My attention was caught just then by Lady Constance's voice pronouncing the word *emeralds,* and so I suppressed an angry retort. I kept my head turned toward Charles but I was no longer attending to his vulgarities. I strained one ear to catch

Sir Roland's response. I gathered, only imperfectly, the essence of their conversation.

"That is correct," Sir Roland said. "Lady Guimont owns a set of emeralds."

I could not hear Constance's reply, for she was speaking very low, but Sir Roland said, "Yes, I believe they are."

To Constance's next comment, I heard, "My dear lady, I own it quite willingly! I did not steal them from Frant, I bought them from our king."

A weight lifted from my heart. The lightness lasted only until I heard him say at the next interval, "As it turns out, you see, I could well afford it."

I supposed he could. He had bought them, it became clear to me now, in anticipation of the money my estate would bring him, since his lands, by his own admission, had been badly managed. Still, the jewels were mine, and if I never wore them, they nevertheless lay ice cold in my strongbox as my security against Sir Roland's death.

Sir Roland presently turned to me.

"I have taken the liberty, my lady," he said, "of sending some of my men to Shrivenham to bring back your father's receiving-chamber furniture. My counting rooms stand bare at present, and I noticed that his was very serviceable. Instead of employing the carpenters to make new, I thought it easiest to use the things at Shrivenham that have no more value there."

I nodded my approval and saw Lady Constance listening to this passage. She leaned over Sir Roland just then to speak to me.

"My dear Marguerite," she said, "I have discovered the perfect solution to your predicament."

"My predicament?" I said.

"Why, yes. Your wedding was such a hurried, private affair, and no one has had the opportunity to wish you well. You remember what we were saying earlier about doing what is proper? I am sure you do, for we have such an excellent understanding between us! And it is most just and proper, now that the Christmas season is fast upon us, that you host the celebration."

"It is too late," I said hastily. "Sir Roland has just returned, and I have too little time to prepare the celebration befitting our friends."

Lady Constance dismissed those objections by offering her help. "Oh, no, no!" I said, and became involved in some rather tangled remonstrations.

My husband came to my rescue. "We shall see," he said. "The idea is not without merit, and I feel quite certain that my wife can handle all the preparations on her own."

Lady Constance knew when to retreat and strategically turned the subject. It was not long before Sir Roland gave the signal that the meal was over and that everyone was free to engage in the evening's leisure. It soon became obvious to one and all what my husband had on his mind for his entertainment. At a very early hour, he escorted me ceremoniously out of the hall.

What we found to talk about on our way to our chambers I could never afterward remember. But talk I did. Torchlight licked the cold stones of the hallways; I shivered.

"Are you cold, my lady?" he asked politely.

We had reached the wing where our suite of rooms was situated. I was too distracted to return an answer. Instead, I stopped abruptly outside the door leading into my own private chambers.

"You have been away almost a full month, my lord," I began hesitantly.

He remained silent.

"A c-cycle of the moon, t-twenty-eight days," I stammered.

"I perceive," he said gravely, "that you do not offer these comments in the spirit of a reproach."

"No, not a reproach!"

The normally harsh lines of his face softened somewhat. "Is this a gentle, wifely hint that I am to busy myself for the next few nights with the accounts?"

"I am sure you have much of that sort of work to do," I said, enthusiastically seconding that idea, "after such a long absence."

"My disappointment on both counts," he said after a pause,

"is mitigated only by the knowledge that there is much time before us."

"Both counts?" I said stupidly and then blushed rosily.

"All things take time," he said calmly, "and there is no hurry."

"Is there not?"

"Not that I am aware of."

"Lady Constance—"

"Is just where I want her," he said meaningfully. I realized then that Lady Constance was to him much like Nan was to me. I liked having her under my nose.

"I am happy that you are returned," I said, relieved to have been understood so quickly.

"I am reasonably content myself," he said, "and have but one small quarrel with my homecoming."

I did not trust myself to speak again. I moved to go; he stopped me by placing his hands lightly on my shoulders. Putting one hand under my chin, he lifted my face to his. He did not kiss me, but he stood close above me, searching my face. After a moment, he let his hands drop and bowed his good-night.

When Nan came to her chamber later, I was still awake. It was to be a sleepless night for me, my repose hampered by cramps and bad dreams and the recollection that Gunhild's prediction that I would get no rest this night had proved entirely correct.

Chapter 10

A new bride is bound to make mistakes, I told myself over and over. This reassurance, however, did nothing to relieve my embarrassment, nor did the dusting and sweeping of that curious chamber I intended for my sewing room. But the vigorous housework did release some of the anger I felt at my own stupidity. What hurt most about it, I thought as I polished and arranged my room, was that I had been trying to do the right thing, and it took several days of cleaning before I could face with any equanimity the unflattering conclusion that I still had a thing or two to learn about being a woman. "You are too foolish for words," I muttered severely to the tapestry in my hands. The green-and-gold finch coming to life on the canvas did not sing out to contradict me.

How had I come to act so foolishly? Was I really so devoid of feminine wiles? I could only wonder at myself later when I realized how stupid—how *very* stupid—it was of me to think to talk to my husband of insignificant domestic details in a formal manner more suited to an exchange between lord and bailiff.

I had been inclined, at first, to blame my stupidity on my relief at Lady Constance's departure, but such an explanation was far too indulgent. She and Charles stayed only four days, and they were nerve-racking days for me. Sir Roland kept his distance from them during the days and played the cordial but slightly disinterested host to them in the evenings. He kept his distance from me, too, and allowed me all the privacy I wanted with Lady Constance, which was really very little. Yet, I was duty bound to entertain her, and therefore had to spend a large part of my days with her. She was wise enough to tread warily on subjects of vital interest to her, and she kept Charles out of my way. She did not even mention Sir Roland again until the moment of her departure.

"An odd thing it is," she said after she had already been handed onto her litter, "to warn a wife against conceiving an *attachment* to her husband, but so it is. His is a sadly unsteady character, my dear, and I hope that he has not affected you too much, for I know how susceptible girls can be!"

"N-not at all!" I assured her.

"Very well, Marguerite," she said with her sickly smile, "you shall see soon enough what I mean. Until Christmas, my dear!"

"Godspeed!" I returned, and promptly forgot her warning, thinking it to be just another of her venomous barbs intended to set me up for Sir Roland's betrayal.

The day of their departure, I learned that Sir Roland, contrary to his custom, would not be riding out at all and was attending to business in his counting rooms. There were certain rooms in the castle whose thresholds I had never crossed. One was, naturally, my husband's private bedchamber, and another was his counting rooms. I knew well enough where the latter were, and when I got there, there were already several people lined up outside the antechamber, apparently waiting for an interview with the lord. I smiled and nodded at them but thought it improper for me to wait outside. I knocked twice on the door, and as no response came, I opened it hesitantly and went in. It was empty, both of people and of furniture, carpeted only by a square of light slanting in through the high window. I suddenly lost my nerve and was about to leave when the sound of Sir Roland's voice traveling easily around the door to the main chamber, which had been left ajar, arrested me. The little devil of curiosity that is in all of us kept me in the antechamber.

"God's throat, man!" Sir Roland's voice was warm with irritation. "Are you telling me that you have returned empty-handed?"

"Beg pardon, Guy, but it was not to be had!" a rough voice countered.

"I have not the least intention of pardoning you until you retrieve it. It is a simple thing, I should think."

"Not if she hasn't sold it yet," the rough voice said.

"Ah! Do you offer me fact or a convenient excuse for your failure?" came the too-pleasant response. There was hesitation. Sir Roland's voice froze with resolution. "Then I recommend that you discover whether or not it is still in her possession and, if it is, find a way to make her sell. Financial ruin is often effective in these cases."

The suggestion of so dire a scheme did not seem to have the same effect on the man to whom Sir Roland was talking as it had on me. "Aye!" the man said readily, as if grateful for the idea.

"I shall expect it in two weeks."

"But, Guy—"

The man was given ample time to voice his objections. None were forthcoming, but at length I heard the man mumble something to the effect that he was afraid that he would not be able to deliver it in two weeks.

Sir Roland's anger flamed out in a savage blaze. "Splendor of God! You shall fear my spurs more! If it weren't for the bargain we've struck, I should have you strung up on the nearest gallows! I've upheld my side of our agreement, with the incontrovertible evidence that you are now a free man. This circumstance may be altered on the moment! You know what I want and why I want it. I do not desire to waste further words on the subject or on your future, which will be short if you do not return successful in a fortnight. Now get out of my sight before I lose my temper in earnest!"

This was my cue to leave, too, for I had lost all desire to see my husband in such a humor. I moved to leave the ante-chamber, but I was not fast enough. Gavin, appearing at the door to show the badly shaken man out of the chambers, saw me and escorted me without question to the door of the inner sanctum. I could hardly say now that I had made a mistake and had no need to speak with the lord. Gavin brought me to the door and stood before me for a moment in an odd, protective stance. I looked beyond him to see my husband seated at a desk that I recognized instantly as having come from Shriven-ham.

Sir Roland did not look up. He was absorbed in a large piece of parchment unrolled on the table before him; one outstretched hand held the curling corner of paper, the other held a quill and moved down the yellowed sheet, writing figures as he went. I was surprised to see him so cool and composed.

Looking at his dark head bent in deep concentration, seeing only the planes of his face against the powerful set of his shoulders beneath his plain blue tunic, I wondered why I felt my heartbeat quicken. I had told Lady Constance that he had not affected me; he had, but I could not say why. I reflected that he had nothing to recommend him but his smile, for he was not precisely handsome. Any woman would rate Hugh Falmouth a far more attractive mate. Then, too, Sir Roland's person conveyed the forcible impression of strength and power; this was hardly a unique quality, however, since the figures of Cedric Hereford and Rannulf Langly, whose names were linked with tourney championships and the martial arts, came so easily to mind. Clearly, I had overreacted to the moments my husband had chosen to practice his unpredictable charm on me. If I had enjoyed little male gallantry in my life, there was still no excuse to lose my head over it, especially when I could not remain blind, or deaf, to his unsteady temperament streaked with violence. He was no different from many another man, I concluded, and probably a good deal worse. But just as I reached this decision, I realized that it was neither his smile that attracted me nor his physical prowess, nor his charm, but something more elemental and hard to define, and that was his blunt masculinity.

"I want him followed," he said coldly without raising his head. "You shall know whom to send. Bring in the next man."

Gavin cleared his throat uncomfortably, bringing Sir Roland's head up. The look in his eyes caused Gavin to blanch and disappear from my side. Exposed to my fate, I swiftly decided on my position. I was somewhat encouraged by the slow smile that came to Sir Roland's lips.

"Good morrow, my lady," he said, rising and holding out his hand in a gesture of welcome. "How can I serve you?"

"Good morrow, my lord," I said lightly and thought to carry it off unconcernedly. "I beg a word with you."

"You honor me."

I sat down in the chair he indicated. "Am I interrupting?" I asked with a smile of inquiry, folding my hands resolutely in my lap to prevent them from fluttering nervously.

"Behold me at work!" he said and then added a bit ruefully, "But you offer a welcome respite: I have not the patience for such industry. How can it be that a man could actually covet the position?"

I was quick to seize what I thought was a note of sincerity in his voice. My heart leapt at it, but his comment stilled my next intended speech, and I hesitated too long in responding.

He said after a pause in an altered, but still pleasant, tone, "Tell me, my lady, what is so urgent that it cannot wait for my ear until this evening?"

"Why, nothing!" I assured him readily. "Just one or two details that have been on my mind for some weeks that I have not yet had an opportunity to discuss with you."

Not a muscle in his face changed, but something in the depths of his eyes flickered, and the thought stole across my brain that I had erred by coming to see him in so businesslike a fashion.

"Shall I await a more suitable time?" Nothing would have made me happier than to have been excused.

"This is an entirely suitable time," he said, his face a mask of politeness. He had assumed the lord's role. "I am entirely at your service. Pray, present me the cases you wish resolved."

"They are trifling requests, my lord!"

"So much the better," he said. "You will give me an immeasurable feeling of accomplishment if I am able to discharge your requests, trifling though they may be."

I had the feeling once again that I would have done better to have mentioned the matters in a more casual context and so did not express myself at first as well as I was able. After one false start, I took a deep breath to compose myself.

"It is Nan," I stated, plunging into the heart of the matter.

"What is your complaint against her?"

"She is totally unsuited for the position of tiring woman. Oh, she is quick enough to learn, but her heart is not in it. She has little regard for the details of proper dress—and it is the small things that count, you know!—she is indifferent to housework and *will* dawdle, and"—bethinking myself of the worst aspect of all—"her needlework is—simply atrocious!"

Sir Roland blinked. "Comprehensive, I apprehend!"

"And so it is! I should have brought you an example of her latest embroidery as proof!"

"I doubt that my examination of it would decide the matter," he said dryly.

"Even a man would be able to detect the flaws in her workmanship!" I retorted warmly.

"Just as a woman would discern all the faults in an improperly cocked crossbow," he replied.

I had to smile at that and accepted the challenge. "Well, I know enough to see whether the—the *thing* is at the end of the—the . . ."

"The stirrup is set at the end of the stock," he supplied helpfully.

"Yes, of course!" I said. "My lack of vocabulary does not indicate complete ignorance, so you see—"

"I concede you the point."

"Handsome of you!" I laughed. "Especially when I have the feeling of having lost it! But that is beside the point. Nan's talents are *wasted* as my tiring woman."

I had, perhaps, phrased the matter somewhat infelicitously, but Sir Roland asked only, with no change of expression, "How may that be?"

"She is wonderful with breads and pastries. Why, just last week I had her show some of the batter boys how to achieve a better crust. Perhaps you noticed—? But the sticking point is: if I were to put her in the kitchens, it might be thought of by the others as a demotion and leave her open to disrespect."

"Yes, I perceive the difficulty."

"That is not the only one," I continued, "for if she leaves

me, which I am convinced she must, I shall be without a handmaiden. There are no women here who can be spared for the post. Hungerford is sorely short of women—as you are well aware! And I do want two tiring women. It need not be Bess and Gertrude necessarily, since you have—certain objections to them, but *surely* there must be two women in all of Shrivenham acceptable to you!"

He had crossed his arms and was regarding me steadily. "Bess and Gertrude, they are called? You shall have them," he said unexpectedly. "I shall attend to it myself and have them summoned here immediately."

It took me a moment to absorb this. "Thank you, my lord," I said rather blankly.

"Do you mean for Nan to return to Shrivenham?"

"Oh, no!" I said quickly. "You—we might—*do* need her here. She has a way with breads. I think I have mentioned it already. That was always my primary reason for keeping her on, not that I did not have reservations about—that is . . ."

"Naturally," he replied, at his blandest. "We shall have to discover a position fit for a former tiring woman in the kitchens. I know not exactly what is involved there, but I do not think it an insurmountable obstacle. I shall leave the title of her station to your ingenuity."

I thanked him for Nan's sake. "She will be much happier out from under my foot. And so, too, shall I be. Thank you!"

He sat back in his chair. "Do not mention it. And now your second request."

"Second request?"

"Come!" he said. "You have me in a receptive mood! You saw how easy it was to accomplish the first of your goals. I urge you not to waste the opportunity to arrange things better to your taste."

"No, no!" I protested. "I have no other requests. I find everything to my liking!"

"When you came in, you said you had two things on your mind," he reminded me with his lazy smile, "and that they had been there for several weeks."

To continue to object in this fashion would only render me

more foolish in his eyes. "Not a request exactly—call it an inquiry! I saw a room that I should like for my own, and I wondered if I might not be—intruding if I took it."

"Is the room in use?"

I said that it was not and had not been for many years. "But the key to the door was still on my trousseau," I added to clarify that I had gone in no room that I should not have.

"Then why would you think to be intruding?"

"I do not know. It simply had a strange feeling about it. But I was instantly charmed by it and thought I might consult you first before doing anything about it."

"Which room is it?"

"Such a strange little nook in the south wing, no bigger than an antechamber, but so interesting! And it looks over the most quaint pleasance. I should like to cultivate the herbs for the kitchen and my essences there. The room wants only a good cleaning to be serviceable."

I felt my color rise under his rather hard stare. "I have told you, my lady," he said evenly, "you are mistress here and may do whatever you please within the castle."

"Then—then I shall want to use it as my sewing room."

"You are certainly free to do so."

"Thank you, my lord."

"Again, there is no need for your thanks."

"You must accept them nevertheless," I said, flushing a little, "because I am very conscious of having trespassed on your attention and for such—minor details, quite beneath your notice!"

"No concern of yours is beneath my notice," he said chivalrously. "And now that you are come, we can discuss our plans for the Holy Season."

I immediately disavowed any prior knowledge to Lady Constance's idea that we host the seasonal festivities and wondered aloud what could have put such a notion into her head.

"Do you find it an unattractive proposition?" he queried.

I could not say that I did.

"Neither do I," he said. "In fact, I find that Constance's solution to our 'predicament' is in many ways most satisfactory.

My only question is about the strain that it shall put on you. If we decide to do so, I believe we must commit ourselves to entertaining the fortnight from Christmas Eve to Epiphany."

"I believe I am equal to the task," I said with dignity.

"Very well," he said, "but we are now almost at the beginning of December."

I paused to consider what would need to be done in the few weeks before Christmas.

"I would suggest also that we keep the number of guests below fifty," he said, gently steering the direction of my thoughts. "Constance must head the list, followed by Charles, I should think."

Our plans seemed already to have taken shape; it was my turn to offer a name for the guest list. "Alicia and Herbert would be happy to come, but only if we also invite the Staffords and the Longchamps."

"They are family friends," he said easily, and from there it was only a matter of minutes before we had a list of some fifty lords and ladies, including Marie-Ange, Yvette, Sir Robert FitzWarren, Sir Bruce Huxley, and Lady Edwina, among others, and I could hardly fail to notice the way Sir Roland so smoothly inserted into the discussion the names of Isabelle and Lord Beauvais, as well as Sir Hugh Falmouth. Their names made my heart sink, for some reason, and yet it was only natural that they be included. When I agreed that Sir Roland should leave the correspondence to me, he opened a large metal box on the top of his desk and handed me the Guimont seals.

Only one small problem exercised my mind. "Do you think, my lord, that on such short notice we should expect many regrets?"

"There may be some who on principle do not come," he said, allowing for the possibility that some might not want to partake of Guimont hospitality, "but I have always found curiosity to be a stronger magnet than propriety. I shall apologize to you now that I won't be able to help you much in the preparations. I will be leaving next week, but will return to Hungerford before the guests arrive."

"Oh!" I said on a note of dismay and caught myself just in time from making a blunder. I continued cheerfully, "Then it is all the better that I have two tiring women from Shrivenham to help me clean and air the guest chambers in the south wing that are now closed!"

Sir Roland was rarely fooled in such cases. "Recent experience counsels you that a week's absence can easily turn into a month," he said with his gently mocking smile, "but I promise to return in good time."

These kinds of comments from him always threw me into a little confusion. "Oh, no! I mean, yes, my lord!"

"Shall I swear it on my sword's hilt, as the Crusaders do?"

I laughed at the suggestion. "No, that is unnecessary. You have promised—surely all that is warranted for the occasion! One promise may lead to another: you must tell me about your adventures in the Holy Land sometime. I admit to having a fascination with the Orient."

He agreed lightly but warned that such talk would bore me excessively. We rose together, and he came around the table to show me personally to the door.

"One last thing, my lady," he said, taking my hand in parting. "May I assume that I am released from my obligation of attending to these damnable accounts at night?"

I believe that I turned various shades of red and could meet his eye but fleetingly. My tongue became unaccountably tied in knots, but I did manage, in the tangle of half-sentences, to convey the idea that, yes, there was no longer any need for him to bother himself with such work.

The next thing I knew, he had summoned Gavin, and I was in the hallway, heading for the day's tasks.

More than a week had passed since my visit to Sir Roland's counting rooms, and he had already gone on another of his unidentified errands, as he had said he would. Before he left, I had had a brief taste of married life: I saw my husband only at the evening meal and then later in the master bedchamber that separated our two private suites. He was gone from my side before the morning light, and I would not see him again until the evening. So it went for the scant sennight before he was gone from Hungerford.

Sir Roland had never mentioned the awkwardness of our interview, and he had acted during it as if what I had done was completely natural, but I had learned enough of him to know that I had stepped amiss. Nevertheless, I could not help noticing, since that incident, his unfailing politeness to me, which was tinged with a certain remoteness and which did nothing to reduce the distance that had always separated us. I could not say that I had determined his behavior by my actions, but I could not but wonder if I could have established a more relaxed style in our discourse, had I chosen to discuss my housewifely concerns with my husband in any of the intimate moments that must naturally arise between a married couple.

"Fool!" I scolded myself again and plied my needle savagely into my tapestry.

At the sound of a footfall at the door, I looked up and found Nan standing there. I hoped, self-consciously, that she had not heard my outburst, and I was vaguely annoyed to be disturbed in my sewing room, which I had staked out as my retreat. It was well past the evening meal, and I could not imagine what she wanted at this hour.

"Yes, Nan," I said unencouragingly, "what is it?"

She looked a little taken aback at my brittle tone. "You told me in the hall to come see you when I was done in the pantry. This was the only place I thought to find you."

"Did I? Oh—! Yes!" I said hastily. "You are certainly very late about your new duties as pantry stewardess. Shall you be every night so occupied?"

"For a while, I think," she said, but not with any displeasure.

"I certainly hope not to have overburdened you," I said, striving for a warmer note. "Now, why did I wish to see you?"

"It was something about a carpet—from your antechamber to this room."

"Of course! How could I have come to forget it? I suppose we may as well be about it, as late as it is. Pray, summon a page—nay, I think it will take two—to roll up the carpet and bring it here."

It was not long before the task was accomplished and the carpet was stretched before the fire crackling gaily on the hearth. I dismissed the pages and stepped back to the door with Nan to admire this finishing touch to my room.

"What do you think of it, Nan?"

She looked around my little room, shimmering in the red-gold flickers from the fireplace, from the newly recovered chairs, the polished tables and little chest, to the tapestry on the wall depicting woman's industry, and the bright cushions in the window seat.

"Aye, it's loverly," she said.

The almost wistful note in her voice prompted me to say, "I know you shall be regretting the many hours you do not spend here stitching with me."

"I'll still live," she said, and smiled with me. Nan had been smiling more frequently of late.

"That is reassuring," I said, "and I hope I have no cause to have you spend your evenings here with me—or to have you sleep in the room off my chambers. Have a care what you are about."

She took the warning in silence. Before she left, she hesitated slightly. "I—I want to thank you," she said, the words coming with difficulty. I wondered when the last time was that she thanked a person.

"For what?" I said. "For improving our fare at table and relieving me of your care, all at once?"

"No," she said, "for never threatening to send me back to Shrivenham."

This was a dramatic comeabout in our relationship; yet I saw no reason to press the advantage. "Then you are very welcome. Allow me to point out to you that you have had a spot on your smock since before dinner. I want you to change it, and I expect you to see to the cleanliness of the girls under you. Your new post is neither a reward nor a sinecure. You may close the door behind you."

I bent over my tapestry, my mind intent on matters other than the green and gold woodland scene before me that was destined to live out its life as the covering for my footstool. My handiwork served a far more important purpose than merely fashioning useful objects for the home. It did much to restore the balance of my mind. I used it, I imagined, in the same way I had seen Sir Roland on occasion absently drink his wine and then toy with his goblet until Gavin came to fill it again for him. I guessed that during those moments he never tasted the wine nor saw the vessel before him on the table. So it was with me and my needlework. It was a matter of concentration, of keeping my hands and the outward portion of my mind occupied with mundane affairs, thus leaving a quiet, inward part of myself free to reflect undisturbed. My thoughts were not kindly toward myself, and I was unable to rid myself of a feeling of inadequacy. The image of Isabelle Beauvais sprang unbidden to mind. Would Isabelle have gone to Sir Roland's counting rooms and have laid her requests before him so coldly? Would Alicia have handled Herbert in such a fashion? Of course not, I told myself scornfully. Isabelle would have waited until she had retired for the night and mentioned the matter casually before slipping into bed, I thought, while Alicia would have touched Herbert's sleeve after the evening meal and melted him with one of her smiles. My artlessness irritated me, and I vowed never again to behave in so naive a fashion. To think that I had admitted having had those details on my mind for several weeks and then had prattled on about it like Dame Ellen! It made my cheeks burn with justified embarrassment.

Someone scratched at my door, interrupting this sober reverie. The fire had burned very low, and the tallows flickered uncertainly; it was an odd hour for anyone to come calling.

Before I answered, Gunhild stood before me. She had never sought me out before, but still I was not surprised.

"Pray, come in, Gunhild," I said unnecessarily, for she was already in the room and looking around rather rudely.

"Do you approve?" I said coolly after a minute.

She turned to look at me, and the dying light exaggerated

the sagging lines of her face, giving her countenance a weird, malevolent cast. "It looks different," she said.

"So I should hope," I said, trying valiantly to keep my courage about me. "After a week's worth of steady work, I think I have achieved some transformation in the chamber."

She looked keenly at me for a moment; I felt some of my mettle trickle away. "So, you have taken a fancy to this room, too," she said.

"Sit down, Gunhild," I invited, "and tell me if the chairs are to your liking."

She made no sign to indicate that she had heard me. "She is dead, you know," she said in a tone that made all my nerves tingle.

I did not ask her to sit again. "She?"

Gunhild's face was turned away from me, but I plainly heard the mockery. "You do not know whose room this was?" She moved in front of the fire, suddenly, so that her shadow leapt over chair and wall.

I shrank back a little in my chair but forced myself to take advantage of an opportunity with the one person who was the least bit communicative. "I would not have asked you," I said, barely controlling my voice, "if I had already possessed this information."

"You're not a very knowing one, are you?" she said bluntly. "I would think that for a new mistress, a little knowledge of past history would be useful."

I did not know how much I wanted to know of it. "How is one to learn?" I asked shakily, hoping to steer her in the direction of answering my question.

"There are many ways open to a clever woman," she replied.

"I fear that I am not very clever, then, for I know only direct methods," I said, trying very hard to keep a clear head, "and can think of no better way than to ask."

"Did you think to ask your husband?"

"No."

"It is just as well," she muttered.

"I have asked you," I said, my throat very dry.

"Ah!" She cackled with laughter. "But you do not like my answers!"

"I have a liking only for the truth," I said, my heart drumming out of rhythm with that statement.

"The truth!" she jeered. I could detect no trace of anything but a bitterness I did not understand.

"Shall you not oblige me by telling me whose room this was?" I persisted.

She cast her eyes about my chamber. Her voice came from far way. "This was Lady Laura's room," she said as if I were not there. "Lady Laura was their mother."

"Sir Roger's and Sir Roland's mother?"

She did not answer that, but she did not have to. She continued to conjure the ghosts out of the past. "She would sit here, like you, before the fire with her needles and talk so merrily of her sons. Little Guy was her favorite. Such a fine lad! And so quick!"

I involuntarily pushed the tapestry frame away from me. "What was she like?" I whispered.

"She was very beautiful. Everyone loved the Lady Laura . . . everyone. Eyes the color of Mary's veil, her hair a mahogany banner, and as slim as an altar candle. Everyone loved her. Everyone."

A thought occurred to me. "Who was Roland?"

"Lady Laura's brother. Roger was named after the lord, and little Guy after his uncle. Roger took after the lord, but little Guy was his mama's son, her love. How she loved him!"

Having put a certain construction on her words, I asked, "Who was Guy's father?"

This surprised a crack of unkind laughter out of her. "The lord, of course. There could be no denying it, little Guy being his brother's twin except in coloring—and in spirit."

Relief swept over me. "Is Lady Laura the woman who rules in my place?" I asked breathlessly.

She turned to me sharply, as if suddenly remembering my presence. "No," she said, her voice losing its trancelike quality, "and you are a fool. Only fools hide themselves from the truth."

"I am not hiding from the truth," I said in an attempt to defend myself. "I simply do not know it."

"Fool!" she repeated scathingly to the fire.

Whether this invective did not offend me as it should have because my sense of the respect due me as mistress was blunted beyond recognition, or because I believed that Gunhild was not necessarily addressing me, remained undecided in my mind. I was not overly concerned with the problem; I wanted rather to discover who, in Gunhild's mind, since Lady Laura was not my competitor, was mistress of Hungerford. Josette seemed a poor choice, as did every other woman within the castle walls. A blunt question as to this person's identity seemed forbidden. I had rather to approach Gunhild through her own way of thinking.

"Was Lady Laura mistress of Hungerford when she was alive?" I asked.

Gunhild looked pleased, in her own way, with this question. "You have a way with queries, in spite of everything."

"And you have a way of not answering them," I returned immediately, emboldened by her approval, however qualified.

"Yes," she said. "Of course she was."

"Was Lady Laura like the other Guimont women?"

The dying flames licked the logs, slowly, silently, wearing them down, while I waited for her response.

"She is dead, you know," she said in that nerve-plucking voice of hers.

I tried to make the best of this unwelcome turn in the conversation. "We were all saddened," I said, entering into the spirit of the occasion, "by the news of her untimely death."

"She did not die! She was killed," she snapped viciously, "and well you know it!"

I did not know whom she thought she was addressing, but I did not want to draw her errant attention to the fact that I was Lady Marguerite, an outsider in her world. Suppressing my shock mingled with intense curiosity, I said soothingly, "I knew it. But I never discovered who killed her."

"Didn't you?" she said sarcastically, turning on me. Her

keen eyes narrowed to slits, riveting me to my chair. "The truth killed her."

"Did Sir Roger's wives also die of the truth?" I asked, disappointed but pursuing.

"No, they just died, like they all do," she said without interest.

This statement alarmed me considerably. "Do all the Guimont wives die in such fashion?"

She apparently became aware of my identity again. "That remains to be seen, doesn't it, *Lady Guimont?*" she said with awful irony and then fell silent.

I drew an uncertain breath. "I have been at the wooden stairs to the back bailey," I said, "and found them most unsatisfactory. I shall have the carpenter repair them soon, to prevent further accidents."

This comment did nothing to rouse her from her abstracted contemplation of the fire.

"Why do you come here?" I asked suddenly. "Why do you tell me these things?"

She looked at me. "You ask too many questions," she said. "You are a fool."

On that depressing note, she left the room.

I gripped the arms of my chair, as if to steady myself. That did not help, and her absence did nothing to diminish the effect of the whirlpool I felt swirling about me. Every time I thought to escape the turbulent waters of doubt and ignorance, Gunhild would suck me down again with one of her revelatory twists and make everything I thought I knew appear fuzzy and without focus.

I had had the feeling that she was trying to warn me—a comforting thought throughout the eerie conversation, but one that was quickly dispelled by the look of acute dislike she gave me before leaving. On the other hand, neither could I quite convince myself that she was threatening me in any way, or amusing herself by taunting me. At her departure, I felt much as if I had just awakened from a bad dream but could not quite recapture what it was in the dream that had so thoroughly disturbed me.

I very calmly rose from my chair, banked the fire, and proceeded to my own chambers, resolutely ignoring the shadows jumping out at me on the way.

I could not fit all the pieces of the puzzle confronting me into a satisfactory arrangement. This, I readily acknowledged, was because I had only half-truths to piece together and depended ·on my very unreliable sensibilities to complete the picture. It was of no use telling myself to trust my instincts, for only innocence can afford that luxury and I had lost mine the night Sir Roland came to Shrivenham and convinced me of my father's duplicity; and worse than useless to try to stop my curiosity from delving into things I would be better off not knowing.

Fortunately, I had too many things to occupy me in the next days than to fall prey to wild overinterpretations of Gunhild's sibylline pronouncements. But my mind had fastened on the word *truth* and would not let it go. Gunhild spoke often of it and with a certain rancor that only some personal misfortune with it could have engendered. Myself, I had always found it an elusive thing, particularly so in the last few weeks. There was a truth, for instance, existing in the relationship between Sir Roland and his mother. Had Sir Roland, a beloved son, changed through his beautiful mother's murder from a spirited, loving child to the cool, self-possessed man I had married? Could the painful memories of a loved one lost have been behind the hard look my husband gave me when I asked him for permission to take over his mother's special chamber? Perhaps this particular truth was unknowable and I had simply misread Sir Roland's reaction. Perhaps, too, Gunhild had misrepresented Lady Laura, mistress of Hungerford and mother. I wanted to believe that Gunhild knew some truth that she was not telling me directly, but I had to wonder if she found truth as slippery as I did. She had certainly given me strange glimpses of her version of it, and I did not know if it could kill.

She also spoke easily of fools. Now, here I felt on firmer ground. A fool, she said, hides from the truth; I thought it more accurate to say that truth hides from fools. But if a fool was a person blind to the truth, then we were most of us fools, and I could not despair of swelling the ranks by one. There were but few among us so privileged to peer into men's hearts and minds and see the truth written therein. Sages extol the sight-giving powers of suffering, and I assumed that Gunhild possessed a modicum of truth through suffering. Yet, I did not understand why, in all of my foolishness, one could not glimpse the soul just as well through laughter, lightness, and love.

I may have been blind to all else, but I was still reasonably certain that we poor creatures performed few acts without motivation. A strange word, *motivation*. I did not mind to shape my mouth around it, but it left an aftertaste I could not like. It smacked of the distasteful aspects of human nature; but we all of us had the motivations that made us human, and understanding them would help illuminate the darker side of the soul and lead a long way to discovering certain truths. It was, to my unhappiness, all too easy to supply motives for Sir Roger's death. Less clear to me was Gunhild's motivation for seeking me out, and the motive behind the killing of Lady Laura could only be a product of my imagination.

A wondrous gift, imagination, and more than just a faculty capable of filling the idle hours and providing entertainment. With it, one could envision new possibilities and grand new worlds, and bring one to better understanding. It seemed, too, that imagination without vision was at best an imperfect tool, like my favorite silver needle, now blunted, which lay useless in my sewing box. I continually sensed that some essential point eluded me and would not be seized by my imagination. Of this I was certain: my imagination was not as rich as reality, nor as vivid as the truth.

Chapter 11

Gunhild was not the only unusual visitor to my sewing room. Just after the noon meal several days later, I was surprised to see Gavin on the threshold. I had accomplished the day's duties in record time and, having surprisingly little to do, I found myself sparring with a persistent feeling of restlessness. I knew that Sir Roland was returning to Hungerford that evening, but even that knowledge gave me no peace. True to his promise to me upon his departure, my husband was not to be gone above a seven-night. Where he went, I knew not, but at least this time he had seen fit to send back a message to me, informing me of his plans for the return. The messenger had arrived late the evening before, and Nan had brought the sealed parchment to my bedchamber.

That morning, my mood had descended with the heavy mists that smothered the keep. Consequently, when I chanced to look up from my embroidery and saw Gavin, I smiled with pleasure and a little relief; I knew immediately the purpose of his visit. He had apparently been standing very circumspectly at my door some moments before I felt his presence. I did not ask him into the room. Instead I rose and crossed to him, saying in all sincerity, "What an excellent squire you are, Gavin McLaughlin! How could you have known that I had no turn for my needlework just now and needed nothing better than some exercise outside? Let me fetch my mantle and my working gloves, and I shall meet you in the gardens below in a minute."

When I met him in my pleasance, he explained to me, with a hoe in one hand and a spade in the other, that since it was a little warmer today, the mists being low, it might be a good time to do some of the ground preparation for the gardens that I had, upon my arrival the month before, mentioned to be necessary.

"I never expected you to respond to the suggestion," I said. "It was hardly an order, you know!"

"Oh," he said offhandedly, "I was used to helping my sisters and mother now and now in the gardens."

I heard the catch of homesickness in his voice. "Well, you could hardly have picked a better day for it. Nothing suits my mood better than working with the earth—not that I would have thought of it on my own initiative! And there is so much here to do that we can make only a start of it today. I never like to leave this sort of thing until the spring, when the ground is wet, particularly since this plot has not been cultivated in so long. It should ideally have been done in September, I suppose, but—well, then, that was impossible."

I knelt down to begin pulling away some overgrown branches from a corner that would eventually become the space for my herbs. I had to stop momentarily to retie my kerchief, which kept falling over one eye. Several feet distant from me, Gavin began to turn over the crusty earth with his hoe.

"So, you are a gardener," I said, "in addition to your other skills. Where is it that you are from in Scotland that things actually grow?"

He laughed at that and lost some of his self-consciousness. "I'm from the Lowlands—Glen More—and I can assure you that many things grow in Scotland besides heather and wild animals that roam at will."

"I confess to the profoundest ignorance of your homeland," I said, "and nourish the notion—no doubt absurd!—that going to Scotland is like stepping to the edge of the world, so far distant and remote it seems. It is a wonder that you do not all fall off, once you have managed to fight off all the beasts. But here you are, very much alive, and I can see that you are entirely civilized, too!"

"We've our claims to civilization," he replied good-naturedly, "although Scotland is as rugged a country as you are apt to find in the world—and as bonny, as well."

"I am sure it is," I said, "and you must be sick to death of your southern neighbors' misimpressions."

"Nay, it's none so bad. Perhaps I'm just used to it, or perhaps after five years in Britain I am no longer considered Scots—although my hair proclaims my heritage louder than any of my words or actions."

"Five years!" I exclaimed. "But how old were you when you first came?"

"Fifteen," he answered.

Suddenly, the age of twenty years seemed vastly young and inexperienced to me, now that I had passed my twenty-first birthday.

"Have you never been back?"

"Once," he said laconically and did not seem inclined to elaborate. I thought not to probe into this subject.

"How came you to Britain and into your present service?—if you do not mind my curiosity," I said after a moment.

"My father has an uncle at King Henry's court," he said, and then explained, "You see, I am the fourth of seven children, with three elder brothers! Wouldn't you just know it! And three younger sisters, none of whom were betrothed when I left. I was given little choice as to occupation, and saw my only opportunity for any kind of life here in Britain. Nevertheless, I recall being reluctant to leave Glen More." He paused to reflect. "It is, after all, one's home and family."

"How I envy your brothers and sisters, despite their numbers! I always longed for siblings when I was growing up."

Working side by side, our hands and eyes occupied with our tasks, it seemed entirely natural to talk of such things.

"And now?" I asked after a while. "Shall you ever return?"

"Nay," he said with finality. "Oh, perhaps to visit, but my life is here now."

I heard in his voice that it had taken perhaps the whole five years of his absence from home to make such a statement with tolerable indifference. He must have grown immeasurably in the past years, I thought, from a boy into a young man and squire. I admired his acceptance of his life, for I knew he had acquired it with no small struggle. I tried to imagine him in another five years, hardened to the temper of the other Guimont men, but without success. I suspected he would always have something of the boy in him.

"If my sisters have their way, I shall be seeing them frequently. And perhaps even too much! Elspeth, the eldest sister, has her heart set on coming to London and marrying an English lord. I gather that she has subverted Kate and Janie, the two youngest, into thinking that this must be the ultimate achievement in life! My sisters!" he said, with an affectionate laugh.

"You must know, Gavin, that if your sisters do travel to London, we would be pleased to receive them also at Hungerford. With or without husbands!"

"Th-thank you, my lady!" he said, and continued on a rather wistful note, "The person I would like to see here would be my father, but I do not think he has any more idea of leaving Scotland than King Henry has of moving his court to Edinburgh! I have fared better than my father's wildest imaginings. The day I left Castle McLaughlin, my father told me, 'You're a scrawny bairn, Gavin, and no good will come of you.' With that on top of my mother's weeping, I did not know if I was happy or sad to go. It did fire me with the desire to prove him wrong, which likely was his intention, now that I come to think of it. In the end, it was nothing I did or did not do that earned me my present position, but something I had not expected: luck."

"How so?"

"I had not been at court a fortnight when Guy—Sir Guy!—appeared there one day. I think he had just returned from the Crusade. Well, the very next day, after talking to me for five minutes, he chose me as his squire."

"What part did luck play?"

"There must have been fifty lads to pick from," he said, still a little overcome by his good fortune, "and Sir Guy was an important knight, even then."

"Are you suggesting that he could have chosen better?"

Gavin flashed me his boyish smile. "No."

"Then it was not luck at all," I said, answering his smile. "Let us rather say that he knew what he was doing, and chose you for all the qualities he obviously saw in you."

"I will agree," he said, "that he is very good at making swift decisions. I have seen him in many a tight spot during a campaign and make the most of it through quick thinking."

"So, you are pleased with your lot?"

"Aye," he said readily. "I have much more freedom than most squires, and Sir Guy has taught me so much!" He colored up a little. "That is not to say that I have never been dressed down, but I suppose that is to be expected. He is very exacting sometimes."

I felt some constraint on this topic. There were a good many things I would have liked to ask Gavin, but I could not bring myself to do so. I thought it wisest to turn the subject.

"I am not so sure," I said lightly, "that the House of Guimont does not have the better end of the bargain. Look! You have managed a whole row already. Are you sure you wouldn't rather be practicing with the quintain or on the archery field than tilling my garden?"

"One tires of that practice on occasion. I thought today one of the last opportunities to help you here, for Sir Guy comes back tonight, and then the Christmas guests will be coming in a few weeks. You will be too busy then to attend to such unseasonal work as gardening."

"You are right, and January will be much too late." I sighed, and added on a brighter note, "But I look forward to the Holy Season, especially now that I have my Bess and Gertrude with me. Have you met them yet? They came two, no, three days ago, and such a weight has been lifted from my shoulders! The proof of my idleness is precisely this afternoon's activity. Why, just look at this perfectly healthy rosebush! It must be cut back immediately in order to save it. How could such a charming spot have been left to turn to seed? At any rate, my women are dear creatures and have been with me forever. Bess has been momentarily assigned to the kitchens to begin planning the feasting, and Gertrude—bless her hard little heart!—

has cowed the few inside women there are into turning the guest chambers inside out. I vow, they have probably not been cleaned like that for a decade!"

"How many guests will we be receiving?"

I had to pause a moment to calculate. "It is hard to say right now, for if the weather turns unusually bad, we might expect fewer people to come. Most of the replies I have received so far have been positive, but I cannot say for everybody."

"My bones tell me that there will be no heavy snowfall between now and Christmas," he said half-seriously.

"You should know all about snow, at any rate!" I remarked. "And if you are right, we will have to count on as many as three score," I said.

"That is a goodly number."

"By most standards, sixty is a small group—intimate, in fact." I laughed. "We had thought to have no more than fifty, but when one is planning for a gathering, one cannot always set a limit and then arbitrarily stop there. I have discovered, furthermore, that planning for a smaller number is practically the same amount of work as for many."

"It must be much work," he said, slightly awed at the thought of receiving as many as sixty guests.

"You can see how busy I am!" I teased. "The worst part has been deciding on the decorations for the Great Hall, worrying about what everyone will do if the weather is too miserable for hunting, and determining the various gifts. The rest is knowing how to delegate authority."

"You sound like Sir Guy."

"Do I? Well, it is simply the truth. I have had much practice running Shrivenham. It is curious, though; Shrivenham is smaller, but I find that I am much more organized here and have more time to spend like this. It is a rare treat to find myself idly gardening!"

"Hungerford does seem more—organized since your coming."

"Shall I say that I am pleased to hear it? I would, if I did not also know that my wonderful organization is due rather to the fact that so many things here lie outside my jurisdiction: the stables, the kennels, the mews, the game, the supply of meat, even the accounts. I assure you, the organization was already here."

"That is only since Sir Guy's lordship," he said.

I swiftly moved on. "Tell me, how is Nan doing as pantry stewardess?" I asked casually, while digging up the roots of a huge bush I thought particularly unpromising.

He did not respond immediately, and I feared the worst. But all he said was, "She seems to fit in, so far as I know. She certainly keeps to herself and knows how to take care of herself."

"That's Nan," I said with something akin to pride. Perhaps Sir Roland had been right about her after all.

His next words mitigated somewhat my feeling. "Gaston has his eye on her, of course, but I suppose she has told you as much."

She had not, nor would I have expected her to, but I saw no reason to admit it. "I hope she continues to take care of herself, then."

"I have no doubt that he'll bring her around to his way of thinking," he said cheerfully.

Keeps were the same everywhere, but it seemed highly probable that Sir Roland held a more relaxed view of moral matters in the keep than did Dame Ellen. I had been unable to determine to what degree he allowed his retainers to consort among themselves, for he had not been around enough for me to know. I personally would not countenance any overt or indiscreet behavior from the retainers; I simply did not know what I would do if the lord himself found nothing amiss with sampling a kitchen maid or two. It was a prospect I refused to consider.

"I shall have to talk to her about her duties in the pantry," I said, "now that she has had some days to become adjusted."

We talked then in a general way about Hungerford and its inmates, but I did not think I would trade on this occasion to pump him for information. And I exercised the strongest guard over my tongue to refrain from mentioning anything about Gunhild. I learned only that Josette and Louise, an inside woman, had never been friends (with the hint that John Potter had somehow played a role) and thought that an interesting enough piece of information to satisfy me for the moment.

"This is a fair afternoon's work," I said, at last getting off my knees. "I am afraid this will just have to do for today. As much as I enjoy this, I must see to the progress on the cleaning of the guest chambers. Talking about the delegation of authority is one thing, acting on it is quite another!" I gestured to the space I was standing on. "What do you think of a flower bed here?"

Gavin gathered up the tools and agreed that the spot would get the right amount of afternoon sun. He then made the excellent suggestion to clear away most of the ivy on the low wall facing my sewing-room window and to train some trailing roses there, and promised, furthermore, to look into the cultivation of a row of straggly fruit trees in the spring.

I peeled off my working gloves and handed them to Gavin, who put everything in a small shed in a shaded corner whose door hung on one hinge. We then proceeded through the small gate in the low wall into the back bailey, where, upon thanking Gavin again for his help, he headed for the stables and I in the direction of the house.

Bess stopped me on my way to discuss the menu planning for the next fortnight. We rapidly came to agreement on the essentials and turned our talk to other matters, foremost among them being to decide whether it was worthwhile to send to Shrivenham for the Infidel's Arm, a problem that did not lend itself to a moment's resolution.

"We need not decide on that right now," I said, "for there are certainly more pressing matters. But tell me, now that we have this moment, what news bring you from Shrivenham? How goes everything? Is Thomas behaving?"

"He's as plaguey a nuisance as ever," she said severely, "and it's God's own truth!"

"Don't tell me Charger has tried to take a bite out of you, too!"

"As if I would let him!" she retorted. "But it's none so bad, and things go along much as before."

"It is somewhat lowering," I said, "to reflect that Shriven-ham can function without me."

"As to that, I can tell you that there has been a distinct change in tone! Mortal envious Hodierne and Avice were, not to mention every other woman in the keep, that Gertrude and I were sent to Hungerford," she said, adding after a slight, betraying pause, "and to you! How they would love to know what is going forward here!"

"Do you think they would be interested to know that Nan is now the pantry stewardess?"

She twinkled responsively but limited herself to saying only, "Aye, that might interest them, for instance!"

"Speaking of the kitchens again," I interjected, "do you serve up some neat's tongue this evening. Sir Roland seems to be so fond of it."

"The master will have as fine a dinner as he's ever had," she assured me, "for I know of no better way of thanking him for sending me here." She then lowered her voice confiden-tially. "And well pleased I am with the way things have worked out. You listen to Bess and never mind what Ellen says! You're doing fine in your new home."

With these words, Bess marched through the door to the kitchen, where I saw her zestfully engage the maids with fetch-ing and preparing. I paused at the door just long enough to watch her stop her labors in order to enjoy with Adam Cook, whom she seemed to have won over within her first hour in the kitchens, a quiet gossip, no doubt about the serving maids, the secrets of Hungerford Castle, and even the lord and master whom she would be feeding that evening.

I shook my head fondly over Bess. It felt good to have her and Gertrude with me again, knowing that they would make certain that everything was done just the way I liked it.

I continued on my way, with the intention of changing my kerchief for a fresh coif to protect my recently washed hair until the evening meal, when I would wear my pearled filet. Before making it to the hall, however, I was waylaid by a very extraordinary encounter. My thoughts on no particular topic were abruptly halted when I felt an arm slide around my waist and a prickly kiss on my cheek.

I whirled around and looked level into the eyes of a man I instantly recognized. He was my height, and wore a day's growth of beard and a leather jack strongly redolent of the stables. At last my knowledge was complete; before me stood the third man of the trio I had met that night in July, and he was surveying me with an interest as lively as my astonishment. I had a mind to call out for some kind of help, but my indignation at his boldness was swept aside by a stronger urge to settle a score.

"Pray release me, sir!" I said in no uncertain terms, and accomplished this objective myself by the simple expedient of pulling myself away from his slack hold. I hurried my steps toward the hall, but not with any desire to rid myself of him. I was not disappointed. He fell in beside me, affecting an easy gait bordering on a swagger.

"I've an uncommon thirst," he said, "and could slake it on a foamy wet."

I supposed he took me for a serving maid; in any case, he did not seem to have the slightest recollection of having seen me before, just as Will had not—which was hardly surprising.

I smiled at him, all politeness. "I invite you to procure one at the brew house."

"Ye're a cheeky wench," he said with a grin, and added on a point of information, "I likes 'em cheeky."

"Then, at the risk of inspiring in you a further liking for me, I must ask you to remove yourself from my presence."

For an answer, he made a movement as if to pinch me, but I outmaneuvered him. One thing was certain: drunk or sober, this man found my charms to his taste, and apparently believed his own to be equally irresistible. I put no store whatsoever in his taste, consistent though it may have been, for I imagined it very easily satisfied when it came to women.

"Where be ye from?" he asked, impervious to any sort of rebuff.

"Shrivenham," I obliged.

"Ah!" he said knowledgeably. "I've heard ye're the new pantry stewardess come with the mistress. There's stories about ye."

This took me a moment to absorb. It was hard to know how to interpret that, and even harder to preserve my countenance.

"What's yer name now, Miss Pantry Stewardess?" he pursued, apparently misreading the widening of my eyes for affirmation of his deduction.

"My name," I said deliberately, "is Lady Marguerite Montcrief. You may address me as Lady Guimont."

He looked me up and down, obviously taking in my kerchief and working kirtle. "Aye," he said, putting his thumbs in his belt and thrusting out his chest, "and I'm the Earl of Guimont."

"Oh?" I said, eyes round with innocence. "I thought he was taller."

"I suppose ye know just how tall he is," he said suggestively.

Here was an opportunity not to be missed. "Do you think I have a chance with the master?"

He winked expressively. "Guy's got an eye for a comely wench, but he don't go blowing his conquests on a trumpet, I can tell you that! Odds are short, though, in the stables that he'll honor ye before too long, that is, if'n he don't mind tangling with yer boyfriend."

"My boyfriend?"

"The Bastard," he said simply.

I let this pass. "But his wife!" I exclaimed. "Has he no regard for her?"

"Hot after him, are ye? As to the master's wife, I'll have to say I don't ken what his feelings are in that quarter. He don't say much about it, being reserved like, and he's never confided in me what he thinks about a woman, but it's not much, I can tell ye! Not that he doesn't consider me one of his friends. I'm one of his closest, in fact! I'm his personal messenger," he announced with obvious pride. "Well, me and Will together," he continued, "but as to his wife, they say she's come with a mort of land, so I draw my own conclusions. It's a law of nature: when a woman's rich, it's a certainty she's got a face like a horse! Not that I ever met her, mind ye, but she's yer mistress, and ye'll be knowing better how to handle her."

I hardly knew whether to be amused or offended. "You're a friend to the master?" I asked, as one impressed.

He affirmed this with a nod and a grin. My imp of mischief prompted me to ask eagerly, "Do you think you could recommend me to him?"

He apparently saw no reason to further my interest in his master, and wasted no time in recommending himself to me. He jerked his thumb to his chest and said, "I'll let ye know, missy, that ye'll not be disappointed in Ben Wickett! Guy and I have often been compared by the ladies—and I've never come off the worse." This last remark he punctuated with a gesture that had all the subtlety of a battering ram.

"In the same way that you are his match at drinking?" I asked.

He did not hesitate to cloak himself with the mantle of hard drinking. "So ye've heard about that, too?" he said, perfectly accepting his own renown. He even went so far as to steal a little of his master's thunder. "Many's the time we've bent the elbow together. Guy's got a hard head—Lord love ye!—but I can tell ye that it takes a man and a half to see me in the basket. It's not just whistling on the parapets to say that I've seen Guy to bed on occasion, if ye see what I mean."

I turned to go, but not before I offered him my brightest smile. "I do see, I assure you! You say Ben Wickett is your name?" I said over my shoulder. "I shall not forget it."

I then passed quickly on through the main portal and left Ben to call out promises of adventure at my back.

I smiled wickedly to myself and hoped that I would be there to witness Ben's discomfiture when he discovered my true identity. Any remorse I might have felt at my admittedly shameless conduct was easily routed by the firm conviction that Master Wickett richly deserved what was coming to him.

My mood of satisfaction lasted just long enough for me to

change my raiment and find Gertrude. It was not too far past the noon, and so I could expect to find Gertrude and several women still engaged in the preparing of the guest chambers, which was proceeding on schedule. I did find them in the south wing, but they were not busy cleaning. Instead, when I entered the chamber from which I heard coming several angry voices, I was greeted with the kind of scene that I had been half-dreading ever since my arrival at Hungerford.

I knew the worst when I spied Gertrude standing helplessly to one side, her face a wooden mask of disapproval. The center of the room featured the usually mild Josette in a fierce altercation with Louise, whom I could not claim to know. It was apparent that the immediate cause of the verbal battle, which threatened at any moment to become physical, was not John Potter; whatever else I could not guess from the words slapped back and forth between Josette and Louise, their belligerent stance told me that they were avowed enemies. A ring of women holding idle dust clouts and brooms framed this tense picture, each face showing a different degree of curiosity and interest in the outcome.

I was up against my first real test at Hungerford. I knew even before I opened my mouth to speak that I would not, in all probability, be able to deal with Josette and Louise fairly, and I had even less hope of winning any allies. The situation had a further wrinkle that would make my participation problematic: they were speaking Saxon and at an alarming speed.

The precise object of contention appeared to be a very pretty embroidered girdle, one that would be reserved for the most festive occasions. Louise was holding it casually, tauntingly in one hand, dangling it before the enraged Josette, much as one would tease a bull with a red banner. Once I had gathered that Louise had apparently taken the girdle from Josette's room on the claim that it had belonged to her, Louise, to begin with, I decided to assert myself.

"What, may I ask," I demanded in an even, authoritative tone that penetrated the hubbub, "is the meaning of this extraordinary scene?"

All heads turned sharply to me, and I noted with a sinking feeling that Josette and Louise were suddenly united against me, the common enemy.

Evidently no answer was to be forthcoming to my question, so I took a step toward Louise. "I think you had best hand that to me," I said to her in Norman, indicating the girdle.

Louise did not move. "And what makes you think you know what is best?" she shot back in that same language so that there could be no misunderstanding.

"I shall remind you but once that I am mistress here," I said flatly, giving her look for look.

"Aye, you're the lord's wedded wife, but that is all, when all is said," she returned, snapping her fingers at my authority.

"Your insolence shall not go unpunished," I warned her ominously.

"You're not mistress here," she spat back insolently, "and I'm not answerable to you."

I was at a loss. To be challenged overtly and in front of my women was a new experience for me, for, from the circumstance of the implicit acceptance of my authority at Shrivenham, I was used to commanding obedience. I was, of course, accustomed to settling squabbles and contretemps of every sort with varying degress of success, but to have my authority completely flouted was something for which I was entirely unprepared. I had been able in my short term at Hungerford to rouse the retainers to carry out my daily orders and to maintain certain standards of organization and cleanliness, but I always knew that I could not expect yet to enjoy unquestioned obedience; and it irked me profoundly to realize that the degree of loyalty given me in the immediate future would not in all probability be determined by my own merit or demerit, but by the perception that my retainers had of my husband's attitude toward me, which they had thus far had little opportunity to gauge.

I had no choice but to hold my ground.

"You are indeed answerable to me," I said coldly and quietly, "but whether or not you will come to realize it in time to save yourself is another matter."

This observation gave Louise pause, but only for a moment. Since this encounter had turned more or less into a test of wills between the two of us in front of the inside women, she tossed her head in smart defiance of me and my authority and resumed her taunting of Josette, who was only too glad, in turn, to accommodate.

There was nothing I could say to stop them or to prevent the shrill voices from spilling into the hallway where several more curious people had gathered, among them Gunhild, to witness my ineffectuality. I had no choice but to resort to physical violence, which I abhorred and which had no guarantee of working, and made a motion forward to check my authority from being disastrously undermined forever at Hungerford, when a sharp voice behind me smote the ears of those assembled.

"Hold hard!" my husband commanded, entering the chamber in one long stride.

His presence instantly altered the room's chemistry. The thin ring of people broke to make way for the master, and then he was at my side. He had caught me unawares, but I had enough of my wits about me to realize that he was in control of the situation and to appreciate his dramatic sense in bowing low over my hand and saying, audibly, with a smooth blend of formality and familiarity, "My dearest lady, it is a happiness to be at your side again."

Fortunately, no response was expected of me, and I suspected that Sir Roland's goal in deferring to me had been to divert attention away from Josette and Louise, for when he rounded on them in the next moment, he caught them a little off balance, but whereas Josette shrank back in real terror, Louise's eye gleamed malevolently.

I, too, had been rocked slightly off my equilibrium and was struggling to regain my own composure, so I was not able to school my wits enough to detect all the finer points that passed between my husband and Josette and Louise. I was aware only that Sir Roland spoke to them in an English as rapid and proficient as their own and that, at Louise's last, unwise burst of defiance of all authority, his anger kindled into a blazing

fire and his hand bit into her arm. It appeared that he was
going to strike her, and I felt an instinctive stiffening within
the group of onlookers as they waited apprehensively for the
blows to fall. But then my husband chanced to look up and
over at me, as if suddenly remembering my presence, and,
incalculably, he stayed his hand. Instead of striking her,
and with no more regard for her dignity than for that of a
wayward stableboy, he flung Louise away from him in disgust.
She crumpled at his feet in a heap, the disputed girdle beside
her, having fallen from her hand.

He did not so much as glance down at her. He addressed
the wide-eyed group in French. "The entertainment is over,"
he said in decidedly unpleasant tones. "Get you about your
work."

No one moved, and I had a good notion that fear and stunned
surprise held each person motionless. Curiously enough, it was
Louise, deeming that now was an auspicious moment to make
good her escape, who made the first move. She picked herself
up and headed for the door.

"Stay here, wench," Sir Roland said in a voice that understandably made Louise wince. "You too, Mistress Potter," he
added, regarding Josette, "for I am sure that your lady has
something to say to you both."

Louise looked at me with every evidence of loathing. "She
does not know anything about it," she hissed with strangled
fury at being so humiliated before her comrades.

He looked down at her with contempt. "She knows a good
deal about it, and since the matter rests entirely in her hands,
you may hope that she will be more merciful than I would be.
Now," he continued, hard eyes sweeping each face, "there is
nothing more for any of you here."

A third dismissal was not needed, and the women dispersed.
I caught only one nuance, which was to nag me much later,
and that was the queer look mingled with dislike and distrust
that passed between Roland and Gunhild before the old woman
left the room.

As the small crowd melted away, my husband bent down

to gather the belt of embroidered cloth and handed it to me. He must have known exactly what he was doing, and he could not have done me a better turn, for more than one person observed the gesture, and it set the seal of my absolute authority at Hungerford. But I should not have been surprised; I should have known that Sir Roland would treat me with unfailing courtesy and deference and that he would demand that the rest of Hungerford should follow his example. I should have learned not to have expected less from this man.

If there were other undercurrents in the exchanged words and glances, I was not alive to them at the time, and it would not be until after the Christmas celebrations that the whole distasteful episode would take on painful new significance.

When everyone had left the room, save the two disgraced women, Sir Roland came to stand behind me, and together we dealt with the issue. Sir Roland held the reins but left the final decisions to me. He made it coldly and stingingly clear that he had no slightest interest in establishing guilt or discovering to whom the girdle rightfully belonged. He had a way, I noted with a healthy respect, of crushing subalterns into their places, and I could readily believe that one would not lightly cross him. That was not my way, but it was effective. He also made it clear that whatever else had happened, Louise's insolence to me had been the far graver wrong-doing, and he apparently considered the matter in a very serious light.

He flicked a glance at Louise. "Shall I have her turned out, my lady?" he asked me when he had done with his verbal whipping.

I was sorely tempted to deal her such a fate. I had a visceral notion that she harbored ill will toward me and that it was something personal, although I could not fathom why that might be, having had little interchange with her. It would have relieved me to be quit of her, but I did not think it the wisest solution in the long run.

"No," I said slowly, "I think not. But I shall request to see her in the morning on the morrow in my solar."

"Very well," was all he replied, but I sensed in his response that I had made the right decision. He had also given me the opportunity, I realized, to appear merciful; at the same time, Louise was not likely to feel any kinder toward me because of it. I only hoped that her resentment would not run too deep. Sir Roland then sent them on their way, having reduced both to tears, and banished Louise from the hall for three meals.

Then Sir Roland and I were alone. He crossed to the window with his back to me and rested his hands on the casement. I hovered over two conflicting emotions: I felt immeasurably better with the length of the room separating us, but a childish disappointment tugged at me that he had not taken me in his arms and greeted me in the same manner as he had in the hall on the occasion of his other return to Hungerford.

"I should have warned you about Louise," he said at length, turning around to face me. His eyes, inscrutable and shadowed, were focused on me. I could not know what he was thinking.

"That she is not given to accepting authority, you mean?"

"She has never been biddable," he said, "but that is not what I had in mind."

"Perhaps you are referring to an association Louise might have had with John Potter?" I ventured. "Something I would not necessarily have discovered in my short time at Hungerford?"

He hesitated. "Perhaps," he replied, but I knew that this suggestion was no nearer to what he had in mind either.

I lowered my gaze and my eye fell on the girdle folded across my hand. I noticed for the first time that it was much finer than anything a maid might ordinarily possess. It was doubtless worth fighting over.

"My efforts to quell the altercation were not crowned with success, I fear," I said with a shaky laugh. "I am usually more effective."

"I am confident that you are," he said politely.

"You see," I said, compelled to explain, "I do not speak Saxon and felt somewhat at a loss."

"It has its uses."

"Your command of the tongue compels one to admiration, my lord," I said, striving for a lighter touch.

He smiled suddenly, and I felt very much less unsure of myself. "Does it, my lady? It is not generally considered a refinement."

"A refinement, no," I agreed, "but I can understand its practicality. Although I do not speak it, I do comprehend it."

"How good is your comprehension?" he asked, with tiny flickers of laughter lighting up the cool blue depths of his eyes.

"Reasonable," I answered. Then, emboldened by his sudden change of mood: "Reasonable enough to know that your knowledge of the language is intimate. I would not admit to a mastery of all the expressions you used, but the context far compensated for any meanings that failed me."

"A result of having learned my vocabulary in the stables," he said gravely. "A circumstance that my mother deplored but my father did nothing to stop. Speaking Saxon has proved, all in all, a valuable asset in meeting the retainers on their own terms if need be, and it dispels their subversive sense of superiority over the master if he is privy to their code. At the same time, demanding certain standards of French keeps them in their place."

He did not allow me to pursue any of these interesting openings. "And since I have returned earlier in the day than I had expected," he continued, "I should like to use this time to make myself fit company for you at the table. There must be at least another hour yet before the horn blows."

I affirmed this and suggested setting dinner back a half-hour, if he so desired, but he declined the need for the upset in schedule. "Shall I send Gavin to assist you then?"

"By all means."

He offered me his wrist and we left the room together.

I was eager to put the recent episode behind us. "It must have been a trifling errand," I said conversationally, "to have kept you away only a week."

"Yes, easily discharged, for a change," he said, "but there are always reasons to keep me on the move, and I could have stayed abroad another fortnight without exhausting Henry's commands. Fortunately, however, I was able to convince him that I was for once needed at my own castle before the advent of the Christmas celebrations."

"I am glad that you brought the king round to your way of thinking, for I am the one who stands to benefit directly. The guests will be arriving in another ten days, and there is still much to do. We are doing rather well, however, in spite of it all—or *were* doing well until this afternoon." I hurried on, "But apparently your errand did not require the services of your squire."

"A squire may always be of service," he replied, "although one is generally more of a convenience than a necessity. However, this time Gavin requested to stay here, and I saw no reason to deny him an infrequent petition."

"Requested?" I echoed, astonished. "Why should he have desired to stay behind?"

"I did not ask him. Mayhap he had something he wanted to do."

"I do not think so! In fact, I had the impression that the poor boy was restless. So bored, in fact, that he was reduced to offering to help me in my garden this morning."

Sir Roland glanced down at me. His face was closed. "And was he helpful?"

"Most!" I asseverated. "We cleared away much of a decade's wild growth in one corner of my pleasance, salvaged some worthwhile bushes along the way, and began to turn several rows of soil. He was really quite good at it and made some excellent suggestions for plantings. I think he told me he was used to do gardening at home in Scotland. And that reminds me that I extended invitations to Elspeth, Kate, and Janie, if ever they should pass this way. I hope you do not mind."

"Naturally not. You were at perfect liberty to do so," he said. "But, who might they be?"

I was surprised. "Why, Gavin's sisters, of course. Had you forgotten?"

"Ah, yes," he said in a way that made me think that he had never heard of the existence of Gavin's sisters. Knight and squire had been together five years, and I thought that Sir

Roland might have remained in happy ignorance of Gavin's sisters another five years, had not I chanced to mention them.

"He spoke of them fondly, and I almost thought that he was homesick. Well! Be that as it may, I hope that he has not regretted his decision not to accompany you."

"I shall remember to ask him," he said with a faint smile.

"It still seems odd to me," I insisted, "to stay here when he could be off and away and free."

"And what makes you cast the decision in just such terms?"

I slanted my eyes up at him. "It is the common notion, is it not, that it is an advantage to come and go as one pleases? I should like it, in sooth."

"Unhappy with your lot, Madam Wife?"

"No, not that!" I said quickly, flushing. "But surely you won't try to convince me that you would easily give up your freedom."

"No man is entirely free," he remarked.

My flush deepened. I had not thought he would be so tactless.

"Not even the king himself," he continued without hesitation, as if he took no heed of the unflattering interpretation of our marriage that I had put on his words. "And the reasons that make a man free—to use your words—may also rob him of life's value. It is a cheap freedom that knows no limits or purpose."

I recovered my complexion. "But I was speaking of adventure and freedom from responsibility."

"Aye, adventure's a grand thing, my lady."

That indefinable quality in his voice, so full of unexpected humor and understanding, made me suddenly aware that he carried a staggering load of responsibility. "But a bit overrated, perhaps?" I asked.

"I wouldn't say that."

"No, but that is what you mean," I said, having caught his eye, and I realized that some ideas communicated themselves far more effectively without the encumbrance of words. "I think you seek to convince me of the worth of my responsibilities.

Perhaps it is merely a question of temperament, for I know that when all is said, the life of castle ways suits me well enough."

He smiled approval at my understanding. "And you have convinced me," he said as we reached the hallway that led to the wing housing our chambers, "that Gavin did not have such a wrong idea after all."

A prettily turned compliment, that, and I could not help but smile up at my husband. "I think I know where to find him," I said, turning to go down the stairs in search of the squire, "and shall send him direct to your chambers."

Just a moment before the horn blew, luck afforded me a very satisfying encounter with a retainer in a day otherwise marred by one of a rather more unsettling nature. I descended to the Great Hall a few minutes ahead of Sir Roland to make sure that all was in readiness for the master's meal of home-coming. I was wearing my best kirtle of Guimont blue and had caught my hair in the beaded silver filet that I dared to think was flattering.

I would have thought that I commanded something of the aura of a chatelaine, but when Ben Wickett, who chanced to be loitering at the foot of the stairs, ran his lively eye over me with no glimmer of possible recognition, I paused to determine whether something was lacking in my appearance or Master Wickett was unusually obtuse. After his opening comments, I decided that I did, after all, have the look of the lady.

"Well, now, missy," he winked broadly, "all rigged out in yer finest. Faith, ye're a comely wench!"

This did not seem the moment to majestically ignore his impertinence and move on. I regarded him coolly. "I should think that I would know what manner of dress befits my station."

"Miss High 'n' Mighty!" he crowed. "The master's just home and already ye're scheming. But I'll be giving you a piece of advice, since ye're so determined, and that's to fill his belly well before ye think to fill his—"

The horn blasted in the bailey, swallowing his last word.

"And to that end," I said, "I am on my way to ensure the smooth presentation of the dishes this eventide."

"Ye're a cool one, you are," said Ben Wickett with a knowing smile. "I've heard it said, in fact. To my way of thinking, though, ye should have been scuttling to and fro this past hour or more."

Innocence widened my eyes. "Why would you think that?" I asked.

"Think what, my lady?" came Sir Roland's voice behind me.

I had to mask my pleasure with effort. I turned to greet my husband with a smile. "My lord," I said and laid a hand on his arm, "you are come to find me dawdling instead of consulting on the last-minute preparations with Nan."

Master Wickett started slightly and paled visibly.

Sir Roland indicated the shaken retainer with a nod. "So you have met?" he inquired of me. Humor was there along with a faint challenge that was too tempting to decline.

"Why, yes!" I responded brightly. "Master Wickett and I met earlier this afternoon in the yard. He was kind enough to identify himself as your personal messenger."

Sir Roland affirmed this, and I chatted merrily on. "And being one of your boon companions, he also mentioned that you were wont to drink together on occasion. Of course, it is such a relief for a wife to know how her husband spends his evenings—and with whom!"

"Surely, Ben, you did not regale my wife with any improper stories," Sir Roland said amiably. "Remember I am a married man now and must look to keep peace in my household!"

Words failed Master Wickett.

"Of course not, my lord! He knows better than to betray you, I am sure!" I replied archly. "Never fear, my lord, we spoke of horses instead."

My husband wisely refrained from pursuing this topic and confined himself to a mere "Ah, indeed!"

Nothing further was necessary. Sir Roland and I turned to go. Master Wickett seemed to slink away, thoroughly abashed, and was presently seen to take strategic refuge in his tankard of ale and to recruit himself with a long quaff.

Sir Roland did not immediately drop the subject. On our way to table he remarked casually, "Ben is known to have an eye for the ladies."

"Is he?" I answered blandly, and could not resist adding reflectively, "But of course you should know, being so well acquainted with him."

My husband looked down at me, not in the least disturbed by my reference. "I offer the observation in case you should feel it necessary to warn Nan, for I know you like to keep an eye on her," he said offhandedly.

I appreciated his knack for the ready answer. However, given what I had just witnessed and knowing the events that led to Master Wickett's discomfiture, I did not think that either Nan or I would suffer any unwanted attention from him. "I have good reason to think," I said with a measure of conviction, "that Ben Wickett is one man who will be staying far away from Nan."

There the discussion ended, but the subject of Nan was to come up later in the evening. The meal was an excellent one: Bess had exerted herself to good purpose, and my husband partook heartily of the flesh and dulcets. I did not suppose that the news of Louise and Josette's altercation and the master's intervention had not reached every ear in the keep by the time the dinner horn sounded, but no one dared make the least sign that aught was amiss. Indeed, as the courses followed one another, I began to wonder if indeed anything was amiss. Louise's absence from the hall was the only difference between this meal and any other, and it was scarcely noticeable. No one questioned the master's authority, so no one questioned his punishment of her, and judging from the occasional explosions of male laughter round the tables from this quarter or that, I surmised that no one really cared. Sir Roland had apparently put the matter behind him; I thought I could, too.

At length the meal was over, and the pages were scurrying to stack the lower tables against the wall so that the evening could proceed. One young man had produced a lute and was strumming idly in a corner, while another pair had placed a chess board between them and were bent in concentration over their moves. The largest crowd of men was gathered about the dicing on the floor at one end of the room, a pastime that Sir Roland seemed to countenance.

My husband had pushed his chair slightly back from the head table, perfectly at his ease, but did not seem inclined to participate in the evening's diversions. Instead, he allowed his men to drift over and greet him, as they desired, and give him informal reports on the demesne's affairs.

After a time I began to feel that I was serving no useful purpose and rose to go about my duties.

Sir Roland laid a hand on my arm to stay me. "Linger a moment, if it pleases you, my lady," he said with the barest suggestion of a smile behind his eyes, "and let your women tend to the cleaning."

I was somewhat surprised by this request, for we had exchanged little conversation during the meal. I had not interpreted this negatively; rather, I sensed that he was withdrawn this evening—tired, perhaps—but content to be back at his castle. And as I was content to remain at his side, I sat back down. His fingers rested heavily on my wrist, but presently he withdrew them and negligently signed for Gavin, who materialized at his side on the instant to refill our goblets.

I was slightly taken aback to see John Potter approach us a moment later, and without the slightest trace of embarrassment or any emotion other than his customary bluff good humor. He exhausted in considerable detail the goings-on at Hungerford during the week past and remained to explain chattily that he and his rib (as he designated Josette) had been out to inspect the holly bushes, in anticipation of the decoration of the hall that would begin the next week for the Christmas holidays, and pronounced them laden with red berries. After the plans and prospects for the coming festivities had been thrashed out, the Bear lumbered off in search of his mate, and I turned to Sir Roland.

"I must imagine that Josette told Master Potter all about what happened this afternoon," I said.

"I suppose she did."

His steady blue gaze on me did nothing to put me at my ease. I could not read by his face if he was trying to encourage or discourage me from the subject. In any case, I wanted to prove to him that I was not too craven to discuss the topic that I knew was uppermost on both our minds.

"And yet he seems to hold no hard feelings against you. I find that remarkable."

"I count John Potter among my men," was his unembellished response, and it told me all I needed to know.

He had also given me the perfect opening. "I wish I could say the same about Josette," I said with a good show of calm conviction.

Something flickered in his eyes. "Have you been plagued with other incidents such as the one you were forced to endure this afternoon?"

"Oh, no! It's just that—" I paused, groping for the best way to express myself. "But it is so very hard to put into words!"

"It seems a straightforward enough matter to tell me if Josette has been disobedient or openly resentful of your presence."

"But she hasn't, you see. She is really most obedient, and as for being resentful, I would say that she viewed my coming here with, well, relief."

"So I would have thought," he said. "She has never been assertive, and you are a very good chatelaine."

"No, my lord!" I disclaimed instantly. Then: "Well, that is, I do *try* to— Thank you!" I managed at last, flushing a little. "But that is not the point. The truth of the matter is that I have always thought that she feared me, for some reason that I cannot quite fathom. It is very odd for me, I assure you! I know, of course, the old saying: 'Be feared and respected or loved and scorned.' That is what Lady Isolde used to say. Sir Reynauld's wife! Our seneschal. You remember him? Yes, of course! How silly of—! Well, *she* used to say that a mistress must be feared in order to command authority and respect, and that if your retainers know that they can push you into any position, they merely end by scorning you. But *I* know that Lady Isolde was both loved and respected—not that that is of the least interest to you—and I—I'm not used to being feared. Not in *that* way, in any case, as if I *beat* them, which I have never done! So I do not know why Josette should fear me, as if I would do anything cruel to her. Oh!—not that some mistresses—or masters—might not find it warranted on occasion to resort to physical vio—physical punishments. I am just saying that it is not *my* way."

"I have no reason to think that you necessarily criticize a way simply because it is not your own."

"No, no," I said hastily. "Of course not! Nevertheless, I find it odd that she should feel that way toward me, although I should not complain, for she always does my bidding. Except, of course, this afternoon. But she was not entirely at fault, and I could see that she was goaded into indiscreet behavior and was thoroughly contrite, whereas Louise," I continued, taking the plunge, "distinctly dislikes me. Nor does she respect my authority, which is only too obvious! Again, it is not her dislike of me that is worrisome. I never deluded myself, for instance, that I was universally liked at Shrivenham, necessarily, but that was entirely different! I do not have the faintest idea why she should take me in dislike, and that is what troubles me. At Shrivenham, I could have named every reason for a dislike, and some of them, no doubt, justified, for I could not have been unerringly correct and balanced in every decision I made. But Louise! I do not know what to make of it!"

I had said more than enough, and I resolutely closed my lips. Sir Roland did not respond for some moments. Finally, he said slowly, "Perhaps Louise was only testing you, as a small child will do to discover his limits. But I have little experience in these matters, and any suggestions I might offer could only mislead your own judgment."

I do not know what I had expected him to tell me. It was entirely my own problem; I knew that much. However, I was sure he had a better idea of what was going on than he was prepared to share with me. I took an absorbed interest in my hands clasped in my lap and tried to convince myself that his response, however politely worded, was not a rebuff. His next question restored my confidence.

"Are you concerned about the effect of the incident today on your effectiveness?" he asked after a short silence.

"As to that, I should think my authority is now firmly established," I conceded. "And it is such a comfort—you cannot guess!—to have Bess and Gertrude with me, since I do not have to win their allegiance and they are accustomed to my ways. Yes, and even Nan seems to be doing rather well, at least according to Gavin, who assures me that she has been taking care of herself. If that means what I hope it does, then I am heartily relieved of the burden of having to spend my evenings stitching with her."

I was looking idly about the room as I was talking, and, by coincidence, when I mentioned Nan my eyes fell on her. She was carrying a heavy tray out to the kitchens, when at that moment Gaston crossed her path and stopped her. They exchanged a few words, and I was glad to see Nan move on, but I was hardly reassured by the stark look of desire in Gaston's face as his eyes followed her out of the room.

"That is, I think I am relieved of having to tie her to my skirts," I said, having observed this by-play.

Sir Roland's gaze had also fastened on the couple. "I have every confidence in Gaston's ability to relieve you of that responsibility," he commented.

He could have meant only one thing. "But I cannot have her behaving indecently!" I exclaimed.

"Can you not?"

I laughed uncertainly and admitted that I did not know.

"I think Nan a very clever wench," he said, "who is well able to look after herself."

I raised my brows in question.

He shook his head slightly and a small smile twisted his lips. "I cannot see for you," he said. "Come, I tire of the hall and desire to exercise the privilege of being alone with my wife in our private chambers."

We rose, and Sir Roland reminded Gavin, who was standing by impassively, to see to the banking of the fires, and we left our retainers to the enjoyment of the diversion that suited them best.

Chapter 12

I had come to look forward to the evening meal in those few days that preceded the Christmas celebration, when Sir Roland and I would be together with our people. I began to appreciate how important those daily gatherings were for the sense of community that prevailed in a keep and how we at Shrivenham, with our sullen, often sour mealtimes, had missed an opportunity to strengthen castle unity. The meals at Hungerford were actually pleasant, I would say, and if they were characterized by a certain masculine roughness, it never became too unseemly for a woman's taste.

I particularly felt the shortage of women at Hungerford during that period. The few women there were had been burdened to the breaking point with chores and preparations. Josette still cast me fearful looks every now and then, and Louise maintained an attitude toward me that I could only describe as mutinous, but I was too occupied to spare much thought for their opinions of me, and their feelings for me certainly did not prevent me from delegating to them their share of the work. I could not, in truth, complain. They were under no obligation to like me, and they had the sense to show only respect to me in public.

Sir Roland, I discovered, was not a great talker at mealtime. He was, as one might expect, always polite and was willing to expand on any theme I might inaugurate, but he never told stories to amuse the company or indulged in what might even loosely be construed as gossip, and would likely have been just as happy to pass the time in companionable silence. I did not attribute this supposed preference of his to temperament, since I had almost immediately noticed that he was naturally engaging with his men and remained at all times very accessible to them. Rather—and he was most unobtrusive about it—he ate and drank while keeping a watchful eye on the proceedings in the hall. I imagined that little escaped his notice and was quite certain that his watchfulness accounted for the remarkable absence of drunkenness and brawling in so male a stronghold as Hungerford. Not that there weren't outbursts on occasion and skirmishes, but Sir Roland rarely found it necessary to intervene. I believed that most men thought it prudent not to provoke the master's ire.

And being so observant of all castle detail, he took a discreet, courteous interest in my affairs and made the proper inquiries into the endless preparations for the guests whom we would soon be receiving. I also related to him the broad outlines of the most unpleasant interview I had with Louise the morning after her orgy of rebellion and thought that he should know that she had shown not the least measure of contrition. He did not comment to this, but merely nodded, and the talk moved on. It was clear to me through these exchanges that he had a reasonable grasp of the duties and dilemmas that daily faced the lady of the manor. It crossed my mind more than once that he was warning me that I would not be able to get away with anything at Hungerford as I supposed he thought I had at Shrivenham; yet his manner toward me was so respectful that I chose to interpret his comments in the light of a lord who let nothing slip by.

Nevertheless, I was surprised when his attention focused on me. When he complimented me one evening on my new hair arrangement, I was in sufficient command of myself to thank him very nicely, but he threw me off my guard later as the meal was finishing. The manchets had been removed and the fruit and nuts and finger bowls set before us when Sir Roland suddenly singled out Gertrude in the act of harrying a page to step more lively.

"Your tiring woman. There," he said, indicating this exacting taskmaster. "What is her name? Gertrude? She has the look of a hunted wolf."

I could not suppress a chuckle. I turned toward him, full

of amusement. "My father once likened her to a skinned rabbit, but I prefer to compare her to an eagle, so sharp are her eyes." I stopped suddenly, afraid I had spoken amiss, and looked down. "But I should not be so unkind as to speak thus, for she serves me well."

When I looked up I saw the little flames warming the depths of his eyes. His hand closed over mine.

"No, you are not unkind but entirely accurate," he said lightly. "And indeed she serves you well, for never have I seen a better pair of tiring women: the one overripe and the other underfed, to set off the most perfect and pleasing lines of their mistress."

This put me to the blush, and before I could recover my composure, he challenged me to a game of chess.

With the uneasy apprehension that the level of chess practiced by Friar Helm or any of the other indifferent players at Shrivenham was likely to fall considerably short of Sir Roland's standards, I immediately bethought myself of all the day's tasks that lay undone, and judging from the look of polite incredulity on my husband's face, I sought to clinch my withdrawal from the contest by adding, in all honesty, "And you would be most disappointed in my play, moreover, it being nothing out of the ordinary!"

"Like your horsemanship, I suppose, or any other accomplishment anyone might wish to credit you with," he said, plainly amused. "Your modesty is most becoming, my lady, but it is a nuisance at times. There is really no reson to berate my poor man's intelligence, either. I am reasonably aware of what needs your attention on the instant and what does not, and since I can think of nothing more relaxing right now than a quiet *partie* of chess, I invite you once again."

"Unfair!" I laughed. "How dare you shame me into accepting you when you know I would like nothing better than to spare myself the humiliation of defeat?"

"But I am not considering your wishes, my lady."

"In defiance of all the laws of chivalry!" I countered.

"They are very dull, and someday I shall even succeed in browbeating you into riding out with me!" he murmured.

The board was set up between us and the play determined by a blind selection of the pawns. I was oddly pleased that he did not automatically accord to me the first move. It was not long before I discovered that my apprehension was well grounded. I knew, of course, that there lay a difference between simply applying the rules that governed play and commanding a firm grasp of strategy, but I had never before sat opposite anyone who possessed the finesse that the game obviously merited. After the opening moves, I found myself at sea and was soon floundering, aware of only enough to realize that I lacked the larger picture and could not, therefore, plan more than two or three moves ahead. Time and again I found each little tactic of mine not only foiled but working to my disadvantage, so that before too long, the end was, mercifully, imminent, and I conceded defeat with a sigh.

"The only thing worse," I said, surveying the slaughter with dismay, "would have been for you to have allowed me to win."

"I would not so insult your intelligence, my lady."

"I thank you for that, at least, my lord!" I answered. "I find very little satisfaction in proving to you that my modesty was not false. In fact, if I claimed my play to be nothing out of the ordinary, I am sure I was being far too generous! Pray, excuse me so that I may put my real talents to good use!"

"What, and leave me in the untenable position of not being able to offer you a grudge match?"

"Surely you do not intend to put us both through this a second time!"

"I do indeed," he said. "You want only practice." He put a black and a white pawn behind his back, mixed them up, and held his fists out to me. "Choose!"

It made little difference in the end which color I defended. I bent my powers of concentration on the game and tried to make a decent account of myself, but I barely managed to labor through the match and felt vast relief when it came to its inevitable conclusion.

"I think it superfluous to point out," I said after this particularly disastrous game, "that I have not the head for moves and countermoves."

Sir Roland looked up at me and smiled briefly. "It is true you are no chess player."

"It is a relief to me that you have come to realize it!"

"I own, however, that it makes me wonder just how you spent your time at Amesbury. Catherine is as canny and as subtle as they come and as formidable an opponent as any I've known."

We had not mentioned the Abbess Catherine since Alicia's wedding. I was happy to have the common ground of a mutual friend between us. I looked slyly up at him. "So I am aware! She is also not one to waste her time. She played with me several times, as she did with all the novitiates, and afterward counseled me that my efforts would be better spent improving my letters. So if you have complaints, my lord, you may address them to her yourself. It is my belief that she thinks you owe her a letter."

"She does, does she?"

"Yes. I wrote her sometime during the second week after I came here to Hungerford. I thought she deserved to be informed of our marriage by me personally."

"I would be most surprised if she had not heard of it through her own sources within days of the wedding."

"As to that, I don't know, but in her return letter she made it clear that she had heard about it before I wrote to her, and she found a few words to say on the defection of former pupils from the dictates of common courtesy. She did not think the suddenness of the ceremony was sufficient reason for her not to have been informed beforehand!"

"Let that be a lesson to you," he replied. "Always know with whom you are dealing, and act accordingly. You should know by now that it does little good to offer Lady Catherine excuses, no matter how compelling they may be!"

"Well, my lord, I take leave to inform you that you did not come off very much better in her estimation."

"Do not spare me. Tell me the worst!"

"I suggest that you write her yourself if you want a firsthand account, but I will say that she seemed inclined to congratulate me on the match."

"This sounds more encouraging!"

"*Inclined*, I said. Her precise words were that she could think of a half-dozen men offhand who would have made me worse husbands."

He took Abbess Catherine's teasing in good part and said that he would write her, for he had a thing or two to say himself on the subject of meddling old ladies, and in this new spirit of friendliness that prevailed between Sir Roland and me, I made so bold the next evening as to beg him to tell me of his adventures in the Holy Land.

He smiled. "Is this your way of forestalling another challenge from me to a game of chess?"

"Of course!" I responded immediately. "How did you guess? It also occurs to me that you should make good on your promise to tell me of your experiences there. Or have you forgotten?"

"No, I remember it well. But I do not expect that you mean to learn about the Saracens' use of Greek fire and the best methods of countering it."

It sounded horrible, and, no, I did not really want to be initiated into the grim realities of war. "Indeed not, and you may spare me the unpleasant details. Tell me first why you went."

If I thought he had been fired with a religious conviction, I was doomed to disappointment. "Do you believe I vowed on my sickbed to go to Outremer like Louis of France? No. The king sent me. I went in forty-six at the beginning. I was in Gascony four years ago in any case, and so it was easy enough to join Louis in Egypt. I stayed with him a little more than a year."

"Why did you come back so soon?"

"I had discovered all that I needed to know."

I waited expectantly, but he did not elaborate. "Do I take that as it stands, or shall I respectfully point out that you have told me nothing so far?"

"If I say nothing on the subject, it is only to spare you disillusionment. I was not the least interested in the securing of Jerusalem for our Pope or anyone else, if you must have the truth, nor in any matters of faith, but in taking the measure of the Mongols, who have harassed much of Christendom to the east of the Holy Roman Empire. Of course, Genghis Khan died a dozen or more years ago, but there is still the Great Khan reigning at Karakorum in Asia, and although his hordes have retired to the steppes for the time being, there is at present another Mongol faction that has been threatening the caliph of Baghdad for several years, and I wanted to take a firsthand look at its strength."

"And what is your estimation of it?" I asked, amazed at the idea of anyone having to think about such things.

"I think that Europe is safe from invasion in the immediate future," he replied, with the ghost of a smile.

"I see," I said, frowning in thought. "But tell me: what do you remember most about the Holy Land?"

"Besides the flies, you mean?" He laughed. Then: "I think it must be the dawn." He paused to consider this. "Either that or the waves of silvery dunes in the moonlight. No, I think it must be the dawn across the great sweep of sands that stretches southward from Acre to where Mount Carmel thrusts its spur into the sea. The dawn in the Orient is not like in England, where the day comes softly, wrapped in mist. You see, the prudent man there must exercise his mount before the heat of the eastern day comes to stun man and beast. I had many mornings to experience the dawn, and the memory of it will remain green for many years to come. It is the coolest time of day, and the cleanest, made all the more invigorating by a brisk breeze off the bay. The day comes upon one without warning. One moment the moon rules the sky, and the next, as if one had but blinked, the stars go out and the east flushes rose and gold. It is as if all at once the heaven is clear, cloudless blue, the sun's edge tips the dunes, and the day has leapt upon one in one long stride."

I was somewhat awed and not just a little captivated, and, with a little prodding, I drew him out on the various aspects of that exotic land and people that had fascinated me for so long. He sketched a fearsome and amusing portrait of that curious, malodorous animal, the camel, with its snakelike neck and oversized paws, that was as likely to be seen wending its sinuous way through the striped tents and gay robes of the markets as it was to be heard trumpeting its weird cry amidst the clash of cymbals and the throbbing drums of battle, spurring storms of sand underfoot to shower banners, standards, and bright mail alike. And then there were the swarms of flies—much more bothersome than the Infidels, so my husband confided to me—and the dust and the searing glare of noon to drive all white-skinned men to shelter. He evoked an enchanted land of azure sky, relentless sun, and seas of sand, and then broke his own spell when he turned toward me and said, "But when all was said, I longed for a rolling meadow, a damp, cold winter morning, and the fresh scent of peat."

My thirst was hardly slaked, but I allowed the topic to shift by remarking on my essences and recounting what I had learned of the Infidels' use of the alcohol base. He seemed to welcome this change of subject, and we fell to talking of this and that until it was time to retire.

The festive spirit filled the keep in the days before Christmas Eve. This was the season of pinching and kissing and mistletoe. I had caught the fun and told my husband in a lighthearted mood one evening after the repast that I thought it high time that Gavin, whom I spied standing aloof, was married.

Sir Roland rolled an eye at me and said with marked diffidence, "Why is that a woman has only to look at an unattached man to be smitten with an unrelenting desire to get him riveted?"

"It's not that! Really it's not!" I protested, laughing and at the same time reddening under his baleful stare. "I just thought that he might be happier to be wed."

"I was not aware that he was unhappy in service at Hungerford."

"I do not think so! Not at all! It is simply that he seems so alone sometimes. Lonely, in fact, and it occurred to me that he wanted only a wife to be happy." I paused. "And you needn't point out that the married state need not necessarily contribute to a man's happiness."

"I had no intention of doing so," he replied gravely, but humor peeped through the stern set of his eyes. "But I am curious: do you have someone in mind for the honor of becoming his wife?"

I had to admit that I did not.

"That relieves my mind, in all events!" he said. "My dear, do you have any idea how difficult it is to find a squire of Gavin's caliber?"

"He can still be your squire if he is married, can he not? And, besides, did you not tell me that a squire was more of a convenience than a necessity?" I argued, rather pleased with myself.

"Yes, but a most necessary convenience, I think! And, yes, it is possible that he might remain my squire as a married man, although it is not customary. But it occurs to me that since he is unlikely to be marrying anyone at Hungerford—we have remarked on the shortage of women here before, have we not? and there is none among them of his rank—he would probably be making an alliance with some handmaiden at court, where it would be natural for him to take up residence, and then I should lose my squire."

"But think! That would be even better! He could bring his bride back here, for we have just said that we could use another pair of feminine hands. There are many genteel occupations for a lady of rank here. I should be most glad of her, in fact!"

"Ah! At last you expose yourself! Behind every innocent face revolves a scheming woman's mind. It would have been more to the point to have said outright that you need another woman here on the inside."

I cast him a look of deep disapproval. "I just this moment thought of that aspect of his marriage."

"And that is what is so particularly compelling about the argument."

"*Will* you be serious? The poor boy is—well, he *is* lonely. He must have met some nice young lady at court who struck his fancy."

There came a disturbing look into Sir Roland's eyes as they

rested on me. It vanished before I could interpret it, to be replaced by a mischievous twinkle. "The lad has but twenty summers behind him. There is time and to spare for him to settle down. I think you would do better to occupy your mind with a more immediate concern of yours." His eyes searched the room and then stopped. "It might interest you to know that Gaston is making excellent progress with Nan."

I followed the direction of his gaze with a distinct feeling of misgiving. Gaston was standing close above Nan, looking down at her. She was holding her hands behind her back, as if she had just the moment before snatched them from his grasp. Her face was stormy. His was slashed by a superior, satisfied smile. They exchanged a few words, the contents of which we could only guess at, and then Nan turned on her heels, deftly dodged his snatching hand, and left the room.

I rose to Nan's defense. "I do not know if I should call that progress precisely. It looks to me that she is doing an excellent job of keeping him at arm's length."

"I have said that I think her a clever wench."

A retort bubbled to my lips, but I managed to swallow it before it was too late.

Sir Roland caught my hesitation. He was a very acute man and had a way of cutting to the core of things. "I hope that you are not going to try to convince me," he said, "that she is something other than what we both know she is. And it is too late for me to believe that you have anything but the most practical view of morality. Given this, I should like to know why you feel so apprehensive about Nan's behavior here."

He had asked me a very good question: I did not know why it had become of prime importance to me that Nan should not fall into the Bastard's net. I supposed vaguely that it was because I sensed that Gaston was a man to be reckoned with and shared nothing in common with the Michel Armorers, the John Cooks, and the Edrics she had left behind at Shrivenham. "I was only thinking," I said with a composure I did not feel, "that she had better watch out or she'll be in over her head."

"Gaston's got not a shred of subtlety about him, I grant you that, but I give him credit for knowing what he wants." My husband tossed off the rest of his wine. "And I don't think she has much choice of it in the end."

These words, lightly spoken, unnerved me, and I made an unsuccessful effort not to recoil. Sir Roland glanced down at me and his expression softened. "You know, my lady, you have only to say the word, and I will tell Gaston to stop his pursuit."

This reassurance, so simple and direct, completely restored my balance. "No," I laughed, mentally chiding myself for a silly goose, "I am sure that she can take care of herself with no intervention from me."

"Good girl," he said and peeled me a nut by cracking it between his long fingers.

I felt suddenly, absurdly secure and was very well content with my lot in life.

It was just such an exchange as this that lulled me into believing that the distance between Sir Roland and me was diminishing and which left me thoroughly unprepared for the disaster that befell me at the evening meal a mere three days before the guests were to arrive on the morning of Christmas Eve.

The keep was already assembled in the hall and the first courses were about to be presented. I had withheld the sign to commence until Sir Roland would enter the hall. He was a few minutes late, but I did not deem that circumstance of any consequence. I was standing on the dais, idly chatting with John Potter, awaiting only the pleasure of taking my meal with my husband. Presently the echo of footsteps rang in the corridor leading to the counting rooms. I looked up with a smile, expecting to see my husband.

I did, but what I saw took me by surprise. Sir Roland's face had been transformed into a white sheet of arctic fury, and the powerful lines of his body were tethered by the loosest of bridles. Gavin came breathless in his wake the next instant and tried to capture his attention, but the boy was shrugged off as if he were the veriest fly.

The hall hushed swiftly to a still, deadly silence.

"Who has had his hand in the till?" the master demanded in a voice I had never heard him use before. Its coldness chilled me to the marrow. He did not move, but his eyes began to scan the room, and I suddenly perceived the unutterable folly of what I had done.

It was such a stupid thing, really, I saw now with nauseating clarity. Such a silly, inexcusably stupid thing, and the worst of it was that I had thought I was doing the right thing. Just after daybreak, Sir Roland and a small party had ridden out in the demesne, and I knew they would not be back until the evening meal. So when, during the course of the morning, an old peasant came to the keep from a far hamlet seeking the lord, wheezing a tale of bargain sealed over a barrel of grain that he had deposited in the bailey and requesting a sum so small as to be insignificant, I weighed the merits of making the man wait for Sir Roland against discharging the debt and sending the man on his way before nightfall. I thought at the time—and it seemed so harmless, given the ease of late between Sir Roland and me—that my husband would want me to use my better judgment and to settle the matter expeditiously. Consequently, I told the old man to wait, while I went to the estate's coffers in the counting rooms, never once thinking, as I tried the endless number of keys at my waist in the lock on the door, that I was stepping amiss. It took me some little time to go through the desk to find the keys to the money chest, but I managed at last to find them and tried to restore them to their original place without upsetting Sir Roland's careful arrangement of the drawer. I could not recall if the keys went to the right or to the left of a box of quills. I finally decided that it did not matter and placed them on top of the box. It occurred to me that I should leave some sort of record of the transaction on top of the ledger in the drawer, but on second thought, I deemed it simpler merely to inform Sir Roland of it verbally at dinner.

If I had not thought of the incident again for the remainder of the day, I had ample time in that split second in which his eyes were sweeping the hall to reflect on the utter folly that had possessed me to go into those chambers without his permission. He could only think the worst of me for it; I had only my miserable self to blame. Then his eyes met mine and stopped.

The words fell out of my mouth, fragile, fearful, crystal droplets breaking against uncompromising stone. "I have, my lord."

"It is as I thought," he grated, and then closed his mouth with the savage decisiveness of a portcullis.

I hardly knew what I was doing. I took several steps toward him. I think I had one arm outstretched. "It was Hradolf the Miller from Saint Phillip's Wood—" I began, but I could not continue. My hand dropped to my side, useless in its gesture of innocence.

I was dimly aware in those few seconds, not longer than the space of two heartbeats, that my husband intended to do me physical violence. I was curiously unafraid, thinking irrelevantly that at last I had seen the man without his yoke of urbanity, that I alone was responsible for provoking his cold fury and must bear the consequences, that such must have been his temper the night his brother died. Fool that I was, I did not even know enough to save myself. I mechanically, irresistibly took another step toward him. I saw something change in him then. Perhaps it was my movement—I could not have said—but his features became arrested, and then his eyes narrowed to slits of blue ice. Without another word or glance, he spun smartly on his spurs, snapping his fingers for his riding party, and vanished down the hallway. I stood staring stupidly after him just long enough to see Gavin cast me an unmistakable look of beseeching intensity. I could not interpret it. Then he too disappeared.

There was a stunned moment of paralysis in the room, as if the breath had been punched out of it. I did not know what else to do, so I signed for the presentation of the dishes, frankly amazed when the pages sprang to life at my command. John Potter, bless his soul forevermore, guided me gently to my seat and sat down at my left. The meal commenced as usual, his lordship's chair conspicuously empty.

I have never cried easily. I have never considered it a particular asset not to cry easily; in fact, I could think of occasions when the release of a few tears might have brought welcome relief. Nevertheless, when I began to eat, I was, perhaps for the first time in my life, profoundly thankful that I was not prone to breaking down in front of the assembled hall and giving in to a hearty bout of bawling.

I could not have made it through the meal without the support of John Potter. My heart was pounding so that I could hardly breathe, my hands were shaking so that I feared to raise my goblet lest I spill the wine, and all eyes were upon me so that I could scarce eat, and yet, through all of this, John Potter kept up a flow of chatter, incredible for its unselfconscious good humor. His was the only voice to be heard, booming along cheerfully, every word discernible above the subdued clatter of cutlery and the serving of the pages. He kept it up for the longest time until finally, toward the end of the interminable repast, other voices fell to talking among themselves, quietly, but they were talking, and I knew the worst was over. The worst of the immediate trial, that is, for the next few days were equally difficult, the only difference being that my fresh pain had dulled to a constant ache, my dogged companion of which I became at length contemptuous.

John Potter had had the presence of mind to request a page to leave a flacon of wine at the table. Thus, we dispensed with the need for another pair of ears to be hovering over us, and when other voices rose to fill the void in the hall, John Potter filled my goblet and lowered his voice.

"You did very well, my lady," he told me.

I unflexed my fingers, feeling the cramp in each one, and commanded my hands very deliberately and very carefully to bring the vessel to my lips. I was immoderately pleased with my success. The wine was sharp; it tasted good.

"I do not have the faintest idea of what I have done," I replied.

"Oh, aye, it's for certain you've escaped a terrible death," he said. His callous cheerfulness momentarily took my breath away.

"Do you mean to reassure me?" I managed after a moment.

He looked at me with a shrewdness of which I had not thought him capable and said, "You'd have us all believe that you've not an ounce of courage."

I did not know what courage had to do with it, and stated as much.

"Not many have stood up to Guy and walked away without a mark," he laughed, "but I always knew he'd never lay a hand on you in anger."

"I did not stand up to him, however," I said, "and I doubtless deserved a beating."

"For what, my lady?" he queried. "There's not a speck of harm in what you did, as far as I can see, and the devil of it is (beggin' your pardon!) that Guy knows it, too! At least he has that much sense! But he's got himself into it now, poor fellow, and will just have to get himself out of it. I shouldn't worry about it, however, if I were you, my lady. You've earned yourself a new name this evening!"

John Potter was at liberty to interpret events whichever way he wanted; I had no intention of explaining to him the depths of my stupidity. I did not think anyone else in all of Hungerford would take so lenient a view of Sir Roland's anger, but I was curious about one thing. "A *new* name?" I asked with a measure of trepidation.

"Up until now you've been dubbed 'Lady with the Scrub Brush,'" he explained with a rumbling chuckle, "but I would wager after today you'll be the 'Lady to be Feared.'"

"You do not seem particularly afraid of me, John Potter," I pointed out.

He laughed, as if I had made a rousing good joke, and the sound of his heavy chuckle brought round several heads in our direction. "You'll see, my lady, " he said. "You'll see."

I did not put much store in John Potter's perception of my status, but I was aware that he alone had spared me much, and I saw no reason to doubt him openly and give him offense. His good instincts carried me through to the end of the meal, whereupon he escorted me out of the hall and handed me conspicuously into Bess's care. This trusty woman was inclined to take a rather dark view of my situation, and could not keep from shaking her head mournfully as she undressed me in my chambers and deposited me, exhausted, sometime later into my marriage bed.

Sir Roland did not return to Hungerford that night. Nor did he make an appearance in the course of the next day.

I did not know what to think, but I rapidly realized what I could do about his absence, and that was absolutely nothing. Our guests were to arrive in a matter of days, and with all my other apprehensions about receiving so many people, I did not even know if they would be greeted by their host.

The next few days may not have brought me Sir Roland, but they did reveal to me that, against all my expectations, John Potter had been right about one thing at least: I might very well have qualified for the epithet "Lady to be Feared." There lingered no question in anyone's mind that I was to be obeyed. Even Louise accorded me a certain grudging respect. I had earned authority now; it had not merely been given to me by my husband.

How I had earned it, I was not quite sure. However, the impression over the next few days remained: I was worthy, in the eyes of Hungerford, of commanding respect. And if I needed a final confirmation of that fact, Gunhild provided it.

She always managed to accost me when I was alone, without another woman at my heels. She caught me the day after Sir Roland's departure on my way to my sewing room. All the major preparations had been completed, and I had summarily dismissed my women so that I could go to my odd little chamber to reflect.

Gunhild seemed to materialize out of the shadows in the south hallway. Her sudden appearance blocked my path and took me by surprise. I stepped back from her with a slight gasp.

She appraised me frankly and at length. On other occasions, she had unnerved me and had inspired in me a certain lack of self-confidence, but now, with all the other things I had on my mind, I did not stop to examine my own deficiencies. Irritation was the feeling uppermost in my mind.

"Well, Gunhild?" I snapped.

A slow, twisted smile spread over her face. "I have said that you were not like the other Guimont women."

"Really? I am sure that I can believe it, seeing that—that a scrub brush was an unknown quantity before my arrival," I said. "At least now we have a keep fit for the peers' eyes."

"'Clean hands, a clean heart,'" she quoted ironically.

I felt very sure of myself. "There is a certain correlation, I should think!"

"But who would've thought the little lamb had the courage of a lioness?" Her tone mocked.

"Anyone with half a wit about her!" I retorted, and swept regally by her and down the corridor to my chamber. I closed the door behind me and locked it.

This was the second time I had been endowed with the virtue of courage. It was not a mantle I was used to wearing; I did not entirely understand how I had come to be cloaked by it. Clearly, something I had done in the hall had been perceived as courage. It apparently had nothing to do with the fact that I had not fled the hall after Sir Roland's departure and buried my face forever under the mound of covers on my bed. I had confronted the situation, yet that had not been a question of courage. I simply had no other choice; I had not fled because the thought had not occurred to me, my brain having been too addled to consider alternatives. No, I thought rather that Hungerford had seen me look upon the face of death without flinching. The thought of merely dying—the giving up of my soul so that it might inhabit another realm—did not frighten me. On the other hand, stamping, snorting steeds, wild boars crazed with blood, Black Death, the bared steel of a raised broadsword, even jousts and tourneys—in short, all the agents of pain and death that threatened life from behind every corner and every bush—these things evoked in me a profound terror. John Potter had not exaggerated, I decided, when he said that Sir Roland had been in a mood to kill me. I believed he would have gladly and with his bare hands. Yet that prospect, as frightening as it was, had been thrust aside when I saw with such blinding clarity the vision of him stripped of every guard that civilization had bred into him. He had loosed himself brutally from the bridle in that moment, and I had been fascinated, as if I had been waiting for such a glimpse, before his reason returned to him and he left the room. I was obliged to give myself a mental shake: the sight of Sir Roland had been awesome, but that was not what had displaced my fear. Mayhap I had felt deep down, as had John Potter, that my husband would not raise a hand against me in anger. Truth to tell, I did not know if I believed this explanation.

Nothing at all made any sense, so I shut it out of my mind, draining it of as much thought and feeling as I was able while Bess readied me for bed on the second evening of Sir Roland's absence. I went to sleep in my own private chamber, it being too humiliating to spend another night of waiting vainly, restlessly for him in our common bed.

The next day dawned with a hint of snow in the air and no sign of my husband. I prayed fervently for the heaviest snowfall in history to prevent anyone from reaching Hungerford on the morrow. I dragged myself through the day, deriving a cynical satisfaction, wholly unworthy of me, from seeing retainers jump at my slightest request. The entire castle was in readiness; I tried to ignore the expectant, nervous glances that came my way throughout the day. Evening came, and I actually forced myself to endure the period of general relaxation in the hall that always followed the meal, thinking that trial less taxing than being alone in my chambers.

Sleep finally caught up with me that night. It was an uneasy repose, filled with weird dreams of fear and death, but sleep, even troubled sleep, was better by far than tense wakefulness in the long, empty watches of the night.

Something disturbed my light submersion into sleep. The click of a door, perhaps, a soft, scraping footfall, a sigh, or all of those things, and slowly I became dimly aware of another presence in my room.

"Roland?" I whispered through a groggy mist of mingled hope and fear.

"Yes, love," he reassured me. His tone was tired and patient and plucked a string in my heart usually closed to him by the defenses of my waking consciousness.

My head sank back into the pillows with drowsy relief. "I thought you had left me," I murmured.

"Never, my heart," he answered softly.

I heard him move silently about my chambers, divesting himself of his heavy clothing. I knew instinctively that he had ridden half the night across frozen fields to reach my bed and drop his aching heart at my feet.

"Art angry with me, my lord?"

There was silence and stillness. "Nay, my love."

I smiled contentedly to myself. I hovered still on the rim of full awareness, languorous in a satisfied drowse, and refused to rouse myself out of it. I lifted the covers back slightly for him. "Come. It is cold and the bed is warm."

"You have lit no fire."

"No, I did not expect you tonight."

"That does not explain why you laid no fire."

"I am used to it when I am alone," I said. "It is an economy. I did not steal any money, Roland."

He made a sound somewhere between a laugh and a groan and slid into bed beside me. He was cold, and I could feel his relief when I slipped my arms around him so that his cheek rested against my breast. The warmth of my body instantly leapt to his, and I was enveloped in a serenity so rapt and tranquil that I would have fallen back asleep on the moment had it not been that the warmth spread to my blood with a fierce, unbearable intensity.

Darkness sheds a special light on lovers, unlocking things too tender or too painful to be expressed by light of day. When he drew himself up into my arms, I could understand that whatever he had said and whatever he had thought of me, he had not left me forever, would never have left me, and I forgave him all, just as I supposed he had forgiven me. What had been inexplicable to me about him in his absence these past days somehow became quite consistent as I lay in his arms this night, and the problem that this morning I had been sure was hopeless had found a fresh, entirely natural solution.

I returned his kisses avidly and abandoned myself to the exceeding sweetness of his touch. My night rail was soon cast aside and with it my self-consciousness, and I blended my body to accommodate the urgent demand of his. Of a sudden there was no more of the awkwardness that I had always felt during what I secretly termed the accomplishment of my wifely duty; it had long since ceased to be a degrading act for me, but submission is a woefully one-sided affair and understands nothing of the real pleasure in giving, much less of receiving.

Within me began to burn a flame with a slow, sweet languor, consuming all fear of him, all will to live apart from his mouth and hands. While the flame flickered and flared out ever more brightly, swelled the head of the familiar wave. So pleasant was it not to be submerged in it that I was content at first to be swept along by its gentle rhythm, but then it gathered force and suddenly, mysteriously, I was released from the depths of those waters and was riding the crest of the wave, white and foaming, churning exultantly toward its pitch, driven inexorably to its point where it broke in sparkling lines along the curve of the shore, and with it was released the welcome crash of its breaking. That was the moment when I came to know the awesome power that physical union holds; it had come spontaneously of its own, surprising me as much as it delighted me with its strength, rendering passion for passion, and filled me with such an aching happiness that I dared not move, desperate to prevent that the wash of time should dilute the moment I wished to hold for eternity. It was as if I had indeed experienced a sort of death in his hands after all—if one may call this intense affirmation of life a death—for once having tasted the most intimate secret of life, I could have expired and been well quit of the world.

At length the floodtide receded, and the sword came back from the sea with a softer sigh. Eddies and whirlpools still ran their course, swirling patterns on the shore, and I believed the moment to have slipped by me. I tightened my bodily hold on my husband as I lay across his chest. He responded with a sleepy, contented sound. It provoked in me a small chuckle that seemed to lift the sealing stone of some deeper well within me and to release a glorious spring of laughter. It came bubbling and leaping up in the most tremendous, unpredictable hurry to reach the surface, so that all my blood danced with it and my breast was suffused with the rush and surge of this extraordinary, unexpected fountain of delight. I felt myself at once ridiculous and audacious. I wanted to sing and begin our love all over again.

Actually, I neither moved nor spoke. I lay still, letting the mysterious rapture have its way with me. Whatever it was, it was something that had been suddenly liberated, and I was intoxicated by its new freedom. It had taken control of me and was behaving very foolishly; its folly enchanted me.

Roland shifted and called to me sleepily, "My love?"

I felt no immediate need to answer.

"Marguerite, love," he repeated, his voice heavy, groggy.

The sound of my name made the fountain shoot sky-high, for it had occurred to me that the epithet "my love" was wonderfully universal and might be used, safely, on any occasion. It was useless to wonder how many women had found paradise in his arms before me, but the knowledge that his desire and pleasure existed for me and because of me endowed me with an omnipotence to which no other woman at that moment could lay claim. I laughed silently to myself, full of my power and folly.

His hand moved and slackly grasped my arm. "Be sure to wake me, love, if I forget to leave," he murmured thickly.

I had no more control over myself than a giddy girl. The bubble of laughter burst forth of its own accord. "I shall do no such thing," I whispered, humor in my voice, "when I consider how long I waited for you to come home."

The hold on my arm became that of a man in full possession of his senses.

"I shall take that for what it is, my dear: an open invitation," he said low in his normal voice. He turned toward me and lounged his head on the fist of a propped arm. I could almost see the gleam in his eye. "And that is the most wifely thing you have said to date."

"How can you say so?" I protested.

"Do not mistake me. I am charmed by the unwifely sentiment."

"No, really, it is not as if I, as a wife, should say that to anyone just anywhere, you know," I retorted, blushing at my boldness.

"I strongly suggest that you do not, in fact, say such a thing to anyone else in even remotely similar circumstances," he remarked pleasantly.

"I perceive that the charm of unwifeliness has its limits."

"Let us just say that the charm of your unwifeliness does."

"Are you never at a loss?" I laughed and thought I would not press the point where another man's wife's unwifeliness might suit him very well. "But the fact remains that I have no intention of waking you up."

"And leave me to be discovered in my lady's chamber on the morrow?"

"Ah! You must look to your husbandly reputation yourself!" I replied. "As for me, I waited too long for you and did not know, in sooth, when I would ever see you again."

"Behold me returned."

It occurred to me that that was about as close to an apology as I could expect.

"Exactly. And that is why I am not eager to have you leave me anytime soon."

"Any more of this, my girl," he warned, "and you shall get what you are asking for."

I was silent. The fountain had become a stream that ran glittering through my body, spreading as it went into a wide river that swept me up and drowned me. To speak of it was impossible, and I thought it a pity to spoil the trance with renewed intimacy, for nothing could improve my state. I merely shook my head and gathered him in my arms, happy just to hold him. He laid his head back down against my breast, and I almost thought he understood my feelings at the moment and shared them. Within the minute, his even breathing flowed into my river of contentment. I realized, as I ran my fingers through his crisp, brown curls, that I had never seen him sleep. I decided that I liked him very well.

I was exceedingly happy and did not think that it would not last forever.

* * *

Two incongruous thoughts drifted and intertwined in my mind, which was drugged with pleasure and sleep and the further pleasure that comes with sleep: one, that it was full morning, and the other, that Roland was beside me. These two realizations provoked, in turn, two still more incompatible reactions: I had hardly a moment to lose and must throw the covers back and jump out of bed; I must lie quietly and not disturb my slumbering husband. I was effectively checked, and could only hope that he would wake up on his own. Then I sensed that he was slowly coming to, as if he were obeying my will. He flung an arm across me, and judging by where he placed his hand, it seemed that he must, on some level of awareness, have realized that he was in bed with a woman.

The opportunity seemed too good to be missed. Still and all, I did not really want to put him to the test, but my little imp goaded me into it. "Good morning, sire," I said in Saxon.

He stirred and pulled me down against him. It flashed through my mind for one sickening moment that I had been too clever, but then he said in Norman, without opening his eyes, "It won't work, my love. You needn't lay traps for my tongue." His hold on me relaxed, and I slid away from him. "Although I am generally heedless of the laws of chivalry, I strictly observe the one decreeing that the knight's first duty is to remember in the morning who it was he took to bed with him."

Then, without warning, he rolled over on top of me, pinning me to the bed. He looked down at me in a way that made my blood beat erratically, and something seemed to have happened to my breath. "You are Marguerite. You are dark and comely and very much to my taste. You also happen to be my wife, but I shall not let that work to my disadvantage."

I laughed and tried to free myself. I could not move. "Roland, let me up," I said.

He shook his head. "I gave you ample opportunity to escape me a moment ago, and I lay trap for trap. You may rise only after you have paid the price."

"But we are receiving guests today," I argued, torn between

alarm and excitement. "I hope that you have not forgotten it is Christmas Eve."

"I have not, love. Let us celebrate."

"There remains still so much to do," I insisted.

"That," he said, "is a most unconvincing statement. I should be sufficiently surprised if you weren't ready as early as yesterday."

"It is true that I have commanded unquestioned authority in the last few days," I conceded.

"So I should imagine," he said dryly.

"It is not as if I were seeking it!"

"One must learn to find advantage in every situation," he replied, adjusting his hold. "Which brings me back to my original point."

Bess chose at that moment to knock twice briskly on my chamber door and to peek her head inside. What she saw made her withdraw in extreme haste, but not before we saw her eyes start from their sockets.

I was somewhat embarrassed. "I hope you are satisfied!"

"Far from it."

I made some further sounds and motions of protest, but these met with as much success as my previous objections.

"I should think that in the course of your dutiful life, you have never savored the pleasure of lying abed in the morning."

"No," I admitted, "and certainly not in the way that you mean, but I hardly think this the moment to initiate me."

"None better! But when words fail, there are more effective measures of persuasion."

He set out then to show me what he meant, and as for persuasion, I learned that he was a master of the art. It seemed that all he had to do was look at me and touch me for the aching fire to spring to life between us. He had much to teach me, and I proved a willing and eager pupil.

It was not until much later that my eyes fluttered open.

"Roland!"

"Heart's lady?"

"We must be about our duties."

"As the cock once crowed: 'I have laid mine to nest.'"

"I suppose you mean for me to explain that to my tiring woman when next she reappears at my door," I said with light irony.

"I do not think you shall have the least need to."

In the event, Roland was right. The moment he slipped out of my chamber after he had done fondling me, Bess entered, catching me in the act of putting on my chamber robe. Words could not have expressed her disapproval as eloquently as did her dark face. She managed to dress me, restricting herself to cluckings and mutterings, but when she turned at last to my hair, she could stand it no longer and broke forth, "It won't be the master's fault if you're not breeding within the year!"

"As to that," I said, "he has been gone more than he is here."

"It is not the actual amount of time here he spends that counts," she retorted meaningfully. "The master in his lady's chamber till all hours of the morning! Hrumph! 'Tis dis— dis—*unseemly,* I call it!"

"No, Bess, really it is—"

"Unseemly! And well you know it. I can just hear what Dame Ellen would have to say on the subject of making free with conjugal behavior in the morning!"

My imagination balked at the thought. "I crave mercy, Bess!" I laughed.

My levity did not help to put me in her good graces. She frowned alarmingly. "Never mind Dame Ellen then! Think what Lady Isolde had to say on the topic, rest her wise soul. Thanks be that she is not here to witness the disgrace of her charge! *I* remember what she said, though it's clear that you don't! If I heard her once, I heard her—"

"I remember very well the Lady Isolde's saying, I assure you! Only then I did not even guess at what was supposed to happen 'at night,' much less the meaning of 'delight,' and until recently I could not understand why anyone *would* want to remain in bed past the matins."

"*My lady!*" she said, gasping.

Her shock was profound. I betrayed myself with a flush,

but replied evenly, "Well, no harm has been done, as no guests have yet arrived."

"None have arrived, and in this you have been lucky," she replied with dignity. "But as for harm, why, the whole castle knows of your conduct!" This, with real feeling. "And how does it look for *me?* Think of that!"

I spent the next minutes and a good deal of effort to calm Bess's exacerbated nerves. I supposed that I achieved a modicum of success when Bess finally conceded, "Well, not but what in this *particular* case it might not be the worst thing."

I understood better some of Bess's distress when I finally made my appearance in the hall. Eyes followed me wherever I went, half in curiosity, half in awe, as if I had been caught at adultery and had miraculously escaped the pillory, instead of merely having acquiesced (willingly) to my husband's desire to lie abed another hour or so in the morning. From the many respectful *Good morrow, my lady*'s that came my way, however, I knew my position to be very secure. It did no harm, as Bess herself had pointed out, for the keep to know that lord and lady were whole again.

The atmosphere had cleared now that Roland was back, and the mood was openly festive. I took heart and was determined to enjoy myself for the next fortnight. It had even begun to snow lightly, but nothing to hamper travelers. Christmas would be very good in the Year of our Lord at Hungerford Castle.

I was even secretly pleased by Nan's reaction to the events of the past days. She was a sly one, was Nan, with a mother wit that managed, I hoped, to keep her from Gaston's clutches and with a very special sense of humor all her own.

"I trust you have found everything to satisfaction, my lady," she said when I drew her aside in the kitchens to discuss the various menus we had planned.

She did not often title me, I had noted, and I did not think her lapse was an accident.

"Do you know the meaning of *double entendre*, Nan?" I asked her pleasantly.

"No, my lady," she disclaimed, as the most dutiful retainer should.

I nodded soberly. "I find everything to satisfaction."

"I am pleased, my lady," she said with deepest respect.

I felt a strange kinship with Nan that morning in the kitchens just before the first guests arrived.

Chapter 13

It is said that the nervousness preceding a dreaded event is far worse than that on the occasion of the event itself. So it was with me. I had viewed the prospect of performing the duties of hostess to so many of the realm's peers with a feeling of trepidation bordering, in my more agitated moments, on panic, sure that some unnamed disaster would strike to ruin all my careful preparations and that I would bring disgrace upon the already tarnished name of Guimont; but from the moment in the early afternoon when the first guests began to stream in, dusting off snow from hood and foot, the ritual of curtsies and baisemains helped to ease my nervousness and gave me a sense of balance. I learned then that to receive the highest praise, all the hostess had to do was to make sure that each guest had a heavy cup of wassail pressed into his hand within five minutes of his arrival. This was easily done. I learned, too, that Roland had been right about the attendance: all the people we had invited came, save the very few who were either too old or too infirm to brave the journey in the cold. Curiosity was a strong magnet, Roland had said, and I did not doubt that anyone who had deemed Guimont hospitality beneath their notice was not really of a mind actually to miss a firsthand account of the festivities at Hungerford Castle.

As the arrivals filled the keep with noisy good cheer, I was swayed into thinking that the fortnight might pass creditably; I was even determined to try to enjoy myself as much as possible. With Roland at my side, calmly receiving the numbers of guests, I already experienced a certain enjoyment in having agreed to hold the year's Christmas celebrations. The last of my fears were swept aside and my pleasure was complete when I spied Alicia enter the portal. Her husband solicitously removed her mantle and brushed the light powder of snow from her hair before he let her rush toward me.

"My dear!" she breathed in awed accents after we had embraced and she looked about her at the hall. "You have wrought wonders!"

"Thank you, dearest! I can always count on you to say just the right thing, but I am sure that it is nothing out of the ordinary," I disclaimed.

I was secretly pleased with the effect I had achieved in the Great Hall, having given vent to all my creative impulses stifled for so many years at Shrivenham under my father's austere eye. The hall at Hungerford looked now like a woodsy fairyland. The huge room was decorated with great bunches of holly, shining ivy, and clusters of mistletoe, the gray berries gleaming waxily in the glow of the two blazing fireplaces, above one of which soared arrogantly the Guimont coat of arms. I judged the whole an impressive sight to greet guests' eyes and had the satisfaction of seeing my opinion reflected in the faces of the arrivals, many of whom had no doubt seen the hall in its dimmer days.

Alicia took my comment for what it was and turned to embrace her host. I, too, turned and gave my hand to Sir Herbert, made a stray remark about Alicia's condition, and discovered this to be a fertile topic that the father-to-be was only too glad to discuss. He confided to me in low tones that his Alicia was a very delicate woman (however, I was not to think that she was not in the best of health!), and it would not go easy for her, but he wondered if things might not go better for her if perhaps I might find it convenient to be with her during her confinement? I told him that I would be nothing more than superfluous at a lying-in, but that I would be pleased to be with Alicia, if only from the selfish wish to be there when the naming of the child would take place, since I had several serviceable names in mind.

He smiled, and his brow cleared with his relief.

Roland engaged Sir Herbert's attention with a query about

the success of his winter crops, and thus Alicia and I were left to talk briefly between ourselves.

"Is everything going well for you, Grita?" she asked me in one comprehensive question.

"I *think* so, but I have found that I never know what will happen. At the moment, however, I feel safe in answering you with a tentative 'yes.'"

"I knew it!" she whispered and gave my arm a squeeze.

"A *tentative* 'yes,' my dear!"

"You were ever cautious, so I do not worry if you can respond in even the most qualified positive. I am sure that you and Sir Guy will do very well for yourselves with this celebration and establish your credit."

"We shall see," I replied. "There are over sixty people coming, you know, and something untoward might happen."

"Ah, yes," she said with a wink. "The roof might cave in— or the sky, for that matter!—for there is no need to try to persuade me that you have left anything to chance in your preparations. And I think you are very clever to have arranged this, for, you know, people generally speak of it as the wedding celebration you were unable to have. It was such an excellent and tasteful idea on your part!"

Honesty compelled me to admit that it was, in its conception, Lady Constance's idea.

Alicia nodded wisely. "She has ever stood in your mother's stead and has loved you as her own. She was very right to have suggested the idea, and I am sure that she must have known how appropriate it would be for you to host the festivities. Ah! Here she comes now. But I must run along and catch my Herbert. Poor dear Lady Constance! See how frail she is! How she suffers so! Brave Lady Constance! Well, my dear, I shall steal a few minutes more from you later."

Alicia gave my arm a last pat and left me. Lady Constance descended on me a moment later with a smile that reminded me of my earlier fears that it was always possible for something to go amiss. I steeled myself against unpleasant feelings of foreboding.

"My dearest Marguerite," she greeted me in her thin thread of a voice that was particularly remarkable for its ability to unwind itself at length. "How good it is to see you in health. Are you well? Of course I see that you are! I do hope that you mean to thank me for having given you the suggestion for this Christmas assembly at Hungerford—or have you forgotten that the idea was my inspiration? No, you would not have, for you are not at all an ungrateful child, are you, my dear? But you need not divulge to whom the credit is due, since it is to be *your* celebration, and I do not intend to stand in your light. No, quite the contrary. I have been feeling very poorly of late— although I do not burden others with tales of my afflictions— and shall not be able to participate fully in the revelry. I almost did not make the journey! But Charles—the dearest son imaginable!—roused me from my sickbed. So good of him to do so! He shall be along in a minute, my dear. You must not think he has not come. Oh, no! I hardly need tell you that he is attending to all the details of my baggage and the stabling of the horses, because you know what a dear boy—*man*—he is. And Agnes has come, too. That should not surprise you. An odd thing it would be if I could not count on her support when I most need it. She has such a way with me when I suffer one of my spasms. They quite incapacitate me—but, no, I am determined not to succumb to any debilities for the next two weeks, knowing how you have doubtless prepared much for the entertainment of your guests. Just let me look around and take in all your improvements. Why, yes! It is lovely, my dear Marguerite, just lovely, and you did not forget to lay new rushes. Very nice, my dear. But do you not think . . . that is to say, well, the hall seems so very—how should I say?—it is so awfully *green,* is it not?

She made the tactical error of pausing to drink in the greenness of the hall, during which I pointed out the obvious.

"Do not say another word, my dear!" she came back, utilizing her thinnest smile to good effect. "I quite see that they are your decorations. Very nice, my dear. Quite lovely, in fact. You must take care, however, to see that they do not catch fire. There was an unfortunate tragedy about fifty years ago at— But why bring up dismal recollections of the past? It is enough that your torches and chandeliers are not too close to the greenery. You are so *careful,* Marguerite. That is what I most admire in you. Now, here comes Charles. My, what an impressive figure he cuts from across a room! Did I tell you that Shrewsbury is most assiduously applying to me for Charles to make a bid for his Joan's hand? Or have you been keeping abreast of all the latest news on your own? But I shall simply intercept Charles and have him take me directly to my room, and I shall send him down to you later so that he may pay you his respects when you are not positively besieged by people, and you may have a few quiet words as brother and sister. That's a good girl, my dear. I am sure that this will be a most satisfactory Christmas, if I do not fall victim to an ague."

Hardly requiring any response to her collection of comments, she melted away from me with an expression of wan interest on her face for the decorations and hailed her son, whose bulk moved obediently to her side.

I had not one minute to recover from the effect of Lady Constance's rather masterful entrance before I was favored with a smooth and warm, almost intimate, salutation from Hugh Falmouth. I had not seen or heard him approach; he simply materialized at my side and took my hand in his, bringing it to his lips, where he held it appreciably longer than was strictly necessary.

"Lady Guimont," he murmured over my hand and raised his liquid eyes to mine, "I have been in a fever of anticipation of seeing you again after Longchamps' wedding, but little did I suspect that when next we met you would be a married woman."

"A fact that you would do well not to forget, Falmouth," came Roland's easy voice tinged with humor from behind me. I had thought him engaged with the arriving Stafford party, but there he was beside me when I most wanted him. Sir Hugh released my hand.

"I am hardly likely to forget while you are playing watchdog," Sir Hugh replied, striking the same easy note.

"Is it not the duty of a host to greet his guests with his

hostess?" Roland returned, brows lifted a fraction. "I bid you welcome to Hungerford Keep, Falmouth."

"God save you, Guimont." This with exaggerated courtesy and a brief bow. "And I congratulate you on your marriage."

"I am indeed fortunate," my husband answered. "How may we serve you? I recommend the wassail; my lady's is most excellent. Tell me your pleasure, and it shall be got for you."

"A poor second to what I had in mind," Sir Hugh said.

"There are wines and ales as you desire, my lord," I interjected.

Sir Hugh smiled at me. He had a very charming smile in a most handsome countenance.

"You trifle, fair cruel one! I was thinking rather of a bridal kiss," he said and glanced slyly at my husband. "That is, if Guimont will allow it."

"By all means," came the response. "It is customary, after all. I imagine that there will be much of that before all is said and done and that the free kissing of his bride is the trial which every new husband must endure. So embrace my wife and be done with it, for I suppose I shall have to grow used to the sight before the evening is done."

"What, under your watchful eye? You do intend to deny me all pleasure, in sooth! But, no! I shall steal it when it suits me best, and you shall be always kept guessing. Such a sore plight it must be to be married to a beautiful woman!"

"It has its advantages, as well," Roland said. "Here comes John Potter with the wassail bowl. You have no choice but to take a cup, Hugh."

"It shall console me," he said with a laugh, as if he were addressing his boon companion. "Until later, Lady Guimont. I do not fear your husband as perhaps I should."

"There is nothing to fear, I am sure!" I said then, adding my part to the nonsense. "And besides, you are his guest and must make yourself free of all that is his, without fear of him."

"Really? Do not tell me that he might not wish to set limits to that freedom," Sir Hugh said provocatively.

I was not going to let that go unanswered. "I might have

something to say in the matter, too," I laughed, I hoped with effect, "for I do not let just anything happen in my keep. I assure you that a woman's wrath is far more to be feared than a man's."

"I shall take a care!" Sir Hugh bantered upon parting.

Roland turned to me and asked me whether I could see to it that Lady Stafford was served the morning and noon meals in her chambers, since she was suffering particularly in her leg. I said that I would certainly arrange what I could to the best of her satisfaction. The subject of Hugh Falmouth was never mentioned between us.

All thought of the words spoken by Sir Hugh left me the moment I saw Isabelle Beauvais enter the portal wearing a red mantle trimmed in vair. She pushed the hood back from her shining tresses braided cunningly around her head and paused to look about her for a moment before starting forward at sight of her host and hostess. She bore down upon us gracefully, her arms outstretched, a smile quivering on her lips. She looked magnificent. I had never thought that a blonde could wear red to advantage. I was wrong. Isabelle was a shimmering flame of beauty, encased in fire from head to dainty toe, and when she held out her hand to Roland for his salute, I noted that on her wrist dangled a slim ruby bangle. She did not look flashy or even inappropriate for all her drama; the over-all effect was very festive and most tasteful.

She acknowledged my husband with becoming reserve and turned to me. I suddenly realized that I had not been looking forward to the moment when I, as Roland's wife, would face Isabelle. I had tried to convince myself that she could not care, or that she might in fact feel relief that he was at last tied down, but I had not entirely succeeded. My stomach pitched and lurched uncomfortably.

Yet Isabelle was smiling at me pleasantly, as friend to friend. "Marguerite," she said, "this promises to be one of the loveliest Christmases ever. I am so glad that you are receiving everyone at Hungerford, and your hall is most beautiful! It puts me in the mood for festivity! And, my dear, you know that you and

I have so much to discuss since last we saw each other." She glanced playfully at my husband. "That is, when there are no men present—especially not Guy!"

The object of the sally took this in good part, and Isabelle squeezed my hand and winked at me. "I must not tarry any longer, however," she continued, "since I have come with my father, who has become terribly infirm and must be constantly looked after."

Roland made a few polite inquiries into Sire Beauvais's health, and Isabelle glided away on the observation that it was a shame that the king would not be participating in the celebration but that perhaps it was "for the best."

I did not know how she might mean that, but I had my own reasons for thinking that it might be for the best. Roland had informed me the week before that the king had sent his regrets to Hungerford just before his departure to Burgundy for the Christmas season, and the queen, who was not accompanying him there, was not disposed to traveling alone and had elected to remain at Westminster for the small, royal celebration there. On the one hand, I was not disappointed, for I had never expected a Plantagenet to grace my foyer, but on the other hand, I had an intuition that Roland could have persuaded King Henry to come if he had wanted to; and this led me to believe that there was perhaps a good reason for the sovereign to stay away, and I could not get it out of my head that it had something to do with the machinations of Lady Constance. Needless to say, Roland had hinted nothing of the kind, nor would I have expected him to, and I had had enough time with him by now to learn that he never did anything without a reason and generally operated so as to cover all possibilities. For all his careless allure and unsteady temper, he was a man of cold, sober reason.

The dinner, except for one disturbing episode from my point of view, was a success and lasted nearly until the midnight Mass that was so special on Christmas Eve. I had planned the meal in traditional fashion, beginning at sundown, by which time almost everyone had arrived, when the great boar's head on its massive silver platter was carried in and placed so as to dominate the head table. There were, lining one table, fat stuffed and roasted capons, wild fowl (trussed neatly according to my orders) steaming from the ovens, and venison that had turned on a spit over the kitchen hearth. There were pies, innumerable pies whose flaky crusts (overseen by Nan) when pierced emitted a wonderful aroma. We had contrived one pie that was so big that it required a special cart and was pulled into the hall by two serving men. And then there was food and more food. I did not anticipate that anyone would lack for anything.

I had seen in particular to a select group of minstrels and carolers who wandered among the tables, and I thought that I had chosen very well. They added the texture to an already colorful gathering, and it was not unusual for a group of diners to join in on a familiar song as the carolers passed by. There was holiday spirit, and to spare, a fact that I attributed in large measure to an abundance of wassail.

Since I was obliged periodically to circulate among the tables, I had ample opportunity to discover the cheer of the revelers, and I had good reason to fear that the Mass would be a none-too-solemn and certainly not sober occasion. It seemed, for instance, that young John Langdon had succumbed early on to the drink. He was not, as I had discovered at Alicia's wedding, blessed with a hard head, and from the circumstance of his becoming excessively absent-minded when drunk and fancying himself in his own castle, he remarked very audibly, as I happened to pass by, on the fine housekeeping.

"My mother," I heard him say with pride, "is a very ex— esh—es—a very fine chatelaine." He apologized for the escutcheon, however, saying that it did not look at all like the Langdon crest and that he did not know how it came to rest above the fireplace; but he noted that it was very handsome and that he would see what he could do about having the family adopt it officially.

I caught the eye of Sir Bruce Huxley, seated next to Langdon's lady, during this passage, and he shook his head and rolled his eyes heavenward in supplication. I did not suppress a chuckle.

Another incident was not so amusing. It was not precisely
unamusing either, but oddly disquieting. It made me realize
how little I really knew about my husband and gave me to
think that I would always be at a disadvantage with him in the
presence of others.

It was after the eating had done and many people had pushed
their chairs back from the tables, satisfied. The drinking continued, as well as the singing, and I had left the table to send
several pages for a fresh supply of tallows. I noticed from
across the room that a small group had gathered about the head
table and was talking and laughing idly; just as I was about to
approach the group, Gavin came up behind me, caught my
arm, and winked.

"I have an idea," he said, and proceeded to catch the first
caroler to pass by and relieved him of his lute. The astonished
caroler was told that he would now see some fun.

Gavin then slipped into the group and dropped the lute into
Roland's hands. He was perched on a corner of the table, one
leg stretched out before him, jesting with Robert FitzWarren,
at whose side stood, not unexpectedly, Marie-Ange Dujarrie,
and on either side of them were standing Alicia and Herbert.
I had seen two others in the group, partially hidden by Alicia
and Herbert, and when I stepped behind Gavin into the circle,
I saw with a sinking feeling that the two were Sir Hugh Falmouth and Isabelle. I acknowledged everyone with a comprehensive nod and smile, while Roland assumed every appearance
of blank surprise at Gavin's gesture and demanded to know
what his squire was about in rather straightforward terms.

"A song, Guy, as if you could not guess," Gavin returned,
unmoved.

"And yet we have hired musicians for the very purpose,"
Roland replied. His face showed no hint of approval for Gavin's
gambit.

"Ah, but they do not know half the interesting songs that
you do," Gavin pursued, knowing that in the tradition he was
protected from reprimand for insolence on Christmas Eve.

"What, a camp song in my lady's hall? Have your manners
gone a-begging, man?" This, with severity.

"It must be the company I keep, sire," Gavin apologized, eyes cast deprecatingly at the floor.

There was laughter all around.

"I do not play, impudent whelp," Roland said, his features a mask of dislike still, and put down the lute with finality on the table.

But Gavin knew what he was doing. "My lord is too modest," he explained to the group, "and fears ill comparison with the professional musicians."

This drew a very dark look from Roland and a volley of encouragement from the prospective audience waiting to hear the master of Hungerford raise his voice to sing. Marie-Ange was the most insistent.

"You must not give us another thought!" she cried, and ran on coquettishly, "It is Christmas Eve, and we beg a song of you. We are the most uncritical listeners imaginable and will not compare you—at least, not for the worse!—to the other singers. I myself do not know a false note from a true one, nor good voice from bad."

"Demoiselle," Roland replied, slanting his rapier glance, "that is poor encouragement indeed, for as Gavin will tell you, I think myself to have a very fine ear and an even better voice and like nothing so much as to hear the sound of it, so that my men are often compelled to beg me quit from sheer distraction. No, I cannot play for those who are unable to fully appreciate my talent. Thus, I need a better reason to perform."

Sir Robert supplied it. "Then teach the wench a lesson in the art of good singing," he said, pinching Marie-Ange's arm playfully, "for the rest of us know full well what it is and are prepared to pass a most refined judgment."

"I needed only that, FitzWarren." Roland laughed suddenly in his most disarming manner and picked up the lute again. He began to tune it.

Isabelle took a step closer to him then. "Guy," she said softly.

He turned to look at her, for he was sitting with his back turned slightly away from her. He had begun strumming and his head was bent over the instrument, but at her interpolation he stopped playing.

"Well, Isabelle?"

His cup sat empty. Isabelle filled it and reached over to hand it to him. "You'll be needing a drink to complete your tuning-up," she said to him as he took the cup from her hands and then addressed the very interested audience. "Guy has such a memory for verse. I have always been amazed by the numbers of songs he keeps in his head. You have remarked on it, have you not, Marguerite?"

I did not want to answer that, since I was totally ignorant of Roland's talents in these domains, and so I merely smiled a little without committing myself.

Sir Hugh had slipped up to me and asked softly in my ear, "Does he whisper poetry to you, my dear?" I looked quickly at him, surprised by his nearness. He caressed me with his eyes and moved a step away from me again.

Roland seemed not to notice the by-play and gave every appearance that he was deep in concentration over the choice of song. He tried the opening notes of several airs, but his first choices apparently did not appeal to him, and so he continued until finally one came to him. He sat upright and looked as if he was ready to begin.

"I know what you'll sing!" Isabelle clapped her hands. "I wager my broach against your armlet, Guy, that I know what you intend to sing."

"Done!" he answered, catching Isabelle's festive mood. He beckoned to FitzWarren to bend over and whispered in his ear. Sir Robert smiled delightedly and clapped Roland on the back. He nodded to Isabelle.

"Well, demoiselle," he said. "What is your guess?"

Isabelle said slowly. "Is it 'La Rose à Noël'? It is one of the Gascon love poems. Why, you used to quote them often, Guy. I thought this one appropriate for Christmas."

Roland grinned, not one wit perturbed by her comment. "You owe me your broach, Isabelle. FitzWarren, tell her what I just whispered to you."

Sir Robert laughed. "You had the right season but the wrong

theme. He's going to sing 'Two Soldiers Return to the Home-fires in Winter.'"

"But that's a duet!" she protested in good humor while she removed the gold broach from the red ribbon at her throat. With her movement, her ruby bangle caught the fire of a torch and blazed for an instant with the red of her dress. She looked very much like a flaming Christmas rose herself.

"And, if I do not mistake," she said, handing over the pin, "it is not very decent."

"You are not supposed to know that," Roland rallied in return, "and it is not so very indecent either." He took his prize and casually pinned it onto the embroidered neck sling of the lute, where it would remain.

"By Mary's veil, you have not underestimated your desire to hear your own voice if you choose a duet!" Sir Hugh bantered smoothly. "I suppose you mean to take both parts."

Roland laughed easily. "Under normal circumstances I would not hesitate, but as it is, I have someone in mind for the countermelody," he said, striking the first notes of the melody and looking straight at Gavin. "When I discovered that the young Scot had a good tenor to my baritone, I instantly engaged him as my squire. Come, McLaughlin, and lend me your voice. We've sung 'Two Soldiers' more than once together."

Gavin colored and made some inarticulate noises of protest. Roland was not going to let him off the hook. "Caught in your own trap, my man. Yet I cannot force you to sing, if you are unwilling," my husband said, a twinkle lighting his eyes, and turned to me. "So we shall have my lady arbitrate. Shall Gavin sing with me, or shall he not, my lady?"

Gavin looked at me and shook his head almost impercepti-bly. "Well, Gavin, it is as your master says," I began. "You have been caught in your own trap. But I suspect that you sing as willingly as he does—though perhaps not so long as he claims to do—and will not fail to entertain us with your tenor. And, besides, you have told me that we were to have some fun and I admit to a great desire to hear this not very indecent duet."

Gavin seemed momentarily distressed by my decision, but

he joined his master with boyish grace. The "Two Soldiers Return to the Homefires in Winter" was a rollicking air and not too indelicate, if one chose to ignore the innuendos and double meanings, and I found that my sensibilities were offended not at all by the kind of tale that would naturally attend the homecoming of two young and (needless to say) lusty warriors. Roland's voice was strong and rich, which surprised me not at all; Gavin's voice was mellow with a masculine texture, which surprised me very much, and their voices blended well together. They made an excellent duet, having a kind of rapport in song that I had never noticed in daily intercourse. They must have sung the air more than once together, as Roland had said, for their interpretation of the verses, illustrated by facial expression and gesture, and some extraneous comments, was subtle and benefited from a sense of comic timing that only practice could have mastered. I was happy to find that my arbitration in the matter had been to the good; and I realized that Gavin's demur had been for the sake of form. In truth, he must have known that he had a good voice, and sang very willingly, and when they came to the end of the tale—by which time a crowd had gathered—Gavin showed no hesitation in continuing with an equally lively tune that required the participation of the audience in the chorus. I sang and clapped with the rest of the merrymakers and would have thought the moment a particularly warm and spontaneous one had I not been haunted by the scenes enacted by Isabelle and Sir Hugh just prior to the singing.

It was so silly of me, really, to give it another thought that I was sure I had no more sense than a wet goose, and yet I could not stop thinking of it.

Unfortunately, the long and most holy Mass pronounced by Friar Obersman that began at midnight gave me more than enough time to review what had transpired during the singing interlude. It was not to my credit that I spared little proper reflection on the event of the birth of our Savior, my most tangible feeling during the celebration being one of relief to have my husband next to me, where I could see and touch him. Since I had always considered him such a man's man, I could readily picture him out with his men, astride his destrier, singing robust songs around a campfire; somehow the image of him quoting love poems, Gascon or otherwise, unpleasantly prodded my imagination, much like the toe of an angry housewife will rouse a dog dozing comfortably on the mistress's best shawl, dreaming of his secret cache of bones. Although I had known of Roland's reputation with women even before I knew who he was and could personally attest to his charms, I had conveniently suppressed until now any idea of him linked to other women. This was pure naïveté, and Isabelle's words: *It is one of the Gascon love poems. Why, you used to quote them often, Guy* made me a little the wiser. They evoked all the many women Roland must have known before me—and would know in the future—and the things I had every reason to believe might pass between them. The existence of Roland's amours should have been obvious to me and not at all startling or upsetting; nevertheless, Isabelle's words tore away one veil and made me remember the day I had innocently asked after the health of the wife of one of my field hands and she had pointed out that she was five months' pregnant: I could thereafter see nothing else in her but her rounded belly. The oversight once recognized gave me an extra sense.

It was not the thought of many women that upset me, I supposed, but the thought of one. Isabelle had tossed off her words like a flick of her ruby bracelet, and it was so well done that it gave me to think that there had been much more to the relationship between her and Roland than I had previously dared to suspect. Alicia, who had also been there at the time, thought nothing of the incident, for I had talked with her about it for a moment that I had snatched with her afterward. She had deemed the comment harmless and the wager a laudable effort to display that there were no hard feelings remaining between the two former fiancés; but then Alicia viewed Lady Constance as my surrogate mother and thought Roland to have married me for love, or at least for preference. I was willing to believe that Isabelle had broken off with Roland out of a feeling of horror at his brother's death; however, I could also believe that it must be excessively agreeable to have Roland quote love poems in one's ear and that it would be a pleasure one would also perhaps not want him to forget. I could understand it. What I could not quite fathom was what Roland's feelings toward her might have been, and I did not really want to pursue that line of inquiry in depth.

It was just as well to let that subject rest, since it did not concern me. I reminded myself that I was only Roland's wife and had no right to busy myself with his past. It was enough that he showed me unfailing courtesy, both in public and in private, and conferred upon me an authority for which most wives could never even hope. I would certainly not be so presumptuous as to make demands on his heart; and just as I came to that meritorious conclusion, he touched my hand, dispelling my reverie, and my eyes raised to his in silent question. He smiled down at me in a way that made me doubt that I would ever be truly satisfied with only the part of him that was strictly husbandly, and passed me the communion chalice, bringing me to a sense of my surroundings. I accepted it and thereafter tried to bend my impious mind to the saving of my soul, but the body has an unruly life of its own, and for the first time in my life I found it very difficult to ignore the warmth of my blood, which could be stirred at the mere sight and touch of my husband.

At length the Christmas bells began to peal their joyous message of life and redemption for all mankind. Roland and I led the procession out of the chapel into the ebony night laced with falling snowflakes and amidst shouts of peace and happiness and even several voices raised to the proposition of more drink. Roland made it known, once we had regained the hall, that his cellar was at his guests' disposal and that the fires would not be banked this night. There quickly formed several reveling parties, but most of the guests, following our lead, sought their beds, so that they could begin again, refreshed, in the morning. We ascended to our private apartment together, commenting on the various aspects of the day. Roland seemed, in general, pleased with my projects, and as we undressed in the light of one candle, I mentally chided myself for my misgivings during an otherwise excellent evening and passed them off as a lingering effect of my initial nervousness. When we came together minutes later in our warm, comfortable bed, all unanswered questions were driven from my head, and I slipped across the brink of consciousness on the resolution that I was not going to become one of those jealous, possessive wives who drive their husbands to distraction with their demands of loyalty and affection.

Christmas Day burst in on Hungerford on a cold, clear blast of arctic air. This did nothing to hinder the holiday spirit; in fact, most people were in agreement that it was a perfect day for a hunt and thought it particularly felicitous that a thin cover of snow had fallen, in which the game would leave their tracks. Not one of the ladies joined the expedition, however, and so it was a very boisterous group of men that rode out of the bailey cat midmorning. I was not sorry to see them go. We women had much to do, and I had discovered in the past months, a little to my surprise, that as much as I liked having Roland present and available at Hungerford, it seemed, inexplicably, that I could get about my work much more efficiently when he was not there. Thus, it was all the better that some two score and ten men rode off to roam field and wood and do whatever it was that they liked best where they would not— to put the matter perfectly plainly—be getting underfoot. The women could go about their business of cleaning and preparing the Christmas feast without hindrance. At the men's departure, the castle was brought to life and hummed like an active beehive, or, better still, like one of those exotic organizations of women I had heard about that existed in the Levant—harems, I believe they are called.

I thought that there persisted much of the harem, then, in every well-regulated castle. In every castle arranged to make the master really happy, that man must always remain a visitor, welcomed, honored, but perpetually a guest. The fact that this must be so has often made me smile, for as much as Hungerford is owned by the Earl of Guimont, Roland lost it the day he married me. Thereafter he might step in from the great outside for rest and refreshment, but he can never again belong. For him, the click and hum of the harem operation stops, but there is always feminine relief when the master departs and the household hum goes on again. The paradox lies in the theory that all the operations exist but for the master's comfort; while, in practice, the castle is mine, and it is much easier to arrange for his comfort when he is not there. If this is also the case in the harems of the Orient, then it must be that women in both the East and the West share an unexpected, and profound, kinship, and that things are not so very different the world over.

Whatever conditions may have reigned in the Great Sultan's harem in Baghdad, Hungerford on this Christmas morning and afternoon was particularly pleasant for me. I had Alicia by my side, and even Isabelle showed herself to be all that was friendly, and there was nothing in her manner to make me think that she was upset, or in any other way affected, by my marriage. It seemed rather that her thoughts were on her own marriage, and we had a small chat on just that subject in the early afternoon. Isabelle was being most helpful to me by personally attending to Lady Constance, who was proving to be a rather contrary guest, and shortly after the midday repast, Isabelle came to report to me that Lady Constance was tucked away taking a comfortable nap.

"For you know, Marguerite, Lady Constance has such difficulty sleeping and needs her repose this afternoon so that she may partake of the evening festivities—particularly on Christmas Day," Isabelle said and then hesitated a moment. When she began to speak again, it was with a lowered voice. "Not that I don't think many of her maladies are imagined! However, do not misinterpret me! She is very frail and does suffer truly at times. But, you know, I think she is much stronger than she suspects or perhaps even lets on to be! Truly I do!"

This comment seemed to me so accurate that I could not help but like Isabelle the better for it. "So I have often thought!" I replied. "It is my belief that after so many years of imagined weakness, she has at last convinced herself of her frailty, so that she is no longer obliged to feign illness. It is most real! And the proof of her real strength is that she is able so well to withstand the wear and tear of her debilities. In my opinion, she is in remarkably good form!"

Isabelle laughed. "I agree, and whatever her physical ailments may or may not be, her mental faculties have not suffered at all. She has the most—the most *irritating* way of being up-to-date on all the latest news—particularly on the things one wishes her to know least about."

"It is true that her ears are everywhere."

"Either that or her spies! Seriously! How she comes to know the things she does, I'll never understand! But in my case, she has a direct source: my father."

"Your case?"

Isabelle clucked her tongue in self-derision. "My case, indeed! It is wretched, and I certainly did not need Lady Constance today to tell me—in her own ever-so-unassuming way!—what to do with my life. Not that she did so directly, but when she gets on her favorite topic—did you know that it is marriage?—she is bound to drag me into it. And it is all so complicated just now."

It was enlightening to discover that Lady Constance busied herself in everybody's business and not just in mine. She also apparently had the same irritating effect on others, and I began to feel that Isabelle and I had much in common. "You and Sir Hugh?" I queried. "Is it not all settled between you?"

"Yes! No—well, that is where my father comes in. He has been acting so unreasonably that I do not know what to do." Isabelle sighed.

She looked troubled, and I had the feeling that she wanted to unburden herself. I was an admittedly strange confidante, given everything that had happened in both our lives, but this seemed not to weigh with Isabelle, who must have viewed me merely as someone with whom she could discuss her problem.

"How has he been behaving unreasonably, Isabelle?" I asked.

That was all that was needed to launch her earnestly into her story, which began with the complaint that it would not be so bad if Sire Beauvais did not think Lady Constance a woman of reason and discuss everything with her, such that she, Isabelle, must then be subjected to Lady Constance's opinions. The long and short of it was that Isabelle's father (along with Lady Constance) did not approve of her union with Sir Hugh and the reason was basically financial. Falmouth's coffers were practically empty, and Beauvais did not want to ally his daughter to a family that must wait for an ailing cousin in Lower Saxony to die. Isabelle made no secret of her own family's straightened circumstances and of her need to marry, as she said with a deprecatory frown, "advantageously."

"But, you know, the cousin may very well die soon," I pointed out.

"It is my belief that he has been 'on his deathbed' these past ten years," she said with a moan.

"Well then, all the better! He cannot live forever, Isabelle, and you must take heart!"

She smiled and shook her head. "And he may just as well live another ten."

I saw her point. "Few marry for love," I felt compelled to mention.

"Just look at Alicia and Herbert," she countered.

"A rare case. Admit it!"

"Then take Marie-Ange. The only obstacle in her way is that she simply has not yet made up her mind which of her swains she shall take."

It seemed indelicate to observe that Marie-Ange had fortune enough to afford the luxury of marrying for love. "And you say that Lady Constance supports your father's position?"

"Yes, although why she should meddle in my life I cannot understand! Except that the notion did cross my mind—that is, it was just a fleeting impression—but, I could have sworn she had me in mind—" Words failed her momentarily. "That she had me in mind for *Charles*."

I laughed out loud. "Calm yourself! I think she has a fancy for Joan of Shrewsbury as a daughter-in-law."

Isabelle looked shocked. "Poor Joan!"

"My sentiments entirely. But better she than you, meaning no slight to Joan, mind you. However, to return to the point:

if worse comes to worst, you and Sir Hugh can always just wait."

Her lovely rosebud lips firmed into a line. "That is the *other* problem."

My lips parted expectantly.

"Hugh feels that he has waited long enough," she said, "and has become rather insistent of late."

"Insistent?" I echoed.

"Let us say, impatient," she explained cryptically.

"Oh!" I said, blushing a little. "Surely he cannot expect—"

"No, of course not! But the problem is that a man's interest does wander with time, if you see what I mean."

"Sir Hugh is sincerely attached to you, I am sure! I cannot believe another woman could take your place!"

"Don't you? It is my opinion that one already has."

"You're joking, Isabelle!" I said, incredulous. "All men have little *affaires,* I suppose—with *courtisanes* or married women—but you cannot think it is anything serious."

"I don't know how serious it is."

"A man could hardly look twice at another woman if he has you, my dear," I said in all frankness. "Excuse my indiscretion, but in order to judge the matter correctly, I would like to know just who you think she is."

"I don't know exactly. It's just the feeling I have that something is happening with him."

"Well, of all the ridiculous starts!" I laughed. "You are merely exaggerating your own uncertainty and impatience. You have nothing to fear from any other woman. How could you?"

"Easily!" she said, her brows raised in surprise as if she did not know to the last eyelash how beautiful she was. "And no matter how attached he may be to me, it is often very hard for a man to resist temptation when it is offered to him, and I should be a silly bird indeed if I did not know that lures past counting have been thrown out to him."

This seemed to call for some kind of comment. "I own he is very handsome—and most charming."

She glanced at me. "There! You see!"

I was slightly taken aback. "But *I* am hardly the object of his wandering attention (if wandering it is!) and certainly not one of your rivals!"

Isabelle's marble brow cleared, and she took my hand. "I did not mean anything so absurd, Marguerite! You are right: I am suffering from my own impatience."

I patted her hand. "You shall see: it shall all turn out in the end. My advice to you is to enjoy your two weeks with Sir Hugh at Hungerford and let the future take care of itself. May Sir Hugh's cousin soon die a just and merciful death!" I vowed solemnly and caught myself. "Holy Mother, what a thought!"

Isabelle laughed gaily, and we returned to our work.

The only other diversion occurred later in the afternoon, when Yvette Mortimer, accompanied by two of her brothers, the only latecomers, arrived at Hungerford. They were blond like Yvette and tall and slim, and I thought that she appeared to advantage next to them. Her arms were laden with gifts, and she was pink from the cold and was smiling. I had not seen her smile in a long while, and it seemed perhaps that she was recovering from her love sickness. This impression was soon dispelled when we had a few moments together while I showed her to her chambers.

"Is Sir Hugh here?" she asked me a little breathlessly.

I affirmed that he was.

"And has his betrothal to Isabelle been announced yet?" she pursued.

I replied that it had not.

"Do you think it shall be soon?"

I did not feel that I could, in all good faith, betray Isabelle's confidence. "I do not know for certain," I said with some difficulty, "but it is my belief that they are quite attached to each other. They are very discreet in their attentions to each other, of course, but it is obvious that they enjoy each other's company."

Yvette took this philosophically. "I am sure they do, but there is nothing in it if they do not marry. My brothers will talk to Sir Hugh next week if it looks as if nothing will come of his match with Isabelle."

She must have seen the look of mild shock on my face, for she continued matter-of-factly, "My dowry is considerable, as you know, and I believe that Sir Hugh would find it an attractive proposition."

I did not know, in truth, what Sir Hugh would think of the whole thing, if he would give up Isabelle and marry for land and wealth. It seemed unlikely, but I knew of one man, very different from Sir Hugh, who had, in a roundabout way, done just that. Yet I could not understand Yvette's desire to marry a man whose heart so obviously lay elsewhere. "But, Yvette, dearest," I said as gently as possible, "is he really worth that much to you?"

She understood what I meant and considered it for a moment. "Yes," she said flatly.

It was hard to respond adequately to her obvious determination to have Sir Hugh at any rate. "Well, we shall see what happens," I said, and gave the conversation a new turn by discussing what entertainments I had planned during the gift-giving that would take place when the men returned. I also thought to put as many eligible young men as possible—preferably tall ones—in Yvette's way. I could see no good for her in a hopeless, loveless match with Sir Hugh, which had every possibility of becoming an eventuality, if Falmouth found it absolutely necessary.

The men arrived back at the castle near sundown. They were a noisy, thirsty group, and several kegs of ale stood ready to be pegged in the hall. All the gifts had been spread out on the tables, and we made a commotion of the giving. There were prayer books, tapestries, and spices exchanged, jewelry, ells of Flemish cloth, baubles, bottles of exotic liqueurs, beribboned baskets filled with fruits and nuts, and cages squawking with all manner of fowl and poultry adding their part to the general pandemonium; then came candles, mirrors, footstools, fur-lined gloves, pelts, pillows, cushions, embroidered slippers, and even stuffed birds. I had prepared the usual vials of attar of rose for all the women with whom I was on gift-exchanging terms, and for the men of Hungerford I had had prepared new tabards; the women were given new aprons. Gavin received a leather jack sewn by myself that was intended more for service than elegance; and for Roland I had made two tunics of his favorite kerseymere, one blue and one gray, and had put forth my best effort to embroider the Guimont eagle motif around the V at the neck and down the sleeve-crease of the arm. They had turned out very well, and I was pleased with the quality and personality of the gift. Roland seemed pleased, too, for he kissed me and somehow in the hubbub contrived to have a toast made in my honor. It was a new, exhilarating experience for me to have so many glasses raised in my name, and I reveled in the moment, thinking that few things could be better than to be at Roland's side as mistress of Hungerford.

He then sent John Potter to fetch his gift to me, and presently a most handsome carved chest from Italy, of Milanese origin Roland told me, was carried into the hall. Not only was it quite the finest piece of furniture I had ever owned, it was also filled with the most exquisite linens I had ever seen. It was truly a gift given with me in mind: it fulfilled my penchant for the practical and appealed to my taste for beauty, which I was unlikely to indulge on my own. I curtsied low to my husband and made the prettiest speech I could muster in my confusion. He took my hand and raised it to his lips.

Before the dinner could be served, the hall had to be cleared of its glut of gifts, and all the guests scattered to their rooms, treasures tucked firmly under arm. I saw to it that my linen chest was stored safely in my odd little sewing room, just beside the window seat, and when I returned to the hall I noticed that Roland had donned his new blue tunic.

The meal was a blur of laughter, juicy viands, smooth red wines, and berry tarts. Then came dancing, gambling for those so inclined, and silly games like Blind Man's Bluff and Catch as Catch Can. This was my hour of fuzzy, self-absorbed in-toxication, a little bubble of delusion that the god of mischief (for I am one Christian who has never doubted his existence) could not resist pricking.

I had no business going down the back corridor off the hall just then, but so it was. It was a cavernous passage filled with dim alcoves and which led to several auxiliary hallways giving access, among other places, to the ramparts, the counting rooms, and, circuitously, to the kitchens. I had thought to run an errand to the kitchens (one that was entirely unnecessary to begin with) and chose this particular corridor rather than the more direct one to avoid the crowds and to give myself a little time to cool off and to settle my pulses, which were throbbing from the heat and the wine.

I was walking slowly, almost dallying, unaware of the stinging, painful voices of reality that stood literally just around the corner.

The sound of low, feminine laughter in one alcove just off the hall caught my ear and stayed my feet. A pair of long shadows were cast across my path by a torch flickering low behind them. They were standing close to each other, without touching. I halted just within the sharp selvage of a black velvety shadow and listened.

An eavesdropper, everyone knows, rarely hears anything to her advantage. What I heard next was just the beginning of what may be said to have been my long winter of darkness.

"A charming gesture, really," I heard the unseen woman say—the voice was unmistakably Isabelle's—"and entirely appropriate for a wife. I congratulate you on your good taste."

"Thank you, my dear," came the deep voice that made my heart stop, skip a beat, and then pound at a sickening tempo. "It is a comfort to have your approval."

I was quick to catch the note of mockery in his voice. Or was it flirtation?

"Ah!" she said softly. "But how very dull to be merely appropriate. Or have you lost your flair for the extravagant? You above all men should know that a woman can never have enough jewels."

"Poor Isabelle! Did you not receive any this Christmas?"

She laughed. "We were not speaking of me. We were speaking of your wife."

"*You* were," he corrected lazily. "I was trying to turn the subject. But while we are on it, what makes you think I have been neglectful in that domain?"

"You are referring no doubt to the Frant emeralds," she said, sounding satisfied. "Very nice, but hardly a personal touch."

"No," he agreed.

"And I had not known you were so wealthy now."

"I am, and I am lost in admiration of your wealth of information."

She laughed again, low and seductive. "But, Guy, you must know that the affair of the emeralds is common knowledge."

"I never doubted it for a moment."

There was a short silence. The tension in the air was a distinct presence. It was a palpable thing, and I could feel it, like the blind man, who, deprived of sight, is also not hindered by its deceptive, distorting tricks and can perceive many things that the ordinary person cannot.

The smaller, slimmer shadow moved a breath closer to the longer one.

"Do you remember the day you gave me this, Guy?" she asked with a sweet smile in her voice.

The shadows did not reveal to me the object to which she referred. I wondered foolishly if the gift had been accompanied by a Gascon love poem.

"I am unlikely to forget it," he replied evenly, no edge of emotion, positive or negative, piercing the smooth finish of his voice. I had heard him use that tone before, to maddening effect.

The slim shadow raised its head. "I do so love rubies," she whispered.

I felt as though the blood in my veins were slowly turning to ice. I should have guessed the moment I saw it that the bracelet Isabelle wore was part of the Guimont collection. I should have guessed, but I had not, and I had been completely taken in by Isabelle's artfully disarming play for my friendship, along with everything else.

"Do you know," she continued, not raising her voice, "that I shall always keep this? It is so much a part of me now! Come what may, I shall never part with it. No matter how much is offered for it! Why, quite by chance, not but a month ago, a man offered me a most fantastic sum for it." She paused. "I refused."

"You must be glad to have the means to have refused him."

"For shame, Guy," she reproached him seductively. "As if you do not know to the last pound how little my exchequer weighs. These things are, we are agreed, common knowledge, after all. No, I refused the sum because I am not at all practical—in fact, I am too sentimental for my own good. We need the money desperately, but I could not sell it when I thought on your words when you gave it to me. Let me see . . . something to the effect that rubies were unexpectedly the most becoming jewel for me, and so conveniently so! But perhaps you have forgotten . . . ?"

Roland did not reply.

"Or changed your mind?" she pursued.

"Why should I have?" he countered.

"By the cross, you have become stingy with your compliments of late," she said petulantly.

He laughed. I knew that easy laughter. "My dear! Do you really need me to tell you that no man would deny that you are the most beautiful woman in the kingdom? Or that no woman can wear rubies to advantage the way you do? Would you feel better if I turned a pretty phrase and said that it is not the rubies that set you off, but you that set the rubies off? If you do need my reassurances, then I shall have to have a word with Falmouth and put him on the right track."

"Why bring up another man, my love? It is not at all appropriate."

" 'But how very dull to be merely appropriate,' " he quoted. "And if it is not appropriate, at least it is to the point. I imagine that I may be congratulating you sometime soon on your forthcoming marriage."

"I find marriage such a sad topic," she said.

"Do you, my love? I cannot imagine why."

"I have already told you that I am sentimental," she replied. "And I had my eye on an entire set of rubies."

"But that was settled long ago, Isabelle," he said. Again the even tone that betrayed nothing of his thoughts. "Finished and finalized."

"Some things are never over, never finalized, my love."

"Death," he said in his mocking tone, "is very final. So is murder."

There was a long pause. Did she need reminding? I wondered.

"I might have forgiven you," she said at length. There was an odd catch in her voice, almost weird and with the hollowness of untruth. I could not understand it, much less interpret it. "I have a forgiving nature. You should know that by now, Guy, and should not have married so hastily."

"But I am known for my hot, hasty temper. You should know that, too, by now, my love."

I had the stomach for no more.

Somehow I made it back to the hall and even managed through a rather tedious evening rendered all the more insupportable by the knowledge that Isabelle and I had much more in common than I had previously suspected.

Chapter 14

The Christmas celebration was effectively ruined for me, although I retained enough of my senses to recognize that my guests were enjoying themselves very well. I fell back on all my weeks of preparation and on Lady Isolde's breeding, which had taught me that a hostess must never allow so much as a crease between the eyes betray to her guests that she is suffering the headache. I believed myself to be fairly successful in my dissimulation, for not even Alicia drew me aside to ask if I was not feeling well. She was naturally helpful to me in every possible way, but she did not evince any unnecessary attentions to the daily routine of housekeeping. I avoided Isabelle whenever possible, which was fairly easy, for she was bent on pleasing me by redoubling her efforts to Lady Constance. I could ask for no more than to have my two least-favorite ladies taken care of at once, and as regarded that latter, captious dame, I could have sworn on several occasions by her cattish smile that she was content that I was beginning to perceive how matters stood between Isabelle and my husband. I could not, of course, be sure, because Lady Constance was far too sly to bring the subject out in the open, but something indefinable in her manner made me think she was able to see my true feelings; but perhaps it was only my imagination. In any case, whenever I saw her, which was, thank heavens, rarely, I remembered the words she had spoken to me at Alicia's wedding: that Roland was in love with Isabelle and was the most jealous of fiancés, so that Isabelle was glad to be quit of him.

I had originally put that scrap in the same rubbish heap as the rest of Lady Constance's gossip, reckoning that it was her

347

way of hinting me away from Guimont. I saw now that there was something between the former fiancés and that whatever else may have been the case, Isabelle was not entirely glad to be released from her engagement. As for my husband, try as I might, I could not rid myself of the notion that if his design had been to tantalize Isabelle, he could not have calculated his responses to her better. Whenever I thought of their tête-à-tête—surely not above ten or twelves times a day—my stomach would flip over, and I would subsequently submerge myself in the conviviality of my guests.

I believed that only Bess guessed my true state of mind, but I soon found out that I was wrong. The evening I discovered that Isabelle's ruby bracelet belonged to the Guimont set, I sought my chambers earlier than usual and begged Bess to excuse me to my husband when he retired and to tell him that I was feeling unwell. Bess naturally believed me to be overworked, thought it an excellent idea for me to go to sleep early and alone, and brought me a hot posset to relax me for slumber. I did not sleep well. The next night, I repeated to her my request not to be disturbed and even went so far as to open a bottle of lavender water so that she could bathe my temples and wrists. If she was not sure that second night that I was suffering more than a mere headache, she must have become convinced of it on the third night when I insisted on remaining alone in my own chambers. She looked at me very keenly and pursed her lips in disapproval, but offered no comment. She sat me down at my dresser and unbound my hair, brushing it at length. The vigorous strokes did me much good, but not so much that I could do without the lavender-water bath. I prepared the basin of water on my dresser and had Bess fetch me several cloths. She rubbed my temples soothingly, and I was just beginning to relax when there came a knock on my antechamber door. It was relatively early and could only have been a servant on some trifling errand. I told her as she was leaving the room to send away whomever it was; whatever it was, it could wait. I continued to rinse my neck and forearms with the warm, scented water.

Several moments later I heard Bess behind me tending to the firewood basket.

"No, thank you, Bess," I said without turning around. "I won't be needing another log. I am going to bed presently."

"Always economizing, my lady?"

At the sound of his voice, I turned around, almost knocking the basin onto the floor. It was indeed Roland, and I was absurdly, unwisely happy to see him.

"I have become used to a cool chamber," I said, somewhat at a loss.

"It is not cool, it is cold," he answered, "and you shall be amazed to discover how rapidly you can become used to comfort, too, and shall wonder after several months of warm fires in February how you were ever able to stand the cold hearth of December."

He crouched down to lay another log across the smoldering embers and commenced to stir them. "And it does not appear, for you at least, my lady, that having become used to the cold has done you any good. You are not hearty enough to withstand this constant chill on your bones winter after winter."

I was too disconcerted to respond properly. "What are you doing here?" I asked idiotically.

He looked up from his work, elbows balanced on his knees. "I am making you a much-needed fire"—with that, small tongues of flames began to lick the stout length of wood—"in that your tiring woman was incapable of seeing the need for one and of overcoming your strictures. You seem to have inherited some of the parsimonious ways of your father, after all. I should like to cure you of them without delay."

"Old habits die hard, and—"

"Yes," he interrupted with a knowing smile, "and wood is expensive."

"It *is*," I insisted, lamely.

"There is not an item in the realm worth having that is not expensive. What is more to the point, however, is the fact that I am well able to afford having my wife's hearth blaze all winter long without fear of draining the coffers. In fact, the cords of wood that have been chopped and stacked for your personal use are in the spare shed next to the stables. You may go there and have a look if you need reassurance. What is there is intended for this winter's consumption, but at your present rate of use, I fear the oak will rot by the end of the decade, and that will be a waste."

I stared at him for a moment or two rather stupidly, then recollected myself enough to thank him for his generosity.

He did not acknowledge my thanks. He simply gave the log a few more pokes with the iron. It spit and crackled its response. Then he stood up and stretched his hand meditatively before the fire.

"I should like to think," he said over his shoulder to me, "that your current indisposition is due merely to your habit of staying in underheated rooms."

I opened my mouth to speak and then closed it.

"Or to the strain of entertaining so many people and so well," he continued, adding, "but I fear that it is not."

"I am not at all indisposed," I disclaimed, "merely tired. It is the exertion—not the strain!—of the entertaining. Not that I mind in the least. Oh, no! In fact, I am enjoying myself thoroughly and can only hope that my guests are, too. So I have taken the opportunity of retiring earlier than my wont these past few nights. That is all."

His harsh features relaxed into a fleeting smile of disbelief. "But you seem to be needing more and more sleep, and I am wondering as to the reason. I thought at first that it was the exertion, as you say, of the Christmas celebration, but you are far too adept at this sort of thing to be affected by it, although Lord knows you had little experience at Shrivenham. In fact, I would have thought that you were in your element as mistress and hostess, save for your preoccupation of late." He paused. "Perhaps you can tell me the cause."

I roused myself to show some animation. "No cause, my lord!" I replied with a bright smile. "I have been very imprudent in the past days and have not husbanded my energies well, so that I run far too many unnecessary errands. By the evening, my poor feet compel me to seek my bed, against all my protests!"

His reaction to my explanation was not encouraging. I moved on. "But perhaps you mean to hint to me that I am being rude by retiring so early?"

"Not in the least," he said, shifting his gaze to the fire. "I note that you do not leave the hall until at least three or four of the ladies excuse themselves. I would be most surprised if you committed even the least social solecism."

"Then mayhap I am leaving some important task undone, and you mean to draw my attention to it?"

"I am not here to reproach you," he said. I was a little surprised by the sternness of his tone. "Everything is perfect, to the last detail." He waved his hand in a careless gesture. "No, do not thank me, for you know it as well as I. As I have said, I am interested in your well-being, and I warn you that I shall not fly from the scent by your attempts to divert my purpose with irrelevant concerns. I do perceive, however, that whatever is bothering you, you do not intend to tell me. But do not think to convince me that your early evenings have done you much good, for it is obvious that you have not been sleeping well."

To my further consternation, I realized that he could read me very accurately. "Not very well," I admitted shakily, "and I thought to spare you my restlessness." I glanced at him, and the look on his face surprised me again. There seemed a vague amusement. "That is all, my lord, and I see that there is little point in dissembling to you. Yet, I cannot help but imagine that if you so readily detect my improper rest, must not also our guests? That would be very bad!"

He shook his head slowly and came toward me. "I am not one of your guests," he said, "and I feel it my duty to ensure your sound sleep. At least I always know that you sleep well at my side. In the future, I recommend that you do not deny my entrance except at the times when you are truly indisposed."

There was a warm glint in his eye that I found very attractive; perhaps it was only a reflection from the fire. I did not have time to consider the matter at length, however; before long, the lavender water was forgotten along with its restorative effects, and I lay in Roland's arms. The pleasure that mingled with my misery was exceedingly sweet, and its effect on my eventual sleep was entirely beneficial. All unpleasant dreams were too far submerged to surface, and I spent the night with the entirely comforting notion that if I was not Roland's love, at least I had an immeasurable advantage in being his wife. This satisfaction lasted throughout the next week of the fortnight of festivities, which I was able to face with equanimity and even considerable enjoyment—that is, when I managed to block out the moments that Isabelle passed at Roland's side.

These came daily. I supposed that there was nothing in it to cause undue comment: my husband also passed time with Marie-Ange, Helvie, and a number of the other unmarried maids, as well as Alicia and the other ladies. By the same token, not a day passed when I did not have contact with Sir Hugh. He had already bestowed on me his bridal kiss, and in circumstances that I believed he deemed enticing. I was not enticed, nor even the least bit attracted to him. He made me extremely uncomfortable besides, and I could not like the heartless way he occasionally flirted with Yvette. I was full well aware that Sir Hugh was playing some sort of game with Roland through me, and I did not like that, either. I might have been naive (a fault I was making every effort to correct), but I was not a simpleton, and it did not take a very worldly woman to understand that by flirting with me, Sir Hugh could also make Isabelle jealous, if he cared to. He must have known, long before I came along, that Isabelle and Roland had had more than a written commitment to each other. It seemed reasonable to imagine that he also knew the provenance of Isabelle's ruby bracelet. Still, she had no wedding ring, and Sir Hugh and I could take heart from that.

Sir Hugh had occasion to comment on my own wedding ring on one of the innumerable times he took my hand, always on the slightest of pretexts, and kissed it.

"Guimont is truly generous," he said to me one evening when he happened to catch me alone. He was gazing at the fine ring weighing on my finger. "I had no idea that his pockets were so well lined. Of course, you did not come to him penniless, did you, my dear? Nevertheless, there was the general, ah, misconception that the Hungerford demesne was in no better heart than . . . well, than mine own! And yet Guimont was able to buy a most precious set of jewelry for his bride. That gives one pause to reflect, does it not?"

He engulfed me in his liquid gaze, and I could well imagine that more than one woman had floundered in its depths and drowned. Fortunately for myself, I was well able to resist the undertow, and on second appraisal I thought his eyes had more the look of a bird of prey or even the snake that is reputed to entrance its victim with its regard, before striking for the kill.

"Does it?" I questioned in return. "It is strange that the ways in which my husband chooses to place his money do not give *me* pause to reflect. I know only that we lack for nothing. But then," I continued on an acidic note, "my desires are minimal. I am not one of those women who crave jewels and furs and new furniture every year to be happy."

"I can see you lack for nothing materially, my dear," he said with his smile, "and I see that you mean to be an undemanding wife. But you are not as simple as you would like me to think and must deal with a complicated man for a husband—and one—will you permit me the liberty of saying so?—one whose desires are many. I wonder if you can live with mere material comfort, my dear."

He was plainly offensive. "I do not understand you, Sir Hugh," I said. "It is not my place to question my husband's desires, and every woman must accept her husband as he is. I think myself very lucky."

"Admirable!" he exclaimed and took my hand again. "You seem to have rehearsed that very well. I confess to a curiosity, you know, to discover what methods the resourceful Guimont used to coerce you into marriage. I cannot imagine him resorting to brutality, that is, where women are concerned, but his wit must have been extraordinary to have captured such a one as you."

"I believe there was an understanding between Sir Roland

and my father," I replied stiffly, and tried unsuccessfully to withdraw my hand, "before my dear sire passed on."

I cast my eyes respectfully to the floor and with my free hand crossed myself in his memory, at the same time repenting my hypocrisy for blessing my father's hated memory.

"You are too good for Guimont," Sir Hugh whispered close to my ear.

"Ah! There is Gavin now!" I cried, thereby gaining release of my hand. I hailed the squire as one would a savior. "I have been watching for him these past minutes, dear sir, to tell him to have the musicians play a lively jig. Oh! Pray excuse my thoughtless implication! If I have been unable to give you my full attention just now, you must understand that I must be always attending to the goings-on with half my brain. I have not been able to devote myself entirely to any one person for more than two minutes running anytime this past week!"

And if that did not signal to him: *Please leave me alone. I find your manner much too familiar,* then the look Gavin gave him as the timely squire led me out to dance with him (for I had let him know that he should remain by my side by the firm pressure of my fingers on his arm) surely would.

Sir Hugh slid away and had enough sense not to bother me again in so obvious a fashion.

Lady Constance, too, kept her distance and practiced few of her die-away airs on me, which was just as well, for she would not have gotten very far with my sympathy, since I had never seen her look so well. She was almost animated; in fact, I even caught a glimpse of her actually laughing at something Isabelle said in her ear. Not a genuine laugh of pure amusement, needless to say, but a laugh of pleasure or satisfaction or whatever it was that Lady Constance could feel on the lighter side of human nature. Her eyes were very bright and lively, too, and darted continually this way and that. I would almost have thought that she was enjoying herself, but I did not flatter myself that it was due to the excellence of the entertainments.

It did occur to me, however, that Lady Constance was plotting something. As the celebration continued, that suspicion receded, and a few days before Epiphany, when the guests would return to their respective castles for a bout of relative sobriety until springtime, I had completely discounted any fear of mischief from her. There simply was not time to organize anything untoward. I had envisioned some horrid scene of disgrace to Roland engineered by her, but that was pure fantasy: whenever Constance moved, it was behind the scenes and I had enough respect for my husband's judgment to believe that he would never be caught to his disadvantage in public.

I was content that Constance made herself marginally agreeable toward the end of the fortnight and that she made sure to keep Charles out of my way. This was not difficult, given the free-flowing quantity of drink available. His perpetual state of intoxication also saved Joan of Shrewsbury considerable harassment: Charles much preferred the feel of the handle of his ale mug to her lithe form.

I did not make the mistake of thinking that Constance would ever forgive me for having let Roland outsmart her in marrying me, but I wanted to think that she had become reconciled to the idea and would have the prudence to let matters rest as they stood.

That did not mean that she could resist a snide comment or two and an unnerving, but not entirely unexpected, reference to the lovely Isabelle at Roland's side.

She chose to make such remarks always at the most propitious moment (from her point of view)—that is, when no fewer than three of my lady friends were there also to hear. It was particularly painful to me that Marie-Ange should have been present to hear Constance sigh and say, while looking straight at my husband in conversation with my rival, "They used to make such a handsome couple, although I was never a partisan of Guimont's for her hand. Oh, no! I believe Falmouth suits her much better, though the poor man fears he shall never regain his fortune! So you see, dear Marguerite, things do have a way of working out for the best."

There was an awkward pause in the wake of that most tactless observation, which Constance seemed not to notice. Then Alicia, I believe, inaugurated the very interesting topic of berry jellies and offered several recipes for jam. It was instantly picked up for general conversation. When the discussion came to its natural conclusion and the ladies fell to talking among themselves, Constance drew me aside and said pointedly, "Well, I must say that you are managing *that* situation very well, my dear! Oh, yes, I quite see that it is a— a—an *inconvenience* for you, if you see what I mean, but you are doing very well."

This was accompanied by her faintest smile that conveyed to me the message: *You poor dear, how you must suffer with Isabelle under your roof. How sorry I feel for you, but do not tell me that I did not warn you.*

Perversely, this passage served to restore my spirits entirely, and if there was anyone to feel sorry for, I thought to myself in defiance of Constance's sickly attempt to get at me, it was Isabelle.

This brave front lasted up until the last evening of the celebration, and it was just as well that I clung to my illusions for as long as possible.

I should never have listened to the little devilries Lady Constance poured in my ear that evening; I should have known that she was just poisoning me, weakening me for the kill— in fact, I am quite sure I did know it—but I was not strong enough to provide myself with an antidote. Sometimes, irresistibly, we do things that are directly contrary to our own best interests, in full or even partial awareness of our momentary weakness, seeing only dimly that we might have to bear the consequences of certain actions or decisions for a long time to come. It is said that experience is the best teacher, but I have often thought that experience is the wisdom of fools, and all the experience in the world would not have prevented me from doing what my better judgment counseled me not to. I was saved, in a manner of speaking, only by a small hesitation on my part, by that tiny reserve of discretion in me that did not, unfortunately, prevail, but which enabled me to escape certain death only by a matter of seconds, much as an archer in the heat of battle will bend down to restock his bow at the very moment that an enemy arrow passes at the precise spot where his heart had been a second before. Comics use such split-second timing for laughter; there was no laughter for me, however, and I rather felt like the lucky archer who, having missed the arrow, was knocked down and singed by a volley of burning naphtha.

The evening began badly. I was in truth a little tired by now; and being something of a perfectionist, I was exasperated out of proportion by the fact that one of the cook's apprentices had managed to burn an entire side of venison. It was edible, and such things were bound to happen, but still it set me off on the wrong foot.

Lady Constance wasted no time in making her way to my side once the meal was over and wasted even less with the polite nothings. Yes, she was sorry to be leaving a most satisfactory Christmas celebration, but did I know that the chimneys in the north wing smoked a trifle when the wind was in that quarter? It was a little thing, she assured me, and easily taken care of by attentive, regular cleaning. I thanked her duly for the household hint and declared myself relieved that I had not housed her in the north wing. I full well expected a remark on the drafts in the east wing, but Constance contained herself. She smiled waxily and came straight to the point.

"You know, Marguerite, an odd thing it would be for me to be telling tales. You know that I am not one of those gabble-mongers like dear Edwina—but it is not my place to criticize, for she is a dear friend of mine! No, I do have my shortcomings, I am sure, and do not enjoy a robust constitution, but speaking of it is not in my character. No, indeed, so you will understand the spirit in which I offer you my comments. And do not forget that I am like a mother to you, my dear—and although I hold a deep affection for Isabelle, I fear that she has been—how shall I say?—led into an indiscretion. And while it pains me to have to say this to you, I am compelled to say that I believe Isabelle (the dear girl!) is meeting your husband this evening in private."

I steeled myself. "Oh, is she? I am fully appreciative of your kind intentions, but I should be a silly goose to lose my head over every tale I hear, for one can never be certain when they are based on truth, and then again, hearing a tale does not always mean that one knows best what to do about it.''

"You are very right, my dear! Yes, I recommend caution whenever possible. You would never jump to hasty conclusions, being so very deliberate (a virtue more of us should cultivate, I am sure) the way you are. And just because Roland and Isabelle have been of late absent from the hall at the same time does not mean that they are away together. There are many people circulating, and when Lady Stafford is absent at the same time Lord Godefroi is gone does not make me suspect that there is anything between them. Of course, Lady Stafford's leg is paining her terribly and the cold is not at all therapeutic, and thus she is mostly bedridden, poor dear! So one would not expect her to indulge in amorous adventuring at this time, yet . . ." She let this sink in a moment. "And, yet, I have been very worried about Isabelle lately. She has not been herself. It makes me think of the time when she was under Guimont's spell and was always out of sorts. I had thought the sad business of the summer and all that had happened had cured her, for she was never in better spirits than in the autumn, and it makes me most unhappy to see her so affected again!''

To say nothing of how it affected me; but then, I suppose, Lady Constance in the office of my mother would think that *my* feelings about the present state of affairs would also make her most unhappy. That, apparently, went without saying.

She sighed. "Yes, Marguerite, I am afraid that there is something amiss, and so I confide to you that it has me very worried!''

"I see that it does," I replied with a distant chill in my voice. "Nevertheless—''

"I perceive that I shall have to make a clean breast of it," she interrupted, "although I shall have to betray Isabelle's confidence. I must do it, truly I must," she said, as if forming a resolve, "for everyone concerned. In fact, Isabelle came to me just before dinner to ask for my advice. She said that Roland had made an assignation with her in his counting rooms for later this evening, which must be almost about now, I would think. Naturally, I advised her against meeting him. I cannot think that it would do her the least good, and then there is her reputation to think of—and her virtue!"

Was I particularly numb not to have been shocked by the implication? Many thoughts jostled in my mind, but among them was not the idea that Constance was at all out of character. The ordinary person would not in general have had the gall to say such things to me, but Constance has an extraordinary amount of gall and no delicacy of principle.

"I am extremely obliged to you for telling me this!" I said with exaggerated sweetness.

"It is not at all agreeable for you, is it, my dear? But so it is. You are a sensible young woman and not given to wild flights of emotion, so I do not hesitate to tell you the worst. Isabelle did not seem persuaded by my arguments and left me in a state of agitation. I wonder if she is not on her way to meet him now."

I looked around, and it was true that Isabelle was nowhere to be seen. Neither was Roland, but then the hall was very crowded and they could have been almost anywhere in the throng. I must admit that I was strongly inclined to believe Constance's story, for I had noticed on more than one occasion that Isabelle and Roland were absent at the same times, but I had tried to write it down to coincidence, except for the one time that I had chanced to overhear them.

"And whatever would you have me do about it, if it is true?" I asked her.

"Well, I should think you might want to go there and stop the rendezvous, my dear. It is not at all the thing, you know, and what could be more natural than your having an errand in Roland's counting rooms?"

I actually laughed at that. "Almost anything, dear lady!" I replied. "I have been in there only once and that was on Roland's receiving day." I conveniently ignored the disaster that had befallen me only recently as a result of my second visit to those sacred rooms.

"Really?" Lady Constance sounded genuinely amazed. "Do you mean that you do not take care of the accounts and pay the servants as you used to do so well at Shrivenham? I would have thought with your head for numbers that—well! Of course, I did not know—I thought that you might have been able to devise an errand to run there, perhaps to pay one of the extras you have hired for the holidays. Something like that. But I see that that would be very awkward. . . . No, it won't do, my dear."

"I should rather think not! And even if I did have something to do there, I would not like to be in the position of spying on my husband—or on Isabelle," I added with some difficulty.

"I did not mean that you should!" Constance exclaimed. "It is simply that— But perhaps my notions are old-fashioned, after all. In short, it is my belief that it is best to minimize temptation whenever possible, and that if you were to hurry, you might well be able to intercept Isabelle and bring her back to the hall on some pretext. She would hardly be able to refuse you, and if she were not to show up, things might just very well resolve themselves for the good. 'Out of sight, out of mind,' I always say. It would be best for everyone to have the two of them separated for good, don't you agree? I see that you do! I am sure you would sleep the better for it."

I was not entirely convinced that my sleep would benefit at all from this night's work, but I was struck by the idea of intercepting Isabelle and spoiling the rendezvous. I had my own reasons for thinking this a particularly wise course of action: Roland and I had seemed closer of late, and I chose to think that Isabelle might have been the instigator of all the meetings between herself and my husband. I would not mind running into her in a back hallway and letting her know that she was, in several ways, off limits.

Lady Constance saw that she was making headway with me, but not for the reasons she had fashioned for me, and added some further words of encouragement. I came to a sudden decision and told her that I would see what I could do, but that I would not take the most direct route to the counting rooms. It would be far better to go around by way of the kitchens and meet Isabelle in the passageway.

She patted my hand and said with surprising sincerity that she wanted only my happiness.

I left her then, determined on my course of action. I had an impulse to turn my head around to catch a glimpse of Constance just before I left the crowded hall, but she had vanished, and with a quickness surprising for all her infirmities. Perhaps it was this that slowed my pace and set me to thinking; I was not sure. Perhaps it was the fact that once away from her and alone with my own judgment, I could consider more clearly what she had said. Or perhaps, and this was the most likely of all, I knew that deep down I was motivated by a jealous curiosity and a basic disbelief that Roland had made any assignation with Isabelle. I wanted to see for myself that it was not true; and, if it was not, why Constance would want to send me in the vicinity of the counting rooms at this precise moment. Then again, if it was true, what point would there be in spoiling their meeting? It would not make Roland desire to see her less, and if he had proposed to meet her in his counting rooms, he had obviously chosen that place as the one least likely to be intruded upon and particularly not by me. I could not decide what to do.

My indecision followed me slowly through the kitchens. I was resolved to turn back, yet I did not turn back. I moved deliberately, inexorably to the counting rooms, but I do not think it was ever my intention actually to enter them to spy (to call the act by its true name) on my husband if I was not so fortunate as to run into Isabelle on my way.

In the event, I was never given a chance to see just how far my jealousy and curiosity would carry me. When I turned the last, fatal corner that led straight to the counting rooms, I saw a shadowy figure move furtively at the end of the hallway. It seemed to be lurking around the door. My pulses jumped. The figure moved again, and I saw for certain that it was neither Isabelle nor Roland. My senses had already registered that its shape was familiar to me as my feet mechanically hastened to confront it.

It was Charles Hartford.

He had seen me, too, and took several steps toward me. No sooner had the words, "What are you doing here, Charles?" left my mouth than, before I knew what was happening, he grabbed my arm and wrenched me to him. He had been drinking.

"You are late," he said with a perceptible slur, "but I do not think that it shall matter much. The essential thing is that you are here now."

"Let me go!" I cried and began writhing in his arms. "What brings you here? You have no business being here."

He laughed a little wildly. "Oh, do I not? We shall see about that, and I am not adverse to waiting a little longer for what I consider rightfully mine."

Then, like the unwary listener to a tale who suddenly puts all the clues together and intuits the end of the story at the very moment that it is being recounted, I understood in a flash what was going on as it happened before my eyes. I knew, too, that Constance's little plan was doomed to failure. She could not have hoped to dupe my husband in his own castle and must have been very desperate to have tried to pull it off.

And there I stood, implicated, imprisoned in Charles's fat grasp, with little hope of redeeming myself. I turned my head at the sounds and the light, and what came next unfolded itself as if everything followed as a natural, inevitable consequence of all that had gone before.

I think I perceived first the heavy scuffling that came from within the counting rooms, the strangled curses and shrill cries. A man darted out the door to the dark antechamber a split second later and ran down the dim passageway communicating with the Great Hall. He must have passed within only three feet of us, but he did not seem to take note of our presence, and then—it seemed to happen simultaneously—the hall end of the corridor was filled with the light of torches and Constance was brought out into the hallway straining in the grip of a large man. To my surprise, she was followed by the frail Agnes, her trusty tiring woman, who was also held from fleeing by a strong man. These two men, along with the one who had run down the corridor, were very likely in the service of the king.

Charles and I stood on the other side of Constance and Agnes in the still-darkened part of the corridor. Charles had released his grip on me and his hands had fallen uselessly to his sides, but apart from this, neither one of us moved. I think Charles was too bewildered to know quite what to do; I did not have the least intention of moving until it was all over. To scurry away now would only have confirmed my complicity in Constance's plans.

The torches approached us slowly, deliberately, and I could see that the first of them was held by Roland. Beside him came the man who had left the counting rooms in such a hurry and three other men who, I guessed, were to serve as witnesses. Roland stopped several feet from the two men from the counting rooms and their quarry; the circle of light that spilled from the main torch fell just at the hem of my dress. Charles and I were left in darkness.

"What is this all about?" Roland demanded of the man at his side, as if my husband did not know perfectly well what was toward and had not himself laid the trap for Constance.

"I am loath to inform you, Guy," the man said, still breathless, "that we discovered moments ago Lady Hartford and her woman in your counting rooms." He paused to gulp a breath. "We apprehended them just as they were about to leave. It is very strange, however, for no money was taken, as you had feared. They apparently wanted only these."

The messenger gestured to the man restraining Constance, and he handed over a sheaf of papers to Roland. My husband placed his torch in a brass cup cinched to the wall and glanced at the parchments. He frowned and asked several questions.

The story came out in the ensuing discussion that my husband had supposedly hired three men to guard his counting rooms for the duration of the Christmas celebration, there being a quantity of money therein and too many people to control properly. I did not really believe that he thought any of our guests would be disposed to robbing us. The men had evidently been planted there to capture Constance when and if she should make her move.

Roland handed the parchments to one of the "witnesses."

"What do you make of these, Sheffield?" he asked.

I had, of course, met Phillip Sheffield and spoken with him on one or two occasions. He whistled low and said that the king would be mightily interested to see them. Sir Phillip looked briefly at Constance, then at Roland.

"How do you suppose these papers come to be in my counting rooms?" my husband asked.

"I do not know," Sheffield said, "except that they were written by Montcrief's hand." He paused. "Did you not tell me once that you had imported your father-in-law's desk and cabinets from Shivenham?" Roland nodded. "Then perhaps they were concealed in the furniture. Lady Hartford apparently knew of their hiding place."

"Ah, yes," Roland replied, "that must be so."

This dialogue clearly had been orchestrated. Constance knew it too and hailed curses down upon the heads of all present. Her voice was strong and shrill and had nothing of her customary artifice of feeble suffering. Her captor held her arms behind her back but did not restrain her voice. Finally it spent itself on the impassive men who stood around her and she was left panting and glaring white hatred at Roland.

"Since there has been nothing of mine stolen," Roland said at length, unmoved, "I am afraid that the matter is out of my jurisdiction. I refer to you then, Sheffield, for a ruling on the matter."

"I have no choice," Sheffield said, "given what I hold in my hand and Lady Hartford's obvious knowledge of the worth of these documents, but to arrest her and her woman in the name of Plantagenet."

Constance was transformed into a raging harpy; the wicked lines of her face were cast into weird relief by the flickering torches. She played what she had hoped would be her ace. "And your wife, Guimont?" she spat. "She is here, too!"

Roland did not so much as look at me at this comment. Neither did anyone else. I saw how she had tried to manipulate me, to use me as her safety measure. She had thought that I would, out of jealousy, actually enter the counting rooms expecting to find Roland and Isabelle, so that if there was a slip-up in her plans and she was caught, then I would be there, too. I imagined that she would think that Roland could not implicate her without also condemning me, and, wanting no scandal, he would be forced to drop the matter. But Constance had miscalculated: I had the chilling impression that had I been discovered within the counting rooms along with Constance and Agnes, Roland would willingly have sacrificed me along with his enemy and with no questions asked.

Roland simply inquired of the guards in a voice devoid of emotion whether his wife had been apprehended within the counting rooms.

The response was, naturally, negative.

"And Charles Hartford? Was he within?"

Again, no.

"Then I do not see what the two of them have to do with this most unfortunate affair," he said. Then, gesturing to the two captives: "Take them away. I shall have to put you in charge of them, Sheffield. I recommend that they be locked in the west tower under guard. We shall have to decide later about their eventual transportation to London."

There was nothing more to be said. Sir Phillip stuffed the incriminating documents into his tunic and commanded the three guards and the two women to follow him down the hallway that led to the ramparts. Constance struggled and grunted, vile, vulgar words spilling from her lips that remained audible until the small party rounded a corner. The two other witnesses faded back toward the Great Hall.

Roland was left facing me and Charles. His face was unusually grim. "Get you gone, Hartford," he said to Charles without taking his eyes off me. "You have chosen a most inauspicious time and place to try to compromise my wife. Every time I turn around, I find another man after her. It is becoming tiresome." When Charles, too stupefied to move, did not react, Roland continued, "Get you gone and never let me see your face here again, Hartford. You are free to leave Hungerford this night. If you do not, I warn you that I shall not be answerable for my actions."

Charles disappeared.

Roland held my gaze for a long moment. I did not flinch from his piercing blue regard.

At length I spoke. "Constance tricked me," I said wretchedly. My voice was barely above a whisper.

"Did she? It is scarce pleasing to me to know that she was able to do so, and apparently so easily."

A wave of that now-familiar nausea swept over me. He thought me a complete fool, if not also an accomplice, but I would not let him know to what depths I had sunk.

"Nevertheless, she did," I said, drawing a breath and squaring my shoulders. "She is wilier than I, and I own it freely. You have said that I have inherited some of my father's traits, but as for his skill at subterfuge, well, I have little head and much less stomach for it."

His eyes narrowed. "Perhaps," he said. "Or it is possible that you have surpassed even your sire's abilities?" He smiled crookedly. "I do not know."

How many times would I be called upon to plead my innocence? The fact was that I had been as close to the scene of the crime as one could get without also being called a thief. I could not have expected him to trust me any better after this. There had been too many coincidences, I had been too preoccupied of late, as if my mind had been busy with intrigue, and, above all, I was too proud and perhaps too unsure of myself even to hint at my motivation for being outside the counting rooms.

I think I shook my head unconsciously and shrugged my shoulders, gesturing my inability to answer his question. I was saddened by the barrier I had managed to create between us. I was also saddened by the prospect of Constance's future. It had been a very sorry evening.

"What shall happen to Lady Constance once she gets to London?" I asked to turn the conversation away from my particular folly.

He said evenly, "I have a notion that she shall be beheaded."

I closed my eyes against this horror. When I opened them again, Roland was still scrutinizing me. "Is it possible? Has she truly done anything so wrong?"

"Treason," he said, "is customarily considered wrong to the king's way of thinking."

We had been over this road before together, he and I. I felt a strange sense of mystery surrounding Roland, which I had felt strongly since first meeting him, that derived from his mastery of affairs just beyond the circle of my knowledge, of matters vitally important to the kingdom and to him and me. I longed to share that with him and to take part in his world.

"What is it all about?" I asked, frustration and desperation peeping through my studied calm. "What can it matter for you to tell me now that she is gone?"

His grim aspect softened somewhat, but not his tone. "There are things, Marguerite, in which you must never dabble. There are some things I don't desire you to know."

"But surely you won't deny that your actions this evening were arranged and very well timed and that you had, in effect, laid an elaborate trap for Constance."

He actually smiled. "No, I don't deny it. You would not believe me if I did."

"Not at all! And neither would Constance. She must have known that Sir Phillip was among the guests and what his capacity must be—that is, I assume he must be a special sheriff for King Henry, or something like that."

"He is, and she did know it, but risk and danger, instead of deterring some people from wrongdoing, inspire them."

"Yet, there was something stupid and obvious—at least to you!—about what Constance did this evening. I thought she had more of the fox about her."

"She has her sly side," he admitted, "but I have always seen her as more of a squirrel. But she tried to line her pockets with too many nuts and finally got caught."

I did not really need to hear the particulars of Constance's crimes to understand that she had caused her own demise. "Well, then, it seems she outsmarted herself, which is, I suppose, a form of stupidity."

"Greed has a way of making people do very stupid things," he said.

I looked up at him suddenly, for he had used his lazy,

noncommittal tone, the one that I had learned to warn me of danger, but I could not imagine that he was directing that comment at me, so I merely agreed with him.

"And yet the greed is always a measure of the character. One cannot be surprised to see it surface in Constance after all," he continued.

"No, but it is sad, and I feel sorry for her." I trembled slightly. "It is hard for me to grasp that she shall be—actually be put to death."

"Your pity is wasted, my dear."

"Better to feel pity," I retorted, "than to feel whatever it is that you feel! That is to say, nothing at all! No, I take that back! It seems almost as if you enjoy her doom," I complained.

He shook his head. "I did not wish it on her, and my only enjoyment comes from knowing that by sacrificing her neck, we have saved others', not least of which, my own. It shall be pleasant not having that itching sensation between my shoulder blades whenever my back is not to a wall. Do not forget that Constance has wanted me as much as I have wanted her, and do I need to remind you what your prize was to have been?"

That reminded me of a loose end. "What about Charles?"

"What about him?"

"Do you not intend to apprehend him in any way?"

"On what pretext?"

"I don't know. Cannot you invent one?"

"Charge him with being the offspring of a conspirator?" he suggested with irony.

That came too close to my own case for comfort. I laughed uncertainly. "Is it not enough that he was involved in it and knew what was occurring?"

"No," he replied. "However, I thought we were agreed that he was not clever enough to be a problem."

"We were also agreed that he is violent," I pointed out.

"Only when he is in a position of power. After tonight, he will have neither position nor any hope of power."

"But what shall he do, where shall he go?"

"I do not know, and I do not care. He may go back to

Downton and drink himself to an early grave, for all it matters to me. In fact, that may be his wisest course."

I assimilated this. "Do you not think . . . ?" I left the idea unformed.

"I do not think that you shall ever be bothered by Charles again."

That was something of a relief, at any rate. It almost made me smile. "I never did like him, you know," I said.

"I cannot imagine that you could have."

"Lady Constance wasn't so bad, although there were times when I disliked her cordially. Still, she had her moments, and a certain style in all her artifice that compelled a certain admiration."

"She would have seen to your death," he said coldly, "if it had suited her purpose. No, there is no need for you, or anyone else, to mourn her."

"Shall not any of the guests miss her presence? Perhaps not tonight, for it is already late, but by the leave-taking tomorrow, or in the future?"

"Something shall be arranged to account for her absence— and death. It need not concern you."

"Yet, if someone were to ask me about it, what should I say?"

"That you naturally know nothing about it. Why should you? You are not responsible for knowing of her whereabouts at any given moment."

"Indeed not. Ignorance is often convenient, is it not?"

He nodded. "The affair is settled, as far as I am concerned," he said meaningfully. "I must go now to the west tower and speak with Sheffield and his men. I am sure you understand that I shall be unable to join you tonight. I shall seek an audience with you, however, first thing in the morning."

I understood perfectly. He bowed low over my hand and left me. I watched him go until nothing was left of him but his shadow, and then even that vanished.

Heavy with conflicting thoughts, I wandered back to the Great Hall. Roland had caught me in the worst of a bad situation, and yet he was willing to overlook the implications of my presence at the scene. It was small consolation to me that I was, indeed, innocent of everything but jealousy.

The hall seemed suddenly bright and gay to me, as if the storm had come and cleansed the air. My guests were plainly enjoying themselves. Marie-Ange was flirting with her various gallants, Alicia was dancing with Herbert, and I felt a certain satisfaction in seeing Isabelle in deep, and apparently amorous, conversation with Sir Hugh. They could not have known that Lady Constance and her unremarkable Agnes were locked in the west tower under guard, nor that her life was forfeit. They could not have known that Charles was preparing a hasty and ignominious departure. They could not have known how matters stood between me and my husband. Nor would they have cared too profoundly, either.

And why should they? If Lady Constance was guilty, as I did not doubt she was, then she deserved her fate, just as my father had merited his. It was none of my guests' concern. It was the eve of Epiphany and a time for celebration. I felt like celebrating, too. This could mark the time of a new beginning for me and my marriage, a time when I could prove to Roland my devotion to him without the poison of doubt and plot and intrigue. Lady Constance had cast a long shadow across us, but now that she was gone, there was nothing to stand in the way of the growth of our relationship. I marveled at how quickly I had recovered from the shock of Constance's swift and brutal end. She had been but a spare hour ago a part of the festivities in the hall. Now, for all intents and purposes, she was dead to the world. Gone without a trace, and with no one to mourn her. It was almost as if she had never existed. The drinking, the singing, and the dancing went on, and there was no reason why it should not.

The death of an enemy is hardly an occasion for joy, I discovered, nor wild happiness. I breathed a sigh of relief, however, and joined my guests in the business of merriment.

Chapter 15

I arose the next morning eager to see Roland and to talk with him about those matters that so deeply concerned us. He did not come to my chambers, however, as I had half-expected, and when I felt I could wait no longer, I left to go about my business, hoping to have a word with him before the day grew much older. As always happens when one gets involved in one's daily affairs, I found I had more than enough things to do to keep me busy, and with running this way and that, I was hardly accessible to Roland, if he should come looking for me. The castle was a confusion of servants and guests, baggage and farewells. The bailey was even worse, but the humor was high, and most of the irritations that frequently attend the leave-taking of a great many people whose schedules can hardly be expected to accommodate ease of departure were passed off with a laugh and a quip or two. Everyone was agreed that it had been a most marvelous celebration, and that was a tribute I accepted most happily. One person in particular, entirely unexpectedly, found reason to think the fortnight spent at Hungerford exceptionally fine.

Yvette Mortimer descended to the hall that morning wreathed in smiles. I had not seen her in such good looks since the day she had come. She was all packed, and her brothers were in the stables, preparing for imminent departure, and so I drew her aside to say some final words. I naturally addressed myself first to the subject of her renewed radiance. She blushed rosily and merely shook her head.

"You need not tell me, you know, Yvette," I said playfully, "and are perfectly free to have me perish from curiosity. I shall take that as just thanks for my hospitality."

"Oh, Marguerite!" she said, laughing. "I cannot! I promised

not to!" She bit her lip in indecision. It was obvious that she was bursting with news, and the more I thought about it, the more curious I was to hear it.

"Tell, Yvette!" I commanded. "Before you explode, my dear! What on earth is it?"

She blushed again and took my hand to lead me to an isolated corner where we could talk. We sat down together in a window embrasure. "It has to do with Sir Hugh," she whispered.

"Does it really? I could not have guessed!"

She laughed again. "I tell you in the most confident of confidences, however, or everything might be spoiled for me."

I crossed my fingers solemnly and placed them over my heart.

"Well," Yvette began, "my brothers have been speaking with Sir Hugh over the past several days, and he has been very encouraging."

"Has he indeed?"

"That is to say, he has not been discouraging, if you see what I mean, and my brothers assure me that they have been very open in what they have proposed to Sir Hugh. They did not want to leave any ambiguities or misunderstandings."

"So they approached Sir Hugh to bargain for your betrothal, and Sir Hugh has not outright refused them?"

"That's right, but there is more to it than that!" she exclaimed, almost beside herself. "Last night my brothers broached the topic of Isabelle, just to bring everything out in the open, you understand, and—and—" she faltered, her tongue a sudden tangle of words.

"And?"

"I do not think Isabelle's chances are very high with him!" Yvette burst forth. "Not high at all!"

This surprised me. "But, Yvette," I said, "my dear! I do not know what to say except to observe that Sir Hugh must be playing quite a game with her. I—that is—this is difficult for me to say—but I think—"

Yvette laid a hand on my arm. "I know," she interrupted, smiling at me with understanding. "They are often seen together. But that is of no consequence."

"No consequence at all," I managed weakly.

"Let me explain," she said, "although I know I should not!" She wet her lips. "The fact of the matter is, Sir Hugh questions Isabelle's purity."

This struck me dumb. I do not know what look I must have had on my face, but Yvette suddenly turned very red and said, "I should not have said it! But it is true! My brothers told me that it was my guarded secret, and I shall tell no one but you!"

"Yes, yes, of course, Yvette. It's perfectly all right. I shall tell no one, I assure you, but it seems to me, well, a little fantastic! How is Sir Hugh to know whether— And whatever would make him think or *say* such a thing?"

"He didn't say it exactly," she said. "He only intimated it. That is to say, when Isabelle's name was introduced into the conversation, my brothers said that Sir Hugh sneered lightly and said, 'It goes against the grain with me to take another man's leavings.'"

"But it is just not done!" I protested. "Isabelle is no *courtisane*, Yvette, and in any case, no woman of our station would compromise herself before marriage and no honest man would compromise her." I thought of Alicia's case. "Unless, of course, the marriage was a certainty."

I stopped. Comprehension came slowly, painfully. Many images clashed in my brain, but only one clear one emerged: the ruby bracelet.

Yvette leaned over and whispered, apparently oblivious to my state of mind, "Marguerite, don't be so naive! You can't honestly believe that! I know your experience at court is not as wide as some, but still—! I can name several unmarried gentlewomen who have had little adventures. And they stand to make excellent matches. It is simply Sir Hugh who is too proud—and upstanding—to want someone who is soiled."

I struggled to control my emotions. I looked down at my hands clenched in my lap and made the unpleasant discovery that my lady's fingers could curl into claws. "Just with whom is Isabelle supposed to have had a little adventure?" I asked.

"Almost anyone, I suppose!" she replied blithely. "Or perhaps more than one. She is no longer so young and—"

"And she was engaged to my husband for about four years, if memory serves."

Yvette blanched a little. "Marguerite! I did not mean it!" she said, her hand flying to her mouth. "It was always said that they never really cared for each other. That was always the strangest of betrothals. I am sure it was not that!"

I could not find the words to respond.

"No, it was not that, Marguerite," Yvette repeated, and rushed on. "Listen, Sir Hugh also said that he would not marry anyone so many men coveted so that he would never know when he would be cuckolded. He was speaking of her in general and not of anyone in specific. Really! You must believe it! It could be anyone! Why, she has so many admirers..."

"That is entirely true," I said, trying to give my voice a light, unconcerned air. "I shall not make anything of it. But I do think you should keep all these matters to yourself. You can count on me to keep quiet, too." I glanced over at her. "I do hope things work out for you, then, Yvette. I imagine they will, if Sir Hugh has made so bold as to air his sentiments about Isabelle in such a way."

Yvette thanked me for everything and made haste to be on her way, saying that her brothers always chided her for being slow, and lost herself in a labyrinth of embarrassed remonstrances, exclamations that she must be on her way, and thanks for all my preparations on her behalf. She rose and kissed me on both cheeks and hastened with visible relief when she saw her brothers enter the Great Hall from the bailey.

I remained where I was. I felt my lip quiver; I looked up from the window seat and stared about me at surroundings that seemed suddenly alien and desolate. I found that I was not able to think very clearly, for when I tried to concentrate on the problem of Roland's affair with Isabelle my brain seemed not to move at all, and the only thought that reiterated rather stupidly in my brain was that Isabelle could wear rubies the way no other woman could.

The room came back into focus, and after the moment I became aware that someone was standing nearby. I looked around quickly and saw Marie-Ange regarding me speculatively. We looked at each other in silence, and I had the light-ning realization that everyone had known of the relationship between Isabelle and Roland. Everyone save myself.

The second passed, and Marie-Ange was giving me her cheeks and smiling and thanking me and saying that she must be on her way. "It was most marvelous, Marguerite. Indeed! I would not have suspected that you were such a competent hostess! Yet all things must come to an end, and it seems that this one is over none too soon, by the look of you, dearest. Or have you just seen a ghost?"

No, I laughed, it was nothing. I was fine, I assured her. It was just a momentary distraction. Nothing of importance, and yes, it was exhausting to entertain in such a fashion, but I had not felt my tiredness until this very moment. Did it show so much?

Marie-Ange made some reply. I was not attending. It did not really matter, and presently she bade me farewell; I me-chanically wished her a safe journey.

I managed to move toward the door that led to the outside to say goodbye to those who were leaving. I was vaguely aware that Roland was nowhere about. Probably he was in conference with Sir Phillip Sheffield. In any case, no one seemed to remark on Lady Constance's absence, nor indeed that of her easily forgettable son.

I distinguished Lady Edwina's motherly stoutness in the happy, noisy, depressing crowd. She came over to me, pressed her cheek to mine, and said, "I applaud you, Marguerite, for the way you have handled everything. It was very *well done*." And as she moved away, I could not help but think that she knew, too. I had the impulse to tell her that my conduct had derived from ignorance and not aplomb, but it did not seem a particularly wise admission, so I kept it to myself.

I glanced around the room and saw a scene that seized me about my midriff and weighted it with ice. I looked for a second with cold, appalling dread at Isabelle fondly embracing my insolent chamberwoman, Louise, and then flicked my glance away. It came to me all in a flash. It was almost too much to accept at that moment, but there it was: the secret about Louise that Roland had not seen fit to tell me. I could appreciate his reluctance.

So, then, it seemed that everyone knew, from the retainers to all the peers, and if it was an exaggeration to say that everyone knew, at least enough knew to make it hurt. I had had ample warning and more than sufficient clues to have determined the lie of the land for myself. Constance had told me in so many words, and even Gunhild had made it plain enough that "another woman ruled in my place," but I had been too blind to perceive it.

I saw perfectly well, now, however, and jealousy had sharpened my perceptions, so that when Isabelle crossed the room to bid me a fond farewell, I saw her for the first time as she really was. Why had I never before noticed that her face was a thought too round for classical beauty? Why had I never before observed the three faint lines that marked her forehead, as if she had spent anxious hours before the mirror, trying to determine whether she was as beautiful as everyone claimed? Why had I never before read her artful smile (for she was smiling at me as she came forward) that seemed to hold so much smug satisfaction?

"Marguerite," she said in her voice of condescending sweetness, "my father and I must be off now. It has been a wonderful Christmas. Most entertaining! I vow I was never bored a minute!"

"I am glad for it," I said as evenly as possible and cocked my bow for the first shot. "And if there is anyone to thank for the smooth operation of the festivities then it must be the Hungerford women who deserve the first praise for having arranged things and been so cooperative. But please don't think to reward them with any gifts or favors, I beg of you! We had the most unpleasant scene some weeks back with Louise and Josette over a very pretty embroidered girdle that you gave one or the other of them."

Isabelle's smile froze slightly. The arrow had hit, whang, in the gold.

"It is not my way, you must know," I continued, pleased

with the control in my voice, "to throw little bits to my retainers and have them fight over them. I do not practice the strategy of divide and conquer, and if I discover that you have bestowed any gifts, I shall just have to confiscate them, as distasteful as that will be to me. I hope you understand that one must respect my methods as mistress of Hungerford."

"Poor Louise!" was all Isabelle ventured to say on that topic. She in turn was, of course, not unarmed. "Perhaps the Hungerford women expected other methods in their mistress, but you are right. By the way, have you seen Guy this morning? I have not seen him since very late last night, and I must see him to say goodbye. He would think it very rude of me if I did not."

"I last saw him in the hallway to his counting rooms," I said with perfect truth. "I suggest you try looking for him there. You know the way, don't you?"

Isabelle knew the way, I was not to bother escorting her there. When she left me, I was trembling slightly and dug my nails into my palms within the folds of my skirts.

Just as Isabelle left the room, I knew, without turning around, that Roland had entered it. I felt him come up behind me and willed myself not to turn around. The next moment, he was in front of me and regarding me gravely. I could command myself not to turn toward his presence in a room, but I could not will my heart, that most disobedient organ, not to leap at the sight of him.

"Good morrow, my lady," he said and kissed my hand. "Circumstances prevented me from seeking you earlier. Pray excuse me."

"I know that you have been more than busy," I said. "There is no need to—"

"Guy!" a voice boomed, and a strong hand came out from nowhere and slapped my husband on the back. It was the Huxley party ready to leave. There were the usual civilities to be exchanged, the reminder for the next meetings at court, and a few hunting anecdotes from the fortnight to be relived, before the group could take itself off.

The interruption had given me a chance to recover. I glanced up at Roland and smiled fleetingly. "Constance?" I mouthed as discreetly as I was able.

"Has hardly begun to vent her spleen," he replied. "But she shall burn herself out eventually. Sheffield will be removing her under guard this afternoon when most everyone has gone. He shall be sending several men on ahead, and their mounts are being prepared now. There are people in London who should hear the news without delay." Roland paused, and then began again. "Sheffield insisted that I accompany him—and withstood remarkably well all my arguments to the contrary."

"Do you fear too close an association with this latest piece of intrigue?" I asked quickly.

"Concerned for my reputation, Marguerite?" he asked. "No, a desire to disassociate myself from Constance did not figure into my reasons for remaining at Hungerford and not accompanying Sheffield to London."

My eyes had fallen to his tunic. One of his Christmas gifts from me. He had never seemed so remote to me, so far from my grasp, and I wished I could have attached him to me as easily as I had embroidered the Guimont eagles around the neck of the tunic and held on to the ends of the silken threads with my hands. I did not think that I would ever be the woman to pull the strings that made Roland operate. Maybe no woman could. I knew he did not belong to me, but did he belong to Isabelle?

I knew better than to ask him when he would be returning, but I did feel I could demand one service of him. "Would you be so kind as to inform me of Lady Constance's fate, my lord?"

He agreed, gravely, to comply with this request.

I then ventured to inquire where he was going, or if he was to stay in London.

He paused and looked down at me with his inscrutable gaze. "I will be in London only long enough to regulate the affairs of Constance with the king. I already have my orders to return immediately to Aquitania," he said in a voice carefully devoid of emotion. "I was hoping I would not be called before the Lenten season, but now I fear that once I am in London, the king will not let me off so easily and will send me directly." He smiled briefly. "The Christmas celebration was a small reprieve for me, you understand."

I understood nothing. All I knew was that he was leaving me, most likely for a very long time. "I see," I said, unable to raise my eyes above his tunic. "Yes, of course, I understand."

"I have the consolation, however," he continued in that cool, level tone, "of leaving you knowing that you are safe from intrigue."

"I am safe," I agreed dully, "although I am not sure how or why. I—I am not sure, either," I said, daring to lift my eyes to his, "what exactly has happened here, but I feel much like a pawn who has unwittingly survived the crossfighting of heavier weapons."

"A pawn, no." He smiled faintly. "There is no need to rate your importance so low."

That gave me the courage to blurt, "Gallantly said! But I know for a fact that Constance used me—*tried* to use me against you, and I cannot believe—well! that is to say, I imagine you have moved me several squares against her."

The smile faded. "I do not know what you are talking about, my lady," Roland replied, remotely polite, and that should have been enough to warn me off my present course, but it was not.

"The Frant emeralds, for one," I said. "She knew—in fact, everyone knew—that you had given them to me, and since she also knew that you were in no position to afford them, she could be expected to believe that you had come across some source of money to purchase them. If you had wanted to bait her into believing that you had discovered the money—or whatever it was besides the documents—that my father had hidden, you could not have calculated better. Your move proved, in the end, to be highly effective."

"The emeralds are yours," he said in a wintry voice that told me all I needed to know about his motivations, "to use as security against my possible demise. I am sorry that, owing to their provenance, my gift of them could be interpreted in such a fashion. I admit willingly to various methods of provoking Constance sufficiently into exposing herself, but I did not imagine that my bride gift to you would also be stained by the unfortunate circumstances that prevailed over our union, and I am sorry for it."

I felt very much like a wayward child who had just been chastened for having flung the generosity of a tolerant parent in his teeth, and was suddenly weary. I could have said that the rubies would have served me just as well, that I would have been content with even half the set, that almost anything would have been better than having served as a useful expedient for my husband; but I was too exhausted to bring up the tiresome subject, and there was little point to it when all was said and done.

But my voice went on, unwisely, against the possibility of silence, against the minutes moving inexorably toward his departure. I heard myself say the first thing that came into my distracted mind: "I have at last discovered why Louise is so ill disposed to my authority."

"Have you, indeed?"

Our eyes met, and I saw the cold, implacable blue of his and suddenly realized that they were always so when the talk turned to Isabelle. Yet that did not prevent me from telling Roland that which, no doubt, he had least desire to hear. It was as if I wanted to punish him a little, to let him know that I was not a complete fool.

"Yes," I said, drawing a resolute breath. "Based on the things that various people have mentioned, it seems that Louise had counted on having another mistress at Hungerford. She and Isabelle had become very close, and so Louise was naturally resentful when another woman came in Isabelle's stead who does not look upon her with partiality—as if I would single out anyone for special treatment!"

His face was closed; my stomach turned and was sitting sideways on my midriff. "So, you have been listening to wagging tongues. Have I ever hidden from you the fact that I was betrothed for some time to Isabelle Beauvais?" he asked.

I had thought the question purely a rhetorical one and vouchsafed no response, but after a short space, while he regarded me silently, I was eventually unnerved to answer softly, "No. Never."

"Then you can hardly be surprised that Louise might have entertained false hopes," he pointed out.

But you never told me you loved her and had compromised her! I longed to cry out. "No, I should not have been surprised, and yet—"

"And yet you were," he finished curtly. "I should like to know why you introduce this subject just as I am leaving for London and the king's side. Does it argue, I wonder, a guilty conscience? Do you fear that I do not honor contracts and shall repudiate you as a conspirator in Constance's schemes? Let me reassure you that I take all contracts seriously and that the one between Isabelle and me was broken legally and at her instigation. You and I are married now, and I am of the opinion that the marriage has gone too far to admit of undoing."

I gasped at the unexpected attack and was left speechless for several moments, confused and unable to see clearly how I could untangle his drastic misinterpretation of my comments about Louise and the beautiful Isabelle.

"I had no thought—"

His gaze was riveted on me.

"That is not at all what I meant, my lord!" I managed at last with a trace of panic. It was impossible, unthinkable, to tell him that, on the point of his departure for a long journey, I needed him to comfort me, to tell me that he loved me and had never loved Isabelle, as if that assurance would ward off the loneliness that would cramp inside me the instant he mounted his powerful destrier and rode away from Hungerford. It was ridiculous to hope that he loved me, much more so to try to maneuver a declaration from him, and I knew that no charm would be potent enough to act against the cold despair that would surely fill me when he left me.

He stood before me, so tall and forbidding. "What did you mean, then, my lady?"

"Only that I know now very well how things stand," I said with, at best, a flimsy courage.

His hard mouth, which could on occasion smile easily, had a dangerous look about it and was unusually grim. He said, almost as if to himself, "I imagine that Gunhild has been enjoying herself in my absence," and then he rounded on me. "Did the wagging tongues also favor you with an account of my brother's death?"

I could not articulate a reply. I was stunned at the question, cursing myself for having opened so disastrous a conversation, desperately unhappy that he had given it such a wicked turn.

"And do you believe that I killed him?" he asked relentlessly.

I looked around me. No one was listening; I would not have cared particularly if they were, since I was too bewildered by his need to inflict pain at just this moment. Perhaps if I had been a little more sure of myself, perhaps if I had possessed the wisdom and vision to peer into my heart, perhaps if I had had a few more precious minutes to understand what he was about, I could have dealt with this disaster. As it was, I remained silent.

"I shall tell you now that whatever the circumstances of his death, they will not provide sufficient grounds for having the marriage annulled," he said brutally.

At least I had the sense to cut through my confusion and pain to give him an honest reply. "It does not matter to me who killed him," I said, letting my shoulders sag, as one defeated. "And I, too, honor all contracts and have no intention—or desire—to seek an end to our marriage.".

Incredibly, something harsh and cold in his face faded away, and his brow lightened perceptibly. "That is something, in all events," he said, "to comfort me while I am away from Hungerford."

My stomach righted itself, and I made so bold as to ask, "And while you are away, do I have your leave to go to Shrivenham, if I so desire, my lord?"

"You are free," he said meaningfully, "to go to Shrivenham, or wherever else it pleases you, my lady. We are agreed, are we not, that it is a wonderful advantage to come and go as the will dictates."

We were also agreed that it is a cheap freedom that knows

no limits or purpose, and I did not bother to tell him that I was hardly free from him, that he would take my heart and soul with him and leave my lonely, uninhabited body behind. Instead, I thanked him for his kind permission and wished him Godspeed.

He bent down and drew me to him. He kissed me once, a warm, gentle kiss, at odd variance with the chill that had not completely left his eyes. I fancied for one, wild moment that he was not entirely free from me either and indulged the thoroughly satisfying notion that I would haunt his dreams and possess his mind as he so thoroughly possessed mine. The warm thought that I would haunt him as he lay camped out under a bright, starry sky, or in a strange bed in a strange castle, or even in another woman's arms, would, I thought while his lips pressed mine, be a fine security against the emptiness and loneliness of his absence, just as the cold emeralds were to serve as a hard gauge against his death.

That comforting vision faded slightly when Roland broke the embrace and left the room with the words "I must go," and vanished entirely when I made the mistake of going to the door to catch a final glimpse of him. Isabelle was awaiting him by his steed and raised her lips to his before he mounted. It was a bold move, although in the commotion in the bailey, no one was attending, and from where I stood I could see the avid look in her eyes. But I could not see Roland's face, and it was just as well that I was spared that much.

During the next few months I came to know my curious little sewing room very well.

Through an endless, dripping, dismal winter I sat there, often at the window seat, gazing down at the dreary, sodden gardens, plying my indifferent needle and wondering how best to avoid doing a great many of my dull duties, the ones that I was used to think so diverting. The castle was still well run—I made no mistake—but my presence was much more shadowy, my authority more remote. I spent as much time delegating tasks as I did actually engaged in meaningful occupations, and I do not know why I was determined to spend so much time

alone in my room, prey to the misery and torment that raged
in my heart, when I could have been out and circulating and
numbed by activity.

Nevertheless, I came to know the number of planks that ran
the floor from my window seat to the door, and the placement
of each weed thrusting its ugly head through the dead furrows
of the cold, wet earth in my pleasance below. I could by heart
have charted a map of the fine, spidery cracks in my white-
washed ceiling; I knew each wrinkle in the gaudy, mocking
stone faces carved around my chimney, and studied with endless fascination the bright, tempting flames consuming each
extravagant log of oak. I learned at length how the moonlight
spilled through the irregular glass to throw dancing, distorted
patterns across my chamber, silvering carpets and hangings,
and the way it would fade into the eerie, gray, blurry light of
winter morning when I could emerge from my tomb, heavy-
lidded and weary, to begin another day of evasion and scheming
to return to that dismal chamber.

I even went so far as to go to Shrivenham once in February,
seeking consolation, but Dame Ellen's motherly bullying did
nothing to restore the tone of my mind, nor did the long walks
I took on the parapets offer my aching heart the solace it craved.
I could remember, in sooth, the time in my life when I could
sit high up in the crenels, shielded from angry north winds or
inhaling sweet summer breezes, and come to terms with whichever one of my selves was out-of-place. I was able, in some
dim past, to harmonize myself, make myself whole, and it
seemed that only a few hours—or even a few minutes—of
calm reflection was all that was needed to put my house in
order before descending to the chaos or the quarrels of my
castle below. But now I moved all in pieces, fragments of a
former self that fused into an imperfect sum of its parts, which
lived in confusion behind a set of features I could recognize
with effort in a looking glass. Pale blue eyes that no longer
saw things the way they were used to remembering them, but
saw a world discomposed. They observed from their great
distance that the castle was no longer a structure, but just a
pile of stones, and irregular stones at that, with no corners with

which one could come to grips. Perhaps it was more accurate
to say that the world had dissolved around me into a gelatinous
blur and that I experienced the continuous queasy feeling of
being at sea in a fluid world.

I toyed with the Infidel's Arm on one occasion with Dame
Ellen's help and wished I possessed the alchemy to distill a
potent *philtre*, like the kind Tristan drank just before he met
Isolde. I knew it would take nothing short of a love potion to
seduce Roland into loving me, but I doubted that even the
wisest witch in the deepest wood knew the spell to make my
wretched charms surpass those of Isabelle; and it was pitiful
to watch the brilliant red of cinnabar, the bright blue green of
larkspur, the deep moonstone blue of hydrangea bubbling and
brewing to their crystalline essence, knowing that their mysterious beauty hid no secrets or magic for me. I would have
been content, in my moments of blackest despair, to have
discovered the counterpotion to the witchcraft of Roland's look,
his touch, and the memory of certain, quiet words spoken
against my throat, and having been denied the one, exquisite
pleasure I could have had in his absence when my woman's
courses came and went only days after his departure, I prayed
for anything to exorcize his presence from me, to empty me
of all thought and feeling, all pain, all life.

I suppose that what defeated me most, when I could drag
my mind from the misery in my heart to concentrate on the
torment in my head, was that Roland had robbed me of my
most powerful weapon against him: resentment. He had brought
me into the marriage with my eyes wide open. It had been a
marriage of convenience; there had never been any doubt. He
had never told me he loved me, and if I had misread a slanted
look, responded to a pleasant sally, or received so much from
the execution of his husband's duty, I had only my foolish self
to blame. He had bewitched me, it was true, but he had em-
ployed no arts to have attached me; he did not quote Gascon
love poems in my ear or spend idle hours at my side or lure
me into his net with the practiced charm of a Sir Hugh Falmouth. No, there was only his vital, masculine presence, the
very essence of his existence, which had charmed me and

breathed life into my soul, and I should have been far more satisfied now if he had deliberately tried to entice me or if he had only flaunted his love for Isabelle, for then I could have fired myself to life with a burning resentment. But he had not. He had never been anything but scrupulously courteous to me in private since our marriage and on occasion, charmingly demonstrative in public for the benefit of those watching us; and after I had sifted through all our encounters, hoping to find some morsel to satisfy my hunger, I realized, painfully, that he had never kissed me without an audience, except within the limits prescribed by the marriage bed.

There was finally nothing left for me but to admit, when every look he had melted me with and every word he had inadvertently wooed me with had been thoroughly examined, that there was aught but irony in my existence and that life had played one of its terribly clever little jokes on me.

Life had indeed passed a very stern sentence on me for the sin of my silliness. What else could I call it, after all, when I bethought myself of all the girlish hours I had spent imagining the life that should be mine or would be mine in marriage? Of course my head had been filled with many agreeable, romantic visions of Ideal Love between my husband and myself, which alternated with the more tragic (and likely) visions of being saddled either with an aging widower of uncertain but highly durable health whose speech whistled through the gaps where his teeth should have been or with a pimply-faced lad in the style of Charles Hartford. Both of these possibilities would obviously have been distasteful to me, and it was equally obvious to me that in either case, the husband would have had the better bargain. Ironically, I had never imagined the one possibility that had happened: in my extravagant conceit, I had never imagined that my husband would receive the bad end of the bargain; I had never once given thought to the possibility that I might not embody for my husband all he might desire in a wife; it had not entered my head that my husband might have reason to chafe against his marriage bonds.

Beyond me yawned a black abyss of desolation when I came at last to the inescapable, sickening conclusion of all my ponderings: I was married to a man whom I loved to the edge of madness, and he did not love me.

It was a thing too grim for tears. I shed none, and it was almost too humiliating to reflect that he tolerated me well enough. I did not think for a moment that he actually disliked me or found me disgusting. There were even times when I knew that I had pleased him. But I must have been a pale second to what he had had—or still had—with Isabelle. He did not pretend that our marriage was other than what it was; he did not insult my intelligence or dupe me into showing him allegiance by making false declarations; he did not degrade me in public or in private. He made our marriage, in short, everything that was comfortable under the circumstances and dignified, and it was this, I think, that made it so unbearable, so dreadful, and underscored the appalling, the so very appalling fact that I was his wife and not his love.

Then, like the proverbial sot who finally awakens from the lurching distortions of drunkenness to the far worse stabbing clarity of plain sight, I desired nothing more than to slip back into the fuzziness of nausea. My one firm resolve during those wretched months following Christmas was to get myself to court, once I was composed enough to face people, and to warn Yvette away from the disaster of marrying Sir Hugh. She could not now know what it would be like wed a man who loved another, and although she deemed any price she paid for him to be worth it, I could tell her better. I did not truly think she would listen to me, but my conscience would not allow me not to try.

I was not, for all of that, so thoroughly blinded by my own personal pain as not to see what else was going forward in my keep. Louise and I maintained cool relations. I had the satisfaction of knowing that she submitted completely to my authority. And it was even a kind of relief to know what was behind her resentment of me, and it took the edge off her insolence. At the same time, I understood now why Josette had held me in fear, expecting the same capricious behavior in me that she had found in Isabelle. I made some friendly overtures in her direction—but nothing that could have been

construed as preferring her to Louise—and was moderately
pleased with the results, so that I was encouraged to think that
Josette and I would rub along rather well. As for Bess and
Gertrude, well, it was enough to say that Gertrude kept all
thoughts to herself, while Bess displayed the tendency to shake
her head mournfully over me.

I think I knew to the day, too, when Nan finally succumbed
to the Bastard's demands.

It had been a long siege, one whose outcome had never
been in any real doubt. I do not know how I came to know,
but I did. There was no talk about it, and I suspected that
Gaston was one who did not relish discussion of his private
affairs. I appreciated the discretion. And in sooth I was not
sorry that Gaston had claimed her, for I could not help noticing
that no other man would dare touch his woman. Perhaps it was
his proprietal air toward her that gave me the clue; however,
I think it more likely that it was a look that Nan and I exchanged
one day in late winter that confirmed my suspicions. It was
early morning, and I chanced to be in the kitchens before Nan.
When she came in and saw me, she paused slightly. She gave
me a quick smile—not quite a guilty one, but almost a conspiratorial one, I would say—and that was enough to inform
me what she was about.

I was, in all honesty, not displeased. Yet I was slightly
discomfitted and felt a need to talk to her about it. And if I
was motivated by a little curiosity, I also wanted to make sure
that all was well. Even Nan might stand in need of support
against so formidable a man as the Bastard. Thus, I bade her
come to my sewing room after the evening's duties were done.
She replied in perfect understanding, and we went about our
day's duties.

Much later that evening, Nan appeared at my open door.
She curtsied perfunctorily and then thrust her hands into her
apron, as was her habit.

I raised my brow at this unwonted show of respect and
nodded. "Well, Nan," I said without preamble, "I hope you
are not in over your head."

A ghost of a laugh crossed Nan's face. "Good eventide, my lady. I hope not, too."

"You may come in," I said, and since I would never ask her to sit in my presence and wanted this to be a more informal interview, I rose and crossed to the chimney and began to warm my hands slowly before the fire. My movement permitted Nan to step into the room and take a lounging position against the wall by the door.

"I did not ask you here to reproach you, you know," I said at length.

"I did not think it, my lady."

"For it would be quite futile," I continued and glanced over my shoulder at her, "and dishonest as well. I have always valued the honesty in our dealings and deem it counterproductive to destroy that now with vain and idle censure."

"I have never doubted the merits o' honesty, my lady."

"Good," I said and drew a breath. "Besides, I do not think Gaston gave you much choice in the matter."

Nan was silent a long moment and then said, "I canna say, in the end, who piped the tune."

I could not suppress a smile. "I, too, have never doubted the merits of honesty! But do not try to convince me that he did not pursue *you*—and rather openly—all winter."

"Aye. It was a long winter."

"But now it is over."

She did not answer that immediately, but merely shrugged. Then: "It did him no harm to wait."

"No, I imagine not. But I am not thinking of the harm to him, for he looks wholly capable of taking care of himself. Rather, I am more interested in your well-being."

Whether Nan was silent on that point because she felt it patently obvious that she was just as capable of taking care of herself, or because she was surprised at the interest I took in her well-being, remained unclear in my mind. In any case, I came straight to the heart of the matter. "My purpose is this, Nan—but I want you to think about my proposal first before you give me an answer! You need not respond immediately—

and do not think I bring it up with any real regard for—for appearances. In short, I wonder if you are interested in having a marriage arranged between you and Gaston."

"No," she said firmly and without hesitation.

"I see," I said. "I had no intention of pressing you into anything. This is not like—the situation with Edric"—I chanced to look at her and caught an expression on her face perilously close to a grin—"and the marriage was to be for your convenience."

"I'm no' put out," she replied slowly, "and if I don't have to, I'd fain no' be pushed into it."

I considered her. "Do you mean, you wouldn't want to push Gaston into it?"

"That neither, my lady."

I did not scruple to abuse slightly our pact of honesty. "Could it be," I asked, "that you have conceived a decided preference for Gaston?"

"He's much like another man," she said, adding in her laconic way, "only more."

I understood her all too well. "That is why I thought you might like the convenience—hardly the necessity!—of marriage."

"I might like it," she agreed. "At first."

I did not mistake her meaning. It was not her roving eye she had in mind, but his. Roland had said she was a clever wench, but I had to disagree: I thought her more brave than clever, for even the stupidest woman in love schemes to keep her man, while only a brave one would risk losing him against the cheaper satisfaction of keeping him against his will. Nan might not be bound by the rules that governed my order, but she was as bound to Gaston as I was to Roland. "For the security, then," I persisted. "You cannot know him very well."

Nan looked me straight in the eye and said boldly, "I share his bed. Naught can tell me more about him."

I lowered my eyes to the fire. Holy Mother, was it truly so simple? I wondered. Could it be that a woman had only to share the bed of a man to know him? I, who had shared Roland's bed by merciless force and selfish, driving need to possess all that was mine, should have known by now that he was neither selfish nor merciless, but I could not, for all of that, lay claim to knowing him. I had been encouraged, on occasion, to believe that I was coming to an understanding of him, but the events of Christmas had shown me the error of my ways. Yet, I credited Nan with a mother-wit and an experience in such matters far greater than my own, and was obliged to admit a tiny twinge of envy that she was able to trust her instincts to such an unerring degree. She had maintained about her all the wariness of a cunning forest animal, and if she had to forgo the next best thing of security, she might just still hang on to the very best thing of having what she wanted.

I longed to ask her if she was happy, but refrained. It was a stupid question and her response would not have told me what happiness is.

"Very well. I am satisfied with the arrangement, if you are," I told her.

Nan nodded and kept her eyes on me. I briefly suspected her of pitying me, but it had only to occur to me for me to dismiss the notion. It was unworthy of her. Whatever else Nan might have felt toward me, it was not pity.

"I am confident that there is no need to ask you if you are suffering from the other men in the keep because of Gaston's attentions to you," I continued, "but I must ask you if any of the women are causing you trouble. Not," I said and held up a hand in a staying gesture, "that you are not perfectly well able to hold your own among the women. You are not tied to my apron strings here either any longer—I am not suggesting it! However," I explained, betraying my conventional self, for I was determined to lend an official cachet to their arrangement, "I would like to know if any woman has been moved to any— any indiscreet comments to you, so that I may drop a word in her ear."

Nan flashed me a rare, knowing smile. "Louise ha' a ready enough tongue in her head, I reckon, but she ha' learned now to keep it betwixt her teeth when I'm about."

Was it possible, I thought with something akin to disbelief, that I had a champion in Nan? I considered her words carefully and decided that I did not mistake the meaning tucked behind those simple words. I had never doubted that there was talk about me, my husband, and Isabelle, but I had never imagined that anyone who was in a position to do so would take my part. Nan's expression of loyalty touched me and brought the first genuine smile to my lips in a long time.

"Well, now," I said, "I'm happy to see you put her in her place, since she has been slow to catch on to Shrivenham's ways. I have excused her partially from the fact that Hungerford was so—so disorderly before my arrival, and I'm glad that you have been so kind as to instruct her in proper conduct. You do me credit."

The grin was unmistakably there now on her face. "Thank you, my lady," she replied, and I supposed that both she and I knew that I had more rightly thanked her.

"Perhaps you can tell me, too, since you're so alive to castle ways, how it goes with Gunhild of late," I inserted into the discussion as casually as possible. "I was aware that she was ailing, and I must make a point of seeing her if it's anything grave."

"She's a viperish owd besom," Nan said with a measure of distaste, "and it's said her venom'll keep her alive another score of years."

"Ah! And what else is said?" I encouraged.

Nan was not a talker. I had often thought of her as an oyster, but I hoped she would be moved on this occasion to open to me any pearls she might be hiding. She could have shrugged and disclaimed any knowledge of the enigmatic Gunhild, but she did not. After the slightest pause she said, "It's said she ne'er got over the death of the Lady Laura."

At least I did not have to shame myself by inquiring into the identity of Roland's mother. "Yes, I believe that she was her tiring woman. But I was also under the impression that Lady Laura was killed."

Nan frowned slightly at this, looked about to say something, and then fell uncomfortably silent.

Something prompted me to add, most improperly, "In fact,

I was under the impression that all the recent Guimont mistresses have experienced rather untimely deaths."

It was an unanswerable comment, to be sure, one that should never have been made to Nan of all people. She flicked a glance at me and simply absorbed this. "I canna say," she replied finally.

I did not go immediately to Gunhild's pallet. I let several days slip drearily by before I screwed up my courage to seek her out. I knew she was suffering from a consumptive disorder, but I also knew that it was not life threatening, and was not quite decided whether I was glad or sad. I could not put it off any longer and went one evening to the common sleeping chambers off the kitchens.

It was a mistake to have gone after dark. The light from the yellow tallows exaggerated the heavy folds of her face, a rumpled devil's mask behind whose slits the eyes, fever-bright, surveyed me with sardonic amusement.

"So the chatelaine comes at last to the sick room," she said in a thin, mocking voice.

"How are you feeling, Gunhild?" I inquired calmly.

"Much better than you have, mistress, for all the aching of my lungs!" she crooned with satisfaction.

Her eyes missed nothing. I would not have expected her to have missed my despair, but there was still no reason not to show her a brave front. "I have been, Gunhild, very hale of late."

"You're a bigger fool than I had thought!" she snapped back. She raised herself feebly on one elbow and regarded me keenly. "I thought you would have learned something by now."

"I've learned a thing or two about the truth," I said with confidence.

"Have you, now?" She cackled derisively. "There was a time when I thought I might be wrong about you, but now I know I wasn't. You know nothing!"

I had seated myself on a stool by her bed, but at that I rose to go. I had no use for all of this, and I regretted having sought her out. "Knowing the truth," I said, looking down at her as haughtily as I was able, "has not helped me face it with equanimity, but it helps to blunt the bitter edges of confusion. I have satisfied myself that you are not at death's door, at any rate, but since fever generally rises at this time, I shall send a woman round to you with some broth."

I had indeed noticed little pearls glistening on her forehead at my arrival, and she was a good deal weaker than I had expected.

"That's the least foolish thing you've said to date," Gunhild said to my back.

"I may be foolish," I retorted over my shoulder, unable to control my tongue, "but I'm not a fool."

"Then you'll know that we're everyone of us at death's door," she said in a voice calculated to stay my feet, "and you have every chance of going before I do."

This brought me around and set the hairs on my neck to tingling. Her face was shiny with perspiration, her eyes overbright. "Do you have good reason for thinking such a thing?" I demanded coolly, fighting the panic rising in me.

Her hawk's gaze pierced me. "You think you'll escape! You think you're different! But you won't escape your fate, my pet, and you'll go the way of the others. If he doesn't kill you, your lover will."

This was pure raving. I was at once perplexed by what she had said and alarmed by her condition. I thought instantly of going to fetch someone to aid me in trying to bring down the fever, but before I left the room I had to try to make her understand.

"I have no lover," I said firmly.

It was to no avail. I do not know if she heard me, or, if she did, whether she knew that it was I who addressed her. Her laugh rattled weakly, ominously in her throat and she went off into wild, incoherent mutterings.

I grabbed her hot, dry hand. Her fingers clung like claws. I tried to reach through her state of semiconsciousness by using my most authoritative voice. "Do not fear. I shall be right back."

She opened her eyes with a lucid gaze that went right through me and said in a perfectly rational voice, "You won't, because you are dead, my lady. I do not fear for you any longer."

My feet flew to find Bess, who was happily nearby in the kitchens, deeming her to be the only one I trusted to hear whatever words might fall from Gunhild's mouth in her fever. I bade her bring tepid vinegar water and cloth and requested Gertrude to keep everyone away from Gunhild until she could be brought under some control.

Gunhild's eyes were closed when I returned, but as she became aware of my presence, they fluttered open slowly. Her eyes were bulging from her head, her face was flushed, and her pulse was rapid. She seemed to know who I was, for she said weakly, "It'd put you in a fix if I were to die, wouldn't it? Then you'd never learn the truth. But you're a fool and it would do you no good in the end."

On these depressing words, Bess came into the room, and that was the last time for several hours that Gunhild had even a dim awareness of who I was. She grew steadily worse; and I did not dare move her, even though her condition prevented a dozen other people from seeking their beds. I had Gertrude announce to the others that they were to double up for the night in other quarters.

There were intervals when Gunhild dozed, but they were never of long duration; and when she awoke, it was always in a state of feverish excitement bordering on delirium.

In one moment of relative calm, Gunhild looked up at me. Gone was the brittle bitterness that I associated with her normal waking state; now her eyes were filled with bleak anguish. "I warned you, my lady. I warned you, but you just laughed your bright laugh and said you would love where you chose. I warned you, I did!"

Bess and I exchanged a long look, but Bess, dear Bess, forbore to comment.

Gunhild fell into a more natural sleep; I indulged the hope that this would endure, but Bess pointed out that the fever had not reached its pitch and offered to brew a mild infusion of linden.

When she came back, I looked doubtfully at the leaves

swimming limply in the cup and fully expected Gunhild to reject it. She did not, however, upon waking several moments later, and it seemed to refresh her. She fell back asleep and then by stages descended before my eyes into the depths of the fever, her thin body racked by convulsions. I had not thought at the beginning of the evening that she was anywhere near death, but toward midnight it seemed almost certain that she would die. It was as she had said: I did not wish her death. Like it or not, she still had many things to tell me that were of vital interest to me. So I frantically bathed her temples and wrists with the water, hoping to draw the fire out of her body, when suddenly she broke into a drenching sweat, thrashing wildly, and then lay still.

She looked so peaceful that I could not be sorry that death had claimed her. I rose, too exhausted to react, and went to wake Bess, who had fallen asleep in an uncomfortable position in a chair. But I had not taken a step before Gunhild's hand shot out to grasp mine.

I nearly died myself of the shock. I looked down, my heart leaping into my throat, to see that, in fact, Gunhild was breathing normally. She opened her eyes a fraction, and I could see in their clear depths that she was in complete possession of herself once again. The fever had broken; she was going to live.

"So it's you," she croaked. "My life wasn't worth it."

"I can see you're back to normal, in all events," I said with a calmness I did not feel. "And it is not I who decides what your life is worth."

Gunhild gave a weary snort. "Yours isn't worth a weaver's brat's either."

I did my best to ignore this. "I shall make sure that you are attended while you stay in bed the next couple of days until you get back your strength."

"My strength?" she replied in a distant voice. "I have no more. Strength is a futile thing for a woman in this world." She focused on me suddenly. "And no amount of it will save you."

"Let me wake Bess, so that she may attend to you."

She smiled faintly. "Aren't you going to ask me?"

"Ask you what?" I replied with a strong premonition of what was to come.

"How my mistress met her fate. I should think that's the question that teases you most."

Had she read my mind? Was I truly so transparent? "I will ask my husband when next I see him, if in fact he knows the truth. You told me once, if I remember correctly, that I was to address my questions to him."

She was plainly satisfied by this. "Aye, he knows as well as I," she answered, "and perhaps better than I, because he inherited his father's black tempers. He's his father's son, there's no denying it, for all he took his mother's quick wit and liveliness. So, ask him, if you dare. Or do you lack the courage?"

I could not resist. "No, just the patience. So now you must tell me about the Lady Laura's end."

Gunhild's thin, ravaged face took on a decidedly malicious cast. "Her lord and master good as killed her," she rattled, "when he had gotten what he wanted from her."

If anything was lacking to set the seal of my misery, this surely was it.

Chapter 16

February sobbed its lachrymose way into March; the skies wrung empty of emotion, March blustered its mournful way into April.

Gunhild recovered; I did not.

It seemed that the spring would not be as beautiful this year, that the leaves would not be as vivid, the air not as fresh and clean as in springs past. I doubted that I had ever before seen the earth so melancholy and gray in its rebirth; nor could I bring myself to care about it very much.

One could cope with pain and wretchedness only so long, I had discovered, before it became a dull, fixed habit, hardly worth noticing except as an agony one had grown used to, and finally it became impossible for me to remember a time when life had been anything but a tedious grind of hours stretching from one dull day to the next.

I had settled down to an acceptance of my state, something like living with a painful limp. There was a comfort in resignation; a predictability, at least, where one's equilibrium was not threatened from one minute to the next, but mine was still precarious enough that I dreaded the inevitability of seeing Roland again. I was not so far removed from my distress that I did not know that seeing him again would renew the pain and make it come alive with all its sharp points.

The horrible implications of Gunhild's words did not have the power either to spur me to a sense of self-preservation or to dispel my feelings for Roland. It should have turned my stomach to have thought that Roland's father had killed his mother and that my husband was capable of the same unspeakable violence. It should have jarred my better self into outrage to have realized that I was in love with a man guilty of the black crime of fratricide. But I had already known that he was capable of murder when I had married him, and I had, in spite of all warning and all knowledge that he desired another, fallen hopelessly, irrevocably in love with a man of such unsteady character. I might not have been able to understand how I had come to commit such a folly, but I saw clearly enough that I could not pluck him out of my heart any sooner than I could will myself to stop breathing. He had come into my life and taken it over so that I was only half-alive when he was not there, and if I was to die by his hand, that prospect filled me with no more fear than I had felt the day his murderous fury had been provoked when I had gone to his counting rooms to pay the miller his pittance. John Potter had called my reaction courage; I had another name for it, one that was hardly as flattering.

I knew what Roland was capable of, I knew he loved another, and yet I loved him. This admission, finally, made it somehow easier for me to bear; instead of endlessly evading the truth or tiresomely searching for excuses for him, I was able to look at the dark side of his nature without flinching and without a zealous desire to change him to suit my narrow ideas. It was an awesome thing for me, who had once craved so desperately an exciting taste of life, to have had the full course presented to me and to have found it not to my liking. If I had known that night in July just before I met Roland that life entailed so much pain and misery, I might gladly have contracted with fate for the temperate comfort and anesthetic security of a passionless marriage. But I had not known that then, and it was now too late to arrange for my comfort. I was a fearful creature at heart, I had decided, but I had looked at the worst life had to offer and would survive my wounds.

I hardly needed reminders of my husband's black character. Nevertheless, one was provided me in the form of the man I had seen when I had presented myself in Roland's counting rooms on his receiving day. It took me a moment to place him, since I had forgotten his existence entirely, and his identity teased me when he came to greet me with a respectful, if awkward, bow, until I realized that I had associated him in my mind with my husband's penchant for hard, cold words and violent threats. And something else: this man was to have brought financial ruin on some woman to obtain an unspecified object, if I remembered correctly what I had overheard Roland suggest that day.

I was mildly surprised to see the man again and supposed that he must have retrieved the object within the specified time, because here he was still walking the earth with the full use of all his limbs. I guessed, too, that the woman in question had been Lady Constance—may her twisted soul rest in peace—yet, I did not know whether financial ruin had brought about what Roland had hoped it would. It did not matter, since she had met her fate in any case, and I could not lay at Roland's door the violent end she had met.

The man, Thomas the Woodsman as he identified himself, begged a word with John Potter, he being the only one of Sir Guy's loaf-men (as he phrased it) to be in the country.

I informed him that Master Potter was abroad for the day in the hamlets, but might I serve him instead?

The Woodsman's face brightened perceptibly and he said promptly, "Oh, aye! As a matter of fact—" and then he broke off in some confusion and a great deal of embarrassment and tried to cover both with a tangle of half-sentences that soon became knotted past unraveling. He had very much the aspect of a harassed hare driven into the thin bush of winter without even the camouflaging protection of a layer of snow.

I had no intention of flushing him out and took pity on him, poor man. Although I was alive with curiosity (and realized, with a sigh, that I would always be so in matters that concerned my husband), I did my best to say blandly that I was really quite unused to anything that did not pertain directly to housework, and might he not be more comfortable in the kitchens by the fire with a horn of ale?

This suggestion found instant favor with him, and I led him back through the corridors, all the while trying to devise a way of subtly prizing the nature of his business out of him. But since my ingenuity fell considerably short of such cleverness,

I personally handed him into the care of a kitchen boy, being none the wiser.

He stayed for the evening meal and was seen afterward in deep discussion with John Potter, who had the highly provocative habit of nodding seriously to what the Woodsman was saying and then flicking me a glance.

I left the hall presently and spent several unprofitable hours over my embroidery tambour. The fire mulled quietly on the hearth, and it took away the cold cramp of chill that still clung to my room on an early spring evening. I stared at it a long time. Something fluttered inside me, something out of nothing, like little bubbles of yeast that come to life on their own accord and rise hopefully upward. I realized with a kind of relieved surprise that it was curiosity stirring inside me; something human and alive, leavening the flatness inside me. I felt almost excited by it.

The Woodsman stayed the next day, too, and went out riding with John Potter. It was then that my unformed, viscous idea of going to court solidified into something I could hold on to and pursue.

I have never been able to understand my impulses. They come like tiny rushes of wind to rumple my hair or to lift my skirts in little unexpected flutters of freedom. I very rarely withstand them, and they are, for the most part, harmless, except of course the one that urged me out of my stuffy chamber July past and nudged me down the cavernous hallways of Westminster. This one came upon me, I think, as I tilled a row of herbs in my pleasance that day. I stood up suddenly to watch an exaltation of larks skim overhead; in that moment, with my head bent upward, kissed by the pale yellow sun, I felt a surge spring from the tips of my toes to the wild wisps of my hair, as if the wooden soles of my sabots had taken root in mother earth and were receiving her nutrients. The moment passed, as did the larks, but the idea had sprouted: I had the tiniest, most discreet desire to know what was going on in the world. The full idea did not come to me until an hour later while I was crossing the back bailey. The laundry was hung crisscross between the buildings and snapped smartly in the wind. It was dazzling white, the way I required it, and rough and fresh and pure. The great squares of linen seemed to dance to the irregular tune of the wind, great, jerky string puppets trying to coax a petulant child out of the sullens; I thought it ungracious not to respond to their efforts, and, without further ado, I had the impulse to leave for Westminster on the morrow. I cannot look on sun-whitened laundry to this day, no matter what my mood, without knowing a small lift to the spirit.

It was decided, then. I left the next day, accompanied only by Bess (having left Gertrude nominally in charge), in a riding party headed by Thomas the Woodsman, who had declared his intention of riding to London, and buttressed by three outriders.

The court was the same, but I was different. With the return of good weather, the continuous entertainments moved out-of-doors. King Henry and Queen Eleanor were as fond as ever of feasting and brilliant pageants; the guisers of Provence still languished gracefully about the castle, sighing of sun and beauty; lips eagerly mouthed the latest rumors, which concerned chiefly the arrangement of a marriage between Henry's brother Richard of Cornwall, whose wife had died recently, and Eleanor's sister Sanchia; and the Londoners continued to drive Henry into royal rages.

The turmoil in the middle of which I entered—and of which Marie-Ange was only too glad to inform me—concerned the business of getting Richard and Sanchia married. The cost of the wedding was chiefly defrayed by the (rather arbitrary, to my mind) levy imposed on the Jews of the country. Even after these "donations" were received, it seemed that the balance of moneys would not be enough to cover the cost of the magnificence that such an occasion called for in Henry's mind. It was suggested then, by some well-meaning councilor no doubt, that Henry sell his gold plate.

This idea required a liberal amount of soothing and persuasion, but finally Henry was prepared to sell his plate. He did not, however, believe anyone could be found to purchase it. The councilors explained to him, "As all rivers flow back to the sea, so everything you now sell will return to you in remunerative gifts," which phrase was widely held to intend an expression of the opinion that the citizens of London were in a position to act as purchasers.

The king was reported to have fallen into a fit near apoplexy. "Those half-wits!" he spat, according to informed sources. "They would purchase and suck up the entire kingdom if I allowed it! If they are rich enough to buy my possession, they can afford to give me the money I need."

Immediately were imposed the payments of tallages, and the court continued to eat off of gold plate.

There was a certain logic there, I had to admit, and a style of governance, but if such economies and strategies were not my way, I was hardly a monarch and in no position to judge.

It did not affect me too much in any case. I was content simply to sit back and watch and listen as it all went by me. My one regret was that Alicia was not at court. Her child was due in another month or so; thus, she was resting comfortably at the Longchamps demesne with her mother and Herbert's cosseting and fussing and making a great bustle about the birth, if Alicia's letters were to be believed. I looked forward to seeing her in the near future.

Marie-Ange, on the other hand, was present and visible at court along with Yvette, who must have read my mind since she avoided all private conversation with me for my first few days; and, mercifully, Isabelle was not on the premises and was said to be visiting various relatives.

The moment I arrived at court I knew my status had changed. I was accorded every courtesy as Guimont's wife and installed in the apartment reserved for him, which happened to be housed in the most fashionable wing of the castle. I knew it was the most fashionable because when I answered Marie-Ange's query as to the location of the Guimont chambers (which she must have known very well), she showed the liveliest interest in seeing the interior and ended the discussion by observing with the palest shade of envy in her voice, "Well, I own that I never imagined you in those quarters! Admit that you have come up in the world and fared better than could have been expected."

I did so readily and, I hoped, politely. And whatever the other drawbacks were that attended my marriage to Roland, which I would never divulge to Marie-Ange, I did have to admit that it was exceedingly pleasant to be treated as a person worthy of the highest respect.

The king honored me one evening by singling me out for prolonged conversation. His mind was still preoccupied with his financial difficulties; but as I led him away from that topic, which had the tendency to bring a dangerous red to his face, I made the rather amazing discovery that Henry was a devoted family man. It was evident that he was genuinely and deeply attached to Eleanor, and it was whispered that he never indulged in a mistress (a strange degree of constancy to find in a son of John Lackland, I thought, but then Lady Isolde was ever fond of saying that "the rotten apple good pips doth hide" to neutralize the more popular belief of "like father, like son") and received from his queen, it seemed, the same degree of faithfulness and affection. He glowed with pride and pleasure when discussing his children, and I was oddly touched that one who carried the weight of the kingdom on his shoulders could love his offspring with the uncomplicated simplicity of any butcher and his mate in the Shambles or any pair of villains in wattled cottage and toft.

The queen herself condescended to talk with me on one occasion and made it clear that her motivation was mere inquisitiveness, for she had heard that Guimont had not done badly for himself after all. This I took in stride as well as the general impression I received from her that she was satisfied I would "do" for him, he being one of her favorites. "Not handsome, but such an air," she said. "You are better than I expected."

I did not know what, in general, had been expected, but I was not so green or preoccupied or dull as not to realize that I was a lively object of interest at court. Curious eyes followed me everywhere, and there were enough people at court who had been at Hungerford for Christmas to relate the various goings-on of that celebration. Suddenly, many people remembered having met me during my brief sojourn the summer before when I had been little more than a nonentity. I might have derived wry amusement from my sudden rise to popularity had I not felt so far removed from everyone, had I not been so locked away in my emotions that I was sure I breathed a different air from everyone else.

I slowly became aware, after several days, of a shadowy figure who could always be found at my side, or at my feet, or at my back when I came into a room. The twang of a lute and the sad, sweet melodies of Provençal love lyrics became insensibly familiar to my ear, such that one evening after I joined a group of ladies, I chanced to look down beside my chair to see the figure disposed languidly on a stool and looking up at me with dark, soulful eyes.

"Who *are* you?" I asked finally in an undervoice, not bothering to mask my impatience with even the barest civility.

The man sighed deeply. He was a young man and handsome, by conventional standards. "I am Raimond of Toulouse, my lady, as I have told you before."

"You have?" I said, startled.

"Yes." He sighed again, exquisitely, and with the slightest crease between his fine black brows. "Two nights ago it was when I sang for you my lyrics to the first of Capellanus's love judgments."

"Yes, yes," I said hastily, not having the faintest recollection of this passage. "Very nice."

Raimond sighed a third time. He had raised the simple act of exhaling to a fine, nuanced art, I noted, but he was a tiresome fellow, a nuisance, really, and I wished he would go away.

"'Very nice,' my lady?" he echoed painfully, as if mortally wounded. "Such tepid praise chills my burning heart! As the first winter frost steals the warm summer's bloom and robs the flower of life's nectar, so I sit before you, my lady, and beg you not to turn your winter's gaze on my heart of greenest spring. You must give me hope!"

"Whatever for?" I replied matter-of-factly, unmindful of my courtly manners and hoping to drive him away with unromantic tactlessness.

Raimond recoiled, stung. He looked deeply hurt. He made some apparently appropriate references to bees, and poets, and Cupid's arrows, but since I was not precisely attending, I did not appreciate the significance of these metaphorical flourishes. Sensing my palpable lack of interest, he cried then, but without raising his voice to attract attention, "Cruel lady!" His voice dropped again to its intimate, caressing, sighing tones. "Capellanus says that 'love is an inborn suffering,' and I had never known until this moment just how accurate he is."

"For heaven's—! Well, sir, why me, after all?"

Raimond's regard assumed a burning intensity. I had plainly said the wrong thing. "Because you, my beloved lady, are the Unattainable, the Perfect Frozen Flower of Winter, the Cold Fires of Love, the—"

"Oh, yes, *that*," I said distractedly, hoping to stem the tide of this promising flow of paradoxes and seasonal commonplace. "Now, run along and admire me from afar, then. I think you might find distance more to your taste."

Raimond unfolded himself to his full, willowy height, every languorous movement suggesting profound regret, and vowed in fervent accents to spirit me away with him to the gardens of Provence where the white mulberry grew.

Raimond's presence, brief as it was, had enervated me so that I was presently obliged to excuse myself from my lady friends—several of whom wore expressions of sly amusement—and to seek my chambers.

This was not immediately to be.

"Fair cruel one!" whispered a well-known voice at my ear as I left the hall. "How can you mistreat the poor poet so?"

"Not you, too!" I exclaimed in exasperation and turned to see Sir Hugh. "Please, I am really in no mood for more!"

Sir Hugh looked momentarily surprised, but the look deepened and spread into amusement. "Poor Raimond! He has been exerting himself so! And to no avail!"

"If I apprehend the matter correctly," I retaliated swiftly, "I am providing him with his fondest wish: unrequited love! Pray, what would he do if I agreed to have him carry me off to where the white mulberry grows? I should think he would be extremely distressed!"

Sir Hugh chuckled unexpectedly, and for an instant I fancied that he lost something of that smooth, inhuman charm I always associated with him. "I do not think poor Raimond was speaking of a place so much as—shall we say?—an act."

I flushed in spite of myself. "Be that as it may, I have it in mind to go only one place at the moment, and that is to my chambers!"

I turned to proceed on my way.

"Your absence only heightens your allure, my lady," Sir Hugh said with a tempting touch of velvet in his voice, "or are you so naive in the ways of love that you had not guessed at even that basic wile?"

I looked back over my shoulder. Whatever it was that he read on my face—puzzlement, interest, skepticism, wariness—caused him to smile his liquid smile. "So, she has not guessed it, the remote, the aloof Lady Guimont."

Is that how I appeared to others, then?

"Who knows what secrets her unattainable heart holds?" he continued, his eyes gliding over me.

"That," I said with a suppressed vehemence that surely betrayed me, "is none of your business."

"No," he said with a bow and melted into the shadows, "I do not presume so much."

I was to see quite a bit of Sir Hugh in the next few days. He had made me the object of his attentions, and I could do naught but suffer them. His purpose was not immediately clear to me, but I was not so naive as not to have ventured some very good guesses: hatred for my husband, his rival in love; a play to get Isabelle jealous (although she was not present, he might be laying the groundwork for her arrival); a way of keeping Yvette at arm's length; or even pique that his masculine charms held so little appeal for me; perhaps all of these things, or none of them: simply an idle game in a frivolous world.

His obvious attentions had only one positive benefit. Raimond ceased his courting of me, bowing to the *force majeure,* and was next observed to favor a very pretty newcomer to court, Sibilla Marshall, I believe was her name.

The dark underside of that benefit, however, was the tacit acknowledgment of Sir Hugh as my premier chevalier. No one ever commented upon Sir Hugh's delicate, but persistent, attentions to me over the next few days. Even Marie-Ange knew when to keep her pert little nose out of dangerous business. And dangerous it was, too, for I perceived that Sir Hugh was slightly shifting his tactics, and the game lost a little of its initial playfulness. I had already shown him that I had no taste for the conventions of Courtly Love as practiced by the men and women of cultured, sophisticated Provence, and so he avoided diverting me with flowery flattery, except for one lapse when he likened my eyes to sparkling jewels.

"Sapphires?" I suggested helpfully. He was about to protest and find a more suitable gem, but I forestalled him by remarking, "You likened them to sapphires once already, I believe."

He did not waste his poetic powers on me again. But he was frequently, yet not always, at my side, entertaining me with stories, squiring me here and there in such a way that I could not decline without gross discourtesy, and generally making himself agreeable to me. It was his change in manner that slowly began to alarm me. When he dispensed with his silken mannerisms, it dawned on me that he was beginning to talk with me as a real person, almost as a friend, and I realized that I might easily succumb to liking him. It was not hard to maintain my guard against him; however, it proved more difficult to sort through the conflicting signals he was sending me. At first, I had to believe that his object was to seduce me. As outrageous—and frankly ridiculous—as it was, I imagined that the compromising of me and my husband's reputation was the only thing that would serve his purpose. Provocative comments, warm regards, a light hand on the waist, a brush on the shoulder were all straightforward enough to interpret. Somewhere along the way, though, these signals ceased and were replaced by conversations with no undercurrents and with the absence of touching, almost a restraint, as if he genuinely wanted to put an arm around me but deemed it improper. I did not know what had caused this change of face, and when I became aware of it, I was more suspicious than ever. Sir Hugh did not move or speak without first having calculated the possible effects of his actions or words; thus, I was convinced that this new, friendlier Sir Hugh was a still more subtle effort to trap me.

Once, but only once, I imagined that Sir Hugh had given up, and I was even inclined, within the bounds of the unwritten rules that governed our dialogues, to congratulate him on at last recognizing the futility of his plan.

I was seated in the gardens (in the same spot where Alicia and I were used to meeting) in the warm, breezy afternoon, waiting for Yvette, and jabbing single-mindedly at my eternal embroidery tambour the way young men must tilt at the quintain. I had finally contrived a private meeting with my lovesick friend, and I was in need of composing my thoughts.

I heard the crunch of gravel and looked up with a half-smile to greet Yvette, but seeing him before me must have altered my expression, for Sir Hugh said with a self-deprecatory twist to his handsome lips, "That is hardly an enthusiastic welcome, my lady."

He had never been so bold as to seek me out at midday and when I was alone. I was not pleased. "But I was not expecting you, Sir Hugh," I said. "I was waiting for Yvette."

"What, no squeak of pleasurable surprise, then? No wide smile of relief to find an unexpected boon in an otherwise tediously dull afternoon?" he bantered and dropped down on the bench beside me. "Besides, what can Yvette offer you in the way of entertainment that I cannot?"

"She is going to tell me the secret of the latest stitch," I said, and clipped a silken thread with the scissors that hung in a sheath at my waist. "She is an excellent needlewoman."

"Is she? How fascinating! You must introduce us sometime. I have been searching my whole life for a woman who plies the needle well."

I put a strong guard on my tongue not to sing Yvette's praises. I did not think it would advance her cause with him just then; in fact, I thought it might sour him on her. In either case, I was not entirely convinced that her cause should be advanced with him. "Do not underestimate the value of mended linens," I replied to his light sarcasm, "when you do at last settle down and bring your household into order."

"Oh, I won't!" he said cheerfully. "Yet I can think of several things that are more important when looking for a wife."

"So can I," I said placidly. "Land and gold."

He quirked an eyebrow at that but refrained himself to saying, "Wise pearls of practical advice, my lady?"

I laughed. "Advice? Certainly not! And how could such commonplace considerations be judged pearls of wisdom? Who does not know that it is best, when possible, to marry for material advantage? It is never, as far as I can tell, viewed in a bad light to do so, and it is generally envied. No, if I offer advice—which I am *not* doing! just a friendly conversation— it pertains more to what I said first about the mended linens. Or a clean castle, for that matter."

"You think I don't know the value of such things?"

"I don't know what you know, sir! I would say that they are, in general, underrated. That's all."

"But can you blame a man for wanting more than just a housekeeper in a wife?"

"No, of course not. However, I cannot imagine a man who would want a wife who is not also a housekeeper."

"You can't?" he responded. "I can! And with very little difficulty!"

"So speaks a man who is not yet married!"

"Are you seriously trying to convince me, my lady, that a clean castle and mended linens are sufficient inducements for a man to marry?"

"Not sufficient. Merely necessary," I said. "And I see little point in pursuing a topic where our ideas differ so widely."

"On the contrary, I am intrigued by it! But tell me, while we are about it: what does a woman look for in a husband, I wonder?"

I folded my hands in my lap and looked him straight in the eye. "Well-protected borders."

Sir Hugh straightened his back slightly and was silent. Then: "Yours are certainly well protected, are they not?"

I relaxed my lips into a small smile. "Yes, I feel unusually fortunate to have hit upon the one thing that women want most of all."

Sir Hugh rose to go. "Thank you for the lesson," he said in a voice slightly stiffer than I had ever heard from him before. "It has been most enlightening."

"Oh, don't go," I protested. "Yvette shall be along soon, and I have already promised you that I shall introduce you to her."

I did not fool him with that comment. I would have been disappointed if I had fooled him. No, he assured me, he had trespassed too much on my time already, and bowed. On the murmured comment that he was beginning to have real sympathy for poor Raimond, Sir Hugh disappeared noiselessly into the gardens.

I had a good notion that I would not be bothered with him that evening.

I was right, and the absence of his unwanted attentions proved something of a relief. I needed the respite, particularly after my emotional interview with Yvette.

She came to the bench under the plantain tree within five minutes of Sir Hugh's departure. I did not know if they had encountered each other, and I did not ask. Yvette looked very pale, and I saw now that she had a haggard look about her. It was probably due to a weight loss, but no matter how many pounds she shed, she would always be round. I did not find her shape unattractive, but I could not see her through Sir Hugh's eyes.

"Good morrow, Yvette," I said brightly. "You look very lovely in that shade of gold. And such pretty designs around the neck and sleeve hems!"

I thought she was going to burst into tears at these innocent remarks, but she managed to hold them back until she had greeted me.

"Thank you so much for coming, Yvette," I continued bracingly, trying to bolster her in her distress. "You know that I have been dying to learn your new seed stitch, and—"

That was all that was needed to set the tears streaming. "It's all gone so wrong, Marguerite!" Yvette sobbed.

"My dear! What can be the matter?"

"It's all so wrong. I—it—I don't understand," she managed on a watery gulp.

"But all these tears! Yvette! Pray get hold of yourself! It can't be that bad!"

"It is! It's worse than bad," she said, moaning. "You can't know what it's like to be—to be—hopelessly in love! It's *agony!*"

My voice cut evenly across hers. "Forget him," I said baldly.

Yvette looked up, blank surprise on her face. I was even a little surprised at myself. "Wh-what?"

"Well, you've stopped crying, in all events," I said. "The only thing—yes, the only *possible* thing I can say to you at this point is that you should forget him. You *must* forget him."

"What are you saying?"

"Have I not made myself plain? Sir Hugh is not for you."

"You want him for yourself, then?" she fired back, her voice scalding through the tears.

It took me several moments to recover from this. Yvette came to her senses first. "Marguerite!" she wailed, with a fresh outpouring of emotion. "I did not mean it! Truly I did not! I would never—you must believe me! You're the only one I can talk to—" Then, on a pleading note: "Please!"

I tried to control the aversion I felt for this scene. I covered her hand with mine and gave her the reassurance I did not feel. "Of course, my dear. You are—simply overwrought. Let us forget that remark."

"Yes! Forget it!" Yvette cried, raising her tear-splotched eyes from her hand linen. "I no longer know what I'm saying! I think I am going distracted!"

"I can see that you are upset, Yvette, and I—I understand, you know, and that is why I think you should forget him. Believe me, that is the only way."

"But I can't—"

"Of course you can, and it will be easier now than in six months, just as it would have been easier six months ago."

"No! It is impossible! How does one go about forgetting? It is not done just like that!"

"Find someone else."

"There is no one else as handsome, as charming, as perfect as Sir Hugh," she wailed.

It would have gratified me in the extreme, at that point, to have made a few choice comments on the perfection of Sir Hugh Falmouth; however, I knew that nothing could be better calculated to set Yvette against me than to point out to her the ruthless way Sir Hugh had been treating her or to describe the games he was playing with me. "He is very attractive," I agreed, "and I am sure that he has many admirers among the ladies. So many, in fact, that I am sure that constant lures are thrown out to him. And since he is so—so busy, I wonder if he has much time for you, my dear."

"That is just the problem! One day, I am convinced that I am the sun and the moon for him. The next day, he does not seem to know I exist."

"His behavior does seem to argue an unsteady temperament. Do you think it wise to marry someone of such uncertain character?"

"This I hear coming from *you*?" she retaliated.

I could not prevent myself from stiffening. "I did not have a choice in my marriage," I said coolly. "And since we are on the topic, you may believe me when I say that it is better to spare yourself the agony, as you say, of entering into a marriage with someone who is unsuited to you. Find someone else! Someone unhandsome, uncharming, and comfortable! Someone who loves you, or at least regards you!"

"Has he mistreated you?" Yvette asked, her eyes round with horror, apparently unable to speak my husband's name.

"Never."

"Then—what?"

She was far from understanding. "You do not want to marry a man who is not in love with you, do you?" I asked at length.

"I will make him love me!"

"How do you propose to do that? You have very strong competition, you know."

"I know, and it does not matter! You think I don't know what everyone else knows? I do! And I am not blind to the fact that he has an eye for the ladies. But it is not his fault if he is attractive! It does not matter! All I want is to be married to him! He need not be faithful—just discreet! That is all I ask."

"You are joking, Yvette! You could never be content with just half a marriage!"

"It is better than none. You *don't* understand, do you? How could you, indeed?" she said in a bleak voice. "But let us say that you were really in love with Sir Guy and not married to him. Wouldn't you want him at any price?"

I could no longer evade the central issue. "Let us just say," I said as evenly as possible, "that knowing what I know now, it would be easier to recover from my—my love, if there were no physical involvement between us."

Yvette's eyes were infinitely sad. "It is too late to go back on that now," she said, her voice devoid of everything but despair.

"No! Yvette!" I cried. "Holy Mother, how could you have been so imprudent!"

"Don't worry," she said, biting off a laugh. "I'm not pregnant, although I wish I were."

I shook my head slowly. "I am quite unable to help you, my dear. I fear I am too late."

It was a depressing day, all in all, to discover that the main purpose of my visit to court had been useless, and I decided that I would return to Hungerford in the next several days. Yvette's outpouring of emotion had drained me, and I suddenly felt unequal to the task of trying to behave as a normal human being in the constant social intercourse of the court.

A brief passage with Marie-Ange was almost my undoing. She was a sly one, was Marie-Ange, but I tried my best to rub along with her. For the most part, I found her lively and gay, and I did not mind her addiction to backstairs gossip; in fact, I enjoyed a good deal of it and thought of it as generally harmless. Not all of it was, of course, but I, as many another frail mortal, did not concern myself over it, until it touched on me directly. I saw her the day after my painful interview with Yvette, and her opening comments confirmed my worst fears.

"You are very clever, Marguerite," Marie-Ange told me that morning. "But perhaps too clever for your own good."

"Marie-Ange," I replied pleasantly, "*will* you stop speaking in riddles? Remember, I do not have as much experience as you at court and so am not wholly conversant with the latest styles of discourse."

"Oh!" said Marie-Ange, and then she regarded me shrewdly. "I think you do very well for yourself, but you're not up to every trick, and so that is why I think to drop a word of warning in your ear." To my raised brows, she said, "Hugh Falmouth is not the man to trifle with."

"I agree with you completely, my dear, but I do not understand you! Could you—do you possibly think that I *have* been trifling with him? I would be most disappointed to hear it, for I have been at *such* pains to keep him away from me. You know," I continued chattily, and lowered my voice confidentially, "it has occurred to me that Sir Hugh would like nothing better than to put my husband out of countenance by pursuing a dalliance with me. Well! I am not usually given to fits of vanity, but it is so *lowering* to reflect that a man's attentions are inspired by a dislike of one's husband."

Marie-Ange looked frankly disappointed but said after a moment, "Surely you do not hope to convince me that you find Sir Hugh's attentions unwelcome."

"But I *do*, Marie-Ange!"

"When every other woman at court is mad after him? You cannot be so particular, my dear."

"Can't I? And that is precisely my point!" I laughed. "I find it hard to be either flattered or seduced by a man who spreads his favors so thinly over—what did you say?—*every* woman at court!"

She made a swift reverse. "Ah! But it is well known that his heart is held by only *one* woman."

"Yes, that *is* well known, isn't it?" I replied dryly. "Isabelle is certainly beautiful, and she and Sir Hugh make a particularly handsome couple."

Marie-Ange, for reasons best known to herself, was determined to disturb me. "I am sure you must think so. In fact, I am sure that you find it to your advantage to have their names linked now, given the person to whom she was allied in almost every way until fairly recently."

"Oh, Marie-Ange!" I said in a light, reproving voice and dug my fingernails into my palms. "Do you think to inform me that Isabelle and my husband were once betrothed? Surely I know that much!"

"More than just betrothed, one might say."

I smiled down at her, a gentle, kindly smile. "Something of a more intimate nature, you mean? Thank you for the information—although I am quite puzzled why you think it should matter to me—but you are not the first to be so *thoughtful* as to bring the subject to my attention."

"I was only thinking that it might be best to know as much about one's husband as one can learn," she said in her own defense, "especially when the man is Guimont."

"Then I thank you for your consideration, but I have little interest in the past."

"And the present?" she prodded.

I summoned all my courage and regarded her steadily for a moment or two. When I spoke, my voice was remarkably normal sounding. "Are you suggesting," I asked, "that Isabelle and Roland still have a relationship? It may well be possible, but I cannot help but wonder at Isabelle! Think for a minute! Roland married me for my land (and I am very satisfied with the arrangement, for what woman could cavil at seeing her lands double?), and if he can have my land and still have her, then she could not have served him a better turn than to have had the betrothal annulled last summer in what must have been a fit of pique! I must say that I am inclined to pity her, for it seems she acted too hastily if she was still of a mind to have my husband. But, ah, well, it is too late for her, and I cannot complain for getting the better end of the bargain."

"You are remarkably cool about it, I must say, Marguerite," Marie-Ange said.

That was the end of that, and I was reasonably content to have fooled Marie-Ange with my display of steady nerve. But I could not fool myself, and the effort cost me so much that I took to my bed for the greater portion of the afternoon, feeling shaken and spent.

I could not fathom why Marie-Ange had been so determined to attack me. I acquitted her of maliciousness, however, and decided that her curiosity to discover the extent of my sentiments overrode any delicacy of feeling she might harbor. Perhaps it was only sport to her, like a joust where opponents square off against each other across a tourney field, visors lowered and lances held mightily in front, and go at each other with all their force. She had not unhorsed me, but she had pierced my ragged mail, my flimsy armor of calm and indifference, and I felt as if I had been severely wounded and needed to nurse my bleeding heart in solitude and repose.

I would have liked that afternoon to have gone to my sewing room at Hungerford. It would have been very comforting to have had that homely refuge to hide in, rather than in Roland's luxurious chambers, so imposing and masculine and alien. I arrived at the antechamber door feeling crushed, even squashed, or perhaps merely flattened, like the black-lined, frozen figures trapped forever between the two faces of a stained-glass window, condemned for eternity to eloquent silence and chosen to witness life in profile.

A Guimont page bowed me through the antechamber to the bedchamber and then circumspectly scurried away. I pulled off my coif and let it fall indifferently to the floor, scuffed the slippers from my feet, and threw myself down on the large bed. For several minutes I stared unseeing at the canopy above me, suspended by a rigging of cords and thick thistle tassles sweeping back the heavy brocade curtains; I pulled a coverlet over my fully clothed body and instantly and thankfully fell into the painless oblivion of sleep.

Two loud raps on the door roused me from the lower rungs of slumber. The page entered on the echo of his knock and rushed in, looking harassed and worried. I had hardly a moment to absorb the oddity of his action before I heard a harsh, irritable voice behind him demand, "What ails you, man?"

My heart flipped over, and I sat up hastily, casting the covers from my legs, but I was not yet ready to stand, being both too groggy and too excited to have control over my limbs.

Roland's presence filled the room. He was on the point of snapping directives at the page but checked himself when he took in the significance of the darkened room. Since my eyes were more accustomed to the dark than his, I could tell that he was bone-tired and suddenly wary. His eyes came to focus on me, and I rose unsteadily to greet him. So taken up was I with the unexpectedness of his arrival that it was not until many hours later that I realized that the page had hastily preceded his master to make sure I was entertaining no embarrassing guest in the bedchamber, and that Roland guessed at it, too. Fortunately, such a thought did not occur to me at the time, so I was able to say with no trace of suspicious guilt, "God save you, my lord."

Roland took my proffered hand and brought it to his lips.

I was dismayed to see my husband compose himself and carefully tuck away behind a calm set of features whatever it was he truly felt. "God save you, my lady," he said. "This is a rude intrusion. Pray excuse me."

He did not release my hand, nor did I make any attempt to withdraw it. The warmth from his strong fingers leapt to mine and set the blood to pounding in my temples with the strength of a herd of runaway horses. "Not at all. You could not have known that I was here, and I could not be better content to see you," I said unwisely.

"I, too, am happy," he replied for the sake of form, and since I could not bear to be so near to him another second without throwing myself into his arms, I moved away. "Am I to assume," he continued, and with a little prick of anxiety, I heard, rather than saw, his tiredness, "that you did not receive my last letter informing you that I was returning to England this month and would stop first at Westminster?"

"No, I didn't," I told him. "I left Hungerford a little over a week ago, so perhaps it was delivered after I left and no one thought to forward it. When last I heard from you, you did not know when you would be returning. Of course, I must thank you for the communication, for even knowing that much was better than nothing."

He inclined his head but otherwise made no response.

"And I also received," I went on, seizing on this topic to fill the tantalizing space between us that made me fairly ache with desire, "your missive in January instructing me of Constance's fate, as I requested of you. At first, it seemed to me that the sentence that fell on her was harsh, although I could see that it was of her own doing. However, upon reflection, I realized that it was prudent to end her career completely, for there was no telling whether she would scheme and contrive again."

"I am glad to hear that your reflections bore fruit. I was not sure how you regarded the news, because I never received an answer from you on the matter."

"It did not occur to me to reply to your letters!" I blurted, quite amazed at the idea that any news from me might be better to him than nothing. "I—it—well, I did not think my opinions were of any urgent interest to you, and there simply wasn't any news to relate of the goings-on at the keep."

He smiled slightly. "I am reassured," he said politely. "I did not anticipate that there would be the slightest hitch in the running of Hungerford under your authority, and if anything truly important had arisen, I am confident that you would have most properly informed me."

He stripped off his travel-stained tunic and tossed it over a heavy, carved chair. His gesture, restrained and casual at once, reminded me pointedly that this was his room, that I was the intruder, and that he was more than just tired. I would try to contrive a graceful exit, but first I felt compelled to account for my presence at court.

"As for that," I said, "I suppose you might be wondering what I am doing here, but as for informing you of my visit by letter, I would not have had time, because I came entirely on impulse. Of course, I could have written you after I arrived here, but then you had already left Aquitania, and— Nevertheless, here I am, and I came specifically—"

"There is no need to give me a reason for your movements," he interrupted shortly. "I gave you free permission to travel as you saw fit."

Despite what he said, I felt a desperate desire to explain myself. "No, really, it is very simple. I came to see someone."

I had paused to compose my thoughts, and Roland turned slightly away from me. I said quickly, "The fact of the matter is: I came to see Yvette. I had something I wanted to discuss with her, but I have discovered that my errand was useless. I was going to return in the next several days. I—I would tell you more, except that I feel I cannot betray Yvette's confidence."

"Naturally not."

"Besides that, I cannot conceive that it would be of the least interest to you!"

"I am sure that it is not without interest, or you would not concern yourself with it."

"Just woman's talk, my lord!"

Roland put his hands on his hips. "Does this mean that I am to learn nothing of what has gone on at my castle during my, what, four months' absence? I imagine you will tell me that there is nothing to relate that would be of interest to me, and I shall in the end have to hear the particulars from John Potter."

There was a touch of humor in his voice, but only the barest. "Dear me, no!" I replied with a laugh. "I shall take great pleasure in boring you to death with a detailed report. Not at the moment, however, for I can see that you desire nothing more than a bath and a rest! I have not even asked you how far you have ridden today, but I can see that it is far! Tell me what I may do for you!"

He smiled again, and this time I felt steadied, reassured. "You have already done your part, Marguerite, by sparing me a trip to Hungerford. I am actually on my way north where I will spend no doubt another few months. With you here, I am saved the trip to see you, and the sooner I can be quit of these matters, the better."

I did not dare read anything into his words. It went without saying that he would have had to come see me. I was his wife, after all. "Unwitting though it was, I am glad to have been of service to you," I said mildly.

His face was closed and his voice expressionless. "Whatever the reasons, unwitting or otherwise, a little escape from the demands of a precarious world from time to time is always welcome."

I may have been blind to all else, given my turmoil in his presence, but I could see clearly that the one thing he wanted now was to be alone. I even strongly suspected that he resented me glimpsing him in his most private moment, when he had no desire to play his role of the deferential husband. He could not, of course, let his guard down completely before me, any more than I could before him, but I had a good notion that if I stayed long enough and provoked him, I could succeed in storming his defenses and in making him behave toward me in a less husbandly manner. I was not entirely certain how a provoked and weary Roland would act toward me, but as tempting as was the prospect of finding out, I could not bring myself to treat him with less respect than he had always treated me.

"Perhaps my absence will also be welcome for an hour or two," I said. "Or do you desire me to attend to you? Shall I call for a bath?"

"You are most wise," Roland commented, as if he had read my mind, and then waved a negligent hand. "No, Gavin will be along soon with my gear, and he has the custom of serving my needs when we are at court. Do not trouble yourself."

It was all I could do to curtsy and murmur the appropriate words of withdrawal. I have no recollection of what I did next, but somehow I arrived at Yvette's room, and fortunately she was there. We spent the remainder of the afternoon together, and I am sure that I said a great many silly things while I maintained a flow of chatter, as unending as it was inconsequent. I even persuaded Yvette to lend me a bliaut to cover the rumples in my kirtle (so craven was I not to return to Roland's chambers) and made up a rather involved story to explain why I was parading with my hair loosely bound and why I needed to borrow one of Yvette's *filets* and a quantity of hairpins. Yvette was, unfortunately, not made of very stern stuff and could not tear her mind away from her own problems for any length of time, but as it turned out, I was just as happy to apply myself to the sorting out of her troubles. I was moderately pleased to discover that I was slowly talking Yvette out of her decision to marry Sir Hugh, love affair or no love affair between them.

Yvette and I presented ourselves in the banquet hall at the approved hour. All talk was of Guimont's return and of the work he had done in the south. I felt a fool for not knowing what he had been about when everyone else seemed to know so well, but even a fool is judged wise when her mouth is shut, and so I kept my lips pressed wisely together. Roland made his entrance rather late, and had I not seen him several hours earlier, his eyes and muscles strained with fatigue, I would never have believed that he was not always so fit and vital and in command of himself.

He was dressed with his customary simplicity, but with a difference: the length of unadorned Flemish blue velvet that covered his back was of a fineness and cut that fashioned the plainness of his tunic into an elegant severity, and in his waist was thrust a jeweled dagger. His hair, crisp and dark when last I had seen it, was an unruly mass of uncut curls; I fancied it longer, I decided, streaked as it was with sunlight. I tried to keep my eyes off him as he made his way through the room, but I observed him just long enough to note a change in his comportment. He moved easily, almost languidly, through the room, greeting whomever came his way, and it occurred to me that he had slipped into the role of the courtier as easily as he had donned his tunic. There was nothing purposeful about his manner, and he did not cast his eyes around the room to see who was there, but still I could not believe it to be happenstance when he managed to fall into brief conversation with Sir Hugh. I would have given much to have heard their exchange of words; it seemed, on the surface, of course, to be entirely cordial, but the look on Sir Hugh's face when Roland moved on was unmistakable. I did not doubt that Roland had heard all about Sir Hugh's attentions to me during the past sennight, and it was monstrous, with all the other events that had conspired to put me at a disadvantage with my husband, that Sir Hugh should have the opportunity at just this time to practice his charms on me. I wondered, wryly, if Roland could be inspired to jealousy. I tore my eyes resolutely away from his tall, magnetic figure and applied myself to maintaining conversation with the women in my immediate circle.

I had not thought that Roland had taken note of me in the large, crowded hall; however, presently he was at my side, and, after the usual exchange, he offered me his arm and led me to the head table where we took our places above the salt.

The mood was festive and the talk ran merrily. I was determined not to be overawed, or tongue-tied, or little-girl awkward, if I could help it. I had spoken with the king and queen before, I reminded myself, and chose a course dictated by good manners: it was far better to enter into conversation, even if I had nothing witty or particularly brilliant to say, than to remain silently glum or sullen or just plain backward. It was extremely difficult to concentrate while I shared manchet and cup with Roland, but his easy manners relaxed me, as did the conversation. I marveled afresh that the lord and ruler of the realm could speak at length on such commonplace topics as the weather and hawking and food.

I knew a bad moment or two when the talk turned to the court and to me. Roland expressed a desire to hear all the latest news, saying, teasingly, that he could not expect to learn any of it from his wife.

The king picked up that frivolous theme and wagged a skewer of meat in my direction. "I'd like to reassure you, Guy, that your wife's reticence argues a discretion not found in many women—or men, God wot!—but you're experienced enough to know that a woman's tongue, when still, hides a guilty conscience."

I successfully fought down a blush. "Surely not, Your Majesty!" I replied with a remarkably convincing lightness. "My husband has only to ask, and I shall tell him anything he wants to know."

"God's truth, man! Here's an opportunity!" King Henry boomed in a voice that brought his queen's hand down on his arm to restrain him.

"Lady Marguerite has an honest face," said Queen Eleanor, sending me a conspiratorial look.

"So do you, love," the king replied, in high good humor, "but that does not mean that I would leave you for months at a time."

"Not so long!" I said hastily, thinking the past four months had seemed an eternity, and belatedly realized how my words must have sounded. "Although I missed him dreadfully!" I added, and forced myself to look up at Roland. "The fact of the matter is, my lord, that there is simply nothing to tell!"

"That is when a women is undoubtedly at her most interesting," Roland said, taking all this nonsense in stride. "I await the full elaboration of that nothing, and anxiously so, my lady!"

"By all means!" I said with a laugh that caught abruptly and suspiciously in my throat when the king interpolated with a broad grin, "Yes, tell him about Raimond!"

"Raimond?" I repeated blankly.

"Such a handsome man," the queen sighed. "Truly one of my favorites."

"Raimond of Toulouse, my lady," the king said with a wink for Roland. "Have you forgotten his persistent attentions? I can tell you that I have not!"

I had indeed forgotten, which was to say that I never really remembered, since his attentions had made so little impression on me. Fortunately, I had a ready answer. "Allow me my measure of feminine pique, sire!" I replied. "When it became obvious to me that Raimond had tired so quickly of me and turned to charm Sibilla Marshall, which he *did* do, if you were attending—yes! I can see that you were!—well, when he did that," I said, glancing up at Roland, "I naturally erased his flattering attentions from memory."

Roland slanted his blue gaze down on me. "Now, why did

he turn his eye elsewhere, I wonder? Did you, or anyone else, hint him away?"

"Oh, no!" I disclaimed instantly. "I think he ran out of inspiration on my dark hair, poor man," I explained mournfully, "and you must know that Sibilla is most fair, and thus she presented him with a whole new world of poetic possibilities!"

The king, for some unknown reason, found that rather amusing. If he had bothered to note Raimond's pursuit of me, then he could not have missed Sir Hugh's; his silence on that particular topic suggested that he had no intention of exacerbating the well-known antagonism that prickled between Sir Hugh and my husband.

It was Roland who pursued the matter. "But then," he said to the king, "it is most difficult, if not impossible, to compliment my wife. Her modesty is—how shall I say?—developed to an unusual degree."

"Is that a compliment, my lord?" I returned. "I hardly recognize it as one."

"For shame, Guy!" the queen chided before he had a chance to respond. "I do not recognize it as one, either. Surely you can do better than that! All women love a measure of flattery."

"But all women are not the same, and a man must match the flattery to the woman," Roland replied easily, and then, to make his point, he paid the queen an extravagant compliment that she obviously enjoyed.

"Look to your own wife, Guimont," the king said sternly, although it was plain that he, too, was pleased to hear the praises of his beautiful wife. "If you've such a glib tongue in your head, you'd do well to flap it closer to home where it would do you some good."

"Majesty," he said with exaggerated deference, "you have not been attending to my argument. I submit that the compliment one pays a magnificent woman and a queen is not the same that one pays a wife. Marguerite is not a filly borrowed for an afternoon's pleasurable hawking such as we described earlier, but part of the Guimont stable, and should be broken in accordingly."

I rose instantly to the fly and voiced objection. "I will

concede that I am not generally receptive to ordinary flattery, my lord, but, on the other hand, I hardly relish the highly uncomplimentary comparison to a horse!"

He looked down at me with a smile calculated to melt my bones. "No? I am become aware of how little I know you and judge my return most timely," he bantered casually. "I should have considered you well flattered, wife, to stand in company with a man's horse, true and dependable."

He knew me better than I had imagined. "I shall have to think about it," I temporized, trying to show some animation.

The queen cried shame down on my husband's head again and declared that no woman would ever get the best of his tongue when he was in such a mood. What woman, she queried, would be taken in by such left-handed tactics?; and without waiting for a reply to her question, she moved the conversation on to more neutral territory. I recovered my composure and tried to avoid looking at Roland for the remainder of the meal, which proved difficult, for my hungry eyes kept straying to his hard profile, and when I could command them to look away, they invariably fell on his arm and hand resting idly next to mine.

So I was to have my taste of Roland the courtier after all. Here was the man who knew enough not to treat all women the same, who could flatter a queen and a wife in the same breath and do it as naturally as he walked and breathed. He was a varied, contradictory man, I thought, and even more irresistible in the flesh and blood than he was in my imagination.

The lengthy repast came to an end at last. I drifted into the general company while Roland lingered by the king's side. I turned back once to watch them in conversation. The king was posing questions with a frown on his face; Roland shook his head several times. The king became more intent, and then Roland held up his hand in a staying gesture. I was surprised to see him make his way straight toward me.

"I shall join you momentarily, love," he said over my hand.

Chapter 17

I hope never again to spend an evening like the one that followed my first meal at court with Roland. I hastened back to our chambers, like a good, dutiful wife, and undressed. I dismissed Bess after she had combed my hair and plaited it down my back. I preferred to wait alone with my thoughts until Roland appeared.

I did not guess just how long I would have to wait. I was excited and nervous and vastly unsure of myself. At first, I prowled about the chamber in my thin night rail. Then, after some little interval, feeling the chill, I shrugged myself into my sendal robe.

Not knowing what to do with myself, I kept my mind carefully blank. I had been avoiding the windows, which opened onto a view of the gardens, as if thereby I could also deny the inevitable association of sweet, desolate pathways with Roland and my desire. But the restless longing was there and refused to be contained by the four walls of the large bedchamber such that I was compelled to give my eyes, at least, room to roam. I pulled a chair over to the window and gazed out over the lovely, lush, hushed gardens. A sword of moonlight cleft the clouds and struck the golden buds below to silver splendor.

It was a melancholy sight, and I came to know it far too wel before the evening was over. My eye, from the superior vantage point of the Guimont chambers, meandered down the paths that led away from the lily pond and came to rest briefly on the stone bench that lately Yvette and I had occupied; it traced the line of tree tops, swaying, sweeping, weeping in the light spring breeze; it sought out in the castle wall opposite the blank, barren windows that had been my suite last July; it followed every shadow that flickered across ground and sky.

I sat there for a time that must have stretched into several hours and knew at last that after all those hideous weeks and months of waiting for Roland and dreading his return, these minutes were by far the worst. I wished that I might learn one day to be free of him; I wished, for a foolish moment, that I had never met the man.

What had he meant, after all, when he said that he would join me momentarily? Had that courteous phrase and gesture been for the benefit of myself or for those around us? Did he truly think that I was so worldly as to know that he did not intend to come to me? Or was that his peculiar form of cruelty to deceive me so? Perhaps he had said it only to divert suspicion in the mind of the court (for surely some soul too had heard him utter those words) and to spare me further humiliation. I could well imagine the whispers on the morrow about Lord and Lady Guimont. "Did you know," one would say, "that Guimont spent the night with Lady——?" "But, no," the other would reply, "I do not think so, for I distinctly overheard him myself tell his wife that he would be with her on the moment." "And yet," the first would sally with a feline grin, "he was seen slipping from the beautiful Lady——'s chambers in the small hours of the morning." "Can it be," the second one would question, "that he was only trying to throw dust in our eyes?" "Very likely," the first would respond, "he being the crafty sort." "I wonder," the second would venture, "if he thought to fool *her* as he tried to fool us?" "Undoubtedly! Have you not noticed that Lady Guimont is mad after her husband?" the first would cry. "And she's as trusting as a lamb." "Poor woman," they would say, shaking their heads, "she is a hopeless case."

I teetered thus on the edge of despair, prey to all my feminine nonsense and my fancies of the hostile world and its gossip. I was hopeless, I thought, as hopeless as Yvette, and I could not guess how I would react when Roland eventually returned to his chambers. Would I, like Yvette, dissolve into a flood of tears or succumb to the wife's role and shriek abuse?

I did not have much longer to wonder. My heart lurched at the soft click of a latch, and suddenly I felt Roland's presence behind me. I turned around to look at him, and the room steadied about me. There was a still, breathless quietude, a moment of enchantment, that came with him, as if the world had taken on an added quality of peace; all the fragments of my being fell into place. I suddenly did not care where he had been in the hours before, or where he would go in the future. All my pain was swept aside; I deemed it a reasonable price to pay to have him with me at that moment and to have him look at me just so. I felt a delicious defection from my sisters on this earth, they who crave security and comfort above all else, to be content with the mere sight of him and the anticipation of his touch.

"I would have thought," he said as he crossed the room toward me, "that you would have given up and gone to bed by now."

Before I had a chance to respond, he took me lightly by the shoulders and turned me toward him, remarking in an equally careless fashion, "There now. I have longed to see your eyes in the moonlight. Just as I thought."

He did not kiss me, but his unswerving gaze upon me was like a caress, and the look in his eyes effectively took my breath away. "You do not mean to tell me what you see?" I asked, looking down.

"I do not dare tell you that your eyes are as beautiful and elusive as moonstones," he said, putting his lips on my hair, "for you have been far too spoiled already with smooth words."

"Not spoiled," I said.

He drew slightly away from me. His hands slid down from my shoulders to my breasts. My heart raced against his palm. "Yes, love, spoiled and bored."

"No woman, according to the queen," I said shakily, "is completely impervious to flattery. I only require that it contain a measure of truth. Just to make it believable, you understand."

"I do, and that is why I chose a modest approach with the moonstones. But I am not entirely satisfied with the image, as apt as it is for your eyes. No, it seems to me that extravagant praise of your face and figure does not quite suit your style."

He was teasing me, tantalizing me, and I knew it. "Am I really so unworthy of the tributes?" I demanded faintly.

He pushed the silk gown from my shoulders to expose me in my thin rail. His hands slid to my waist, where they rested lightly. Where he touched me a flame streaked along my nerves. "Fishing for compliments," he said, "does not become you, love."

"I see," I said, thinking to have understood him at last, "that you strictly distinguish between a queen and a wife."

He shook his head. "No, whatever you may think of me, I am not so ungallant as to confuse the woman with her role." Tiny flames in the depths of his eyes flickered to life. "You, my love, prefer tokens to words, and if you must have truth, I think that your name calls to mind several possibilities for appealing to your taste for the studied gesture. I must remember next time to favor you with a bouquet of daisies."

I chuckled, pleased. "A modest flower, in sooth, and disgustingly appropriate. I accept the bouquet with a gracious curtsy, but surely, sir, you would never come to see a lady without the fitting gem."

"Pearls," he said without hesitation. "I had it in mind on my first trip to Shrivenham to bring you a set of pearls, knowing that you might appreciate the thought behind it. But then the Frant emeralds came my way, and I could not resist them. I have long regretted the mistake."

"Have you?"

"Until now," he said, and began to kiss my brow, my cheek, the base of my throat.

Mind and body were at direct odds. I could hardly endure his kisses without responding fully; neither could I bear not to continue the conversation we had entered into. "Am I to forgive you the error? I am hardly in the mood for forgiveness, you know, since you have kept me waiting for such an inhuman time, abominable man."

He did not respond to the precise scope of my comment. Instead, he said into my neck, "That I know only too well, but you must understand: it is not usual for a man to bed a woman before he seduces her."

"Poor husband," I said with a throaty laugh, "I had no idea you found yourself in such an awkward position."

"That I also know, and it's been the devil of a nuisance for me," he said. "Many's the time when I've thought we'd have done better together if you had had a husband lurking in the background."

This caught me unaware. "You would be here all the same if you weren't my husband?"

"Aye," he said quietly, his hand now moving over my hips and pulling me firmly against him, "and if I weren't, you'd have had the daisies and pearls by now."

Foolish woman, I thought, as I surrendered completely to the desire I had been fighting for such a long time, you are not the only one he has seduced so easily and so well. He has had more practice at this than you can dream of. I did not stop to analyze the charm of Roland the courtier and the lover, so taken up was I with the extraordinary feeling of being the woman who inspired his desire, if only for a night, and the sweet conceit he fashioned that I might relish being his lover and not his wife. Yet, if I were to guess at the secret of his success, I would have to say that, while he had obviously had much practice, there was nothing practiced about his manner, and he had discovered what it was about me the woman that I wanted most to be appreciated. It was hard, that is to say impossible, not to respond to such a man, and I did not try to resist him.

His ruthless mouth was very sweet against mine when he kissed me thoroughly and at length. I had never held such a delightful discussion; and if I was eager to force the pace, he was not and kept me back with yet another kiss and then still another. All doubt and all hesitation were routed by the pale, private moonlight, the gentle surge of a breeze, and Roland's warmth around me. He had set out deliberately to seduce me, aye, to drive from my head all thoughts of other men. I could have told him that he needed no further arts to make me his than to put his hand on me, that no woman who had known him would ever be satisfied with less. Would he, I wondered, have gone to less effort if he had known that I had not met the man who could take his place?

He drew me to the bed, his shirt and chausses discarded, my night rail a formless heap on the floor. He put his mouth on mine and showed me how gentle his strong hands could be. Perhaps Raimond of Toulouse commanded the poetry to express what it was like to lie in the arms of a lover, but I doubted that mere words would capture the experience that spilled recklessly beyond the confines of ordinary existence and shook the very bones in my body. My trembling happiness was proof enough that I had been given a share of earthly heaven. This was paradise, however fleeting; nothing better could exist in this world.

When next he raised his head to look at me, his face was so close that I could just barely discern the tiny image of my face reflected in the depths of his eyes stained midnight blue. I realized with mingled surprise and delight that not only had he led me to this little kingdom of paradise, he had also made me its queen. *Now,* I thought exultantly, now his defenses are down, and he is mine to command as I will. But with orb and scepter thrust in my hands, I was reluctant to take hold of power and call my empire my own.

He was unguarded and vulnerable in that moment, it was · true, and I had only to ask and he would give me what it was I wanted. And, yet, I somehow vaguely intuited that I was being tempted by some devil known only to woman who prompts and cajoles her to use that moment for her own selfish ends. I had a hold over Roland's passions just then, but it seemed no fairer to take advantage of him at that point than it had when he was weary and in need of privacy and rest earlier in the day. I think I could have won from him then the declaration that I most longed to hear, but I could not bring myself to ask him outright. It could not be so difficult to ask him: "Do you love me?"; still, in the end, I did not think his response would bring me comfort when he was not at my side. Perhaps I was only a coward.

In the event, I chose an indirect route, and whatever else it brought me, it most certainly was not comfort.

We looked into each other's eyes for a long time; at length, I began with a tentative, "I'm glad you're back, Roland."

He smiled. "You're a sweet wench to come home to, Marguerite, and I, too, am glad to be back. I look forward to the day when I can be quit of my errands and apply my energies to my lands."

"I do not suppose that day comes soon?" I asked in what I hoped was an even voice.

"Not before the end of the summer," he replied.

"And then?"

"We shall see," he said. His face was all planes and hollows and shadows, but I saw that he smiled still.

I longed to ask him what business would occupy him until the end of the summer, but he had told me once that there were things he did not want me to dabble in, and I guessed this was one. I said merely, "You go north, I believe?"

He nodded assent. "North, south," he said with a long breath that bordered on a sigh, "it's all one. Just put me on my horse and point me in the right direction."

"Do you not like what you do?"

He laid his head on a propped hand. I lay below him, looking up. "I do, but one grows tired of endless adventure, I think you would call it. No, there are other things in life that require a man's attention."

I made a wry mouth. "'Require'? The word sounds dreadfully dull and no better in the end than 'endless adventure.'"

He did not respond for a space. When he did, humor was just barely discernible in his voice. "I come to realize just how long I have been away. I had not guessed how bored and spoiled you had become, and I see you need my stringent quality to bring you back to a sense of yourself."

"How can you say so?" I said, torn between amusement at his teasing and puzzlement at his approach.

"I have already said that I am glad to be back," he pointed out.

It was so: I wanted him to turn a pretty phrase for me. I saw no harm in the wish and, furthermore, it seemed entirely appropriate for the occasion. "Well," I said with mock indignation, "it shall be difficult for me—being so spoiled and bored—not to fish for compliments, however mild."

"Yes," he agreed, "I have come back none too soon and shall begin my plan of daily beatings on the morrow."

"Chivalrous!"

He cast me a rapier glance that nigh well melted my bones. "How well you understand me," he murmured.

I could not resist trying my hand at coquetry. "Is that—is that *really* the most amorous conversation I am to get from you?"

Roland paused. "Words are dangerous, wife," he said casually.

I felt that brief interval of time, when passion had warmed his eyes and brought a look of tenderness to his lips, slip by me. "More dangerous than actions?" I countered.

"In some cases, yes."

"In all cases, though? Let us say that I were to declare love for you. Would that be dangerous?" I asked, suddenly desperate to recapture him.

"But I do not ask it of you," he said evenly.

There was the heart of the matter. That sick uneasiness gripped my stomach. He was a maddening, contradictory man, one minute in my possession, and the next gone. I could not believe that he would talk to me so. I had little taste, at that moment, for the truth.

Then, to my surprise, he reached out and ruffled my hair. It was an affectionate gesture, and I regained a measure of assurance. "I was hoping that you had learned a thing or two about me since our marriage," he said in a lighter tone.

"I have learned a great many things in the past months," I said with the barest touch of feminine pique that he, experienced with women, could not fail to notice.

"I think sometimes," he replied, "that you know no more now than you did that very first night I met you here."

I could only stare up at him, eyes wide.

"Poor Marguerite," he mourned, "I cannot see for you."

Our intimate talk, such as it was, came to a close on this ambiguous note. Even within the safe pillow of his arms, I was not wholly at ease, for, any way I turned it over in my mind, I could not get his words to sit the way I would have liked.

I saw a good deal of Roland in the next few days. He was often found at my side; Sir Hugh was thereby effectively held in abeyance. I tried not to think about Roland's motives for honoring me with his presence: it was enough, for the moment, to have him near me, and I was weak enough to delay my plans to go to Alicia until Roland also left Westminster.

Those three days and nights were for me an idyll; Roland showed me what it was like for a woman to be properly loved by a man. I simply forgot about everything else. Isabelle did not exist; neither did Sir Hugh. Hungerford might well have been swallowed into the earth without so much as a cry of protest from me. Roland spoiled me with no words of love, but I did enjoy his teasing and the times we laughed together.

But when he left Westminster for points north on the morning of the fourth day, my laughter ceased. What happened after he rode off, leaving me desolate with only the memory of his lips on mine, is as foggy and unclear in my mind as the morning mists that creep around the pleasance below my sewing-room window. He had told me that he was going north; now, just before his departure, he thought to inform me that he was on his way to Isabelle Beauvais's demesne. He did not say why he was going, but he must have seen the pain on my face, for he kissed me very gently and looked on me as if I were a muddled child. I had thought at first that he was being deliberately cruel in having so bluntly told me. Later, however, when I mastered my initial misery, I came to appreciate the fact that he had informed me himself, lest I be appraised of it from another, perhaps malicious, source. Needless to say, Marie-Ange brought it up several times.

Nevertheless, I had been too unwary once again, and even while my body yawned with the loss of him, I had to reconcile myself afresh to the knowledge that he was not mine. I thought I had already suffered enough. I was mistaken.

Once I had beheld the shining peaks, it was not possible to descend slowly and comfortably to the placid meadows below where another woman might be stable and content with half a husband. No, I fell into and was sucked up by a swamp of unrequited passion and gloom, and could only, by the coincidence of Alicia's baby's birth, bring myself to think of something other than my own miserable self.

I am reluctant, especially now that Roland is his most inaccessible to me, to think of the long hours that followed my learning of his destination when he left Westminster. There were, of course, the familiar tears, born of despair and feminine foolishness, followed hard by tortured musings that are not to be spoken of in the clear, clean light of day; those thoughts belong to the dark, wicked hours of the night, to strange waking nightmares that expose the cankered corners of the soul. I am sure that I could have led a full, meaningful life without having had to examine the depths of my humanness, but I was not spared this exercise in impotent fury and rage and magnificent self-pity. I do not know if coming to terms with it has made me what the well meaning call a "better person," but then, I have not yet found it in my heart to repent.

Alicia, dear, dear friend for life, came unwittingly to my rescue. The day after Roland's departure from Westminster, I received a letter from her that had been forwarded to me from Hungerford. I had, in fact, been about to make my weary way back to the Guimont demesne when her plea for my company reached me. I was more than happy to avoid Hungerford, and so my little traveling party set out instead for Longchamps where Alicia would be lying-in.

I soon discovered, to my considerable amusement, that the birth of the Longchamps heir had acquired all the trappings of an Event. I was greeted at Longchamps not only by Alicia's in-laws but also by her parents, Lord and Lady Stafford, as well as the Dowager Stafford. It became apparent, as I threaded my way to Alicia's apartment escorted by no less than five persons all talking at once, that while the mere birth of a child could not require the elaborate preparations of a wedding in Alicia's style, it would lack nothing in general bustle. I could not quite conceive what everyone found to do a full two weeks before Alicia was due, and when I said just that moments later to Alicia herself, she rallied me, wryly, for my deplorable want of imagination.

I found her in her bower, swollen with new life and plumped on a cushioned chair. Several attendants were hovering about her, fussing and cosseting, and I could tell from just one swift glance that her sweet disposition was being sorely tried. Her normally serene countenance was determinedly cheerful and just barely concealed what I guessed to be an honest, and justified, harassment. When I remembered her early words that she wanted no to-do about the baby, I had to suppress a strong desire to laugh.

"Alicia!" I cried, gulping down a bubble of amusement. "You have grossly deceived me!"

"Grita!" she exclaimed in return, perking up on sight of me. Then, with a puzzled frown: "Whatever do you mean?"

I crossed the room and bent to kiss her cheek. "You know very well," I replied, laughter welling up in spite of myself, "that your letter to me conveyed the distinct impression that you were pining for company, and here I arrive to find a hundred people falling all over themselves to administer to your slightest whim!"

She pursed her lips into a pretty moue of irritation. "It is beyond everything!" she admitted, and seemed inclined toward an impetuous outpouring of the absurd lengths that two sets of families were prepared to go to secure the succession, but caught herself up and shooed the attendants out of the room before unburdening herself. I was soon laughing in earnest, as much at the excesses to which her family was going to provide

for her "comfort" as at Alicia's well-founded exasperation.
Poor thing, she probably wanted nothing more than to be left
alone, and I said so.

"A little peace and quiet would be more than welcome!"
she responded with conviction.

I rose to go.

Not in the least diverted by my ploy, she tugged at my
sleeve. "How you tease me! No, you must know that I sent
for you—and you *did* say you would be with me when the
time came, dearest!—for some—how shall I say?—rational
conversation. The others are driving me distracted! It's no
wonder," she said, folding her hands over her girth, "that little
Herbert is in no great hurry to come into this hubbub. It's as
if he knows what's in store for him and is biding his time. I
can't blame him, really, but I've come to the point that I would
prefer for it all to be *over!*"

"How is the baby? I mean—I know so little about such
things!—do you have any signs?"

"He's kicking like a Welsh warrior," she replied with a glow
of pride. "He's a healthy one, I make no mistake, and as soon
as there is some calm and quiet, he will make his appearance."

"I'm happy for you," I said with a smile. "But tell me: just
how are you planning to create this atmosphere of calm and
order?"

"Oh, I depend on *you* to do that! You're *very* good at managing people!"

"Clever Alicia! *I* am to be the ogre to keep everyone away
from you. Oh, yes, I can see that I am to be very popular in
the next few weeks here."

"No, no, no, not that! Everyone was looking forward to
seeing you again. Herbert—dear man!—suggested it, in fact,
and Mother, who adores you, thought the idea excellent. But
I don't expect you to keep everyone away from me precisely,
although I do need you to *talk* to me."

"That would normally be a relief to me. However, I fear
you have something far more sinister in mind for my role in
this drama."

"Well," she admitted, "it would be most helpful if you

could—that is, if you could keep the peace between the two families. Not that they aren't good friends! Never think it!"

"I see perfectly!"

"But there are so many of them, and they tend to fuss and fret together so much that it puts me in the fidgets! Why, even Herbert is acting like a lad in leading strings, and he is normally the most composed of men! But I should not talk so, for they all *mean* well—"

"May the saints preserve the world from the well intentioned," I interjected.

"But they *do!*" she insisted. "Even if they do make me cross as crabs sometimes!" A dark look crossed Alicia's face. "Why, just yesterday, Grandmama Stafford fell into the most ridiculous quarrel with Herbert, who, I might add, in all the months of our marriage has never been quarrelsome. And why *she* had to come is beyond me!"

"Ah!" I replied with a wink. "I'll warrant the Dowager Stafford has come to bring her dear granddaughter's husband to a sense of his folly, uselessness, and total irrelevance, my dear! As Lady Isolde used to say: 'When a woman's in the straw, a man can do naught but chaw.'"

"You made that up!" Alicia accused.

"I didn't! But it's not my most favorite of her sayings," I owned, "although it is to the point. I think a man would be entirely useless on such an occasion, and so I can see that my first duty will be to entertain Herbert and to keep him from vexing you to death! I can be quite ruthless in my methods, and if he has the effrontery to think that *he* had anything to do with this baby, I will not hesitate to correct him."

This drew a laugh from Alicia, who then begged me to give her the latest gossip. I was at liberty to discuss any topic I chose, I was told, as long as I did not mention the word *baby*.

I was happy to oblige her. It was easy enough to divert her with the latest stories, and I carefully chose the most inconsequential among them. I passed lightly over Yvette and completely omitted Sir Hugh, Raimond of Toulouse, and Roland from the conversation. Alicia exclaimed over some things, clucked her tongue over others, and seemed generally satisfied with my chatter. I left her presently so that she could take a nap, and went in search of the father-to-be.

I found Herbert in the Great Hall absorbed in earnest conversation with his mother. I did not have to strain my mind very much to guess at the subject of so serious a discussion.

"I just left the invalid, Sir Herbert," I said as he took my hands in a warm, painful grasp, "and I think the prognosis is very good. Excellent, in fact!"

"Marguerite will have her joke," Lady Longchamps said, torn (I suspected) between amusement and the feeling that no effort should be spared her very pregnant daughter-in-law.

"Thank you for coming, Lady Marguerite," Sir Herbert said, wonderfully oblivious to the point of my comment. "Alicia is doing well, isn't she? I *knew* that your coming would be beneficial to her spirits." His brow wrinkled, and he continued heavily, "The health of the spirit is so important at such a delicate time in a woman's life, I think. We have all done our best to ensure Alicia's physical comforts, but we must also think of her mental comfort. That should not, *must* not be overlooked, dear Lady Marguerite!"

"I couldn't agree with you more, sir!" I said. "Come, tell me of the ways you have devised to ensure the comfort of her spirit so that I may learn them, too. I am fascinated, and you must instruct me without delay!"

Lady Longchamps looked momentarily surprised, but as comprehension dawned, she nodded approvingly and left to go about her business.

Sir Herbert and I took a turn in the gardens. He was mightily preoccupied with Alicia's health and that of her child, and I came to the rapid conclusion that he should be kept away from his gentle wife as much as possible. It put me in a fret simply listening to his concerns, and it was forcibly brought home to me, as I heard the most loving of husbands express his worst fears, that nothing could be more disastrous than to bring two families together, each represented by three individuals, and to have these six persons exacerbate and feed on one another's anxieties. I suddenly saw the wisdom (however misguided the reason for doing so) in sending for me, since it would become increasingly necessary to have a nonfamily member keep the peace among the six adults, who were displaying little more sense than a group of three-year-olds.

Midway through Sir Herbert's ponderous recital of his worries and schemes for Alicia's well-being, he mentioned the one point that I guessed had greatly exercised his mind. "The Dowager Stafford, for instance," he said, "though a wonderful woman and so devoted to Alicia, does not entirely understand the seriousness of Alicia's condition."

It required a conscious effort to preserve my countenance. I bit my lip hard before I trusted myself to say, "I fear you must excuse her the miscalculation, Sir Herbert, for from the circumstance of her having survived the birth of numerous offspring and of witnessing the fortunate good health of her own daughters and daughters-in-law, you must admit that she perhaps takes a more hopeful view of the case than you do."

"That is precisely my point!" he replied without a blink. "She knows nothing of what can go wrong! There are many things, I assure you!"

"I do not doubt it, but I think it far more likely that the Dowager Stafford, knowing what good stock Alicia comes from, has a reasonable expectation that everything will go well for her."

"She's an irascible old woman," Sir Herbert said with his own measure of irritation, "and has no conception of the delicacy of Alicia's constitution. The woman's a menace!" Then, to my look of surprise at his vehemence, he retreated slightly: "Not that she doesn't mean well, mind you!"

It seemed that there were far too many well-meaning but meddlesome people in residence at Longchamps Castle, but instead of saying what was uppermost in my mind, I applied myself to the role of peacemaker. I bent my energies toward convincing Herbert that everyone was concerned about Alicia's health and the birth of the baby, but that there were as many ways of showing that concern as there were people. I was having some difficulty in tactfully hinting to Herbert that perhaps he was being too possessive and overanxious, so I tried another approach entirely.

"Now tell me the girls' names you've thought up," I said innocently. "All I have heard so far is about little Herbert."

Big Herbert's brows flew up.

"Just thought I'd mention the possibility for a girl, you know," I said with a mischievous smile.

This Herbert would not allow. It was to be a boy, and that, I was told, was that.

"But, Sir Herbert, don't you want to dandle a maid on your knee?"

"Oh, yes!" he replied. "Next time around!"

My ploy worked like a charm. At least, if I was not able to convince him that he alone knew what was best for his wife, I was able to funnel his thoughts into more pleasant and productive channels, which included a thorough discussion of the bright future that was to be Herbert Harold Longchamps's, and I was not at all surprised to see that Alicia's husband was going to make the perfect father, once the baby decided to make an appearance in this world.

I was thoroughly occupied in the ensuing few weeks and had, fortunately, very little spare time in which I could give myself over completely to my misery. I began to think, as the days slipped by, that I was suffering from a spell of exhaustion—both physical and spiritual—for I began to lose my energy and to feel generally unwell.

I have never ailed physically in my life and so was able to dismiss my general indisposition as pure imagination. But if I was able to ignore my pallor and weakness, Alicia was not. She mentioned it to me one evening after supper when the two of us had some time to ourselves.

"I am conscience-stricken over you, Grita," she said in a manner so serious that it surprised me and left me incapable of diverting her attention from me. I had been careful, up until that point, to keep all conversation away from me personally.

"Whatever can you mean?" I asked.

"My dear," she said gently. "You look so—that is to say,

you do not look at all your usual robust self. I fear that I have overburdened you with the task of keeping Grandmama Stafford and Herbert from coming to physical blows."

Since this was not what I had expected, I laughed, half in relief. "Relieve your mind of care, then! I have—well, to be perfectly frank—I have almost *enjoyed* doing it! It has kept my mind off other things," I said unwisely and hastily moved on. "It's been a challenge to me, really, to apply my ingenuity to soothing their ruffled nerves. I do warn you, however, that my bag of tricks is just about drained, and I cannot keep them apart from each other for much more than a few more days. So, please, contact little Herbert and tell him to hurry on."

Alicia merely smiled serenely and folded her hands across her belly in a now characteristic gesture. She looked radiant, and certainly as beautiful as any Madonna I had ever seen.

I suddenly realized that her time was near. "The nest is ready and your feathers are smooth as silk, I perceive," I replied to her smile. "Is the little bird ready to be hatched soon?"

"I think so," she said. She did not betray the least fear or even anxiety. I marveled at her calm and thought that somehow her present state was nature's way of preparing for the emergence of life. It was perhaps due to the fact that her body had taken over the beginnings of the birth process that she was able to focus her attention on me. "But what do you mean," she continued without hesitation, "by saying that your occupations here have kept your mind off other things?"

"Why, nothing! Whatever should I mean?"

"That is what I was hoping you would tell me."

"But surely you cannot mean to ask how *I* am doing at a time like *this?*" I protested.

"What better time than the present?" she replied.

"My dear, your baby—!" I exclaimed, thinking I was making an excellent argument.

"Will come on his own accord, and it won't be for a while yet. That much I do know, but what I *don't* know is what that has to do with anything. You must be sick to death of hearing about it!"

"Not at all! I—"

Alicia held up a hand. "And you've already told me all the latest news from court."

"Yes," I said on a note of mild triumph, "I *have* told you everything, haven't I?"

Alicia regarded me steadily for a moment or two. "You have not once mentioned your husband, my dear."

I am sure I blanched a shade or two. "No?" I said in a slightly strangled voice. "I had not noticed."

"I have," she replied. "I began to notice it only a day or two after your arrival, but did not think it odd until a few days ago."

"What is so odd about that?"

"It is only natural to speak of husband and castle. Why, you haven't once mentioned Hungerford, now that I think of it."

"Well," I said, "I'm sure I must have mentioned that I saw my husband at Westminster before coming here."

"No, in fact you did not."

It seemed ridiculous to insist that it must have slipped my mind. In truth, almost every diversionary tactic that came to mind seemed equally ridiculous, and pointless as well. "I suppose that all I can say," I said slowly, "is that it is a very painful subject for me."

"That much I have gathered, but my question is why? I cannot conceive what the trouble is between you."

"Can you not?"

Alicia looked blank. "No, indeed I cannot. Do not tell me that Sir Guy mistreats you, for I will not credit it!"

I shook my head. "No, he does not. He is the model of the polite, courteous husband. Really, I consider myself most fortunate."

"And so you are, my dear. But," she continued with a small frown between her wide eyes, "I am having difficulty understanding the problem. Could it—could it possibly be that you do not, somehow, *fancy* your husband?"

A sound remarkably like a groan of pain was heard in the room. It took me a second to realize that it had come from me. "The problem, Alicia, is in the phrasing of your question,"

I said quietly after a long moment of studying my fingers. "It should not be *what* is the problem, but rather *who* is the problem."

"I am in the dark! If the problem is neither with you nor with Sir Guy, then *whom?*"

I stood up abruptly and turned to cross toward the window. My stomach lurched queasily. By strength of will, I commanded it to right itself.

"Almost anyone at court could answer that," I replied with a bitter laugh. I turned to face her. "You cannot guess? But we've been over this road before! My husband is in love with Isabelle Beauvais."

Alicia's face underwent no change of expression. She evinced neither surprise nor dismay. "That is not true," she said simply.

"But it is!"

"You have a very active imagination, Grita! I do not know where you come by your notions!"

"Shall I tell you, then?" I cried, once having launched myself on this path unable to stop. "Let me begin by mentioning that it is practically common knowledge that he and Isabelle were—or still are—lovers."

Alicia considered this for a brief moment. "I am not at all surprised if they were in the past," she said.

I could only stare. *"Not* surprised—!"

"Oh, but I doubt they still are, you know, now that he is married to you."

I was too taken up with her simplicity actually to be angry with her, but first things first. "How can you not be surprised that they had a relationship before they were married?"

"These things do happen, Grita."

So I was the only naïve one, then. "Yes, to married men as well as to unmarried ones," I countered.

"As to that," Alicia replied with unbelievable confidence, "I doubt Sir Guy is interested now that he has you."

I hovered between exasperation and incredulity. "Let us get one thing straight! He married me for my land, and I have it on very good authority—his own, in fact—that he married me in a fit of jealous pique, to boot!"

"Marguerite, I'm surprised at you! You forget that I had the privilege of attending your wedding and saw with my own eyes how Sir Guy conducted himself. Never have I see a man behave less like someone indulging in a fit of jealous pique!"

"He is a very calculating man and knew just how to act."

"Now you are contradicting yourself," she pointed out.

She plainly did not understand. "Appearances are deceiving," was all I could think of to say.

"They certainly are!" she agreed roundly.

It became very important for me just then to convince her of the rightness of my perceptions. "I may as well tell you that Isabelle has in her possession the ruby bracelet that is part of the Guimont collection." That admission hurt more than any other, and while I was about it, I added, "And I think he is at the moment paying Demoiselle Beauvais a social visit."

"Are you positive?" she asked, rather struck by these two pieces of information.

I nodded glumly.

I had the grim satisfaction of seeing that I had at last succeeded in arresting her attention. She was frowning in concentration, as if trying to gather an elusive thought. "The ruby bracelet," she murmured. "Now why should I be wondering about that? I wonder if I haven't heard something about it in the past months."

I told her, wearily, that it was probably in her mind because she had seen Isabelle wearing it at Hungerford during the Christmas festivities.

"No, that's not it," she said, shaking her head. "Now what was it? . . . Oh!" she exclaimed as something flashed across her face. I felt she had been about to tell me something vitally important, but with her next movement, the moment was gone forever. She clutched her belly and said with a mixture of excited anticipation, relief, and satisfaction, "My time is come!"

I immediately dropped the most distasteful subject, and my curiosity in the particularities of the ruby bracelet was displaced by the more immediate needs of new life. I said that I would fetch Lady Stafford on the instant.

Before I left the room, Alicia grabbed my sleeve. "Before

you go," she said, favoring me with a searching look, "I want
to say something to you now—in case the occasion does not
return. You must promise me something."

I thought, morbidly, that she meant that I should look after
Herbert and son if she were not to make it through her labor
and birth. "What is that, dearest friend?" I asked, patting her
hand solicitously.

She smiled slightly, almost secretly. "You must promise me
to take care of yourself during the next few weeks," she said
with a significance that baffled me.

I did not ponder at length the promise that she had exacted
of me, for I, as much as anyone, was caught up in the ab-
sorbing, and lengthy, process of birth. The men were banished
to wherever it was that men went when women were in labor,
while we women were left to attend the mysteries of life. The
Dowager Stafford was in high croak over the birth of her first
great-grandchild, the Ladies Stafford and Longchamps were
taking very seriously their roles as attending mothers, Alicia
remained calm and controlled, and I began to feel progressively
more nauseated as the night wore on.

The birthing chamber had been set up long since. It was to
be a while yet before Alicia would take to bed. She sat comfortably for the first hours of the night in a long chaise. The
women chatted of this and that and did not have anything
specific to do besides keeping her company. Toward midnight,
however, her pains came at more regular intervals and closer
together so that she was at last persuaded to lie down. I hovered
about for some minutes, feeling more and more unwell (thoroughly convinced that it was my own fear of the dreaded
process of child-bearing that affected me so), until Lady Stafford looked at me and told me crisply that since I was serving
no purpose whatsoever, I would be better off in bed.

I arose betimes the next morning to discover that there were
no new developments in Alicia's condition. Nature was taking
her time; Alicia was bearing up well. The hard pains had not
come yet, and from the looks of things—so said the various
voices of experience—it would be many hours more.

I entered the birthing room to be greeted by a sight for

which I had, fortunately, prepared myself. Alicia was lying, pale and drawn, on the bed, racked every few minutes by contractions. I spent the next several hours trying to make myself useful and desperately trying to avoid thinking of Alicia—or even looking at her. When she entered another, more intense stage of her labor, I found that I was unable to bear her cries one minute more, so I slipped out of the room and sagged against the wall, entirely incapable of understanding why I had suddenly become so squeamish. Nothing before had so affected me.

A minute later, the Dowager Stafford, supremely composed and confident, also left the room to run an errand. She caught sight of me just at the moment when I was dashing the back of my hand across my eyes.

"Thinking of your own mother, I suppose," she stated matter-of-factly. I nodded. "Well, I don't claim to have known her well, but she was always a frail thing. Not like Alicia, in all events, who, despite all appearances, is very hearty. Now, your mother was going to have a hard time of it no matter how much she pampered herself, which is a course of action," she said, her thin bosom swelling with conviction, "I never advise for *any* pregnant woman. Alicia has followed my advice admirably, in the face of all the silly opposition from her husband (who is a dear, but knows *nothing* about such things, as I have been at pains to show him for *weeks!*), with the result that she should experience *no* difficulty whatsoever. There is nothing for you to worry about, Marguerite, so I suggest you go back in and show your dear Alicia some support."

"I am sure that you are right, my lady," I croaked in a voice barely above a whisper, "but I think that, at the moment, I am most selfishly thinking of my own fate, were I ever to—to conceive a child."

"Oh, pooh!" she said, as she ran her eyes over me. "You were built for child-bearing. I don't doubt that you will have at least four—two boys and two girls, if I know anything about it! But don't look for a lad the first time around."

Her authoritative manner reassured me and momentarily

calmed my fears but did not cure my nausea. I went back into the room and made myself as unobtrusive as possible.

The infant, a boy (as predicted), came into this world in the early evening. He announced his arrival with a lusty cry that turned into contented gurgling when he was presented to Alicia's breast. He was pronounced healthy, and the proud father was ushered, trancelike, into the room. I did not linger to spoil their intimate family moment with my presence, but I was heartily glad that I had remained with Alicia until the baby was born, for I discovered that at the end of all the pain and waiting was quiet and contentment; and, contrary to all my expectations, I saw that Alicia looked, in the few minutes after the birth, even more beautiful than I had ever seen her. She was truly a woman now.

We all left then to let the new family have time to themselves, and I wondered vaguely if I would be so well surrounded by love and loved ones when I would have the infinitely complicated pleasure of bearing Roland's child.

When the baby was a week old, it became time to move on. I could have departed several days before, but somehow I was avoiding leaving Alicia, the baby, her entire family, and comfortable Longchamps Castle. I had been avoiding the issue of facing Hungerford, I finally admitted to myself, and each day that passed made it that much harder. I thought at first that my lengthy and unaccustomed indisposition was making me reluctant to travel, but since I could not believe that there was anything truly wrong with me, I resolved to return to my own keep without further delay. I ignored all denials from Alicia that I had overstayed my welcome and gathered my traveling necessities, my tiring women, and the outriders. We were on our way by sun-up the next day.

The trip itself was uneventful, but upon my arrival at Hungerford, it seemed that events conspired to twist and wring my emotions until I felt as if I hardly recognized myself. It was not easy to accept that nothing about my life with Roland would ever be simple or straightforward, that no joy would be without its dark, disturbing underside, or, for that matter, no deflation so complete that it was without its leaven. So it was in the week of my return, a wildly erratic, highly contradictory week, which left me confused and exhausted.

I was elated out of all proportion, for instance, by the gift that Roland had waiting for me in my private chambers. He had apparently sent it to me from points north—a small circumstance I thrust momentarily to the back of my mind.

I opened the small package to find, with a lurch of my heart, a string of perfectly matched pearls. The note, left unsigned, that accompanied this most exquisite gift puzzled me at first. I had to blink and realized that my intellect was always disordered where Roland was concerned. Then I turned the page right side up to read the message he had written in Greek. I labored through the lines, shaking my head slightly over the elaborate phrase whose syntax eluded me. But the real content did not: I culled four references to *margaritēs*, or "pearl," each time in a different case, among the bold, black lines, and knew the lovely warm pearls in my hand to be for me the woman, Marguerite. I felt very happy indeed.

That pleasant sensation stayed with me through the day and into the night but was dispelled on the morrow when Sir Hugh Falmouth's presence at Hungerford was announced to me by a very sly and smug Louise.

I was in my sewing room at the time and remained there a good while after I had dismissed Louise. Having been taken so much by surprise, I needed some time to marshal my wits. Before I could sort out the problem of how I was supposed to receive Sir Hugh alone or even had a chance to speculate on the reasons why he had come, I looked up to see him standing at the door to my chamber.

I no longer made any effort to think; I simply reacted. My immediate feeling was revulsion. I absolutely did not want Sir Hugh in my most private, personal room, and felt so strongly about it that, even before properly greeting him, I rose from my chair on sight of him and said a little too curtly, "No, not here. Let me escort you to your chamber and get you settled before I meet you in the Great Hall."

I crossed to the door as if to block his entrance. He had

made no move. Then I recalled myself. "Pray excuse my rudeness, Sir Hugh," I said, trying unsuccessfully to inject a note of warmth into my voice. "You have taken me by surprise." I proceeded with the conventional greeting.

I was heartily glad that he did not take my hand and kiss it, as he had done on so many other occasions, for I am sure I would have recoiled at his touch; and if I had been less vexed by his sudden and unwanted presence, I might have detected in his voice the edge of bitter hurt that I, at the time, interpreted as offended feelings.

"The rudeness, my lady, is entirely mine own," he said, "for having burst in on you so unceremoniously."

I was not equal, as I led him away from my room, to arguing the point or making the expected remonstrances. We chatted noncommittally on indifferent topics, before I remarked, "You shall be disappointed to learn, Sir Hugh, that my husband is not here at this time."

"I am aware of that fact, dearest lady," he replied.

I might have supposed he was, but why he should admit it, I did not know. My anger, as sudden and inexplicable as Sir Hugh's presence at Hungerford, flared. I was betrayed into saying, irritation warm in my voice, "Then what, Holy Mother, are you doing here?"

Sir Hugh paused slightly. He said with extreme politeness, "My lady, it grieves me that you mistake my motives. I know that you could not do otherwise. It also pains me that you are not particularly, ah, delighted by my visit. Nevertheless, I am here and shall stay until it is no longer necessary."

His unaffected sincerity—and his honesty—left me silent. I searched his face for clues to this extraordinary speech, but his features wore an impassive mask. I suspected him of anything and everything. I did not know precisely what his object was, but one thing was clear: he had as much as told me that he would not go, even if I ordered him, which I had had a good mind to do.

I was in no mood to expend any energy in being polite to Sir Hugh. That much, at least, was obvious from my next words. "You may stay as long as you like, sir," I said at last, my voice stiff with distaste, "but I warn you to stay away from me as much as possible. I am without the company of my husband, as you already knew before you came, and I want there to be no possibility, no *breath* of a possibility, of leaving the impression that you have come here to see me. I want that clearly understood."

"I understand completely, revered lady," he said with a deep bow.

I was sure that my ears deceived me. I simply could not credit the accents of humility uppermost in his reply. He was so sly in his attempt to manipulate my sentiments that I nearly hated him.

True to my request, however, and somewhat to my surprise, Sir Hugh did not approach me once in private during the next few days. He was making an elaborate and convincing show of spending as much time as possible during the day with John Potter and the other men of Hungerford, while after the evening meal he conspicuously dallied with the ladies and retired early.

I did not begin to understand what he was about. The less time I spent trying to overcome my nausea (it had lessened in the week of my return), the more time I passed in a state of mingled anger and confusion. I tried hard to keep myself as busy as possible, but I was unable to rid myself of the feeling that something was about to happen. Louise was suspiciously biddable and had an air of expectant triumph—not unlike Lady Constance's satisfaction (premature and unfounded though it was) during the Christmas celebrations. I felt I could deal with Louise; I was not so sure that I could withstand too many interchanges with Gunhild.

I knew that she was keeping her eye on me and Sir Hugh, a very close eye. I was therefore thankful that Sir Hugh did not behave improperly once. Nevertheless, Gunhild seemed to be enjoying a kind of malicious satisfaction at Sir Hugh's presence. I could not guess why. Because my husband and Gunhild cordially disliked each other, I thought it unlikely that Gunhild would attempt to get away with going to Roland with lies about me and Sir Hugh. She did not even seem the type to stoop to fabrication to serve her ends, whatever they might have been. She had an odd regard for the truth. In any case, her close scrutiny unnerved me and made me unwontedly fretful.

At least I now knew the partial cause of my fretfulness. Gunhild knew it, too, and her knowledge rattled my nerves all the more.

I was crossing the bailey alone on the third day of Sir Hugh's visit, my mind preoccupied with my errand, when Gunhild appeared at my side.

In the bright light of day I saw clearly the years etched into her face. She was unusually alert.

"Good day to you, Gunhild," I said steadily.

"You're a brave woman," she returned. Her sarcastic tone indicated that she was not paying me a compliment.

"I thought we had already established that fact," I said bravely.

"You'll never get away with it," she said. She seemed completely lucid, even prophetic.

Unaccountably, my heart started pounding irregularly. "I do not know what you mean," I said slowly, clutching at my dignity as one would to a chamber robe in the presence of strangers.

"Do you not?" she snorted and then drifted off into reverie. "If you're like all the rest, you think you can get away with it. But you won't! None of them do! If someone else does not get you for it, then Guimont will."

"That is plainly absurd," I stated flatly.

This comment snapped Gunhild back to the present. Her eyes took on their keen, hawklike regard and moved over me, slowly, meaningfully. "I wonder if you'll live to see the babe born," she said in a horribly detached voice.

It was full noon. The sun was shining benevolently overhead on the cloudless, last day of June. It was glorious weather. I shivered.

I did not even consider disclaiming her implication. That would have been futile; but I could not imagine how she had come to learn of my condition when I had only just allowed myself the luxury of acknowledging it. I struggled against letting Gunhild frighten me or ruin the one thing in my life I desired so fiercely.

It took me too long to respond. Finally I said, "I have recently been told that I was made for child-bearing, so I do not fear death in childbed."

I absolutely refused to let Gunhild get the better of me. As I held her gaze, her eyes narrowed. "Death has many shapes and many guises. Do not say I did not warn you," she said harshly.

"You've warned me of many things, Gunhild," I replied clearly, "but I have yet to discover the meaning of it all." I held up a hand. "And there is no need to point out that I am a fool. I am sufficiently aware of that fact."

"Aye, a fool," she repeated bleakly. "And if you're as blind to the truth as I think, you will surely die by jealousy."

Her pronouncements never failed to catch me slightly unawares. This one startled me as much as it puzzled me. "I hope that I have too much strength of mind to die from jealousy."

She opened her mouth to speak but evidently changed her mind. Then: "Let us see how much strength you have tonight," she murmured.

Thinking of my own miserable self first, I decided that it was highly unlikely that I could actually be consumed physically by my jealousy. I was horribly jealous, it was true, but I did not think that it could kill me; it occurred to me, however, that Gunhild might have something completely different in mind. I felt immediately unwell. One man's jealousy, at least, was legendary, and it had taken him to murderous lengths before.

"Do you think it possible," I asked intrepidly, "that my husband could *really* suspect that I have a relationship with Sir Hugh?"

"I could not say what he does or does not suspect," she answered.

"You told me once that the truth can kill. Do you now propose than an untruth can kill, too?"

Gunhild gave me a shrewd look. I felt that I had scored significantly. She shook her head slowly. "No, I've not changed my mind. It's still the truth and jealousy that will kill you, too," she said as she withdrew, a tight, slightly malicious smile curling her lips.

"I thank you for the warning, Gunhild," I said to her retreating back.

I spent the rest of the afternoon trying to determine what she meant. No matter which way I interpreted her words, I could not find an answer that added up to the way everything seemed to be. I deemed Roland perfectly capable of killing me for infidelity; I flatly rejected the notion that he would do so without having absolute, firsthand evidence; and I would have thought, unless I grossly misjudged the matter, that he knew I loved him to the exclusion of all other men.

Half of my brain continued to consider the implications of my conversation with Gunhild throughout the evening meal, but the problem ceased to exercise my mind when the pages had hardly done stacking the tables in the hall and Isabelle Beauvais was announced as the latest visitor to Hungerford Castle.

I knew instinctively that she and Sir Hugh had prearranged her arrival. I could not guess at what their game was, but I did not like it one bit.

Gunhild's words *Let us see how much strength you have tonight* flashed across my brain, and I gathered what flimsy courage I had about me to face the beautiful Isabelle.

She had never looked more lovely. Dressed in virginal summer white, she was a fair, ethereal vision of feminine beauty.

I felt my heart wither with jealousy, but death certainly did not claim me.

She glided forward, arms outstretched to greet me, and when she presented me with her two cheeks, it took all the strength I had to offer her the kiss of friendship.

I noticed then that the ruby bracelet was tactfully absent. A small concession, that.

"Why, Marguerite," she said, her voice husky, "I hope you're not too surprised to see me."

"Not at all," I replied with perfect truth.

"You cannot conceive what shifts I had to employ to get

away," she began, and before she had the chance to develop this most interesting theme, Sir Hugh appeared at my side.

"Hugh!" she cried joyfully and flung her hand out to be taken. "I have kept my promise to you after all!"

Sir Hugh bowed over her hand. It was a formal gesture.

"You see," she continued, turning back to me, "Hugh and I agreed to meet here when we last saw each other." She tossed her head to Sir Hugh. "Didn't we, love?"

Sir Hugh affirmed this.

She added, soulfully, "It was the only place we could think of to—to be *together!* We have been apart far too long, and I have become quite desperate, so that I must compel Hugh to marry me—*here!* You see, Hungerford is so conveniently close to London and far from my father!" She paused artfully. "You *will* 'aid and abet' two runaways in love, won't you, dearest friend Marguerite?"

She played her part well, and since I did not really think she meant for me to sanction a marriage without the consent of her legal guardian, I replied that I would be most happy to be of service. I supposed that I would have been happy to see her wed to Sir Hugh; in all honesty, I did not think it would alter the complexion of things very much.

"I have been in *agony* without you, love," she went on to the apparent object of her desperate desire. "How have you been getting on without *me?*"

"Tolerably well, Isabelle," was Sir Hugh's rather uninformative reply.

She made a pretty moue and said archly, "Flirting with all the ladies, no doubt."

I felt something was expected of Sir Hugh at this point. "You must know that I have eyes only for you, Isabelle," he said with his customary silken charm.

She cocked an eyebrow. I would almost have said that she looked disconcerted by his reply, but the feeling was as fleeting as her expression. "Have you, darling? How reassuring!" she said lightly, as if entirely satisfied by Sir Hugh's avowal.

Sir Hugh said nothing to this. I was too preoccupied by the thoughts crowding in on me that Isabelle had just spent the past few weeks in my husband's company to take real notice of any strain in the atmosphere.

Isabelle smoothed over her loved one's ungallant silence with an airy, "But we can talk about all that much later."

"Yes," I agreed, "and I am sure you would like to spend some time with Sir Hugh alone to discuss whatever it is that needs to be done if you are to be married. I am sure that you must be bone tired and in need of rest before doing anything else, so, pray, come inside and I shall see to the preparation of your chambers and one for your tiring woman."

Isabelle thanked me very kindly, and with a sincerity that made my stomach flip over, and accompanied me to the main portal.

"How lovely to be back—at Hungerford," she said when she stepped across the threshold and into the Great Hall, and I thought for a moment that she had meant to say "home."

Chapter 18

Dinner had to be endured. I was sufficiently numbed by all that had happened to me in recent months to spare little energy imagining what Sir Hugh and Isabelle were about to be both at Hungerford at this time. For whatever purpose they had come, I was hardly in a position to hinder them, and I had decided to let the pair conspire to their hearts' content. It occurred to me during the meal that they did not seem to have much to say to each other. I did not understand why that was, and it did not particularly bother me. I cared very much more for my own personal health and had determined that my delicate condition would best be served by not worrying about unpleasant people and their possible activities.

They behaved, outwardly, as they had always done. It might have been, I thought by the time the dolce was served, that they had in fact come to marry each other in secret. If Sir Hugh appeared a touch more formal than I remembered him to be in Isabelle's presence, and if Isabelle's customary charm and composure were a shade forced, these deviations might well have been due to a nervous anticipation of the enormity of their marrying without Lord Beauvais's consent.

One passage sounded a false note, if their reason for being at Hungerford was indeed marriage. I intuited from it that their meeting had somehow not been prearranged, although I did believe that they had expected to find each other at my home.

Upon giving the signal that the meal was at an end, I rose and gave consent for the evening's general entertainment. I was about to excuse myself and retire for the night, pleading a very real fatigue, when Sir Hugh hastened to help me from my chair and gave the conversation an abrupt and curious turn.

"Do you know when your husband will return, Lady Marguerite?" he asked as he handed me solicitously from the dais.

I was surprised by the question because he knew I did not know. Still, I did not think his purpose was to embarrass me before Isabelle. I appraised him briefly. Evasion did not seem appropriate in the circumstance.

"No," I said directly.

I had expected Isabelle to be smug or satisfied by my ignorance, but she did not evince either of these reactions. Sir Hugh turned to his betrothed. "Isabelle?" he queried.

Again I experienced a queer puzzlement at his tactics. He did not need to ask her in my presence about my husband's movements, unless the scene was being played for my benefit.

Isabelle smiled. "How should I know such a thing, dearest Hugh?" she countered with a smoldering look that was almost successful.

"Because presumably you have seen him of late," Sir Hugh replied with all his smooth, silken charm.

I would have said that Isabelle was disconcerted by this disclosure. I knew where Roland had been. Obviously Sir Hugh knew it, too, but our knowledge—or perhaps Roland's visit—gave Isabelle no pleasure. In fact, it struck me singularly odd why, if Roland had just been to see her, she found it necessary to come to Hungerford.

Isabelle became evasive. "But, love," she expostulated, "I have no more control over Guimont's movements than anyone else in the kingdom. Who could possibly know where he is now?" Her voice implied: *And who could possibly care?*

Sir Hugh apparently did. "He might be on his way to his castle even now," he suggested. The reply sounded an unmistakable warning note.

Isabelle made her own interpretation. Sir Hugh received the full force of her wide, provocative eyes. "Do you think that our marriage would anger Guy?" she asked. "Do you fear for our safety? He is well known for his jealous rages, after all."

I could have been roused to my own jealous rage at such a bold comment in my presence, had I not heard the taunt in Isabelle's voice, just as there had been the warning in Hugh's.

Sir Hugh said nothing, and I suspected that his silence piqued Isabelle into an admission. "But you needn't worry, love," she said sweetly, "Guy mentioned something about being on his way to London."

Sir Hugh bowed briefly in acknowledgment of the information and let the subject drop. Of course, it hurt me that Isabelle should be in possession of the facts with regard to my husband's directions, but I was too exhausted to dwell on the matter.

I remembered to give some final directives to Nan before retiring. I found her conveniently by the wide stone stairs that led from the Great Hall up to the bedchambers, and thus I was spared the necessity of going in search of her. It seemed almost as if she had been awaiting me, but other than simply being on hand, she gave no indication of needing to see me for any specific purpose. She had an alert look about her, despite the long day, and I was pleased that I did not have to repeat any of the instructions that I had in mind for her in the early morning.

She was regarding me so peculiarly—or mayhap it was only so intently—that I was moved to ask, "Is anything toward, Nan?"

"No, my lady," she replied. She did not lower her gaze, however, and this unnerved me slightly.

I spoke at random. "You will feel better when your Gaston is returned."

"Aye, my lady," she said, and thrust her hands into her apron. She did not ordinarily volunteer extraneous comments, but this evening she chose to say, "I donna fear for him when he is out with the master. Still and all, I hope they return in haste."

I smiled faintly. Nan had an uncanny knack for echoing my own sentiments, but I could not believe that she wished for the return of the Bastard for the same reason I wished for the return of Roland. In spite of everything, I desperately wanted him to be here to deal with Sir Hugh and Isabelle as he saw fit. I had no taste for entertaining visitors just then, and the most appealing prospect at the moment was my bed. I think my hands went to my back in an unconscious gesture of strain.

My weariness prompted me to add, "I do not think that it will be anytime soon, unfortunately. Lady Beauvais has informed me that Lord Guimont and his party are on their way to London."

Nan's look sharpened. Then her eyes slid over to a far corner of the hall. So drained of energy was I that I had no will of my own, and my eyes automatically followed Nan's. I glimpsed the beautiful Isabelle deep in conversation with the once beautiful Gunhild. I felt a childish pleasure that Isabelle was receiving no more satisfaction from the conversation than I had ever received from Gunhild. It gave me a queer sensation to see them talking, although surely I would have guessed that they knew each other well. It hardly mattered any longer. It was enough that Isabelle seemed to be getting the worse end of the bargain, if her look of dislike was any indication.

I composed myself. I absently patted Nan's hand and climbed the stairs heavily.

After shedding my bliaut and kirtle, I had Bess bind my hair in one long plait. I dismissed her for the evening on the assurance that I would need her again before morning. I lay restless for long minutes awaiting the comfort of sleep. When at last it began to steal around me, far-off masculine shouts outside the walls penetrated the selvages of my consciousness, and I awakened on the involuntary thought: *Roland!* Just when I wanted him most, he and his men had returned to Hungerford. I doubted my ears for a moment in the ensuing silence, but then came an answering call from the watch, and I was sure the men had come home. It was normal that I should feel some conflict about seeing my husband again, but my first, most honest reaction was one of profound relief.

I rose on the instant, scrambled into the handiest kirtle, and cast a heavy shawl across my shoulders. For all that it was late June, it was still chilly within the castle walls. I slipped into soft leather shoes and padded out into the corridor and rounded the corner that would take me down the long hallway to the stairs. In my haste, I nearly collided full force with another body.

I gasped slightly and took a step back. It was Isabelle.

The torches cinched to the wall had burned low and were flickering uncertainly. I saw well enough, however, and I had the distinct impression that Isabelle looked peculiar. I could not have defined it, but she looked somehow suddenly out of control of herself. Logic convinced me that she was merely lost, since she had no possible reason for being so far from her own chambers and so close to mine. Before I had a chance to redirect her, Isabelle opened the discussion on a topic I would never have dared.

"The dutiful wife off to greet her returning husband?" she asked mockingly.

I was never good at games. "Yes, I am," I replied levelly.

"You poor thing," she said, shaking her head mournfully. "How sorry I feel for you!"

"Do you?" I said thoughtfully. "Why should you, after all? My husband treats me well enough. I should rather feel sorry for you, if you had a mind to have him for yourself." This unnerved her sufficiently to give me courage to go on. "Of course, I have no reason to feel sorry for you, since you did not want him, evidenced by your rejection of him last year."

Isabelle's overly brilliant eyes narrowed at that. Was she perhaps feverish? I worried that it was something she had eaten.

"There is certainly no need for you to feel sorry for me, my dear," she said in a perfectly normal voice, which convinced me that I had misjudged the state of her health. "No, none at all! Still, as brave as you are, dear Marguerite, is it not difficult when you are alone to know that he is with another woman?"

Difficult as it was for me, I found her triumph then rather pitiful, and I was woman enough to let her know that, in one very important sense, I had won.

"It is sufficient comfort," I said, "that I carry a part of him with me now."

Isabelle's eyes swept my slightly ripened form. I would never have dreamed that she would ever appear anything less than lovely. She looked positively ugly in that moment. She made no effort to mask her emotions.

"Congratulations, my dear," she said acidly, then hesitated artfully. "Or is it cause for congratulation?"

My heart began to pound irregularly. I needed to get away from her. She did not appear to be in possession of herself. "I think it is, in all events," I said.

"But whom am I to congratulate?" she simpered in mock innocence. "Your dutiful husband—or Hugh?"

I favored her with my coldest stare. My first impulse was to pass along down the hallway in silence. There was no need to dignify the ridiculous implication with a reply. That surely would have been the wisest course, but this was not a discussion governed by wisdom. I said the one thing that I knew, instinctively, would hurt Isabelle most and possibly check her from poisoning my husband's ears with lies of my infidelity.

"Isabelle," I said with a calm satisfaction I did not feel, "haven't you guessed yet that Sir Hugh would not lay a hand on me?" I smiled derisively and continued unwisely, "Of course, I thought at first that he meant to compromise me, but I was proof against his charm. Perhaps you mean to imply, then, that he took me by force? Surely any man can take a woman by force, but I do not rate Sir Hugh's self-respect so low, do you? No, I can see that you do not. So I think that you will just have to acknowledge that Sir Hugh has given up his pursuit of me. What exactly the two of you are doing here at this time, I do not know. Perhaps indeed he has come to marry you. If that is the case, then I wish you joy of him. I will take pleasure in congratulating you."

I had already said far too much. Voices, the jingle of bridle, and the scrape of spur on stone were heard now in the back bailey. I turned to go, as much to welcome the returning men as to escape the frozen, malevolent look on Isabelle's face. I started for the main staircase, which swept down into the Great Hall. When I arrived at the end of the dimly lit corridor and saw pages and serving maidens still at work below, I capriciously reversed myself. I decided to go instead down the back ways to the bailey, in order to avoid as many castle folk as possible. I retraced my steps, and when I passed the darkened corner, now empty, where Isabelle and I had minutes before crossed swords, I shuddered. I guessed that Isabelle had strategically retreated to her chamber. My feet took me noiselessly through the maze of back hallways.

The castle was slowly rousing itself to greet the newcomers. Muffled, indistinct noises came from all directions. I felt a clammy sweat bead out on my forehead and palms and pulled my shawl closer about my shoulders. I had no business taking a chill at this time, I chided myself, and while I was in the mood for self-reproach, it seemed a rather unnecessary venture seeking Roland out in the stables. He would come, in his own good time, to our chamber, and there was really no urgency to my informing him of our guests. He would have heard about them by now anyway and would even, possibly, be on his way to our chambers through the front of the manor house. I paused uncertainly and almost turned to go back to bed, where I should have been in the first place.

Some whim drove me on. Perhaps it was panic. I could not say. Yet, one thing was clear to me: I needed to see Roland before anyone else did. I quickened my pace and cursed my shoes for their slippery soles.

The last coherent thing I remember thinking, when I stepped out at last onto the landing of the wooden staircase, was that the cool, clear night air felt immeasurably good. I looked down into the shadows and thought I perceived a shape lurking below in protective darkness. I did not have the barest second to sort out the unknown movement, for just then I felt the thrust at my back, and the handrail slipped inexplicably through my grip. The stairs had an odd, evil way of plunging at me, and insensibly I realized that at any moment the hard ground far below me would come up and hit me smartly in the face.

It did not. Scarcely had I the wit to understand that I was falling before I had stopped. The ground had miraculously eluded me. I was lying in a pair of arms. I looked up into the terror-stricken face above me.

"Well, Nan," I said politely, "thank you very much."

Then, never having fainted in my life, I swooned. I must have drifted in and out of consciousness over the next few hours, because tatters of perceptions remain with me: there was a scuffling of steps, some shouts, and then finally strong arms carrying me. I am sure that I foolishly tried to speak but was told by a deep, familiar voice—I wished devoutly that it were Roland's—to hush. My reasoning became very labored, and I remember working through the notion that if I did not say anything about losing my baby, then that would be my charm against a miscarriage. I did manage to articulate quite distinctly, to my own ears at least, "Do not dare drop me, sir."

When I awoke, it was broad daylight and I was in my own bed. My lids felt too heavy to open fully, so I merely cracked my eyes against the sun. Oddly, however, the light was streaming directly through my window, indicating that it was the afternoon. I felt immediately remiss for having been so tired and sleeping through the morning. I could not imagine that Bess and Gertrude had possibly forgotten to awaken me. Then I recalled our visitors, and Roland's return. But I could remember nothing more.

I shifted to lift myself and felt two hands against my shoulders, hindering my progress. It was Nan, and she looked unwontedly concerned. She was also very disheveled, and I was most displeased.

"Your smock is a disgrace," I said, "and what, may I ask, is the meaning of a crumpled coif at this time of day?"

Nan actually grinned at the rebuke. I had never thought she would be insolent to me.

"I sleep through one morning," I remarked, "and this is what happens."

Her features darkened again and she reached for a bowl and offered me hot broth. This puzzling action triggered my memory, however, and suddenly events began to take shape once again in my mind. I pushed away the broth in disgust and asked after our visitors.

"They have all gone, my lady," she replied woodenly.

"Sir Roland, too?" I asked, surprised. Again Nan looked concerned, so I hastily added, "That is, he did return, did he not?"

"Aye," she replied.

"But then he left again?"

Nan considered her response for a moment. Then: "Before he left, the master spoke with you. I was here, too, and there dinna seem cause for alarm. After he'd gone, though, you, ah, went back to sleep again."

The memory of a conversation with Roland danced about the borders of my memory, but the cloud was too high and I could not catch it. In any case, it was good to know that Roland had not simply abandoned me, if I had appeared gravely ill.

"Very well," I said, and then in a moment of panic I laid a hand on my flat stomach. My glance flew involuntarily to Nan.

"You suffered no harm," she said, and I sensed that she was pleased.

My relief was profound. "If I came to no harm," I said, "it is because I have you to thank for it."

Nan's face remained characteristically impassive. "Aye, it was a lucky thing that I found myself at the foot of those dangerous stairs."

I wondered what part luck had played, but there were so many other things to determine first that I did not want to expose my fears and fancies before knowing what I was up against. I felt perfectly sound of mind now, so I did not fear for my reason.

"How long, exactly, have I been out of awareness?" I asked.

Nan hesitated fractionally. "About three days," she said.

"Holy Mother! No wonder I am so hungry!"

Nan put the bowl to my lips again.

I became suddenly impatient. I was fearful at having gone so long without proper nourishment and told Nan to fetch me a sirloin and some peas. She looked doubtful, but I assured her that I could force down the food. Watered wine would have tasted good, too.

"I cannot leave you, my lady," Nan said with deepest respect, "until Bess is come to take her turn with you."

I cocked a brow at this piece of information. Did they, too, suspect that someone wished me harm? Or was it only that they had feared I would awaken with no one to tend to me and that I would be disoriented and foolishly try to get up? I chose the latter interpretation.

I smiled my most authoritative smile and spoke deliberately. "Nan," I said, "I am very hungry. I am not used to lying in bed. Neither am I prepared to have my orders countermanded, not by you, not by Bess, nor by anyone else. I have no intention of getting up at the moment, for in fact I feel as weak as a newborn colt, if that is any reassurance to you! If the purpose in staying by my side is so that I will not upset myself, I can assure you that it is far more upsetting to me to find you here with me when I have made it clear to you what I desire."

The ploy worked most effectively. She hastened out of the room. I could not resist adding, just for good measure, "And do not forget to change your smock and coif before returning."

Nan had not been gone a full minute when I had another, less welcome visitor to my room. I believe that Gunhild must have been lying in wait to get me alone. Had I known that, I would never have sent Nan to fetch me food before it was Bess's turn to watch over me. The sight of Gunhild was upsetting enough, and when I learned what she had to say, I saw the wisdom that Bess and Nan had shown in wanting to guard me from distress.

She entered without knocking and stood wordlessly at the door regarding me with her hawk's eyes.

"So you see," I said at last, to break the uncomfortable silence, "that I had the back staircase strengthened only to fall down it myself. I should never have been circulating at that hour in slippery leather shoes."

She bit back a laugh and said, "Still hiding from the truth, are ye?"

If she was prepared to cast aside all pretense, so was I. "No," I said, "just testing the terrain. I was pushed, and well you know it. But I am still alive, and so is my child, despite all dire warnings."

"So you are," she said sharply. "Do you have any ideas about who pushed you?"

"I have a great many ideas, Gunhild."

"Do you have any about where your husband was when you were pushed?" she asked maliciously.

"In the stables, I suppose," I replied coolly.

"He was seen coming down the back stairs within minutes of your fall," she informed me baldly.

I flatly refused the implications of that remark. "It makes no matter where he was, and I am glad that he was at hand."

Gunhild was determined to pursue the matter. "Does it matter that another died in your place?"

I had no idea why she had to inflict such pain. I had a strong mind to ignore the question, but my need to know was as desperate as was her need to wound.

I regarded Gunhild levelly. "Who, in your estimation, has died in my place?"

"Isabelle," she said, a half-satisfied smile exposing even teeth.

My heart ceased beating. I must have voiced my most intimate fear aloud. I was not aware of forming the words *Who killed her?* but I saw Gunhild's lips compress in a tight line. Then she opened her mouth to speak.

"Hugh Falmouth," she answered.

The last day of June thus crept to an end. July has come again, and the path of the moon has brought the earth to its rich, splendid fullness. My garden, meticulously tended, is in bloom and spread out below me. It is a full year since I first met Roland, and I doubt that I am any nearer understanding him or the ways of the world than I was last summer. I am surely no closer to an appreciation of a blessed, earthly state that should be mine by virtue of my marriage to the man I love and the child whom I am proud to bear. Happiness, if such exists, must surely be a quiet, peaceful eternity, empty of the need to accommodate doubt and despair, and devoid of the wild imbalances of vain hope.

I am alive, however, and Isabelle is not. To do myself justice, I never wished her dead. The Lady Isolde maintained, and with good reason: "Be careful with your wishes, for they may come true." I see little advantage in a rival, now dead, whose golden beauty will not dim with age. It is even more disturbing to me to be bound now to silence. What is to be gained by accusing a dead woman? It is clear to me beyond a doubt that Isabelle's hands were the ones to have pushed me to an uncertain fate.

I have come to some other conclusions, too, but it will do me no good now to cast unpleasant, perhaps even spiteful, suspicions on one who no longer breathes. I have no taste for ghosts and wish her the rest and peace I do not hope to find.

Nevertheless, my suffering cannot have been futile. I trust that the hard-won center of my being can withstand the aftermath of so much misspent passion. I can only hope that I will be wife enough to give Roland what he needs.

Roland is gone from Hungerford. I do not know where he has gone or when he will be back. Try as I might, I cannot remember the conversation we are supposed to have had. Presumably he informed me of his movements on the day after my fall, and I am sure that, if I was speaking as lucidly and coherently as I am told I did, I assured him I was fit and hale. Bess has given me to understand, however, in the most oblique terms imaginable, that Roland has gone in search of Hugh. She also informed me that Hugh rode off in search of Isabelle who fled Hungerford after she had pushed me down those treacherous stairs; and when he found her he killed her. My heart tells me that Roland did Hugh no harm; my head cries out not to trust my heart. It has taken all my courage to accept the possibility that Roland has gone to grieve over Isabelle in private. It may be some time yet before my restless spirit will cease its practice of evasion and stop long enough to consider the possible reasons for Isabelle's destruction by Sir Hugh's hand. I have not had time in this last eternity to spend myself completely. Has it truly been but two days?

I have passed too many hours in my sewing room not to have become comfortable enough to stir up some of the spirits and memories that haunt Hungerford. It has been a fine, sunny day, in sooth, and being in the mood for cleaning, I have taken the unprecedented step for Gunhild to help me clear away some of the shadows.

When she arrived at my door, I knew that I had not miscalculated. I guessed that she would not like me to exercise my authority so purposefully.

"Good morrow, Gunhild," I said, rising from my writing table. I was still too caught up in my own audacity to feel any qualms under her hard stare. When she said nothing, I thought to press my advantage. "Thank you very much for coming. I need your help with some cleaning."

She moved a step into the room. "I know nothing of cleaning," she said warily. "Mayhap you should summon Josette or Louise. Or even Nan, since she is such a prime favorite with you."

"Nan has served me well," I agreed, "and I think that she shall always remain a prime favorite with me. Josette is far too busy in the gardens, and Louise . . . How is Louise faring in her state of, shall we say, mourning?"

"It's a sad day when a maid loses her mistress," Gunhild said evenly, but she was not able to keep the bitterness out of her voice. "She'll grieve for a long while"—she looked up slyly at me and continued—"and may not be accountable for her actions in the future."

"I can sympathize with her grief, but I'm not alarmed that she, or anyone else, will come to harm because of it."

"Can you be so sure?"

"Of course not. Who can predict the lengths to which grief or anger or jealousy will take a person? I cannot, nor would I think anyone else could for a certainty either. As for Louise, would you have me turn her out?"

"Some have suggested you might do it, my lady. And wisely so."

I had heard that rumor through Bess. It would have been impossible that my fall down Hungerford's unlucky stairs would not occasion speculation. Apparently some pinned suspicion on Louise, perhaps remembering her stiff rebuke over the embroidered girdle that preceded the Christmas celebrations. Perhaps others guessed that Isabelle still had a mind to be mistress of Hungerford and had used Louise to try to achieve her ends. I acquitted Louise of all but her dislike of me. I believed it possible that she was the only other one, besides mayhap Gunhild, to have guessed that Isabelle had tried her hand against me. Grief was hard enough to bear. I wondered if disillusionment might not prove worse and turn a spirit sour and bitter.

"I'll not punish loyalty," I said at last.

"And walk with your back to the wall henceforth?" Gunhild suggested.

"Come now, Gunhild! We are decided, are we not, that I have more courage than it seems and do not fear ghosts. Surely you can appreciate the awkward position that I am in." I paused and drew a breath. "Certainly I appreciate yours."

Gunhild glanced up sharply.

"As I said," I went on, "I will not punish loyalty, but the ghosts have accumulated of late, and I feel the need of clearing some away."

The queasiness that still comes upon me occasionally forced me to sit down. I chose the window embrasure for its wide seat and comfortable pillows. It was reassuring to have the warm sun at my back. Truth to tell, I felt a little drained by recent events, but the belief in the rightness of my actions, both for me and for Roland, gave me courage.

"Do you think to dispose so easily of Isabelle's ghost?" she asked me shrewdly.

"I do not know," I confessed. "But I am not thinking of her particularly. I am thinking rather of the Lady Laura."

Something akin to approval was barely evident in Gunhild's eyes. "What might the Lady Laura have to do with it? She's been dead a full score of years."

"I don't know," I said again, "what she has to do with it. But you once told me that the truth killed Lady Laura, and I am now wondering if, in your estimation, the truth killed Isabelle."

"Why not ask Hugh Falmouth?" she answered evasively.

"Why not just answer me yourself, Gunhild? Or does your dislike of my husband prevent you from dealing honestly with me?"

Gunhild grunted and looked a little tired. "You have become very clever, for all your innocence," she commented. "It is a wonder that you ask me anything."

"And you are very evasive, for all your knowledge. I cannot help but wonder myself what truths you are hiding. You have said that Isabelle died in my place. So be it. I cannot alter that, as much as I would like to."

"You find no satisfaction at her death?"

I was startled by her derisiveness. "Very little, if you must know. But that is of no moment. We are agreed, are we not, that I am not like the other Guimont women. It is also evident that I have not shared their fate. Now, how have I escaped?"

My eyes followed Gunhild's movements across the room to the fireplace, now gaping silent and cold on a warm summer's day.

"Perhaps you are cleverer than they were and did not get caught at infidelity."

She was deliberately being ambiguous. "If by that you mean I did not stray, then I will say that I felt no desire to do so. I do not think that particularly clever. Call it instead want of temptation."

Gunhild cracked an unpleasant laugh. "You are not that naive, surely, my lady! Hugh Falmouth would be considered by most to be sore temptation indeed."

"I do not find it flattering," I said clearly, "to be the object of one man's revenge against another. That would be truly naive to fall into his lap for so unsatisfactory a reason. Allow me my measure of feminine vanity. I have never thought to vie with Isabelle."

"Perhaps she thought that she had to vie with you."

"Then she was more of a fool than I have ever been."

"Do you truly think so?"

"I have no reason to think otherwise," I stated simply. "But I have yet to discover how and why the Lady Laura died. Or have you already told me as much? Her death was a result of the fact that she was not faithful to her lord."

"She did not love him!" Gunhild spat suddenly, venomously.

"Then she was to be pitied," I said. "But that is no excuse for faithlessness."

"As if you are in a position to judge!" Gunhild retorted savagely.

I was effectively silenced. I suppose that it is obvious to Gunhild, and everyone else, that I am in love with my husband to the exclusion of all other men. She was right: I was in no position to say how I might succumb to temptation if Roland were not my husband and of a mind to seduce me, as he had been the last time I was with him at Westminster.

"Be that as it may," I said as calmly as I was able, "you once intimated that her lord was the one who killed her, but perhaps not directly."

"There are many people who contribute to a death," she said mournfully.

"Yourself included, Gunhild?"

She rolled a malevolent eye toward me, but I refused to cower. "She needed protection! She needed protection!" she raved. "I gave it to her! I did everything I could do to protect her, but in the end I couldn't stop her! I couldn't protect her from *him!*"

"From whom, Gunhild?" I prodded, thinking to come to the bottom of it at last.

"Gunhild has always held me responsible for the death of my mother," came a voice from the door.

My eyes flew around to discover that my ears had not deceived me: Roland stood there, regarding Gunhild through cool blue eyes, looking not one jot different from when I last had seen him. He was fit and at his ease, leaning casually against the doorjamb. In spite of everything, he did not look the man who grieved the loss of his lady love, but I had surely learned by now that Roland would never expose himself so idly.

I did not know how much he had heard; however, it was evident that he had heard the last passage.

"So you are," hissed Gunhild.

"And if I were to accept that responsibility," he replied in lazy tones, "would you sleep better o' nights?"

She eyed him shrewdly, suspiciously. "Yes!" she hurled back, on a challenge.

"Then I accept full responsibility for my mother's death," he said carelessly, "and suggest you make your peace here and now. There is scarce a topic that tires me more. You are dismissed."

Gunhild stared at him wordlessly for a frozen moment. "Do you think it such an easy matter?" she said at last.

He affected mild surprise. "But, Gunhild! You have blamed me all these years, why balk now?" The lazy, indolent tones left him then, and he rapped out with wintry effect, "Do not, I beg of you, blame yourself—or the Lady Laura—for her impetuous folly! Certainly, if you will, I was the unwitting precipitator of her death. I have paid for it—and dearly! Of course," he continued, dispassionately now, "I am hardly accountable for the fact that my mother chose such an unwise course of action to begin with, or that I was in the wrong place at the wrong time, but if we are sticking to points, then let us agree that I killed her—not in deed, but in principle!"

Gunhild was not at all pleased by such plain speaking. Roland perceived this, too. He continued ruthlessly, "It is something of a check to have it stated so openly, isn't it, Gunhild? Whispers and innuendos are so much more to the purpose! They divert attention from your own miserable role in the whole affair!"

Gunhild made one last stab: "And shall you announce your opinions at dinner tonight, for all the castle folk to know? Shall you dredge up events years past to exonerate yourself and cleanse the effects of your vile temper? Who would believe you?"

"There is only one person's opinion which matters to me now," he told her flatly. "All else may continue thinking as they have done these many years past."

Gunhild's eyes slid to me. My heart was pounding irregularly. I rose slowly to my feet.

"You are dismissed," came the command again. This time Roland's tone brooked no refusal. He was entirely capable of throwing her out bodily. Gunhild left the room, beaten and spent.

Roland turned to me. "What else did Gunhild tell you," he asked abruptly, "about my mother, save for the fact that I was responsible for her death?"

I had no time to adjust to his remarkable presence. "That she was very beautiful," I said.

"She was."

"And that she was loved by everyone," I ventured again, saying anything that came to mind.

Roland's lip curled. "She was," he said again. "By every passing squire and every passing knight." The scorn in his voice touched my nerves and made it impossible for me to open my mouth to respond. "I discovered her one day—quite by accident, I assure you—in the arms of some handsome, gaumless lord. In this very room, in fact! Gunhild was standing guard outside the door. I think this made me as suspicious as many other things I had been noticing for some years."

Roland paused and then continued again in full possession of himself. "In anger, I hauled the fool by the seat of his half-buttoned chausses into the bailey, and would have beaten him to death had John Potter not stopped me. As it was, the man was crippled! Nevertheless, the cause of the brawl was widely and instantly known in the keep. My mother, in fear and guilt, one might suppose, saddled her horse and rode faster than hounds in the direction of London. My father caught wind of the whole and went after her some hours later. I believe he would have wrung her neck, and taken great pleasure doing it, if she had not already broken it jumping a high hedge. As it was, she was dead, by a flight precipitated by my reportedly false accusations. Gunhild made sure to protect her beloved lady's reputation. She had an easy time of it: Lady Laura was considered something of a saint, and I a traitorous son. I joined the king's service shortly thereafter. My father was only too happy to see me go, for I shall tell you that he never recovered from the incident and never quite knew whom or what to believe. He died two years later, leaving Roger to grievously mismanage the lands."

So, it was out. Though a tragedy, Roland's part was not so very terrible, or inexcusable, after all, and I was sorry that he had had to live with it all these years.

"You did not tell your father your side of the truth?"

Roland shook his head slowly. "His grief was profound. I saw no advantage in confirming what he already knew: that my mother was a beautiful, lying, cheating baggage."

"Perhaps you judge her too harshly," I said.

Roland raised his brows at that.

"I mean only, of course, that perhaps she did not love your father—perhaps he gave her no reason to love him!—and sought consolation elsewhere, as women do."

I realized, almost before the words were out, the construction he could so easily put on that statement. "Gunhild suggested as much to me recently when I condemned your mother's faithlessness," I added hastily, "and pointed out to me that I was in no position to judge."

Roland considered me a moment. "You take a large-minded view of the situation, I perceive."

"I am only reluctant to judge her, her actions, Gunhild's, or even yours," I said. "In any case, it happened a long time ago, and I think it should be over and done with."

"Is innocence so simple a thing, then, and can be acquired with the passage of time?"

"Partially, I suppose, especially if one has paid for the crime. There are limits to the length of time one can be accused and must be eventually pardoned. Depending on the crime, of course!"

"That is encouraging, in all events! Wish me a long life to be pardoned of all my crimes!"

"I do wish you a long life, but not to live down your so-called crimes," I ventured. "You have been falsely accused on more than one occasion."

"Have I now? My record is not a blameless one, as you well know, nor is my temper a well-guarded secret."

"But you are no murderer."

Roland smiled. "You cannot make me as innocent as yourself, Marguerite, no matter how hard you try," he said. "I have killed many men, and shall probably kill more before I am through."

"There is not a knight alive who has not killed someone," I countered, and took the fateful plunge, "but you did not kill your brother."

I could not read his face. He said, "How have you arrived at that conclusion?"

I could have said that the same person who pushed me down the stairs pushed Sir Roger, but I chose not to. I could have said that Roland might have killed his brother with his bare hands, as he might have killed me, or just as his father might have killed his mother, had he been given the chance. However, he could never, even in the grip of fury, do anything so calculated or so cowardly as to push someone down the stairs. I did not offer that explanation, either. I said merely, "I just know you did not."

"And when did you decide my innocence?"

"Not recently," I said, to disassociate my knowledge from my recent experience with Isabelle. "Not at first, either. It came to me slowly, but very clearly, so that now I believe it most implicitly. I do not think you capable of it, and I do not think you will tell me otherwise."

Roland looked very pleased. "No, I did not kill Roger," he stated simply. "He was my brother."

Gunhild had said that one man mourned Sir Roger's passing, and that one man was, of course, Roland himself. It was not more complicated than that. Still, a point or two eluded me.

"But," I said slowly, still struggling to comprehend the whole, "but you allowed everyone to think that you had killed your own brother, just as you did not defend yourself against your mother's death."

"I merely allowed everyone to think as they pleased. Protesting one's innocence is a wearisome affair—and so unconvincing."

"You must have known that suspicion would fall on you. Yet you did nothing to have anyone think otherwise. And do not say that you are used to the blackguard's role—"

"But I am."

"—For I can see very well that you are, in addition to being generally indifferent to the opinions of others. But to accept the stain of fratricide! That is going a bit too far!"

"I fear," he said, shaking his head sadly, "that you shall always be poor at ciphering. If you think a little more clearly, you may arrive at the correct sum."

We stared at each other a long moment. I could succeed in my goal only if we spoke her name between us. I did not want to be the one to bring it up, but there was, finally, no avoiding it. He lived up to his namesake's reputation, after all.

"You did it to protect Isabelle."

"Perhaps partially."

"Well, you did," I insisted, and hardly faltered as I went on. "You did it because you had a relationship with her, and," drawing a long breath, "contrary to popular readings of your character, defending her was very chivalrous of you."

He laughed at that. "Acquit me of chivalry! Given my relationship with the fair Isabelle, a true knight would have insisted on marriage. Don't you agree?"

"Not necessarily," I said doubtfully. "Not in all cases."

"Should not the physical always be sanctified by marriage?"

"No," I said, feeling my way.

"Which brings us back to your original observations on my mother. I had not thought your notions of intimacy and fidelity to be so elastic. I have apparently deluded myself that I was fortunate to have found a wife with rather strict notions on these vital matters. I find now that I should have a care what I am about."

"Fidelity is given at the marriage ceremony," I said. "Thereafter it must be earned. And, in any case, my notions are no less elastic than yours."

"That is reassuring! My notions are as strict as I thought yours to be."

"For both parties!" I said. "It works both ways!"

"Assuredly."

I was backed into something of a corner. We were at the heart of the matter. I would no longer evade it, but I could not quite meet his eyes. I studied my fingernails. "But if one loves elsewhere . . ."

"Are you perhaps referring to Hugh Falmouth?"

I fell easily into the trap. "No, rather Isabelle Beauvais!" I replied swiftly.

"My tacit acceptance of Roger's death," Roland said evenly, "was the price I paid to force Isabelle to annul officially our betrothal. Had you not guessed it, innocent Marguerite? But now she is dead, and I need protect her no more." His mouth twisted into a wry smile. "My motives were not so chivalrous, after all."

These words scarcely penetrated. "But she did not give you up! She had reason to think that you might go to her again. She persisted! And she loved you! I know she did, and I do not see how you could resist her!"

"Easily, I assure you," he said. "Aye, she loved me after her own false fashion. But she would not have me without also having Roger's land. I was not enough for her. I was determined, even before Roger's death, I think, that she should have neither, if it came to that."

"I myself was burdened with a tremendous amount of attractive land," I said petulantly, relieved at last to have done with it.

"You did not come," he said with a teasing smile, "without your land." He paused then and looked down at me. "Let me tell you true, Madam Wife, ever since that first night at court when I saw you looking frightened and dignified and voluptuous all at once—mind you, ever since then, I've looked at no woman twice."

My eyes flew to his. "You have been faithful to me?" I asked incredulously.

He smiled a quick, mercurial smile that held all the charm of the man. "I have not looked at another woman twice. Is that not sufficient loyalty?"

I could not resist a smile in response. "But I did not earn your fidelity and did little, in truth, to make you trust me."

"I, like you, have come to some slow, sure conclusions of my own. Of course, there was that first time I met you, when circumstances did not argue in your favor. I came to realize since then that you did not fully know what you were about. An improbable explanation to my mind, but the only one that finally made sense." His eyes were warm with intimate laughter. "You are, I decided, as innocent on all scores as I wanted you to be."

It must have been a difficult conclusion for him, so contrary to his experience of women and the evidence that militated against me.

I could not speak at once. I could only look at him and think many long thoughts about torment and delusion and jealousy and love. I began to understand what had escaped me these long months. I began to see what had been before my very eyes all along. Here was the hard core of his integrity, his dignity, and he had enough self-understanding to grant me my own share of integrity and dignity. It might have been no easier for him than it had been for me in the year past, but he had trusted me, and, once again, he had not erred.

Isabelle no longer hovered between us. Now all ghosts needed to be put to rest. "And Sir Hugh?" I asked, somewhat ambiguously. "What of him?"

"He has gone into exile. Self-imposed."

"Has he? Does it—does his self-imposed exile have anything to do with Isabelle?"

"That, and other things. However, if you mean that he had to leave before any legal action could be brought against him for her death, then the answer is no. I think that I could have spared him any prosecution."

"You?"

"Does it surprise you so much?"

"In a word, yes! Not that I do not think you capable of

accomplishing it. I'm sure it is simply a matter of a word here and there in the right ear and quickly hushing the whole! But to think that you would!"

"Falmouth seemed far less amazed than you when I suggested it to him."

I was now bewildered. "You spoke with him?"

"Indeed. It was unavoidable, in fact. He was the one to have informed me of his decision to live in Navarre where he has family. You might say that it was our first honest conversation—and doubtless our last."

"I gathered that you had gone after him, but I did not think it was to talk."

"Well, now, I am a jealous enough husband," he said, favoring me with a smile, "but not, I hope, a fool. I did not go after him to bring him to book for the seduction of my wife. Rather, I thought he might have something I wanted."

I felt an involuntary blush stain my cheeks. Roland did not fail to perceive it.

"At last you betray yourself," he remarked. "I did not think you could remain unmoved by the flattery of one such as Falmouth. Nevertheless, although I did not need to hear it from his lips, he assured me that you remained stalwart against his assault. A true citadel."

I struggled to command my voice. "But, Roland, do you call it flattering to be courted by a man who had in mind only the discredit of my husband? You say that you are no fool—well, I hope that I am not so vain as to have fallen victim to empty flattery and ignoble motives!"

Roland smiled kindly. "No, love. Falmouth unexpectedly got caught in his own trap. It was he who fell victim to an honest emotion, putting him in the unprecedented position of being truly in love with another man's wife. Most unnerving for him that it should be mine."

I choked out a protest.

He shook his head slowly. "Even Isabelle knew it in the end, and I found myself, for once, having to thank Falmouth for having come here to save you from her."

"Nan did that," I pointed out.

Roland grinned and opened his mouth to speak.

I held up a hand in a staying gesture. "Don't say it! You showed infinite wisdom in having her brought here from Shrivenham. I could not have managed here without her. I owe life and limb to her—not to Sir Hugh."

"Still, he was more alive to Isabelle's hatred for you than I was. Despite past experiences, I had forgotten Isabelle's habit of harming those least capable of defending themselves. She threw me off the scent when I went to see her in Northumbria, and I rode off to London while she came here. Otherwise, I would have been here days earlier. As it was, Falmouth guessed her intentions better than I."

"I think Isabelle was not well in the end, and Sir Hugh knew it. That is why he came. For all his immoral ways, he still possesses a conscience. Besides which, he knew that Isabelle was just using him, and he did not like it. No one would! I really do not believe that he—that I was—that is to say—"

Roland put his hands on his hips. "I do not suppose that you will ever admit that Gavin is deeply smitten by you, either."

"Gavin? No, don't be absurd! He's not but a lad!" I said. When Roland did not reply, I asked warily, "Where is Gavin now?"

"I took mercy on the poor fellow and sent him away." Roland shook his head sadly. "It is a black day when a woman comes between a man and his most trusted squire."

"If that is true—which I doubt!—it was most unintentional on my part, I assure you!"

"Which makes your charm all the more fatal," he riposted quickly. "It is not a comfortable notion for a man to take with him that his wife stands in constant danger."

I had to laugh at that and put this lighthearted topic aside. I became serious again. "Do you not grieve for Isabelle? Not just a little?"

His face was sober. "At the risk of endangering your good opinion of me," he said, "I confess I do not. Neither do I rejoice."

"I should suppose not!"

"But you see," he explained, "I had come to hate her, until

I met you. Then my hate for her became indifference."

I perceived then what had undone Isabelle in the end: the knowledge that Roland's passion for her was spent, never to be revived. His indifference must have been unbearable. Anger and hatred were signs of life and could be teased and roused again to a blaze. Absence of emotion is death, and a part of Isabelle died when she realized, finally, that she had well and truly lost.

I looked up to find Roland's eyes on me.

"I have told you all now. Have you nothing to tell me?" he asked.

"My conscience is clear. I have absolutely nothing to confess."

"I was not thinking of confessions, love. Is there really nothing far more important to tell me?"

It is hard to describe, when I told him of the child I was carrying, how, instead of answering, he took a long stride across the space that separated us and closed his arms tightly around me. It was an embrace free of troubling doubt, a warm, comforting, husbandly embrace.

He had told me that he could not see for me. The shadows and the blind spots had disappeared, and all was in focus. I saw Roland the man in perfect clarity. I do not know if others will see him as I see him, but perhaps they will say, "Yes, I understand how she loves him."

Much later, Roland sat down in the deep chair before the hearth. He withdrew from his tunic a velvet sack and positioned it carefully on the small table beside him. He said nothing, offered no explanation. He did not need to. The silk cords of the pouch were loose, and I could see the edge of the ruby bracelet winking at me from where I sat. This became as clear as all the rest. He had gone to Isabelle to retrieve it and had, in fact, tried several times, unsuccessfully, to get it back from her to give to me, its rightful owner. It was truly that simple; as simple and understandable as the sight of Roland in my room, in my chair, his legs stretched out before him, very quiet and at rest.

He has given me to see that there are many different forms

of love: that of Roland for his brother, that of Gunhild for the faithless Lady Laura, that of Isabelle for Roland: and all these forms were crossed and recrossed, so that the hopeless knot past untangling had had to be cut. There are many faces of love, ugly as well as beautiful. I see, too, that the strange passions that ruled Isabelle and Hugh, Gunhild and Roland and myself, need not consume themselves and die cold and bitter, but can continue to burn steadily and brightly in the ordinary: shiny copper bowls, a well-placed stitch, striped satin pillows, the crunch of autumn leaves underfoot, a baby's dimpled cheek, a husband's familiar kiss in greeting.

The summer sun, soft and yellow as warm butter, is slanting through the open window at my back. The trill of the thrush is on the air. There is peace and balance and fullness in the world. Roland sits before me, a tired and contented man, and his child is at home just below my heart. I need search no further, for I know now that this is happiness, this is grace.